Available in February 2010
from Mills & Boon® Intrigue

THE SHARPSHOOTER'S SECRET SON

He had one chance to prove himself worthy of being a father.

She hadn't seen him in eight long months, although she'd come close to telling him about the baby. Then she'd thought better of it, decided that she and her child would be better off if she never got sucked into his self-destructive life.

Seeing him now, she wasn't sure she'd made the right decision.

Loving Deke was a recipe for disaster. Not that her heart cared. Nor her body. He'd always been the sexiest thing on the planet. From his sun-streaked brown hair to his startling sea-blue eyes. From the hard line of his jaw to his broad, leanly muscled shoulders. Even his battered shearling jacket couldn't hide the power and grace of his six-foot-plus body.

She squeezed the hand that held hers and knew she had no other choice but to give in with a whispered "Take me."

FURY CALLS

Blake had been an outsider most of his life.

And yet the fact gnawed at his gut. As he stood behind the restaurant where *she* worked, he reminded himself that he had no need of humanity with all the attendant emotions, especially love.

Love only complicated the whole undead-demon gig.

Then *she* emerged.

Meghan's blonde hair glistened beneath the light of a bright full moon. She wrapped her arms around herself, as if to ward off the chill of the early spring night. Not that vamps like them really felt the cold, he thought. It was probably a lingering human habit.

Meghan had only been a vamp for three years, eleven months and ten days, but who was counting? Besides Meghan, he would be the one to know.

He had turned her, after all.

Meghan rose from the stoop as he made himself visible, her body tense and seemingly poised for flight.

But this time he wasn't about to let her run away…

All the characters in this book have no existence outside the imagination of
the author, and have no relation whatsoever to anyone bearing the same name
or names. They are not even distantly inspired by any individual known or
unknown to the author, and all the incidents are pure invention.

First published in Great Britain 2010
Harlequin Mills & Boon Limited,
Eton House, 18-24 Paradise Road, Richmond, Surrey TW9 1SR

The Sharpshooter's Secret Son © Rickey Ricks Mallory 2009
Fury Calls © Caridad Piñeiro Scordato 2009

ISBN: 978 0 263 88199 8

46-0210

Harlequin Mills & Boon policy is to use papers that are natural, renewable
and recyclable products and made from wood grown in sustainable forests.
The logging and manufacturing processes conform to the legal environmental
regulations of the country of origin.

Printed and bound in Spain
by Litografia Rosés S.A., Barcelona

THE SHARPSHOOTER'S SECRET SON

BY
MALLORY KANE

FURY CALLS

BY
CARIDAD PIÑEIRO

◉™ MILLS & BOON®

THE SHARPSHOOTER'S SECRET SON

BY
MALLORY KANE

Mallory Kane credits her love of books to her mother, a librarian, who taught her that books are a precious resource and should be treated with loving respect. Her father and grandfather were steeped in the Southern tradition of oral history and could hold an audience spellbound for hours with their storytelling skills. Mallory aspires to be as good a storyteller as her father.

Mallory lives in Mississippi with her computer-genius husband, their two fascinating cats and, at current count, seven computers. She loves to hear from readers. You can write to her at mallory@mallorykane.com.

For Debbie and Lorraine

Chapter One

They called them ghost towns for a reason.

Black Hills Search and Rescue Specialist Deke Cunningham wasn't afraid of anything. Not anymore. But the late afternoon shadows spooked him. They moved with him, reaching out like gnarled fingers across the empty, dusty main street of Cleancutt, Wyoming. He tried to shake off the feeling, but it wouldn't shake. Probably because today he wasn't working a routine assignment to rescue a deserving but nameless innocent.

Today he was searching for his ex-wife.

He glanced at the GPS locator built into his phone, then at the two-story building with the letters *H E L* barely readable above the door. The *O* and the *T* had long since faded.

This was it. The location where BHSAR computer expert Aaron Gold had finally managed to triangulate Mindy's last cell phone transmission.

Mindy. She didn't deserve this. She hadn't deserved anything she'd gotten for loving him.

And he'd never deserved her.

Deke approached the two-story building, doing his damnedest not to swipe his palm across the nape of his neck, where prickles of awareness tingled. He was being watched.

No surprise there.

He even knew who was watching him. The same person who'd kidnapped his ex-wife. Well—who'd *ordered* her kidnapped, anyhow.

Novus Ordo. The infamous international terrorist who'd already targeted another member of the BHSAR team, Matt Parker.

We've got your wife, the obviously disguised voice on the cell phone had said.

Alarm bells had clanged in his head and his gut had clenched with worry. Still, he'd had to smile a little. Whoever the kidnapper was, he had no idea what he'd gotten hold of when he'd grabbed Mindy Cunningham.

"Ex-wife," he'd muttered, working to sound bored and uninterested. "And be my guest. You can have her."

"This is no joke, Cunningham. We've got her and we'll kill her if you don't do what we say."

"The only thing I think you've got is her cell phone and a death wish."

The kidnapper had taken the bait. He'd put Mindy on the phone.

Deke Cunningham, don't pay them one red cent! It's a trap—

Tough words. Exactly what he'd expected from her. But beneath her brave words he heard fear—a soul-deep terror he'd never heard in her voice before. And that, more than anything the kidnapper said, scared him to death.

Something was wrong with her. Something beyond being kidnapped. While that alone would be enough to terrify any woman, his Mindy was made of stronger stuff.

In the twenty years since he'd first spotted her hanging by her heels from the top rung of the elementary school jungle gym, he'd never seen anything she couldn't handle.

Except him.

Her tight, strained voice, cut by static, still echoed in his head as he paused at the bottom of the dilapidated wooden steps of the only hotel in Cleancutt, Wyoming.

He'd heard about the ghost towns of Wyoming all his life. Eighty years ago, Cleancutt and other coal-mining camps had been booming towns. But by the 1950s, underground coal mining had given way to strip-mining, so today Cleancutt was a ghost, a dying piece of history located near the city of Casper.

A vibration started in his breast pocket. *Damn it.* His phone.

As he retrieved it, he glanced around him, in case he could catch someone watching him, waiting for him to answer. But the display read Irina Castle, his boss, not Mindy. He pressed the talk button without saying anything.

"Deke, where are you?" Irina asked.

"I'm busy," he said quietly.

"You did it, didn't you? You went after Mindy alone. I told you to wait until I could arrange a meeting with Aaron Schiff."

"Irina, do *not* get the FBI involved in this. It's too dangerous for Mindy. I'll handle it. Besides, you know the drill. They threatened to hurt her if I brought backup."

"And *you* know the drill. My specialists never take unnecessary risks."

"This one was necessary."

Irina blew out a sigh of frustration. "You told Aaron not to tell me where you are." Her voice was accusatory.

"It's for your own good, and Mindy's. You can't know. It's too dangerous for you. Besides, there's nobody alive who's better trained to run a covert rescue mission than me." He'd meant the comment to be reassuring, but it hung in the sudden silence between them.

Irina's husband, Rook Castle, had been the best until he'd been assassinated by Novus Ordo two years ago.

"Aaron and Rafe have my projected timeline," he continued. "They know what to do. You've got to trust me, Irina."

"I don't like it."

"You think I do? I should have known what was going to happen as soon as Matt told me he'd been followed back here from Mahjidastan. I should have anticipated that Novus would go after Mindy."

Novus Ordo was desperate to find out why Irina had suddenly called Matt Parker back from assignment in Mahjidastan and announced to her employees that she was ending her two-year-long search for her husband—or his body.

"It's not your fault, Deke."

"The hell it's not. I should have taken care of her, put her in protective custody." He shook off the feeling of failure. He'd let Mindy get captured. Now he had to rescue her.

"Don't worry, Irina. I know more about Novus than

anyone alive. You listen to Rafe and Aaron and Brock. They each have their instructions. Their primary mission is to keep you safe." He paused. "And Irina, don't leave the ranch without one of them with you. Make sure all three of them know where you're going and who you're going with."

Irina sighed in frustration. "You sound like you don't trust your own team."

"My helicopter was sabotaged. I don't trust anybody but you and me."

"You mentioned your timeline. What is it?"

"I plan to be out of there with Mindy in less than twenty-four hours."

"What's your drop-dead time?"

"Seventy-two." He had his timeline. He wished he knew what Novus's was.

"Be careful, Deke."

He hung up and started to pocket his phone, then hesitated, looking at the display.

Two days ago, the BHSAR recovery team, along with the FBI, had found the body of the man who had tried to get his hands on Matt Parker.

Papers and a prepaid cell phone found on the dead man proved his involvement in terrorist activities, with ties to Novus Ordo. It was bad enough that it took only a couple of hours for Novus to find out that Irina had recalled Matt. What made it so much worse was the ruined helicopter rotor on the floor of Deke's hangar that proved his bird had been sabotaged. The grounded helicopter had caused Deke to miss a critical rendezvous point and had almost cost Matt Parker and Aimee Vick their lives.

There was only one explanation for those security breaches.

Both the sabotage and Novus's intel had to have been engineered by someone who had unrestricted access to Castle Ranch. They had a traitor in BHSAR. Someone who was working for Novus.

Deke had put his most trusted specialists to guarding Irina. He just wished he could trust them without reservation.

But there was only one man in the world, other than himself, whom he could trust with Irina's life.

Trying to ignore the fact that his fingers were shaking, Deke dialed a number he'd thought he'd never call.

Irina's innocent action had negated everything Rook Castle had done to keep her safe.

Deke listened to the electronic message, hoping he was doing the right thing. He spoke quickly, quietly, then hung up.

It was done. Two years ago he'd made a promise to his best friend, Rook Castle. Today he'd broken it. But he'd had no choice. It was time to raise the dead.

DEKE CAREFULLY CLIMBED the crumbling steps and put his shoulder against the weathered front door of the abandoned hotel. He stopped dead in his tracks when it creaked loudly. Clutching his weapon in both hands, he listened.

Nothing. Not a scurrying rat or the buzz of a disturbed insect.

He'd expected Novus to come after him. He'd hoped the terrorist wouldn't be savvy enough to go after his ex-wife. Hell, they'd been divorced over two years.

It disturbed him that Novus knew that much about him. Mindy was his weakness.

His only weakness.

The air force had done what nothing else ever had—it had made a man out of him. He could fly a helicopter. He could shoot a housefly off a general's lapel at two hundred yards—hell, he could take that shot *while* flying a bird.

Being a Special Forces Op had taught him there was nothing he couldn't face and conquer.

But with one disappointed look, and the sparkle of a tear, Mindy could reduce him to his pathetic, arrogant high-school self, trying to bully his way through school and drink his way through life.

He stood outside the hotel's door and wondered what kind of traps Novus had set for him. He'd have preferred a face-to-face confrontation, but he already knew the publicity-shy Novus wouldn't do that.

There was a reason the terrorist wore a surgical mask in every known photo. An excellent reason. And only a few people knew what that reason was.

Yeah, he was walking into a trap. But Novus had baited it with the only lure he couldn't resist.

His ex-wife.

All those thoughts swirled through his mind in the two seconds it took for him to flex his fingers, retighten them around the grip of his Sig Sauer, and take a deep breath.

Here goes.

He nudged the door another inch and slipped through.

The hotel lobby could have been lifted out of one of the Western movies his old man had watched when he wasn't passed out from cheap vodka.

When Deke stepped inside, eyeing the ornate desk and curved staircase, glass crunched under his boot. Shattered prisms from a broken chandelier.

Then something moved at the edge of his vision.

Startled, he swung around. His finger tightened on the trigger.

A raccoon. It scurried across the room, claws clicking on the worn hardwood floor like faraway machine-gun fire.

Deke's breath whooshed out and his trigger finger relaxed. He took another step, eyeing the dark room beyond the arched doorway. He figured it was the dining room.

What was the raccoon running from? He crossed the lobby and angled around the arch so his back stayed to the wall.

Heavy curtains revealed only slivers of the late afternoon sun. The smell of mildew and rotting wood tickled his nostrils. He held his breath, resisting the urge to sneeze as he moved silently across to the shrouded windows and reached up to push the drapes apart. Too late, he saw the flash and heard the report.

Something stung the curve of his cheek. He whirled, ready to shoot, but whirling turned out not to be such a good idea.

Things got real hazy real fast. A fuzzy shadow loomed in front of him. He aimed, but as hard as he tried, he couldn't make his fingers hold on to the gun, and he couldn't make his legs hold him up.

As the room tilted sideways, the haze before his eyes turned to black.

DAMN, HE HATED THE WAITING. He liked to be the one making the phone calls. When he had to wait to be called, he couldn't control who might be listening.

He paced back and forth in front of the big picture

window, with its panoramic view of the Black Hills, until he couldn't stand it any longer. He yanked the blinds shut. He despised those desolate looming mountains. He'd seen enough of them to last him the rest of his life and beyond.

The prepaid cell phone hidden in his shaving kit rang.

Finally.

"Everything's in place here."

"No change here."

"There better be a change soon."

"I'm working on it. Do you have any idea of the level of security around this place? It's tripled since—"

"Do you have any idea of the time constraints we're facing?"

"I think I'm close—"

"You think? You'd better know! We've only got one chance. I'm guessing you remember what'll happen if you fail me."

"Why all the mind games? It'd be a hell of a lot easier to just go in and get it over with."

"Are you questioning my methods? Because you're not indispensable. Nobody is."

SOMETHING SOFT ROCKED against his side, rousing him. His mouth felt stuffed with cotton and his stomach clenched. Beneath the nauseating smell of mildew and rotten wood, he noticed a sweet, familiar scent.

He tried to push through the drowsiness, but whoever had filled his mouth with cotton had put lead weights on his eyelids. He wanted to turn over, but he was too tired.

The unmistakable supple firmness of a female body rocked against him again. "Eee!"

"Mindy, sugar," Deke mumbled. "Move over."

Whoa. A sharp blade of reality sliced through his mental fog. That wasn't right—on so many levels. For one thing, his tongue wasn't working, so all he'd managed to do was grunt unintelligibly.

"Eee, ake uk," she retorted.

What was she saying? Maybe she was dreaming. Maybe *he* was.

"Okay," he whispered, smiling drowsily to himself. "You know what happens when you don't move over." Anticipating her giggles and kisses, he turned—or tried to.

He couldn't move.

He wasn't in bed. He *sure* wasn't in bed with Mindy. That hadn't happened in a long, long time.

So where the hell was he?

More shards of reality ripped through his brain. The flash of gunpowder. The biting sting in his cheek.

He forced his eyes open. It was dark. Totally dark.

Danger! His heart rate skyrocketed and his Special Forces training kicked in.

Judging by the way his head wobbled like a bobble-head doll, he figured he'd been drugged. He clenched his jaw and worked to gather his thoughts.

The gunpowder. The sting. He'd been shot with a tranquilizer gun. Ah, hell.

He bit down on his tongue, using the pain to clear his brain. Giving in to drugs—or fatigue, or torture—in combat rescue missions could be fatal. Not only to the rescuer, but also to the innocents depending on him for their safety, their protection, their very lives.

Before he could help anyone else, he had to assess his own condition. He needed to take inventory.

Blood? No stickiness or wet warmth.

Broken bones? He shifted enough that his arms ached and his legs cramped. No.

Other injuries? Nope. Just the sting from the tranq dart. That and the drug it had delivered.

Location? Somewhere dark and damp.

Position? Tied up—arms behind his back, and gagged. He pushed his dry tongue against the cloth in his mouth. Gagged tight. Then, gingerly, he moved his legs—and nearly fell off the crate.

That explained the cramps. His ankles were tied.

Mission? Not quite as easy. What was he doing here, tied up and drugged?

"Eee!"

Mindy. Her voice ripped the haze from his brain. That was it. He'd come here to rescue her. Novus Ordo had kidnapped her to get to him.

Her soft warmth was close—way too close for comfort. Her shoulder was touching his. Judging by her restricted movements and incoherent mutterings, she was tied up and gagged, too.

He wanted to reassure her, but that would be a waste of breath with the gag in his mouth. So he spent his energy getting rid of it. He rubbed his mouth and chin against his shoulder, not easy with his hands tethered behind his back.

His neck and jaw ached like a sonofabitch, and the skin on his chin was raw by the time the cloth peeled away from his tongue and lips.

His throat was too dry to swallow. "Mindy? You all right?" he croaked.

Her answer was a frustrated growl.

"Okay, okay, just a second." He scooted closer and twisted until he was leaning heavily against her shoulder.

Another not-so-good idea. But this time it was because he got a whiff of that tangerine bath stuff she always used. He bent his head and nuzzled her cheek, feeling for her gag with his mouth.

Soft, warm, tangerine sweetness. That solved the dry-mouth issue. Her familiar scent made his mouth water and his body tighten in immediate, familiar response. He clenched his jaw and swallowed a groan of frustration. Sex had never been the problem between them.

It sure as hell hadn't been the solution.

Mindy stiffened at his frustrated moan, slamming his brain with a harsh reminder that this wasn't old times, it was deadly serious.

But she didn't lash out at him or try to move away. In fact, she angled her head to give him better access to the cloth that gagged her.

He bit and tugged at it with his teeth until it began to loosen. He tried to hold his breath, tried to ignore the soft, sensual tickle of her hair against his nose and cheek.

After a lot of tugging and nibbling and some extremely uncomfortable brushing of his mouth against her lips, cheeks and chin, he finally got her gag loose.

When he straightened, his head felt clearer, although wherever they were was dark as the cargo hold of a C-17 transport plane at midnight. The only light was pitifully dim and came from a window high above their heads.

The smell of mildew and dirt chased away Mindy's familiar, evocative scent.

"Basement," he muttered. They had to be in a basement.

Mindy groaned and wriggled against him.

"Min? Are you okay?" he asked, squinting in the darkness. He could barely make out the silhouette of her face. Her dark clothes blended into a pool of shadows just below her shoulders. "Did they hurt you?"

She shook her head. "Just practically broke my arms when he tied me up." Her normally husky voice was soft and raspy.

And sexy as hell.

Deke cursed to himself. What a chump he was. After all this time, his ex-wife could still turn him on just by talking.

She coughed. "By the way, thanks for involving me in your little adventure."

And she could still tick him off.

He took a deep breath and winced when the blast of air sent a piercing ache through his temples. "Here we go again," he muttered.

"Don't even try to tell me this doesn't involve one of your rescues," she rasped.

"You think I'd put you in danger if I could help it?"

"What I think is that you've gotten yourself in over your head again. You're never going to learn that you can't save everybody. And even if you could, it wouldn't fill up that hole inside you."

Deke grimaced. It was an old argument, and he'd be damned if he let her lead him down that road again.

He raised his gaze to hers and curved his lips in a confident smile, prepared to give her back a smart retort. But even in the dimness he could see the fear that darkened her olive-green eyes. The same fear he'd heard in her voice. It knocked the confidence right out of him.

"Min, are you sure you're okay? You don't sound too good."

She focused on a point somewhere behind him and to his left. Then she arched her neck, and sonofagun if she didn't stick the tip of her pink tongue out to moisten her lips.

Do not go there, he ordered his brain. But it went there anyhow—to all the amazing things Mindy could do with her tongue. Not the least of which was cut him down to size with a well-chosen word.

"I'm—okay," she rasped, then coughed again.

He knew how she felt. Her throat sounded as dry and sore as his. "What the hell happened? How'd they kidnap you?"

"I got a call about some—something addressed to me that had been delivered to the wrong place." Her voice gained a bit of strength as she talked. "When I went to pick it up, they grabbed me."

"Damn it, how many times have I told you—don't go to strange places alone. You know how dangerous it can be."

"Right," she croaked. "Because of your dangerous profession. Well, silly me. Since we've been divorced for two years I was kind of hoping your danger wouldn't rub off on me anymore." Her hand went to her throat.

"Besides, this was a young woman. She told me she was also pr—" She stopped.

"Also what?"

After a split-second pause and a brief shake of her head, she continued: "She said a store had delivered some things to her by mistake. They were addressed to me. She asked if I could pick them up because she was— ill."

"Damn it, Min. That's an obvious scam. I can't believe you fell for it."

"Would you listen to me?" she snapped. "She said the sender's name was Irina."

Deke's scalp prickled. More proof that Novus had deliberately targeted Mindy. He'd expected it, but that didn't mean he liked it.

"The girl said that?"

She nodded. "I should have been suspicious, because Irina wouldn't know— I mean, there's no reason she'd send me a b— a gift out of the blue."

"What's the matter with you? Did they drug you, too? You sound strange."

"As soon as the door opened, somebody dragged me inside and stuck something in my neck. The next thing I knew, I woke up here."

"Did you get a look at them?"

"No. I was blindfolded until they brought you in this morning. He took my blindfold off right before he left. I never saw him."

"But it *was* a man? What did he tell you? Anything? What made you think it had anything to do with me?"

Mindy made a small, impatient noise. He knew the look she was wearing, as well as if she were standing in a spotlight. He'd seen it too many times before. It was her *do not treat me like an idiot* scowl.

"What made me—? Maybe because I've never done anything that would cause anyone to kidnap me. You, on the other hand—"

"Me what?" His evasion was automatic. He'd practiced evading the truth from the time he could talk. It was ingrained in him—part of his survival tactic.

But he knew she was right. He'd done plenty in his lifetime that might make him the target of revenge. Not the least of which had been just two years ago.

A lot of people, including Mindy, would want his head on a pike if they knew what he'd done—for and *to* his best friend. His only friend.

However, what *a lot of people* thought meant nothing. He'd do it again. That and more, for the one man who'd always believed in him—who'd trusted his life to him.

His life *and* his death.

I just hope your sacrifice wasn't in vain, Rook. Because here they were battling Novus Ordo again. And this time he wasn't going to give up.

"Okay, fine," he snapped at Mindy. "Supposing for the moment that I've screwed up your life yet again. I can't change that. But I can do my best to get us out of here. I promise, as soon as I can manage it, I'll get you back to the normal, safe life you like so much."

Chapter Two

If her mouth didn't hurt so much, she'd smile at Deke's words, Mindy thought. *The normal, safe life you like so much.*

She'd give anything for normal and safe right now.

But as usual when Deke was around, normal and safe had left the building.

His words were on target. She'd loved him most of her life, and loving Deke wasn't exactly a recipe for normal. Certainly not for safe.

Loving Deke was a recipe for disaster. Not that her heart cared. Nor her body. He'd always been the sexiest thing on the planet. From his sun-streaked brown hair to his startling sea-blue eyes. From the hard line of his jaw to his broad, leanly muscled shoulders. Even his battered shearling jacket couldn't hide the power and grace of his six-feet-plus body.

A wave of nausea reminded her that this was no time to be ogling her ex-husband. She swallowed against the queasiness that was fast overtaking her. It had plagued her ever since the moment yesterday morning when she'd rapped on the apartment door. Even before the door opened, she knew she'd made a mistake.

Deke had warned her often enough not to wander around strange places by herself. But the message had been so simple, so innocent sounding.

Hi. Mindy Cunningham? I just received a delivery from Babies First that belongs to you. It's from an Irene or Irina Castle. I'd bring it to you, but I'm on bed rest for the last month of my pregnancy. Can you pick it up?

When she got to the address, the person who opened the door wasn't a pregnant woman. Wasn't even a woman. It was a man. Something about him—the expression on his face or the gleam in his eyes—confirmed that she'd screwed up.

Before she could react, he'd grabbed her arm and pulled her inside, slamming the door behind her. Then he'd shoved her up against a wall and stuck something into the back of her neck.

He'd drugged her.

She was terrified that whatever he'd given her might hurt the baby. It was her worst fear—that something might happen to her little Sprout.

As if he knew what she was thinking, Sprout kicked. She rubbed her tummy and smiled sadly.

Until she'd acquired this tiny passenger that depended on her for his very life, she'd have said her worst fear was that she'd never be able to get over the man sitting next to her.

Deke Cunningham, air force veteran, sharpshooter, alcoholic, adventurer and ex-husband.

Once their divorce was final, her plan had been to never see him again. But the best-laid plans…

Just over eight months ago, he'd come to her mother's funeral. One of about three times in his life she'd seen him in a suit. He'd been handsome as a *GQ* model, and more gentle, sweet and protective than he'd ever been before.

For that one night, he was the man she'd always known he could be.

At the end of the evening he was still there, at her house. Just to make sure she was okay, he'd said.

When he got up to leave, somehow she'd asked him to stay. They'd somehow ended up in the bed, and she'd somehow ended up pregnant.

So much for getting over him.

"Mindy, you're not okay. They hurt you, didn't they?"

His voice was controlled—barely, but that was all about him that was. His intensity and anger washed over her like scalding hot water. Anger, not at her, but on her behalf.

"No, I'm not injured. Just tired and hurting."

He'd never understood why she hadn't wanted him to be angry for her. He'd never realized that his anger—even when it wasn't directed at her—still scared her.

And that was why, although he needed to know what he was up against—deserved to—she couldn't tell him. Not until she absolutely had to.

Like the coward she was, she planned to put off that revelation as long as she possibly could, because scalding water didn't begin to describe what Deke would throw at her when he found out she was pregnant—with *his* child.

"Deke, we've got to get out of here. The guy told me he'd be watching me. He'll be back anytime."

"Yeah, we do. Can you move? Turn around. Let me see your hands."

Could she move? Hah. *Not too well,* she wanted to answer. Like an overloaded supply plane, she was carrying heavy on the front end.

She twisted until her back was to him, working to suppress the grunts and groans that went with everything she did these days.

By the time he said "That's good," she was breathing hard.

"Min, are you sure you're okay?"

She squeezed her eyes shut and nodded. "It's the drug," she said as evenly as she could. "It's making me light-headed. And I'm hungry."

He chuckled. "No surprise there."

Mindy bit her lip against the poignant memories that bombarded her. The sweet teasing, the tickling matches, the kisses. Dear heavens, she'd missed him. It didn't matter how many times her head reminded her heart that they were as compatible as jet fuel and an ignition source.

He twisted on the wooden crate until he was facing her back. Then he bent double to look at the ropes binding her hands.

He uttered a short burst of colorful curses. "Damn it, I can't see anything."

"Can you bite them like you did the gag?"

He sniffed in disdain. "My teeth aren't that good. Stay still."

Mindy waited. It soon became obvious that Deke was scooting around until his back was to hers. Then he shifted closer and twisted some more, until they were pressed together like bookends.

She felt his hands on hers, big, warm, protective, as they explored the ropes.

He let go a string of colorful curses. "…Those sons of bitches," he finished.

Mindy's pulse skittered. "What is it Deke? What's wrong?"

"Nobody's this stupid. Everything about this, from the moment you called, has been too easy," he muttered. "Too pat."

"Too easy? How is this easy?"

"They used your phone. Didn't even bother to keep the call short. Like they were telegraphing their location. And now, these knots are just strong enough to be frustrating. If he'd wanted to, he could have used knots I'd never be able to untie."

"That makes sense," she rasped. "I tried to warn you that it was a trap to lure you here."

"Trust me. I'd already figured that out."

Deke's hands moved over hers, touching and manipulating as he worked to loosen the knots.

"Ow!"

"Sorry."

"No, I'm sorry. My thumb got a little twisted."

"I'm almost done."

She listened to his labored breathing as he worked. "Deke, why do they want you? You know who they are, don't you?"

She winced as the knots began to loosen and the circulation increased in her fingers. "This is connected to a case, isn't it?"

He shook his head. She had her back to him and she knew he'd done it. Was it a movement of the air, a rustle of his clothing? Or was it the connection they'd always shared? Even when they couldn't share their dreams or their heartbreaks.

"I'm not on a case right now. I'm trying to stick close to the ranch. Irina's not doing well. She's stopped searching for Rook."

"What? Oh, Deke. I can't believe she'd ever— Did she find out something?"

"Ran out of money." He pushed air out between his clenched teeth, a sure sign he was frustrated about something.

"She stopped because of *money?*"

"She either had to stop the search or fire at least two specialists and cut back on voluntary cases."

His fingers strained against hers as he picked at one of the knots. His breath hitched and he grunted quietly.

Mindy knew what he was feeling. His arms were tied behind his back, just like hers were, and she couldn't even imagine the pain in his wrists from working against the stiff ropes. She wanted to say something, to at least acknowledge the pain he was going through. But Deke Cunningham would never admit pain. Not pain. Not hurt. Not heartache.

"But Rook's her *husband.* I can't believe she'd quit for *any* reason. I'd never—" she stopped, biting her tongue—literally. *Never give up* was what she'd been about to say.

But she had. She'd given up on them.

"Well, she did." Deke's curt answer told her that he hadn't missed what she'd almost said. His breath hissed out between his teeth again. A sure sign that he was hurting.

Not knowing what else to say, she kept talking about Irina Castle. Maybe if he got irritated enough with her, it would distract him from the pain in his wrists.

"She must be devastated. It would be bad enough to

give up if she knew it was useless. But not to know, and to have to stop because of money. When did she make that decision?"

He didn't respond, just kept working silently.

He didn't want to tell her. Dear Lord, she knew him so well. "When, Deke?"

At that moment she felt the ropes give, releasing the strain on her shoulders, arms and wrists. Pain shot through her muscles as they relaxed. She bit her lip and tried to suppress a groan.

"Easy," Deke muttered. "Don't move too fast. You'll regret it, trust me."

It was one of the cryptic remarks that reminded her how little she knew about this man she'd loved as long as she could remember. She slowly flexed her arms and shoulders, clamping her jaw against the pain, as her brain filed that tidbit of information away with the others she'd collected over the years.

He knew how it felt to be tied up for hours—or days.

He twisted around. "Turn around this way. I need you to get my knife," he said. "It's in my left boot, *if* they didn't strip-search me while I was out. They took my gun. Thank God I ditched my cell phone."

She twisted awkwardly around until her shoulder bumped his. "They didn't search you after they brought you down here. They didn't have time. One of them got a phone call, but he obviously didn't want to talk in front of me, so they left." She looked down, but the tiny window didn't provide enough light for her to see that close to the ground. Still, she knew she couldn't bend over far enough to reach his boot.

"Good. See if you can grab my knife."

"No," she said flatly. "I can't."

"Come on, Min. It's sticking down in the side of my left boot. You remember where I keep it."

"I *can't*."

"Why not?"

She bit her lip. She'd put off the *big reveal* as long as she could.

"Are you injured? Too stiff? What?"

She almost cried. He assumed she was hurting. And she let him think that. Dear heavens, she'd never realized what a coward she was.

"These knots are so slippery, I'll bet I can loosen them." He kicked his feet back and forth, working the ropes. "There." He inched around.

Mindy could see his head and shoulders in the dim light. She'd already felt the comforting softness and smelled the old-leather smell of his jacket. So it was no surprise that even with the darkness leaching the color out of everything, she could see the way it bunched across his constrained shoulders. She could even see the shadow of his too-long hair on the sheepskin collar.

He straightened his leg and barely missed brushing her tummy with the side of his boot. She flexed her cramped fingers and rubbed the indentations on her wrists. Then quickly, she wrapped her right arm around his calf and got her hands behind the boot heel and tugged.

"Pull your foot backward against my hands."

"You got it, sugar."

Her heart twisted until she wanted to cry out. "And don't call me sugar," she hissed.

He pulled backward, inadvertently pushing his heel into her tummy. "Hey—" he said.

Mindy cringed. "What?" she snapped.

"Have you gained weight?"

"Deke, this is serious."

He didn't say anything for a couple of seconds. "I know it is."

Tugging harder, she finally got a purchase on the boot heel and jerked it off his foot. His knife fell into her lap as something clattered against the crate and onto the floor.

"There," she said, breathing hard as she pushed his foot off her lap and picked up the knife. She pressed the button that sprung the blade. It snicked into place.

Deke jumped at the sound. "Hey, careful. It's sharp."

"I remember that, too." She slid the knife blade between his wrists. The blade sliced through the thick rope as if it were warm butter.

Deke carefully relaxed his shoulders and moved his arms. He grunted a couple of times.

She knew what he was going through. He hadn't been tied up as long as she had, but she figured the kidnappers hadn't been as careful with him as they had with her. His hands had to be on fire as the blood rushed back to them.

She handed him the knife, her heart pounding. When he leaned over to cut the ropes binding her feet, would he see why he'd gotten the impression she'd gained weight?

She held her breath while he cut the ropes. "I had a cigarette lighter in my boot with the knife. I think I heard it fall."

Mindy felt around with her foot until she touched a small cylinder. "Here it is." She kicked it toward him.

He grabbed it and sat up, grunting. "Whoa! I can understand why you didn't want to bend over. I'm still

kind of woozy." He reached a hand out to the wall beside him and stood. His shadow loomed over her "Can
you stand up? We need to get out of here."

Mindy crouched there, her shoulders hunched. Right
now, he couldn't see anything. But as soon as she stood—

*Dear God, please help me. When Deke sees me, I'm
going to need all the courage you can spare.*

He was about to find out that she was pregnant. She
had no idea what he'd do.

She *did* remember what he'd said he'd do.

Years ago, when they were seventeen, she'd had a
scare. She was late, and the pregnancy test had read posi-
tive. When she'd told Deke, his reaction had been immediate. Shock and abject terror had darkened his features.

*You're pregnant? No. No way. You gotta do some-
thing. There's enough screwed-up Cunninghams in the
world already.*

She'd been stunned and frightened. But she'd understood. If she'd had the baby, Deke would be gone. But
the issue was moot, because a few days later she'd
started her period. They'd never spoken about it again.

Now here she was, six weeks away from bringing a
Cunningham into the world. And six seconds away
from Deke finding out.

"Stand up." He held out his hand. "You'll be woozy,
but I won't let you fall."

Mindy sucked in a deep breath and took his hand.
Struggling, bracing herself against the wall, and with
a lot of grunting and groaning, she managed to push
herself upright.

When their gazes met, his expression softened and
his fingers tightened on her hand. "Hey, Min. It's been
a long time." His mouth quirked.

She swallowed hard. "Long time," she replied, with a nervous nod.

"I'm so sorry they hurt you," he whispered. He leaned in closer, a gentle smile on his face.

Then he stopped—dead still. His gaze flickered downward.

Her mouth went dry. She couldn't move. All she could do was stand there.

She knew what he saw. A dark wool peacoat, navy blue pants and low-heeled boots. Pretty standard wear for this weather.

But the peacoat stuck out to *there,* and he'd just bumped into her tummy.

Her hands moved to cradle the baby. She couldn't stop them. It was an innate reaction, a protective instinct. Shielding her baby from what was to come.

Trembling with trepidation, she braced herself.

Deke stood frozen, his face lit by the fading beam of light from the tiny window. As wan and dim as the light was, she still saw the color drain from his face. His blue eyes widened and his mouth dropped open.

Mindy cradled her belly tighter.

"Min—?" His voice broke.

She bit her lip as her heart broke.

He shook his head as if to clear it—or to deny the truth before his eyes.

Then it hit—the storm of Deke's anger. His brows lowered until his eyes were dark and hooded. "Mindy, what the hell have you done?"

She tried to hold her own against Deke's fiery gaze, but she couldn't. She had to look away.

"Deke, that kidnapper is coming back anytime. It's been hours since he checked on me."

"I'll deal with him when he gets here." His voice was tight with what? Confusion? Shock? Fury? She couldn't sort out all the emotions. For the first time since she'd known him she wasn't sure what was behind his clipped words.

"How did you—?"

The baby kicked, probably feeling her distress. She rubbed the spot and he calmed down. "How? The usual way."

"So who's the lucky guy?"

And there it was. Deke Cunningham's patented defense system. More efficient than any antimissile missile the government had ever dreamed up. It was as effective and high-tech as the Starship *Enterprise*'s shields, and as quick to rise to protect his heart.

Although she understood why he did it, his words still hurt. She braced herself. "You are."

Chapter Three

Mindy sucked in a deep breath as she watched her ex-husband and waited for the explosion.

His face was still lit by that small rectangle of light. If he realized it, he'd move—cover his reaction with darkness. But right this second she had a unique opportunity to watch his face as he processed what she'd said.

His eyes widened in panic for a split second, then narrowed. His brows knit in a frown and he blew air out between his clenched teeth. "That's impossible. We haven't even seen each other in almost a year."

"Eight months plus a week, to be exact," she murmured.

"Eight—oh. Your mom's funeral." He shot her a look before he turned away, out of the wan spotlight. Then tightly, "Why didn't you tell me?"

"You know why. Look at your reaction. Now can we focus on the kidnapper, who's going to show up any minute?"

"Fine," he snapped. He wiped a hand down his face and around to rub the nape of his neck.

When he turned back around, his features were carefully neutral and his voice was all business. "What do you know about this place? Where's the door?"

She ignored his curt tone and pointed behind them. "There's a staircase back there. I hear the door open. I see light until he closes it. Then he comes down the stairs. Twelve. Twelve steps."

Deke tried to concentrate on her words. She was absolutely right. They needed to get out of there before their captors came back.

But all he could think about was her…condition. And she was right about his reaction. Years ago she'd come to him, worried that she might be pregnant, and he'd lost it. Yelled at her.

Scared her. His heart twisted with regret for an instant, then leapt again in renewed panic.

The idea of having a kid scared him. More than anything he'd ever come up against—before or since. And he'd faced a lot.

But a baby. His mouth went dry and his chest tightened.

Damn it, he didn't have time to be distracted by emotion. He had to focus. He squeezed his eyes shut and forced himself to concentrate on the danger. To forget that his ex-wife was carrying his child.

He growled under his breath and looked in the direction she'd indicated. He recognized the stairs. Their shape stood out as a darker shadow ascending into blackness.

The basement was so damn dark, and the light from the window above was waning. He was pretty sure, based on his instinctive sense of direction, that the window faced east.

He'd driven in from the east, from nearby Casper.

He wasn't sure what good that information did him, but at least he was oriented now.

"It's getting dark out. What else have you seen? Did the man bring a light with him?"

Mindy's hands were cradling her belly and her head was inclined. A serene expression made her face as beautiful as a Madonna. Amazingly, even in the darkness of the basement, she glowed. She was lush and beautiful. He wanted her so bad he ached.

Stop it!

She looked up, frowning. He could see her processing his words. "No. The last time, he and another guy were dragging you. I couldn't figure out what I was hearing until you grunted." She smiled. "No mistaking that growl. Anyhow, when they took off my blindfold I tried to take in as much as I could before they left and closed that door. I saw something over there, beyond that stack of wood. Maybe a door, or an opening of some kind."

"Stay right there," Deke ordered, pointing at her feet. He moved carefully toward the place she'd indicated. The entire floor was dirt, and littered with boards and logs along with pieces of broken furniture.

Within minutes it would be too dark to see, but his senses took in the shapes of the shadows and the musty smells. He figured that there was very little down here newer than fifty years old.

Finally, his outstretched hands touched the wall. Mindy was right. Complete darkness had already encroached on this end of the basement. He ran his hands over the rough-hewn boards. If there was a door, he couldn't find it.

He rapped on the wood, listening for a hollow echo. No luck. Every place he knocked sounded solid as a rock.

Finally, as a last resort, he reached in his pocket and pulled out the disposable cigarette lighter. He shook it. Fairly full. Striking it with his thumb, he used its light to quickly examine the wall.

"Deke?"

Mindy's scared voice, harsh with the strain of holding herself together, tore through him.

"Just a minute, sugar," he said, studying the crevices between the boards. If there was an opening in this alcove, he couldn't find it.

The lighter was beginning to burn his thumb, so he let go, then turned around and made his way back to her.

"Okay. I'm going upstairs and check things out. You stay here. You were right about the alcove, but I can't find a door anywhere, and we're almost out of light."

"Deke, you can't go up there. You said they wanted you to get out of the knots. That means they'll be waiting up there to ambush you."

"I'd be surprised if they weren't. But I'll deal with them. When I call you, we'll make a run for it."

Mindy shook her head. "No. It won't work. You can't—"

"Have you got a better idea? Because I don't. Our only other choice is to wait until they come back, and I'm not going to fight them down here so close to you. You could get hurt. Now give me my knife and stop arguing. You're wasting time. Nothing's going to happen to me."

"You don't know that—"

"Nothing ever has."

"We both know that's not true."

Deke clenched his jaw. The arguing had always come so easily. Just like the sex. Two things they'd always gotten right.

They'd learned early how to push each other's buttons.

"My knife, Mindy."

She handed it to him.

He closed it and stuck it in his pocket. Then he dropped the disposable lighter down inside his boot.

"Grab those ropes and sit back down. I'll wrap them loosely around your hands and feet, so you'll look like you're still tied up if they—" he paused "—get past me."

"Wait. I don't understand."

"If they come down here, I want you to look like you're still tied up. That way they can't blame you for trying to escape. Just me."

Mindy slowly bent down, reaching a hand out to steady herself against the wall.

Deke grimaced. This was going to be harder than he could have imagined. She was so handicapped by her pregnancy that she couldn't even bend down. He cupped her elbow.

"Okay, never mind." He led her over to sit on the wooden crate and fetched the ropes.

"Put your hands behind your back."

He took her hands and carefully looped the rope around them. Then, bending in front of her, he wrapped the second rope around her feet.

He straightened. "Good. In the dark, it'll look like you're really tied up."

"I *feel* like I'm really tied up. Are you sure about this?" Her voice was edged with panic.

"Trust me, sugar." His mouth flattened in a grimace, just like it did every time he said those words to her. She couldn't trust him. He knew it, and she knew it. He'd let her down too many times.

"But how—"

He placed into her palm one end of the rope that was wrapped around her hands. "Hang on to that end of the rope. When you pull it the ropes will fall off. The ropes around your feet aren't secured at all. Just kick them."

"Deke, I don't like this."

He glanced at the lone window, high above their heads. Then, closing his eyes, he formed a mental blueprint of the main floor of the hotel in his brain. "If the desk is there, and the stairs are there—" he muttered, tracing the most likely route out of the building.

"Listen to me, Min. That window faces east. My car is out there. Whatever you do, keep yourself oriented. The front of the building faces south." He pointed in that direction. "Which means these stairs are on the north side. That door probably opens into the kitchen."

He laid his palms against her shoulders. "Relax," he said, massaging the muscles there. "You can let your hands rest against the ropes. They won't give unless you jerk the end you have in your fingers."

"The dining room is through an arched doorway to the right—east—of the desk. I want you to wait down here until I call you. If you don't hear anything within a half hour, undo the ropes and run up the stairs. If you see a clear shot to a back door, take it. Otherwise run through the dining room into the lobby and hightail it out the front door."

"Hightailing is not so easy these days."

Deke grabbed her arm. "Listen to me, Min. Your life and the life of—" He couldn't say the words. "Whatever happens, you *have* to save yourself. Got it?"

She bit her lip and looked up at him. "Deke, I—"

"Got—it?" he bit out.

"G-got it."

"When you get to my car, you'll find a spare key and a cell phone under the driver's seat."

"Who's supposed to be there to help—?"

"Drive like hell due east. Call Irina. Her number is first on the call list."

Mindy stared at him, wide-eyed. On her face was a mixture of trust, fear, doubt and a shadow that didn't come from the dim light in the room. It came from inside her. Slowly, she nodded.

He turned toward the stairs and stopped.

He was leaving Mindy undefended. Mindy and his unborn child. A strange mixture of pride and abject terror weakened his knees.

He'd saved a lot of innocent lives, and while he understood that underestimating his enemy could be fatal, he'd never once doubted his own ability.

Okay—once. Right now, he felt like a rookie who'd been handed two equally deadly choices.

For the first time in his life, he hesitated over which course to take. For the *second* time ever, the awful consequences of failure slammed him in the face.

There was a reason Deke Cunningham never thought about losing. Because to consider the results was unbearable.

If he went out there armed with a four-inch switchblade, he had a very good chance of succeeding—against one or two, maybe even three opponents. But if he failed—

If he failed, he left Mindy and his child vulnerable. That was unthinkable.

He turned around. "Here's what I'm going to do," he said, stepping over to her and bending down until his lips were next to her ear. "Keep the knife."

She looked shocked. "But—"

"Shh."

"But Deke," she whispered. "That's your— No. I mean, no, you can't go out there with nothing."

He held out his hands in front of her face. "I've got these. Now, where do you want me to put the knife? In the pocket of your coat?"

She shook her head. "Everything I put in those slanted pockets falls out. Put it in my bra."

"Your—?"

"Shh." She smiled wryly. "It's not like you don't know where it is. Do you want me to do it? And then you can retie the ropes around my hands?"

He shook his head, rubbing his face against her silky, tangerine-scented skin. "I'll do it." He opened her coat and unbuttoned the three buttons at the neckline of her sweater, then he pulled the knife out of his pocket.

"Okay," he whispered, feeling like a kid about to cop his first feel. He felt that awkward, that shy, that excited.

Quickly he slid his hand down through the neckline of her sweater. When his fingers slid over the rising mounds of her breasts, he almost gasped. They were so full and round and firm.

Her body was preparing for her child. Awed and speechless, and working as fast as he could, he slid the knife between her breast and the cup of the bra.

"Does that feel okay?"

Her head inclined slightly. "It's good," she murmured, sounding a little breathless.

He extracted his hand and rebuttoned her sweater. Then he pulled the lapels of her coat together. When he lifted his gaze, she was looking up at him.

He wanted to kiss her so badly he ached. Not a lover's kiss. Just a gesture of caring, a promise that he'd do anything to protect her and the child that she sheltered inside her.

But he'd made her so many promises, and he'd broken them all.

So instead, he made a vow to himself. A simple vow. Yet one more difficult to keep than any promise he'd made to her, kept or not.

He vowed that when she was safe, he'd get out of her life and stay out. He grinned as pain stabbed his heart. Leaving her meant leaving his child. Still, she and the baby would be better off if he was out of their lives. And she knew it.

She deserved a chance to make a new life with her baby. The kind of life she'd always wanted but never had with him.

A normal, safe life.

"Ready, Min?" he whispered.

She lifted her chin and her eyes drifted shut. After a second, she opened them again. "I'm ready."

After one more tug on the lapels of her coat, he left her there and climbed the stairs. At the top, he turned around to check on her. He couldn't see her. Everything below him was a lake of darkness.

That was good.

He nodded in her direction, knowing she could see

him, then reached out toward the doorknob. His hand stilled just millimeters from the knob as qualms assailed him.

"Here we go, Min," he whispered. "Be ready for anything." He turned the doorknob carefully, repeating the warning to himself. Then he pushed open the door.

The room in front of him was nearly as shrouded in darkness as the basement below. He took a careful step forward as his eyes sought the source of the faint light he'd seen under the threshold. It seemed to be coming from behind the open door. Probably daylight from the dining room and lobby.

Without moving, he listened. *Nothing.* Still the uneasy feeling that had prickled his nape—the feeling that someone was watching—wouldn't leave him.

He took a step forward so he could pull the door shut behind him. A blinding bright light flared in front of his face.

He squeezed his eyes shut and whirled toward the light, swinging his clasped fists like a sledgehammer, hoping to take down whoever was holding it.

Fireworks exploded inside his head, snapping it backward. He grabbed at the doorknob, but his hand barely brushed it.

He managed to get his feet under him, even though the blow still rang in his head and his eyes were still blinded. He swung his fists, seeking a target, but just as he connected sidelong with what felt like an arm, something heavy and forceful hit him in the middle of his chest.

He fell backward through the open door. He managed to grab the stair rail, but it didn't hold. Nails screeched as the wood gave way. He heard a scream. *Mindy?*

His butt bumped down a couple of stairs before he managed to stop himself.

He still couldn't see, but over the years he'd honed all his senses. Now they came to his aid as he reacted instinctively, like an animal.

He heard a heavy step on the hollow stairs, felt the swish of air that indicated movement close to him.

He scrabbled to get his feet under him and prepared to launch himself at his attacker. Before he could do more than tense his thighs to spring, a dark figure loomed in his blurry vision and swung something shiny at his head.

MINDY KNEW SCALP WOUNDS BLED a lot. That was Nursing 101, but she'd been an administrator for so long she'd forgotten a lot of the everyday side of nursing, like how bad a little bit of blood could appear.

The cut on Deke's forehead wasn't little. An inch-long diagonal slice was laid open above his right eyebrow, and he looked like he'd lost a fistfight with a heavyweight.

The guy standing over him wouldn't have made middleweight soaking wet. He was medium height and skinny, and dressed as if he'd stepped out of a B Western, down to the curled-brim black hat and the red bandanna tied over his nose and mouth. He still clutched the big six-gun he'd used to coldcock Deke.

As she watched, he cautiously nudged Deke's ribs with a silver-toed cowboy boot.

Deke stirred and groaned.

The man jerked his foot away.

Mindy held her breath, trying her best to stay still. She'd almost given herself away by jumping up when Deke tumbled down the stairs. She *had* screamed at him.

He'd rounded on her and warned her in a gruff, fake Texas drawl that if she didn't shut up he'd stuff a rag in her mouth and blindfold her. She'd nodded meekly and stayed as still as her worry and agitation would let her.

"Get up, Cunningham," the gunman growled. He stood over Deke, watching him warily, one hand pointing his gun and the other resting on what looked like a stubby billy club. "You think you're pretty smart, don't you? Getting yourself untied. How come you didn't untie your girlfriend? Oh, wait. She's your wife, ain't she? Or is that your ex-wife?"

Deke pushed himself up to his hands and knees and shook his head, slinging droplets of blood in a semicircle around him.

"Min?" he rasped.

At that instant the cowboy reared back and kicked him in the gut. He dropped with a pained grunt.

Despite her resolve, Mindy gasped aloud.

Deke's grunt stretched out into a growl. He bowed his back and dropped his head.

She watched in stunned awe as he got his feet under him and sprang up like a big cat. He hurled himself at the gunman.

The gunman barely sidestepped in time to avoid being bowled over. Deke checked his lunge, twisting and falling on his shoulder.

The man turned toward Mindy, pressing the barrel of the gun into her temple. "Don't make another move," he yelled. "I'll kill her. She's disposable now that I've got you."

"Stop!" Deke shouted, as he rolled and shot to his feet. His hands spread in a gesture of surrender. "What do you want? Just tell me what you want."

Don't, Mindy wanted to cry. *Don't give in to his scare tactics.* But even if she could have spoken, she was too terrified to put up a brave front. She was terrified—for herself, yes, but more for the baby.

She closed her fist around the piece of rope in her hand, wishing she could figure out a way to surprise the gunman.

Something of what she was thinking must have shown in her face, because Deke shook his head, a subtle movement worthy of a major league pitcher refusing his catcher's signal.

Meanwhile, the gunman thumbed his ridiculous hat up onto his forehead. His little beady eyes crinkled. The red bandanna tied around his nose and mouth stretched, suggesting a grin.

"Whadda I want?" he growled in his silly Texas accent. "I want answers—"

"Fine," Deke broke in, spreading his hands wider. "Let Mindy go, and I'll give you all the answers you could possibly want. Fire away."

The man shook his head slowly from side to side. "Not yet. If I ask you now, you'll just lie to me. I figure it'll take a couple days to wear you down," he drawled. "By then you'll have tried everything you can think of to escape or get the drop on me, and you'll fail every time. You'll be hungry and thirsty and tired. Even better, your gal there'll be pretty darn sick from hunger and exhaustion, seeing as how she's *that* close to whelpin' that pup. It yours?"

"That's none of your damn business. Who the hell are you anyhow?"

"So it ain't yours." He chuckled nasally. "She been sleeping around on you, ain't she?"

Deke went still. Mindy knew he was about two seconds from a firestorm.

"Deke—" she said quietly.

He shushed her with a wave of his hand and lowered his head. His dark eyes glowed dangerously. "Who are you?" he growled.

Mindy watched his fingers curl—not into fists. They curved like claws, ready to sink into the soft flesh of the man's neck. His knees bent slightly, like a cat about to spring.

The gunman took a half step closer to Mindy's side and pressed the gun barrel into her flesh. "I'm asking the questions here, Cunningham. You'll find out who I am soon enough. Meanwhile, you can call me Frank James." He chuckled. "Now it's time for you to get a taste of what's to come."

"You come near me again, you'll regret it for a long time."

The bandanna stretched again, and the black eyes crinkled. "Don't worry, Cunningham. I'm not planning to come near you. Not right now."

He cocked his weapon slowly, drawing out the *snick-snick* of metal against metal. Mindy felt the end of the barrel scrape against her skin.

Deke's head jerked slightly and his face drained of color. "Wait!" he snapped.

She closed her eyes involuntarily, and her shoulders tensed.

"Wanna play a game? How about Russian roulette? How about you Mrs. Ex-Cunningham?"

"Put the gun down," Deke warned. He stepped forward, his hands still out, and still curved like claws.

Mindy pulled the end of the rope Deke had left in

her hand. Just as he'd promised her, the ropes immediately loosened and dropped silently to the floor. She
had no idea what having her hands loose would do for
her chances. But if an opportunity presented itself, she
planned to be ready.

"Don't move!" Frank James shouted. Coward that
he was, he moved behind Mindy, and put one hand
against the side of her head while he pressed the barrel
into her temple with the other.

Deke hadn't taken his eyes off James since the instant he'd cocked his gun. His expression was a mask
of fear and nausea. He believed Frank James would
shoot her.

The realization of how afraid Deke was sent panic
fluttering into her throat.

Right now they were in a standoff. Deke couldn't
rush James without fear that he'd pull the trigger. James
couldn't easily lower his gun without the fear that Deke
might jump him. And she couldn't do anything.

Or could she?

Her hands were free, and James didn't know that.
Considering his position, if she interlaced her fingers
to form a double fist, she might be able to slam him in
the groin and get away.

Okay, maybe not get away—not constrained by her
bulk as she was. But at least she could give Deke a
chance to jump him while he was doubled over with
pain. Maybe Deke could even grab his gun.

Of course she could also get herself shot in the head.
But at least she'd be shot trying to do something. Frank
James didn't sound like the most stable kidnapper on the
planet. He could accidentally pull the trigger at any
second.

Here goes. She looked up at Deke and slowly winked at him. His brows drew down slightly. He gave her another of his World Series-caliber head shakes.

But she couldn't obey him. She had to try something. With excruciating slowness she pushed her fingers together, moving her shoulders as little as possible.

She moaned loud enough for James to hear her as she drew up carefully, until every muscle and tendon in her arms and shoulders were tense and poised, preparing for one ultimate purpose—driving her fists into Frank James's groin.

"Shut up," he snapped.

"But I'm hurting." She made her voice small and hesitant. "I need to move my legs. Please?"

James made a growling sound in his throat, but he eased off the pressure of the barrel at her temple.

Mindy shifted position, using the movement to brace her feet on the floor. Then she took a long, slow breath, and sighed, as if in relief.

Deke's body tensed expectantly. At that instant, she rammed her fists backward, putting all her weight and all her determination behind the blow.

She connected.

James squealed and dropped his gun.

Deke dove forward.

Mindy froze, staying as still as possible. She felt Deke's hands sliding under her arms. He lifted her up off the crate and out of the way.

But by the time he'd turned back to James, the man had retrieved the short baton from his belt. He flicked his wrist and it telescoped.

Deke stopped in midlunge and backpedaled. He held up his hands, palms out, and glanced back her way.

James flicked his thumb and a faint crackling hum filled the air.

Mindy stiffened. What *was* that thing?

Then he lunged, as if with a fencing sword, right for Deke's solar plexus. Deke tried to pull back, but she was too close behind him, so he took the full brunt of the attack. His spine arched sharply and he growled between clenched teeth. Then he flopped to the ground like a discarded rag doll.

Chapter Four

"Deke!" Mindy screamed, as he collapsed to the dirt floor of the basement. "What did you do to him?"

"Shut up, honey, or I'll give you a dose of the same."

She cradled her belly and glared at Frank James, or whatever the heck his name was. She was so damn helpless.

I love you, Sprout, but you're crippling me.

Deke heard Mindy's scream, but he couldn't make sense of what she'd said. He had to get to her.

Cold dirt scraped against his cheek.

What the hell was the ground doing there?

He tried to lift a hand, but his hand wasn't paying attention to his brain. Nor were his feet. Even his eyelids seemed stuck open.

He saw a movement in front of his eyes. Something glittery—silver? James's damn cowboy boots. Fake and all show, just like the lowlife who was wearing them.

Kick me again, bastard, and I'll make you regret it. At least that was what he wanted to say, but his mouth wasn't cooperating, either.

From somewhere he smelled the aroma of tangerines, mingled with dirt, mildew and the faint odor of burnt hair.

Then, more static filled his ears, his muscles spasmed in unbelievable pain and lightning struck his head.

WHEN HE GOT BACK TO HIS ROOM it was almost midnight. The strategy meeting Irina had called had lasted a lot longer than planned, mostly because they couldn't agree on a course of action.

He'd tried to sound helpful but neutral. Trouble was, everybody else was doing the same thing. Ultimately the only decision that was agreed upon was that Irina would not leave Castle Ranch until the threat from Novus Ordo was over.

He could see in the other guys' eyes that they were as skeptical as he was that she'd be able to stay put that long.

He bolted his door and put the chain on, made sure the blinds were closed, then went into the bathroom and dug in his shaving kit for the miniature cell phone.

Sure enough—a missed call. Reluctantly, he pressed the callback button, wishing he had good news to report.

THE INSIDE OF DEKE'S EYELIDS screamed with pain.

It was that damn sand. It got into everything. Slowly, he opened his eyes to a narrow slit. The tent was dark, so he had a few hours before Novus's man came to torture him again.

He came every day. Every damn day. With that laugh. That gun.

That sound.

An icy shudder of helpless terror crawled up his spine as he relived those awful few seconds. They never varied.

First, the pressure of cold steel against his temple. Then the split second of screaming panic and soul-wrenching sorrow before the hammer clicked against the empty chamber.

The sound triggered a cold sweat of relief, and the casually curious question of whether he would hear that same clicking sound if the hammer impacted a live round.

Finally came the regret that he'd lived through one more day. Because that meant tomorrow he'd have to face the same fate again. The inside of his mouth turned to sand-blown desert.

Taking a deep breath and cringing against the antici- pated agony of his dislocated shoulders, he moved. Pain shrieked through him, but not the pain he'd ex- pected.

What the hell? He hurt everywhere—not just his shoulders. His hands weren't even bound behind his back.

Something had changed. But why? He'd been in this hell called Mahjidastan so long he'd lost count of the days. The predictability, the inevitability, had be- come as torturous as the pain and fear.

He carefully lifted his head, which hurt like a son- ofabitch. Taking a cautious breath, he coughed.

Dirt, mildew, old wood—completely different from the stink of urine and camel dung he'd expected. This wasn't Mahjidastan, the tiny disputed province in the region where Afghanistan, Pakistan and China joined.

He opened his eyes. Not easy. They were matted with

dried blood and caked with dust. Blinking and wincing as he stretched his sore neck tendons, he lifted his head again, even more cautiously this time, and looked around.

Slowly, his brain gathered up his scattered, disorganized memories.

He was in a ghost town, in the basement of an abandoned hotel. He'd come here to rescue Mindy. *Mindy and their unborn baby.*

He stiffened at that thought, causing his muscles to seize in bone-cracking pain, bending him double. With a superhuman effort, he unclenched his fists. Holding his breath, he stretched his legs. As long as he moved with unbearable slowness, the spasms stayed away— for the most part.

Frank James had slugged him, kicked him and then Tasered him.

"Mindy!" he croaked. The last thing he'd seen was James holding that damn gun at her head. The sight had come closer to breaking him than anything he'd ever faced in his life. Because he knew the dread, the fear— the sound of that hollow click. He would give his life if it meant that Mindy never had to experience that.

Immediately, that image was replaced by another one. The image of shock and agony on James's face when Mindy hit him in the groin.

Deke chuckled, which knotted his neck muscles and sent a painful spasm through them. That was his Mindy. She'd acted with the ingenuity and determination that had made him love her from the moment he'd first laid eyes on her when they were ten years old.

Then reality sheared his breath. Where was she? Had that weaselly coward Tasered her? Had he hurt their baby?

He'd kill him with his bare hands if he had.

By moving slowly and stopping when a twinge foreshadowed a muscle spasm, he got his feet under him. Damn, but everything hurt.

He'd been Tasered before, in training. But that was nothing compared to this. He spread his fingers carefully. The amount of voltage Frank James had used could do serious damage. Hell, it could kill. The spasms caused by the electric shock could stop the heart.

He had to find Mindy, make sure she was all right.

He leaned against the wall as his knees threatened to buckle and his head spun dizzily. Bile burned in his throat, and nausea sent acrid saliva flowing into his mouth.

He forced himself to think rationally. Chronologically. First things first. How long had he been unconscious?

He looked at the shadows on the floor. Light was coming in from somewhere above and behind him. He turned his head, squinting through his aching eyes.

That window. He recognized it. He was still in the hotel's basement. The way the light streamed in, and its bright yellow color, told him it was daylight—morning. At least he could see better than he'd been able to last night.

There were the crates they'd been sitting on, and in a tangle on the dirt floor were the ropes that had bound them.

"Mindy!" he croaked, then stopped and listened.

Nothing. A knot of fear tightened in his gut. "Mindy, sugar? You've got to answer me. Where are you?"

If that ridiculous cowboy had hurt her—

Frank James had to be working for Novus Ordo. It was the only thing that made sense, given everything that had led up to this point.

"Damn you, Novus!" he growled. "This is your doing. I know it."

He knew Novus and Novus knew him. It was Novus who'd had his helicopter shot down during a covert rescue mission over northern Mahjidastan. Who'd had him tortured, made him reveal how he had found his camp, and how he knew Novus was holding Travis Ronson, the only son of Wyoming senator Frederick Ronson. The senator had been a great friend of Rook's dad, and Travis, who was a journalist with the Associated Press, had disappeared while embedded with American troops in Afghanistan.

Rook had come after Deke in the middle of a windstorm. That's when he'd gotten a look at Novus's bare face without the famous surgical mask he always wore.

Novus knew him—knew that no matter what he did to him, Deke would never break. He also knew the lengths Rook and Deke would go to in order to rescue each other.

So all this, the cleverly tied ropes, the near escape, were Novus's revenge on Deke for escaping and his proof that he was stronger and smarter than Deke.

He was toying with him, like a cat with a mouse. Waiting for him to break.

It didn't make sense to Deke that a man with a goal of destroying the United States would spend time toying with a man just for revenge. Didn't he have better things to do? Like achieve world domination?

Now, he'd taken Mindy away again and left Deke to

find her. It was a deadly game of hide-and-seek—with life or death hanging in the balance.

He knew Novus Ordo was a smart guy. He hadn't gotten to be the most feared terrorist on the planet by being sloppy. He'd worked fast and smart to get this complex plan in place in the week since Irina had stopped the search for Rook.

He'd lured Deke here by using Mindy as bait. It was exactly what Deke should have expected. He'd said as much to Irina two days ago.

"You surprised Novus when you suddenly called Matt back from Mahjidastan. He knew he had no chance of getting to you through all your security, so he targeted Matt first, figuring the reason you stopped was because Matt had found him. But Matt outsmarted his man."

Irina had nodded as Deke went on. "So Novus goes after the next obvious target. Me." He'd ground his fist into his other palm in frustration.

"He knows if anybody has information about whether Rook is still alive, I do. So he approaches it the easiest and most logical way, just like he did with Matt. He goes for the most bang for his buck. With Matt, it was his best friend's baby. With me, it's Mindy."

"Your Achilles' heel," Irina said matter-of-factly.

The three words echoed in his brain. She'd hit the nail square on the head. Mindy was his weakness.

His only weakness.

He'd promised Mindy he'd save her. And he would. He may have broken promises before, but he couldn't break this one. If he did, Mindy would die.

He licked dry lips as his gaze roamed around the basement, studying the layout. He hadn't gotten a chance to search the whole thing last night. There might be other alcoves or secret doors.

Before he'd headed out alone for Cleancutt, he'd spent as much time as he dared studying maps and satellite photos of the area.

His heart had sunk when he realized the call had come from an abandoned coal-mining town. A big one. It was one of the few that had actually grown rather than died around 1950 when underground coal mining had given way to strip-mining.

So it made sense that some of the newer buildings, like the hotel, had been built over old mining tunnels. It was highly likely that this basement connected to at least one of them.

Pushing away from the wall, he took a step, relieved that his muscles were no longer spasming, although they still trembled. So he concentrated on putting one foot in front of the other, taking it easy until he could be sure his knees wouldn't collapse.

He started his search of the basement under the window. It was the best-lit area and therefore the easiest to search.

He examined every wall, every nook and cranny, holding to his grid pattern. Finally he ended up on the far west side, where he'd looked for a door the night before.

In the dim daylight, he saw that the timbers lining the wall of the alcove looked different from the wood on the other walls. In fact, they looked like a door, except there was no handle.

He rapped on the wood with his knuckles. Yep. Solid as a rock. Cursing to himself, he moved his hand a few inches and rapped again.

His instincts had always been excellent, and combining that with the maps he'd studied and the local history of the area, he figured this was the most likely place for a door into the mine.

The mine he wasn't even sure was there.

Just as he moved his fist another few inches, preparing to rap again, he heard something. He froze, his knuckles millimeters from the rough wood. Closing his eyes, he listened.

There it was again. A faint rapping—muffled, barely audible.

He rapped again. And again heard the muffled answering rap.

"Mindy?" he called softly.

Nothing.

He drew a breath to yell, then paused. What if Frank James heard him? Yeah? So what? He'd bet money this was part of Novus's cat-and-mouse game, anyhow.

As he prepared to knock, the muffled rapping began again.

"I'm here, Min. Where are you?"

Was he projecting or, worse, hallucinating? He had to believe he'd really heard her. If she was on the other side of the wall, then there was a way through it. And he'd find it.

He rapped on every square inch of the alcove wall, starting at the top. The sound remained flat and solid.

He stopped again and listened.

There it was again. The answering rap. It didn't sound like she was knocking on the same wall he was.

"Mindy! Can you hear me? Is there a door?" He kept on, testing every inch of the wall. When he got down to knee level, he sat on his heels, wincing as his knees trembled and his leg muscles protested.

He knocked again. And got a different sound. A hollow sound.

Yes! His pulse pounded, sending pain arcing behind his eyes. *Damn Taser.*

"Mindy?" he called.

He heard something! A faint low murmur. It was her. He knew it.

Immediately, doubt sliced through him. What if it wasn't Mindy? What if it was another trap designed to wear him down?

Then he'd crawl right into it. He wasn't about to ignore even the smallest chance that Mindy was on the other side of the wall, counting on him to save her.

He examined the boards with his eyes and fingers. If he had to, he'd break it down with his bare hands to get to her.

He couldn't see anything unusual, but he sure as hell felt something. A slight difference in temperature—a slight movement of the air. Digging the lighter out of his pocket, he thumbed it.

Sure enough, the flame wavered. There was air behind the rough planks.

After a few frustrating seconds of digging at the corners of the boards, he thought of his knife. He reached toward his boot and then remembered. He didn't have it.

It was inside Mindy's bra. A thrill slid through him as he thought about how warm it would be from the heat of her body. He shook his head.

"Get out of my head," he muttered under his breath, and focused on digging out all that wood putty with his fingernails.

A long time later, with his fingertips scraped and sore, he called out to Mindy again.

"Mindy, if you can hear me, move back. I'm going to kick these boards in." He banged on the wall with his fist. "Right here. Okay?"

A faint tap answered him.

He sat back and drew his knees up to his chest.

"Okay," he hollered. "On three. One—two—"

He braced himself with his hands behind him. "Three!" He slammed the heels of his boots into the planks as hard as he could. The thud echoed through the basement.

Propelling himself forward, he examined the damage. *Not much.* "Min, stay back."

He rocked backward and stomped the wood again, and again. The fourth time it gave, with nails screeching as they separated from wood. Although his legs quivered with fatigue and reaction to the Taser, he kicked at the splintered wood until he'd opened a hole big enough to crawl through.

For a few seconds he sat quietly, listening. Had the deafening noise alerted Frank James? He waited, but nobody came.

If the fake cowboy wasn't sitting back watching his efforts through a hidden camera, Deke was certain he was listening and waiting, and probably laughing at Deke's efforts.

Lying down on the dirt floor, he peered through the opening, which was barely wide enough for his shoulders. "Mindy?" he whispered.

No answer.

He eased a bit farther in, holding his breath.

It could still be a trap.

A movement at the corner of his vision drew his eye. He tensed.

"Deke—?"

He clamped his jaw against the flood of relief that closed his throat and stung his eyelids.

She was there. And her voice sounded strong. But it was still undercut by that same terrified, desperate tone he'd noticed on the telephone. At the time he'd known something was horribly wrong, but he hadn't known what. Now he did.

She was afraid for her baby.

"Everything okay in there?"

"Yes," she answered.

"You alone?"

"Yes."

She sounded terrified. He hoped she was telling the truth. Once, he'd been able to tell by the timbre of her voice. Could he still?

What would he do if Frank James had her?

Nothing different. He was making himself vulnerable to attack by crawling through the small trapdoor, but he didn't have a choice. If he were alone, he'd reconnoiter, figure out the best place to defend his back and ambush his enemy.

But he wasn't alone. He had to get to Mindy.

"Stay back. I'm coming through." He ducked his head and slithered through the hole, then stood. It was damn dark in here. Darker than the basement with its tiny window. He wished he had something more than a disposable lighter.

Deke could barely make out her silhouette. "Min, honey? Are you okay? Are you alone? Did he hurt—"

Suddenly a firm, round tummy collided with him, and slender but strong arms wrapped around his waist. "Deke, I was so scared. I was afraid he'd killed you."

Deke's throat seized. He swallowed hard against the lump that suddenly grew there. Carefully, feeling as if he might break her if he squeezed too hard, he wrapped his arms around her shoulders.

She laid her head in the hollow between his neck and shoulder—her favorite place to sleep, she'd always told him.

"Nah," he croaked, then had to stop and clear his throat. "You know me. Nothing can break me. I'm fine. What about you? He didn't Taser you, did he?"

Mindy clung to Deke for dear life. If she could crawl inside him she would. Body to body, especially through clothes, wasn't enough. No matter how many times she'd feared for Deke's safety, even his sanity, she'd always known he would never hurt her. She'd always felt safe with him.

Almost always.

She hugged him tighter. His strong arms tightened around her—a little. He was holding back. Partly because he was still stunned and angry about her pregnancy, she was sure.

But that wasn't the whole reason. In all the time she'd known him, he'd never opened up to her—not completely.

She knew him so well—probably better than anybody alive. So she knew there was a deep core to Deke Cunningham that she'd never been able to penetrate.

She would bet a lot of money that nobody ever had. Or would. It broke her heart. It was the one thing she'd wanted from him that he'd never been able to give her—his complete trust. It was one of the reasons she'd finally given up and gotten a divorce.

"Min?"

She shook her head against the soft cotton of his shirt. "He didn't hurt me."

"How'd you get here? Can you find your way back?"

"I'm not sure. He blindfolded me again and we walked—it felt like hours. When he left me here it was so dark. I don't know how long I've stood here. I was afraid to sit down." She shuddered.

"That's right. You're pretty paranoid about creepy-crawlies, aren't you?" She felt his chest rumble with soft laughter.

"Don't laugh at me. And no. Not this time. I was so tired I'd have gladly sat in a nest of cockroaches. But I was afraid I wouldn't be able to get back up."

"Sorry." The amusement was gone. "Tell me everything you remember. Did you have to crawl through anything? Bend over to get through a door?"

"No. We went upstairs and then down again—twice. I think he was trying to confuse me. But once we went outside, I think into a different building. Then down a different set of stairs. Did you come from where we were tied up?"

"Yep. The old hotel. How'd you keep up with which building you were in?"

"Mostly by smell. The building we were in smells like mildew. The other one—wherever it was—had more of a smoky odor to it."

"Good! We might be able to find our way out by following our noses." Deke bent his head and kissed her forehead.

His lips moving against her skin took her back to those innocent high school days, when they'd been good together. Before they were old enough to understand that love alone couldn't always conquer fear or fill the hollow places left inside by an uncaring parent.

"You've got dried blood all over your face." She brushed at his temple and cheek, then ran the pad of her thumb gently across his closed eyelid. "And that cut needs to be washed and bandaged." She touched the skin around the cut and he winced. "Plus, you're going to have a bruise on your forehead."

"Yeah? Well, it'll match the rest of them."

Tears stung her eyes and she squeezed the lids shut.

"You getting hurt is not funny to me." She pushed away from him.

He let go immediately.

When he did, she swayed. She knew what was wrong. She was tired. She was hungry. The *baby* was hungry. He got so restless when she didn't eat. "I need food."

"So what's new?"

"I mean for the baby."

He stiffened. "Oh. Yeah." He straightened and looked around. "Got any idea which way you came in?"

"I think we came from somewhere back there." She gestured toward a heavy wooden door on the north wall. "But I could be totally turned around."

"Okay." He wrapped his fingers around her upper arms and set her gently away from him. "Do you still have my knife? He didn't search you, did he?"

"No." She unbuttoned her sweater, retrieved the knife from her bra and handed it to him.

He closed his fist around it, soaking up her warmth. "You stay right there. I want to explore a little."

"Don't leave me," she breathed. She clutched at his white shirt. "If I lose you in the dark, I'll go crazy."

"You'll be fine. I'm not going far."

"Deke, what if he's waiting for you again?"

"I'll be ready for him. You stay right there."

Holding his knife in his right hand, he fished out the cigarette lighter with his left and struck it, then took a second to get his bearings. The trapdoor he'd come through was on the west wall of the basement. So he turned south, following the dirt wall until it curved around to the west. From the hollow sound of his footsteps and the whisper of air in his ears, he figured he was in a tunnel.

He walked a few feet farther, but nothing changed. The tunnel looked totally abandoned beyond the tiny circle of light cast by his lighter.

After extinguishing the lighter and pocketing it, he blindly examined the walls, but all he felt were thick, rough boards, like railroad ties, and dirt walls. In a few places his fingers brushed across some sort of mesh screening, probably designed to hold the dirt in place.

He felt along the ground with his feet, from wall to wall, but found nothing. No rails for the coal cars. This tunnel had probably never been finished. It was a dead end.

He retrieved the lighter and struck it again as he turned to retrace his steps. He'd felt steel rails under his boots in the alcove where Mindy was waiting. The rails led into the tunnel on the north side of the alcove. That was their only hope of getting out.

Just as he rounded the curve, back to the area where he'd left Mindy, light flared, revealing two dark silhouettes. Deke smelled the phosphorus smell of a match and the unmistakable odor of lantern oil. Alarm pierced his chest.

James. He had Mindy.

"Mindy?" He cautiously pressed his right arm against his side, hoping to conceal his knife. He didn't want to take a chance that James would catch a glint from the steel blade.

"Howdy, Cunningham," Frank James drawled. "Nice of you to join us. I've been waiting for you."

He hung an oil lantern on a nail above their heads with one hand, while his other aimed a Colt .45 revolver directly at Mindy's head. The red bandanna across his face stretched as he grinned.

Terror sheared Deke's breath for a second time. Previously, when he'd seen the steel barrel pressed against her temple, he'd sworn that if it killed him, James would never again get her into that life-or-death situation.

But here they were. And just like before, his consciousness was split in two. Half saw her precious head, once again threatened by the 9 mm barrel with its lethal cargo. The other half spun through a whirlwind of memories—the hot metal cylinder pressed against his own skull, the distinctive *snick-snick* of the hammer cocking, the slow grind of the barrel turning, and finally, the hollow click as it hit the empty chamber.

He knew the horror of waiting to hear those sounds. A shudder rocked his whole body.

He shook his head and stared at her. He had to stay here, in the present, on alert.

Her wide green eyes sparkled with tears as her hands cradled her tummy. "Deke, I didn't know—"

"Shut up!" James yelled.

Deke wanted to reassure her with his gaze, but he didn't think he could pull it off. So he turned his attention to James so she wouldn't see how scared he was that the man might be dumb enough to actually shoot her.

His only chance was to distract James and turn his anger toward him and away from Mindy.

"You're a coward," Deke growled. "Hiding behind a woman—a *pregnant* woman."

"You better watch yourself, pardner. You're not the one in charge here."

"In charge? Are you saying you are? Give me a break. You don't even have the guts to use your real name. You're named after an outlaw—hell! Not even a real outlaw. You're named after the *brother* of an outlaw."

Frank's eyes narrowed and his gun hand shook. "You shut up. Frank James was a great outlaw. As great as his brother."

Deke felt triumphant and apprehensive at the same time. He'd gotten to him. He'd struck a vein with the remark about the cowboy's moniker.

The guy was obviously under somebody's thumb. Most likely Novus. Frank was exactly what he looked like. A hired gun.

"Yeah, not so much. The only thing I remember about Frank James is that when people talk about Jesse they sometimes say, 'and Frank, too.' I know something else, too. I know you're ashamed of something or else you wouldn't be wearing that ridiculous bandanna over your face like a bad TV cowboy."

"You don't know anything about me." A red spot appeared in the center of James's forehead. And his gun hand shook.

That scared Deke. Nobody could trust a nervous

gun hand. Still, he had no choice. Somehow, he had to catch the guy off guard. All he needed was two seconds.

"I know enough to know you couldn't pull this off alone. You're working for Novus Ordo, aren't you?"

The gun barrel shook even more at the mention of the terrorist. "Shut up! You think you know so much. You don't know nothing." Dark spots dotted the bandanna where sweat rolled down James's pinched face.

Deke shifted to the balls of his feet and curled his fingers, ready to attack. *One second.* He only needed one second.

The cowboy was breathing hard, practically gasping, and the bandanna was fast becoming soaked. He looked like he was on the verge of panic.

Deke concentrated on keeping his own breathing even as he studied the other man. He'd bet money— hell, he was betting his life and Mindy's and her unborn baby's—that the coward had never killed anybody.

At least not face-to-face.

He could do this. He was bigger, stronger and faster. He *could* stop James before he got off a shot.

He had to.

As if he sensed Deke's resolve, James looked him dead in the eye. His beady pupils gleamed with malice as he cocked the hammer. He turned his head toward Mindy, still holding Deke's gaze.

Then his finger squeezed the trigger.

Chapter Five

Horror closed Deke's throat as he watched James's finger tighten on the trigger.

The sound of metal sliding against metal made him cringe. The chamber slowly turned.

Knowing he could never beat the bullet, and propelled by terror, Deke slung his knife underhanded at the cowboy's arm, then lunged at him with full-body force.

All hell broke loose.

Mindy screamed.

James squealed as Deke slammed into his skinny torso, pushing him against the timbers that lined the mine shaft. Gravel and dirt rained on their heads and peppered the dusty floor.

Deke shouldered James in the solar plexus as hard as he could. They crashed against the wall, and James's breath whooshed out. Deke closed his left hand around James's right wrist and beat it against the timbers, again and again.

Finally, the gun thudded to the dirt floor.

"Grab the gun, Min, or kick it away." He drove his forearm into James's face, trying to crush his nose and slam it up into his brain. James grunted and tried to shove Deke off him, but Deke wasn't about to let go.

He fisted his hands in James's shirt and dragged him forward, then body-slammed him against the wall again.

"Mindy!" he yelled.

She didn't answer.

Terrified that she was hurt, he threw the cowboy down to the ground, slamming his face into one of the steel rails, and whirled.

"Mindy!"

The oil lantern's flickering light sent shadows chasing around the tunnel. But none of them looked like her. Deke blinked as he scanned the small space.

"Deke—"

A wave of relief washed over him, so sharp, so spine-tingling, that it almost drove him to his knees. He turned toward her voice and saw a shadow move.

"Min," he breathed. She was on the ground. "Are you hurt?" He reached for her.

"I don't think so." She wrapped her arms around his neck as he lifted her.

"Stay back," he whispered, and set her gently against the far wall.

Her eyes slid past him and widened in the flickering lantern light. "Look out!"

When he whirled, Frank James was diving for the gun.

Deke dove, too, landing on top of the smaller man. He shoved him out of the way and reached out to grab the gun.

When he did, a searing pain slashed up his arm. Shocked, he fell backward.

Behind him, Mindy cried out.

He rolled and dove for the gun again, but it wasn't there.

James had it.

Deke was on the ground and James was standing, so he wrapped his arms around the silver-toed boots and jerked, hoping to knock James off his feet. Deke got his right foot under him for momentum and stability, but when he threw himself forward to unbalance James, his foot slipped.

He tried again and managed to head-butt James in the stomach. The man's breath whooshed out as he tumbled backward.

A thrill of triumph filled Deke's chest. He spotted the gleam of the knife blade at James's feet. He lunged for it.

At the very instant his fingers closed around its hilt, the heavy wooden door behind James opened and a big shadow loomed in the doorway.

Deke tried to check his momentum, but his feet slipped again. As if in slow motion, he saw the blue-white arc of the Taser coming at him.

MINDY WATCHED IN HORROR as a large, dark man appeared from nowhere. The light was behind him, so he was barely more than a silhouette, but she saw the blue light and heard the static.

The Taser.

Helpless to do anything, she merely stared as Deke's spine arched and the fine muscles hidden under his smooth, golden skin trembled. Then he dropped where he stood, his legs collapsing as if they'd turned into rags.

Then the big man kicked him out of the way. "Where's the woman?"

Deke had set her against the far wall, in the shadows. But she knew they'd spot her any second. There was no way she could defend herself, so instinctively, she closed her eyes and pretended to be unconscious.

"I don't know," James gasped, struggling to breathe. He coughed. "Forget her."

"Here she is."

Mindy's muscles tensed, and it was all she could do to keep from cringing.

"Leave her!" James yelled breathlessly.

She heard the bigger man's footsteps, felt him standing over her. She didn't know why she thought it was so important to keep up the pretense that she'd passed out, but she did.

"She's out cold. I can grab her."

"No! What did I just say?"

"But they could get away."

James's breathing was almost back to normal. "Get over here," he ordered.

Mindy heard the man's heavy footsteps recede.

"Now pay attention," James whispered.

She held her breath, listening.

"They're not going to get away. This isn't about capturing them. They're already captured. It's about—" James lowered his voice even more, too low for Mindy to understand.

She opened her eyes to narrow slits. The two men had their heads together. She could hear the hiss of James's whisper, but couldn't understand a thing.

The big man nodded. "I'll get the knife."

"Leave it. It'll make him think he's smarter than us." James coughed again and took a deep breath. "Let's get out of here."

He opened the door on the north wall, and the two men disappeared through it.

Blinded by the bright light from the open door, Mindy scooted blindly across the dirt floor toward Deke. Several times, her bottom bumped against the raised metal rails.

As her night vision came back and she made out his silhouette, she noticed the blacker-than-black pool that was spreading under him. It wasn't just a trick of the shadows.

It was blood.

Deke's blood. That's why he'd kept slipping as he'd fought James. She'd seen James jerk Deke's knife out of his side with a roar and brandish it as Deke dove for the gun.

The lantern's light had reflected off the blade as it sliced an arc through the air. Behind the blade, red droplets had scattered in a fine spray that caught the light like tiny rubies.

Then Deke had gone down.

"Deke," she whispered, touching his forehead with her fingertips. She knew it would be foolish to assume that their kidnappers were gone for good. So she kept an eye out for the least hint of light.

"Deke, wake up. Are you okay?"

He groaned and stirred.

"Deke? Answer me."

He made a low growling noise in his throat and tried to push himself to his hands and knees, but his right arm wouldn't hold his weight. He collapsed again.

She didn't know what to do. Watching him struggle helplessly sent fear burrowing into her—soul-deep fear. She'd never seen him weak or injured. The sight was like a slap to her face.

Deke Cunningham was flesh and bone, just like everyone else. Just like her. He was breakable.

She pressed her palm against his forehead. "Wake up," she pleaded. "I'm going to need your help. I don't think I can stand up by myself."

He made a noise. It could have been a groan or a brief snort of laughter. Carefully, holding his right arm against his side, he rolled up into a sitting position, got his legs under him, and pushed himself to his feet.

Mindy looked up. His face, distorted by the wavering lantern light, was a grimacing mask of pain. She had no idea what being Tasered felt like, but if it could do this to her ex-husband, it had to be bad.

But what really worried her was the knife wound in his arm.

In typical Deke fashion, he composed his face, then looked down at her and crooked his mouth into a half smile. He held out his hand.

"You can't just give me a hand up," she said wryly. "I'm way beyond that. This is not going to be pretty." She rolled over to all-fours, and slowly, using the wall for support, she carefully pushed herself to her knees.

"Can you come around and get your left hand under my arm and lift?" She was embarrassed by her helplessness in front of him, and he picked up on that.

"What's the matter, Min? I've seen you in more interesting positions than this." He moved to her right side and hooked his elbow under her arm.

"This is different."

He lifted her with a grunt. "Yeah. You weigh more."

"Not funny," she grunted, as she managed to stand with a whole lot of help from him. "I'm sorry. I know that hurt you."

"No problem," he muttered.

She stepped to one side so the lantern light shone fully on him, and gasped when she saw the amount of blood that soaked the arm of his jacket.

"Oh, no, Deke. All that blood."

"It's okay," he muttered. "What about you? Did that bastard hurt you?"

She shook her head. "You took care of me. Now I need to take care of you. Take off your jacket."

Once he'd managed to peel the jacket off, she lifted the slashed cotton fabric away from the wound and hissed through her teeth.

"It's nothing," Deke protested, pulling back.

"Oh, no, trust me. It's *something*," she retorted. "You've got at least a six-inch gash. You need stitches."

"How do you suggest I get 'em?"

She winced at his gruff tone. He didn't like to show weakness—any kind of weakness. Not physical, and certainly not emotional. He never had. He'd learned early that weakness drew predators like a shark to blood. So he'd long ago decided that the best defense was an impenetrable shield and a strong offense.

Over the years she'd watched him learn those lessons, from his alcoholic father, from the other kids in school, from life. She'd been there for every brick he'd laid to fortify his heart.

She understood that his anger wasn't aimed at her. She just happened to be in the way. Just as she'd been many times before.

With the ease of long practice, she ignored his words and his attitude. "I can't sew up the wound, but I can wrap it."

"Min, we don't have time—"

"Just shut up and take off your shirt."

With a frustrated sigh, he complied. He kept his right arm still as he undid the buttons with his left hand. When his shirt was hanging open over his bare chest, she took his left hand. "I'll get this button," she murmured.

He let her undo the sleeve, then he shrugged the shirt off with a groan, and carefully slid it down his right arm.

"Oh, Deke. Look what he did to you." Dark bruises covered his side, where James had kicked him with those silver-toed boots. His right forearm was coated with blood, and in taking off his shirt he'd smeared the blood all over his abdomen and chest.

He shrugged, sending ripples along the muscles of his shoulders and arms.

Mindy couldn't take her eyes off him. They'd been married for nine years and lovers for two years before that. She knew every inch of his body. Every curve of muscle. Every scar.

He seemed leaner, harder, and yet at the same time less harsh. Every bit as handsome, though. And every bit as sexy.

Memories washed over her—the feel of his hot, naked body against hers. That silk-over-steel strength and the unimaginable thrill of being filled by him.

As she'd told him many times, their problem was never the sex. She was just as turned on by him as she'd always been. Maybe more.

She still wanted him. She was eight months pregnant, cold, hungry and terrified, and yet the desire was still there, humming, vibrating, singing, inside her.

Stop it. The stirrings she felt were just hormones. Hormones and habit.

Even as she lectured herself, she knew she was lying. Deke's golden-tanned skin, his sleekly defined muscles, the slope of his broad shoulders and the harshly beautiful planes of his abs, hips and flanks, were as familiar to her as her own body.

Actually, more familiar right now. Considering that for the past eight months her body had been in a constant state of change and still was.

She rubbed her tummy where his son was wiggling around. Her little Sprout was proof of that. Even on the day she'd buried her mother, the one thing that had succeeded in drawing her out of the poignant sadness was Deke, with the sweet gentleness that he revealed only to her.

Dear heavens, she loved him.

No, I don't, her rational brain responded immediately.

But arguing with herself was useless. She might not be able to live with him. But she would always love him.

"Well?" he grumbled. "Are you just going to stand there while I bleed to death?"

His voice sounded irritated, but his eyes held a spark of amusement, and his mouth a ghost of a smirk.

Her face burned with embarrassment. Damn him, he knew what she was thinking. *Great.* Something else that hadn't changed. A splinter of irritation stung away some of her desire.

"Sorry," she muttered. She yanked the shirt out of his hands and ripped it into strips.

"Min, I didn't mean—"

"I need something to wash out the wound." She spoke briskly, not giving him time to apologize. She glanced around, her gaze stopping on the lantern. "The oil."

"No. No way."

"Why not? It's hot, and it's a good disinfectant."

Deke shook his head. "It's a better fuel source. As soon as you're done playing nurse I'm putting that sucker out and taking it with us. We'll need it."

"I don't want to wrap your arm without washing it."

"Wash it later. Wrap it now. That sonofoabitch is going to come back, once he licks his wounds. I don't plan for us to be here."

"Did you hear James and the other man talking?" she asked as she quickly and efficiently wrapped his arm, doing her best to keep the edges of the wound together without tying the bandage too tight.

"Talking? When?"

"After he Tasered you."

"Seems like I heard something, but it didn't make sense. It's hard to think when electricity's frying your brain. I think I passed out for a few seconds." He rubbed his temple with his left hand. "Why?"

"They had a perfectly good chance to capture us both again. You were paralyzed by the Taser and I was on the ground, helpless. But James told the other guy not to. He said 'it's not about capturing them.' Then he said to leave you the knife. He said, It'll 'make him think he's smarter.'" She looked up. "What's going on?"

Deke shook his head. "He's playing cat and mouse with me. He wants me to believe I can get us out of here."

"*I* believe you can."

He gave her a ghost of a smile. "Thanks. But I have

a feeling I'm a little outnumbered. I'm pretty sure there are more than two of them. I'd bet money that every exit is guarded."

"So—we're mice in a maze? And if we run the maze correctly our reward is death?"

"Something like that."

Those three flat words frightened her more than his anger or even his fear ever could. He was the bravest man she'd ever known. So why was he accepting the inevitable now, after all the things he'd endured?

Endured. That was it! He knew they were outnumbered and outflanked. His only choice, given the handicap of having to worry about her, was to conserve his strength and hers—to outwait and outwit the enemy.

Something he'd said earlier, when he was trying to stop James from shooting her in the head, niggled at the edge of her brain. But she'd been so scared that her brain had been incapable of processing what he said. She tried to replay his words in her head, but they flitted away, leaving her with nothing but a question.

"Who is the enemy?"

"What?"

She jumped. "What?"

"You said something."

"No, I didn't." Had she spoken aloud? She savagely ripped the ends of her makeshift bandage, berating herself for not watching what she said.

"Ouch. Where's the knife? Cutting the fabric would be easier—and less painful than tearing it."

"It fell over there." She gestured in the direction of the door."

"Hurry up. I need to get it. And by the way, yes, you did say something. You said, 'who's the enemy?'"

She tied the torn ends of the bandage to keep it in place.

"Did I? Well, it's a good question. You never did tell me what you did that made Frank James kidnap me, and why he's playing cat and mouse with you. He obviously knows who you are."

He looked at his fingers and flexed them, as if the most important thing in the world to him was making sure the bandage wasn't too tight.

"Deke, look at me. Who's behind all this?"

His head ducked a fraction lower, then he raised his gaze to hers. "I've never seen Frank James before."

Mindy studied his face. This was her childhood sweetheart, her lover, her former husband. The man she knew better than anyone in the world. The set of his jaw, the tiny wrinkles at the corners of his eyes, the flat line of his mouth, told her he was holding something back.

She almost laughed. *So what's new?*

He swiveled and headed toward the wooden door.

"Deke, what are you—?"

Then he held up the lighter and kicked around in the dirt. He was looking for his knife.

She watched him and tried to remember what he'd said back there when Frank James was holding her with a gun to her head. He'd tried to bluff James out of pulling the trigger by distracting him with insults and playing on his obvious cowardice.

He'd said something that hadn't fit with the rest of his verbal jabs. Something that sounded real—and disturbing. She could almost hear it in her brain. Almost, but not quite.

Suddenly, the memory hit her. His voice echoed in her head.

You couldn't pull this off alone. You're working for Novus Ordo.

Novus Ordo. "Oh, dear heavens," she choked out through the hand that had flown to her mouth. The realization stole her breath. The man who'd captured and tortured Deke. "It's Novus Ordo."

"What?" He looked at her suspiciously.

"Don't even try that 'I don't know what you're talking about' innocent tone with me, Deke Cunningham." She took a step backward, as if distance could protect her from the knowledge that was swirling around in her brain.

After Deke had come back from Mahjidastan, he'd been a different man. He'd never told her what had happened to him over there, but his best friend had.

Rook had told her how Novus Ordo, the infamous terrorist, had captured Deke when his helicopter went down. He'd described some of the torture Deke had endured at his hands.

Rook had begged her to stick with him, to help him heal.

And she'd tried. But Deke had refused her help—or anyone else's. Refused vehemently. Then he'd gone away and left her alone.

The empty shell of his body had still been there, but the man she'd loved all her life had disappeared—into drink, into depression, into self-loathing. The man she'd believed was unbreakable had been broken.

So in self-defense, before he sucked her into the abyss with him, she'd filed for divorce.

Then Rook had been assassinated, and the speculation had started—on a national scale. Novus Ordo, the most feared terrorist since Bin Laden, was rumored to have ordered the death of the highly decorated former Air Force colonel Robert Kenneth Castle because of a personal grievance.

Mindy had feared that Rook's death would send Deke over the edge, but through Irina she knew that he had moved to Castle Ranch and had taken over BHSAR operations, while Irina handled the business aspects and searched for proof that Rook was still alive.

It seemed that Rook's death had brought Deke back to life.

"That terrorist is behind this, isn't he?"

"Come on, Mindy."

Mindy lifted her chin pugnaciously. "No. You come on. Don't treat me like an idiot. Irina stops searching for Rook and a week later here we are, being held captive because you know something that you're not telling me. I heard what you said to Frank James. I can put the pieces together. Novus Ordo thinks you know where Rook is, doesn't he?"

Deke's eyes narrowed and the tiny wrinkles between his brows deepened. He scowled at her.

"Oh my God, you do!"

For an instant, Deke stared at her as if she were a ghost. Then his mouth and jaw relaxed. He shook his head. "No. I don't know where he is."

Mindy frowned at him. "Why are you—?" One look in his eyes and her question died on her lips. Without moving his head, he shifted his gaze above her, then to his right and his left then back to stare at her.

She understood immediately. He suspected that they were being watched or listened to. She gave him a small nod and took a deep breath.

"You really don't know?" she asked, doing her best

to sound like she believed what she was saying. "But what about all those rumors that he's still alive?"

"They've stuck around because Irina wouldn't give up. But now she has. Rook Castle is dead."

"So what about Frank James? Do you think he's working for Novus?"

"He could be. I'd have thought Novus was smarter than that, but maybe not. He may have ordered Rook assassinated, but the body was never recovered. If I were Novus, and I thought my nemesis was still alive, I'd probably panic if his wife suddenly quit searching for him." He made an impatient sound. "Are you done playing nurse yet?"

She gave the bandage on his forearm a final inspection. "Fine. I'm done. But if it doesn't stop bleeding. I'll have to put spiderwebs on it."

"Hell, no, you won't." Deke stared at her. "What are you talking about—spiderwebs?"

"They can promote clotting. They work by—"

"Min." Deke held up his hand. "I don't care how they work. I won't bleed anymore."

She shot him an ironic glance. "You'll control it with your steely resolve?"

He nodded. "Damn straight I will."

Mindy chuckled. "That's my hero."

Deke winced at her words. She'd said them unintentionally, he was sure. She'd called him her hero ever since high school. Ever since the first time they'd made love, when she was seventeen.

He'd been careful and slow, determined to show her what sex was all about. Afterward, she'd lain in his arms, panting and spent, and awed by what had happened to her.

Eventually, she'd turned toward him. She'd touched his cheek and murmured, "You're my hero, and I will always love you."

He blinked and shook his head slightly, pushing the memories back—way back—to the place where he kept them locked up. That was a long time ago, when she'd loved him.

He was no hero now. *Hah.* Never had been. He'd never brought her anything but heartbreak. No wonder she hadn't wanted him to know about her baby. She'd tried to protect herself and her child from more pain.

And what had he done? He'd left her alone and vulnerable against attack. He was the one who'd gotten her into this, and now he had to get her out.

Without a scratch.

"Let's get out of here. I'm sure James already knows where we'll end up. But hell, there's nothing I can do about that." He carefully shrugged into his shearling jacket and grabbed the oil lantern off the nail.

The first thing he did was examine the slatted wooden door on the north wall. There was no knob, just a keyhole. "This is where they disappeared?"

Mindy nodded.

He pushed against it, but it didn't budge. Then he transferred the lantern to his right hand and tried to get a grip on it by inserting his fingers into the slats. "It's locked."

"What did you find in the other direction?" Mindy asked.

"Pretty much what I expected. I'm guessing this hotel was built here so they could use this tunnel junction as its basement." He pointed toward the south tunnel. "No coal car rails in that tunnel. So I'm thinking it's either closed or it's a dead end. I didn't go very far. I didn't want to leave you." He grimaced. "I left you too long as it was."

"You didn't know—"

"I should have." He gestured at the floor. Unlike the south tunnel, this branch had two sets of rails on its dirt-and-rock-covered floor. They extended down the corridor as far as he could see. "See? These rails have been used. You can see where they're worn. Obviously this tunnel has seen a lot of people come through it."

"But why would they need rails here? This looks like the end of the line—or the beginning."

"Look at that." He pointed at the planks and boards surrounding the trapdoor where he'd crawled in. "That was a door into the hotel basement. This other door may be to the mine foreman's office, or some other administrative type. They probably used a man car to travel from here down into the belly of the mine."

"Man car?"

"Traveled on the rails like the coal cars, but held passengers—the miners, of course—to carry them down to the deeper parts of the mine. But the inspectors, the bosses, the foreman, would travel down there, too."

"How do you know all this?"

Deke sent her a wry smile. "I read up on it as soon as I figured out where your phone call came from."

He bent over and picked up his knife, and then pointed to the trapdoor that led into the hotel basement.

"Can't go that way," he said, conjuring up a picture of Mindy getting on hands and knees to crawl through to the hotel's basement.

Not happening.

He pressed his bandaged arm against his side and

clenched his teeth against the stinging pain as he looked at the two tunnels. His instincts had always been excellent. They'd gotten him out of dangerous situations many times.

But right now he had no idea which tunnel to take. What would Novus expect him to do? Take the south tunnel, which appeared to be abandoned and might lead to a dead end, trapping them? Or follow the coal-car rails, which careered down a steep incline to a tippling station, where they'd dump the coal into the larger railroad cars?

He cursed under his breath.

"What is it?" Mindy asked. "What's wrong?"

He pointed to one of the tunnels. "What do you think, Min? The lady? Or the tiger?"

Chapter Six

"I don't think I can go any farther," Mindy said. She hated to tell Deke that. Hated to let him down. Her fingers were cramping from holding on to his belt and trying to stay directly behind him.

He'd been guiding her in the darkness, warning her of rough patches or a curve. They were walking on a steep downward incline—going deeper underground.

When he'd chosen the abandoned south tunnel over the north one that appeared to be open, she'd been surprised. But she'd kept her mouth shut, trusting him.

Twice already, he'd stumbled over broken boards and piles of dirt and rocks. Once he'd hit his head on a sagging roof beam.

She'd never been afraid of the dark until now.

This darkness was *total*. The sensation was claustrophobic, dizzying, terrifying. She couldn't see anything, not even her own hand. Even holding on to Deke's belt, she found herself drifting off to the right or left. And sometimes she felt like she was leaning—not standing up straight.

When that happened, she'd suddenly jerk upright. That earned her a bout of vertigo.

The vertigo would trigger panic, which would disturb Sprout, and that increased her nervousness. Especially when she thought about how deep underground they were.

Not even having Deke with her helped.

"Hang in there a little longer, Min." His voice sounded strained.

If Deke was worried, then it was seriously time to panic. "Deke—I can't!"

"Just a little more, Min. I think I hear something."

Her heart pounded. "What?"

He reached behind him and touched her hand. "Water running. Listen."

He stopped, and she stepped up closer to him. "I don't hear anything."

"I've got specially trained ears."

She heard the smile in his voice. And appreciated it. He was trying to keep it light. For her. Trying to help her through the blackness.

She sucked in a deep breath that hitched at the top like a sob. "You do—have nice ears."

"Nice? They're superb." He gently extricated her fingers from his belt and pulled her close, wrapping his strong arm around her waist.

"Listen," he whispered in her ear.

She started to tell him that as long as he was breathing that close to her ear, it didn't matter what was out there. She wouldn't be able to hear Niagara Falls.

As if she'd spoken aloud, he held his breath. She held hers, too.

And heard a faint ripple.

"There it is," she whispered in awe.

"Told you." His arm tightened around her waist. For

the first time he seemed, if not comfortable, at least not especially uncomfortable with her rounded, unfamiliar shape.

Then, to her surprise, his head dipped and he nuzzled her hair.

"Let's go find that water," he said, straightening. "If we're real lucky, there will be another lantern there. Or some torches."

"Can you—" Mindy paused and took a breath. "I'm sorry, Deke, but can you light the lantern?"

"As soon as we get to the water, okay? I don't want to waste the oil."

Mindy felt like crying. She was so tired, so hungry, and so afraid that she'd never see light again. Her skin was clammy and cold. The air had been growing a little warmer as they went deeper, but suddenly, her neck felt cool—cooler than normal. She shivered as Deke took her hand and tucked it into his belt at the small of his back.

"Deke? I think I feel something."

Deke froze in midstride. "Something with the baby? Are you okay?"

"No. I mean, yes. I'm fine. It's not the baby. It's like air. I feel air on my neck."

He stayed still. Yet she knew from the change in the tension of his back muscles and from her familiarity with his body that he had his hand up and was testing the air.

"Come on," he said, and moved forward.

As they got closer to the running water and the sound increased, Mindy started thinking she saw something. Which was impossible, since there was no light anywhere.

She blinked, making sure her eyes were open.

Sure enough, there was something not quite hellhole-black in front of her. All at once she got her balance back, and the vertigo went anyway.

"Deke, do you—?"

"Shh!" His hand reached back and connected with her tummy. She felt him flinch, but he didn't jerk away. "I need to check this out," he whispered. "Stay here."

Terror gripped her, causing her little Sprout to stir restlessly. She grabbed Deke's hand and squeezed it. "Deke, please. Don't leave me. Not in the dark."

"Stay here!" Deke's voice brooked no argument.

Mindy stayed. She trembled and hugged her tummy. Her eyes devoured the faint hint of less-than-total blackness in front of her. Her ears strained to hear the smallest sound that would tell her that Deke was all right. And her pulse drummed so hard and fast that she thought she might pass out. But she stayed.

Suddenly, a shadow moved directly in her line of sight. At first she wasn't sure she saw it. She attributed it to the darkness and her fear and anticipation. But it kept coming closer.

Looming, menacing, like a spectre out of a dark lagoon, it stalked toward her.

Her pounding heart sped up even more, until she could feel the throbbing in her temples, in her wrists, even in the restless movements of her baby inside her. Then Sprout kicked her—hard.

She gasped.

"Mindy?"

Deke. His precious voice was right there. In front of her. It was Deke.

"Deke?" she breathed.

"Yeah. I was counting my footsteps. I didn't mean to scare you."

"What did you find?"

His hand touched her upper arm and slid down until he found her fingers. He clutched them.

"Wait and see." He couldn't disguise the excitement in his voice.

Mindy's pounding heart calmed down immediately. Right now, here in this menacing, dark place, she caught a glimpse of the handsome, cocky teenager she'd fallen in love with so many years ago.

He'd been supremely arrogant—certain that there was no obstacle he couldn't conquer, no mountain he couldn't climb. Happy and teasing and gentle, excited to show her a new discovery. From the moment she first laid eyes on him, he'd been her hero.

She hadn't seen him in eight long months, although she'd come close to calling him a dozen times to tell him he was going to be a father. Then she'd thought better of it, decided that she and her child would be better off if she never got sucked into his self-destructive life.

Seeing him now, she wasn't sure she'd made the right decision.

She squeezed his fingers back. "Take me." She heard the tremor in her voice.

He put his arm around her waist and led her forward and around a curve. As soon as they rounded the corner, Mindy saw a silvery-blue light shining down from above like a spotlight. In the light's circle was the spring they'd heard. It warbled and bubbled, its shimmering water reflecting the light like something magical as it flowed over pale rocks.

"Oh—" She was speechless.

Deke's hand tightened on her waist and he nuzzled the delicate skin right in front of her ear. "Welcome to your fantasy forest glen, my lady," he whispered, a smile in his voice.

"This is so beautiful. How—?"

She felt him shrug. "Best I can figure, this is a major artery of the old mine. They put it here, where the underground spring carved out this natural cavern." He started forward, guiding her at his side as he talked.

"The light comes from what looks like a wooden chimney way above us. Look." He pulled her close to the stream and pointed above their heads.

Almost too distracted by the sheer incredible relief of seeing light before her eyes, Mindy finally assimilated what he'd said and looked upward.

"I think it's a ventilation shaft. They sometimes had problems with the air quality in these mines. So they'd build shafts to let in fresh air."

"And light!" she exclaimed.

Deke's finger touched her chin and his thumb urged her to raise her head.

She did. When she met his dark gaze lit by blue fire, her knees grew weak.

"And light," he murmured. Then he bent his head and kissed her.

His kiss was like coming home. Like heaven. Like life. She melted into the warmth and sensuality of his mouth on hers, and responded. He kissed her more intimately, and a thrill slid though her entire body, settling in her sexual core.

Then Sprout kicked her. She drew in a small, sharp breath and instinctively pressed her palms against her side.

Deke backed away instantly. "What was that?" he asked. "Are you all right?"

Mindy smiled sadly. "It's our son kicking. He likes to get me right here, in the side."

"Our—" Deke looked down at her tummy, then back up. His eyes glittered in the pale blue light that barely managed to chase the shadows away from the circle under the ventilation shaft.

"Our son," he whispered, an expression of awe lighting his face.

His words, his voice cut through to her heart. She heard fear, but along with the fear was a note of wonder.

And there he was—the man she'd never seen, the man she'd always known he could be. If he'd ever learn to trust her, or himself, enough.

She nodded and lifted her hand to touch his cheek.

But he took another step back, straightened and turned away. He walked over to the edge of the stream.

"You need some water," he stated matter-of-factly without turning around. "I found an old candle bucket in the corner. I cleaned it with sand and anchored it between some rocks so the flowing water would rinse it out."

Mindy felt like he'd ripped her heart right out of her chest. She'd always wondered what it would take to break through the wall he raised whenever someone got too close. Her love had never been enough. She'd hoped little Sprout would be.

But his damn pride and fear had overpowered him.

So he'd forced his feelings—what he considered his weakness—back behind the wall that shielded his heart.

He kneeled and picked up the bucket and brought it to her, half-filled with water. His face was expressionless, his voice remote. "Here. I'll hold it while you drink."

She held the sides of the bucket between her palms and guided it to her lips. The galvanized metal rim was icy-cold, and she had trouble swallowing the water past the lump in her throat, but the few swallows she managed to get down tasted heavenly.

It was sweet and cold and thoroughly refreshing. It ran over the edge of the bucket and dripped down her chin onto her breasts and tummy.

Deke held the bucket patiently. As soon as she'd finished drinking, he turned on his heel and with his back to her, he drank his fill.

"Come over here," he said without turning around.

As she followed him over to the wall, she took in what was around her. There was a small stack of railroad-ties against the wall that was obviously intended as a crude bench. Buckets were scattered around, sitting up or overturned. On the ground to the side of the railroad tie bench sat a large metal tray covered with a piece of steel screen. Several feet beyond the bench stood an old vehicle that looked like a wagon with a cover over it.

"What is all this?" she asked Deke.

"I think this was probably a popular lunch spot with the coal miners. Somebody took the trouble to build the bench and the stove. And check that out." He pointed to the vehicle.

"That's a man car. Covered with a blanket. Look at

the lanterns attached to the sides. They look like they still have oil in them."

Mindy turned her head to look, but she must have moved too fast, because dizziness overwhelmed her.

Deke caught her arm. "Whoa. Sit down over here. You're exhausted, and I am *not* about to try and get you back on your feet if you faint."

She made a face at him as he tugged on her arm until she followed him over to the bench. He gently pushed her down.

"Now stay there. The miners who worked down here had a pretty clever setup. We'll have some dinner in a few minutes."

"Dinner?" she said weakly. As if on cue, her stomach growled and Sprout wiggled and pounded against her side.

"Yeah. Do you see the silver flashes in the stream?"

"No." She squinted. "Maybe."

"They're fish."

"Fish? There are fish down here?"

"I haven't figured out what kind they are, but I'm about to."

"What are you going to do?"

He picked up one of the buckets and brought it over for her to see. "Somebody punched holes in the bottom of this bucket."

"A lot of holes," Mindy agreed.

"I'm thinking they used it to fish—like a net. With any luck, I can anchor it in the water and come up with a few fish."

"Fish," Mindy breathed. "I'm so hungry I could manage to eat them raw. But—?"

Deke grinned at her and pointed at the pile of ashes and twigs. "Don't worry. We'll cook them the old-fashioned way."

WITHIN TWENTY MINUTES, Deke had a bucketful of fish, and the legs of his jeans were soaked through. He climbed out of the stream, shivering when his bare feet hit the air. The spring was quite a few degrees colder than the surrounding atmosphere.

He brought the dripping bucket over to the campfire site and set it on a piece of railroad tie.

Raising his head, he started to speak to Mindy, but her eyes were closed and her lips were barely parted. She was asleep.

Compressing his mouth into a thin line, Deke sat on his haunches and watched her for a few minutes. Her soft mouth, her delicate brows and the eyelashes that lay on her cheeks like big fuzzy caterpillars, all the little parts of her that were tattooed on his heart.

His gaze slid down her neck and breasts to her tummy. Pregnant, she looked and acted so different. She had a contentment about her that she'd never had when they were together.

Just the sight of her soft, serene expression made his heart hurt. Why was she serene and happy now? Was it because he was out of her life? Why hadn't he been able to bring that look to her face?

As soon as the question rose in his mind, he knew the answer. It was simple. He could never give her ease and contentment, because he was a breaker. He broke promises, broke vows, broke hearts.

He sighed. Even if he couldn't give her contentment, he could give her his protection. He owed her that much. He'd brought her into this mess.

He resolved to let her sleep until he got the fish cooked, then once she ate, he'd make sure she slept some more.

For several minutes, he explored the cavern. It wasn't huge, but it was like a vast, empty auditorium compared to the dark, narrow tunnels that fed into and out of it.

The main tunnel had eight sets of rails that ran downhill, parallel to the stream. Four of the sets came from the tunnel behind him. Its incline wasn't nearly as steep as the north one. The other four came from the east—the tunnel from the anteroom in the hotel basement—and joined the first four just above the sharp downhill incline.

He continued northward, examining the walls for other tunnels. In a pocket close to the rail intersection, he found a pile of branches and twigs. Beside the pile was a bucket of kindling and one about half-filled with candles.

Deke propped his fists on his hips and looked back toward the ventilation shaft, thinking about luck and co-incidence.

A cozy campsite with readily available fuel, a water source and a light source. *It was too good to be true.* It could easily be the latest in a series of traps set by Novus Ordo. Force them to take this tunnel, bring them to a veritable underground paradise complete with everything they needed to fill their stomachs and calm their minds. Then attack them while they were asleep.

He had to hand it to Novus. It was amazing what he'd managed to put together on a moment's notice. Amazing and frightening. Deke wondered how many men Novus had in the U.S. who were available and willing to drop everything on an hour's notice to carry out a focused and unrelenting attack.

Oddly enough, he no longer felt that prickle on the back of his neck. Maybe Novus's men hadn't managed to wire this section of the mine.

He thought about what Frank James had said to him.

You'll be hungry and thirsty and tired. Your gal there'll be pretty darn sick from hunger and exhaustion.

It made perfect sense, knowing Novus. He was wearing Deke down, as he'd done before. After his capture in Mahjidastan, Deke had been trussed so tightly his shoulders had been dislocated, then he'd been thrown into a filthy, stinking tent. Each day at the same time, a robed man brought him a bowl of foul-tasting mush and one of dirty water. Then hours later, another robed and masked man would come in, order Deke to rise to his knees, spin the cylinder of a revolver, and fire it at Deke's head.

Those two visits took about six to eight minutes out of his day. The other twenty-three hours and fifty-odd minutes, he was left alone to think about the next day, when they would come again.

Deke pushed his fingers through his hair and rubbed the back of his neck as a deep shudder racked him. He wanted to give Novus and his ridiculous toy cowboy something to think about. He wanted to leave this lovely, compelling little cavern behind and spend the night poised for ambush, waiting for them to come looking for him.

But Mindy was already dog-tired; her face was drawn and pale. Right now, the most important thing was to make sure she got nourishment and rest. For herself and her baby.

He brought a pile of branches back to the campfire

and, using a candle stub for a starter, soon got a nice fire going. He washed a small piece of screening to put the filleted fish on, then set it on the stove to cook.

By the time the fish were cooked, Mindy was stirring. Deke took the makeshift plate over and set it beside her on the railroad-tie bench.

"What's this?" she murmured sleepily.

"Dinner. Unfortunately, this is the entire menu. I don't even have any salt—or utensils."

"This is perfect."

The fish was tender and fell apart easily. Deke held back and let Mindy have as much as she wanted. She downed at least six of the small filets. When she sat back and sighed with contentment, Deke, who had been busying himself with the fire, finished them off.

Then he brought her a bucket of water. "Drink first," he said, "then wash up."

She obeyed, then glared at him. "Now, you bring some fresh water up here and some sand or gravel."

He frowned at her.

"I'm going to wash your arm. *And* I want some of that lantern oil to disinfect it."

"I told you, Min—"

"I don't care!" She held up a hand. "You said yourself the lanterns on that car had oil in them. Now bring me some. And get those bandages off and use the bucket with the holes in it to wash them in the stream."

It was Deke's turn to obey. By the time she'd scrubbed the gash in his arm with sand and water, and poured lantern oil into it—which burned like a sonofabitch—he was cold and strangely tired.

"Long before we had modern ways of cleaning and

disinfecting wounds, people used kerosene, gasoline, even gunpowder, to clean wounds."

Deke uttered a short laugh. "I guess I'm lucky we don't have a gun. I can hear you now, telling me that fire is the best disinfectant."

"Don't make fun. If it gets any worse, I may have to burn it. See the inflamed areas at the edges of the wound?" she asked.

Deke didn't want to look. He felt like his arm was on fire, and yet the rest of him was shivering with cold.

"That's cellulitis. It means your wound is infected. I'll bet you have fever. Damn it, Deke. If you'd let me clean it when I wanted to, this wouldn't have happened."

"It's not a problem."

"Yes, it is. I've got to keep an eye on this. If we see red streaks starting up your arm, that'll mean the infection is serious."

"I'll be fine."

"You're already not fine. Now bring me those bandages."

It took only a few minutes for Mindy to wrap his arm. Afterward, he quickly cleaned up the campsite, doing his best to make it look as if it hadn't been disturbed. Then he helped Mindy cross the shallow spring.

During his exploration earlier, he'd found a pocketlike alcove in the wall on that side of the spring. It was deep enough that they could sit in the shadows and see into the tunnels without exposing themselves.

"I'm going to have to sit you on the ground," he told Mindy. "But I promise there aren't any bugs."

She chuckled quietly. "Don't worry. Bugs are the least of my worries right now."

Deke looked at her, wondering how he was going to get her to the ground. If it weren't for his arm, he'd pick her up and lay her down, but she was right about his wound. It seemed to be getting hotter and more tender. He shivered.

If her efforts didn't stop the infection, he was terribly afraid he might not make it much further under his own steam.

But he didn't tell her that.

"How do you want to do this?" he asked.

"If you can hold my hands, I can lower myself to the ground. Getting up will be a different story, though."

He helped her to the ground. "Are you cold?"

She shook her head. "Not too bad. It's a lot warmer over here than on the other side of the creek. Wonder why?"

"There could be a fire smoldering on the other side of this wall. I don't smell anything, so I'm not sure."

"A fire?"

"Sometimes the coal in these underground passages catches fire. They can burn slowly for years before anything happens." He put his hand on the dirt wall behind them. The wall did feel several degrees warmer than the wall on the other side.

"Years? And what kind of anything?"

"Yep, years. Like fifty or so in some cases. Eventually the fire will use up all the air in the mine and can burst through the surface."

Mindy turned her head to stare at him. "It won't happen today, will it?"

He couldn't help but smile. "Not if we're lucky."

"Why couldn't you have just said 'Who knows?' when I asked you why the wall was warm."

"Ask me again."

She laughed quietly and Deke felt her shoulders move. He lifted his left arm and slid it around her.

"Why don't you try to sleep," he said. "I'll keep an eye out for predators."

Mindy's shoulders stiffened. "Predators? You mean Frank James? Or are there bears and things around?"

He tightened his arm around her and bent to whisper in her ear. "You let me worry about bears and things. You just worry about getting some sleep. You're exhausted, and you've got to rest so your baby can rest."

"*Your* baby," she murmured.

The two words ripped through him like a bullet.

His baby.

He still couldn't make those two words work together. *He* didn't have a baby. He couldn't.

Not with his legacy. Not if he was anything at all like his father. *If?* Hell. There was no if about it. He *was* like his father.

His dad had been a mean, abusive drunk. Deke knew that his own battle had taken a different turn. He'd drunk a lot and tried drugs a little. But early on he'd discovered that he was a surly drunk rather than a violent one, like good old Dad. He didn't lash out physically, but he definitely lashed out verbally, with hurtful, cutting jabs at anybody who happened to be in his way.

No. Fatherhood was not for him. No innocent child should ever be subjected to what he could dish out when he was under the influence. A very good reason why he never drank anymore. Not even beer.

"Deke?"

His thoughts slammed back into the present, and he

realized he was squeezing Mindy's shoulders. He relaxed his hand. "Yeah, sugar?"

"You don't have to be afraid of him."

The image of his father, eyes black as night and deep lines in his scowling face, rose before his vision for a few seconds before he realized she was referring to the baby.

"This little Sprout is a lot like you already. And he's only just getting ready to be born."

"Sprout?"

She laughed. "I call him that. It just came out one day when I was talking to him." She rubbed her tummy with both hands. "Do you want to feel him move? It seems like he moves almost all the time now. I don't know when he sleeps."

"I, uh—"

"Come on. Give me your hands."

Mindy took his hands and placed them on her rounded tummy, which was much firmer than he'd expected it to be. He'd always figured a pregnant tummy would be sort of springy and mushy. But hers felt like a basketball, round and hard.

"Is that how it's supposed to be? All hard like that?"

Mindy laughed, and her laugh slid through him like old times.

Then something moved. Deke jerked his hands away.

"Okay, you big scaredy-cat, it's just your son."

Just?

She pressed his hands down again and slid them over to her side. "Here. Here's his foot. *Mmh.* Feel that? He just kicked me. It's his favorite pastime."

"He kicked," Deke whispered in awe. "That was his foot."

"See? You can tell he's very healthy. He's pretty big, too. The doctor thinks he'll probably weigh at least seven pounds."

"Seven pounds."

Mindy inclined her head and gently bumped Deke's chin. "You're funny. All you're doing is repeating what I say. Is Sprout here that intimidating?"

Slowly, he nodded.

Mindy yawned, so he extracted his hands from hers and put his arm around her again. "Lean against me and sleep. I'll keep watch."

Mindy tucked her head under his chin and settled against him, with her tummy pressed against his side. "Then you have to wake me up to stand guard while *you* sleep."

Deke settled gently back against the warm wall and watched the tunnel in front of them, wondering how long it would take for Frank James to find them.

Chapter Seven

He drove the SUV along the fence line, using only the moon's light to examine the chain links for tears or breaks. Headlights would ruin his night vision. Besides, although everyone knew it was his shift to guard the remote perimeter of Castle Ranch, at least without headlights they couldn't see exactly where he was or what he was doing.

Everyone at the ranch was getting cabin fever, so Matt Parker had suggested that the specialists patrol the perimeter. All of them had jumped at the idea. It wasn't their nature to sit idle while one of their own was in trouble.

He drove over a ridge—and there it was. Exactly what he'd been looking for. On a spread the size of Castle Ranch, there had to be sections that were totally hidden. And this one was perfect for his purposes. The top of the ridge had a clear view of the front of the ranch. Its other side was completely hidden from all directions by scrub brush. A sniper could hide out here for hours—days, if necessary.

His hands shook on the steering wheel. At least, the vengeance he'd longed for all these years was within his reach.

MINDY SLEPT LIGHTLY. It had been weeks since she'd slept well, thanks to her little Sprout. Now her bed consisted of hard-packed dirt in an underground cave in early April. Which meant the nights were still quite cold. If she didn't have Deke to lean on and snuggle up against, she'd be half or maybe three-quarters frozen by now.

But she did have Deke. At some time while she was asleep, he'd managed to maneuver so that her head was on his chest and her tummy rested in the cradle created by his thighs.

She closed her eyes and relaxed against him. Her right ear was pressed to his chest and his strong, steady heartbeat set a rhythm for hers.

And her Sprout's. She could feel the baby. He felt like he was gently rocking himself to the comforting drumbeat of Deke's heart.

The spring provided a lilting melody to the bass beat of Deke's heart, and water dripping somewhere close by added a sweet accompaniment. Above her head the pale light of the moon lent an idyllic glow to the underground cavern.

Right here, right now, Mindy could believe that she and Deke had escaped the tethers of the real world and traveled to a fantastical alternate universe.

Mindy took a long breath, and the scent hit her. Her heart skipped a beat and a thrill rolled through her. Leather, soap and heat. *Deke.*

Dear heavens, how could she face losing him again?

Sprout kicked her in the side. She grunted, and Deke stirred.

Mindy straightened, preparing to move away, but his arm tightened around her shoulders.

"Where are you going?" he asked sleepily.

She lifted her head. "I'm sprawled all over you. I figured you might want to change positions."

"Um, not right this minute. In fact, you may not want to move, either. You might be embarrassed."

"Why? What are you—" She stopped, because she knew what he was talking about. He was erect. The sensations her stretched-out tummy were sending her were different from her normal nonpregnant self, and so until she'd moved, she hadn't noticed.

Now that she had, the strangest feelings roiled through her. Feelings that she hadn't had for a long time. Okay, maybe she'd had them, but she hadn't acknowledged them. From the moment she'd accepted the fact that she couldn't live with Deke and his self-destructive ways, she'd done her best to curtail all of her feelings—bad and good.

She'd felt as if to admit that she was sexually frustrated was to admit that she was still in love with Deke.

So now, lying in his arms with his erection rubbing against her tummy, the feelings that had started with warmth and comfort and safety morphed into desire.

And that was ridiculous. She was over eight months pregnant. She shouldn't be feeling like this. In fact, according to all the books, she should be working up a good-size dose of resentment and irritation toward him right about now.

"What are you thinking about?" Deke asked.

Mindy's throat seized. Did she dare tell him that she was fantasizing ways they could make love on this dirt floor?

"Min? Everything okay?" He touched her chin with his fingertips and tilted her head so he could see into her eyes. When he did, his blue eyes widened slightly and his mouth quirked up.

He knew. Damn him. He always knew. Once, it had fascinated her that he could tell with a glance when she was turned on.

Now, it embarrassed her and left her feeling vulnerable. She lowered her gaze, but not in time. He made a soft growling sound deep in his throat that rumbled against her ear.

"Min, I didn't mean to get you involved in this." He spoke against her hair, his breaths warming her skin.

She nodded. "I know."

His fingers under her chin pressed harder, urging her head up again. "I'm so afraid I'll hurt you."

She opened her mouth to offer up the standard protest, but he dipped his head and stopped her words with his lips.

Dear God, she loved to kiss him. His kiss was a perfect reflection of who he was. Hard, determined, yet with an undertone of such gentleness that it made her want to cry with joy because he'd shared it with her.

She needed to stop—for her own sanity. Needed to pull back, physically and emotionally, from the precipice of sublime insanity that making love with him always plummeted her over.

He bent forward, pulling her closer, holding her mesmerized with just the touch of his mouth on hers.

She'd gotten used to the vagaries of her hormone-suffused body, but in the entire eight months she'd been pregnant she hadn't once had a lascivious thought. In fact some days she'd felt so uncomfortable and lonesome that she figured she'd never have sex again. And she'd been okay with that.

But right now—

Deke's mouth moved over hers with the confidence and strength she'd learned to depend on, until he'd proved to her that he wasn't dependable.

She kissed him back. She couldn't help herself.

He ran his thumb across the underside of her chin and then cradled her cheek in his palm. His kiss grew deeper, more intimate, more demanding. Her heart pounded and her insides thrilled as she tasted his tongue and the inside of his mouth for the first time in way too long.

Trailing his fingers down her cheekbone, he traced the line of her jaw. At the same time his lips slid across her cheek, caressing the tender skin in front of her ear. Deep within her core, a rhythmic throbbing began and grew, swelling like a symphony.

Inside her, Sprout wiggled and kicked. Her deepening arousal was disturbing him. She cradled her tummy and glanced down.

When she did. Deke pulled away. "Sorry," he muttered.

"Deke, don't."

Don't what? She couldn't answer her own question. Don't apologize? Don't stop kissing her? Don't make her remember how it felt to love him?

Ignoring the voice in her head that told her how foolish it was to go down that road, she slid her fingers around the nape of his neck and pulled him closer.

"Don't apologize," she said. "I need—" She couldn't verbalize what she needed, but he seemed to know. With a pensive, solemn expression, he sat up and shrugged out of his shearling jacket.

"Sit up for a minute," he said. When she did, he

placed the jacket behind her back, then leaned over her and kissed her again.

He was so strong. She ran her hands along the corded muscles of his forearms, shivering when she encountered the damp bandage. Then her palms slid up to trace the shape of his biceps and triceps. She lifted her head and pressed her lips against his throat, feeling the pulse thrumming there.

Balancing his weight on his arms, he lowered himself until he could nip at the curve of her jaw, at her earlobe, at the sensitive skin just beneath her ear. His breaths sawed in and out in a deep, steady rhythm that called to something visceral inside her.

"Min?" he whispered into the curve joining her neck and shoulder. "I can stop."

She shook her head. "Not yet," she murmured. "Not now."

He took in a deep breath that hitched at the top. "Then you'll have to stop me before I—before I hurt you."

She swallowed an ironic laugh. *Too late,* she thought. That ship sailed a long time ago.

Deke wanted to push away. He wanted to be the stronger one. The one who kept his head.

But he knew he was doomed to failure. He'd never been able to resist Mindy's soft, full mouth or her sexy, made-for-loving body. Or the sweet way she always made him feel like a hero, even though they both knew he was anything but.

They'd been together since junior year in high school. They'd been lovers since graduation night. She knew everything about him.

She knew where he liked to be kissed, to be touched.

She knew how to bring him to the point of no return with nothing more than a brief caress of her fingers. She knew that although he'd never admit it to any of his buddies, he loved for her to touch his nipples. The sharp, erotic sensation of her fingertips and nails on them nearly sent him over the edge.

As if she knew what he was thinking, she slid her palms down his biceps and over his pectorals. Then she rubbed his nipples until they stood erect. He gasped, and she chuckled.

Okay, then. He knew everything about her, too. This would be tit for tat.

Like right now. He buried his nose in the little curve between her neck and her shoulder. If he ran his tongue along the apex of her shoulder, right over the little bump covered by golden skin, she'd moan and squirm.

He did.

And she did.

His throat closed with laughter—and sweet, aching nostalgia. Her hands tightened around his muscled wrists. Absently, he remembered that her fingers didn't reach all the way around.

He shifted his weight to his left arm and began unbuttoning the buttons at the top of her sweater. He didn't dare look up. He was afraid of what he'd see in her eyes.

Excitement, anticipation or apprehension?

When she pushed his hands away, his heart sank all the way to his boots. His logical brain, however, reminded his heart that they were in this place because she was in danger, and it was all because of him.

He had no right to take advantage of her. She was at his mercy. Dependent on him for safety, for comfort, for strength—for her very life.

Which made her vulnerable. And he was exploiting that vulnerability by letting his body overrule his brain. What he needed to be doing right now was figuring out their next move.

He knew perfectly well what this idyllic refuge was that they had found. It was bait—to lure them into a false sense of security.

Novus Ordo was still out there and still plotting to wear him down, still playing cat and mouse. For the moment he'd lifted his paw, giving them a taste of freedom—a false belief that they had a chance to escape. As soon as they tried, he'd clamp down on them again.

Her fingers brushed across his again, reminding him that his hand was resting near her breasts. He pulled away, but she stopped him. He watched with bated breath as she guided his palm to her waist, and then slid it up until his fingers curved around the bulge of her tummy. Against his palm, her satin-smooth skin seemed to vibrate with life—hers and the life of the tiny child inside her.

He closed his eyes, and for a moment he existed only in the sensations that flowed through the nerve endings on his fingertips and palms. He didn't think he'd ever felt anything so alive, so vibrant, so awesome.

To his surprise, tears stung his eyes, so he lowered his head, unwilling to let her see his weakness. He'd never even dreamed of being a father, never once considered that a precious, innocent child could spring from these loins of his. From the same DNA that had produced his cruel dad, and himself.

He pressed his forehead against the warm bulge of her tummy and silently prayed that one day he might be worthy of her and her baby.

He felt the tears leaking out from beneath his lids. He couldn't let her feel the salty drops on her skin. He hadn't cried since he was in junior high school and his dad had showed him what happened to crybabies.

So, under the pretense of nuzzling her tummy, he managed to wipe his eyes on the tail of her sweater.

Her abdomen moved as she sighed. Her fingers tightened around his, and she slid his hand across the slope of her tummy and farther up, toward her breasts.

His breath hitched and he raised his gaze. "Mindy—"

"Hush, Deke," she whispered. "Please don't spoil this with logic and reason. It's nothing more than a moment stolen out of time. It's not like we've never done it before." She made a quick head gesture toward her tummy.

"But you're—"

She put her fingers to his lips. "Shh. Don't even go there. Please don't *think*. For once in your life, just feel. I need you to take me somewhere outside of here. Outside of myself, because if I keep worrying about what's going to happen, I'll go insane."

As she talked, she continued to slide his hand upward, to the underside of her breast. Then she gripped his wrist and guided him over the fullest part to the peak, pressing his fingers to her nipple. She gasped.

And sighed again.

Deke's first instinct was to jerk his hand away. She was pregnant. These weren't the small delicate breasts he'd teased and nuzzled so many times. These were big breasts, pregnant breasts. They were firm and full, and the nipple was large and erect, waiting for the hungry little mouth of her son.

Their son.

His body instantly hardened—muscles, tendons, bones—all stiffened in sharp, aching hunger. His mouth watered to taste the distended tip.

He caressed the nipple with the gentle touch of his fingers. As he did it hardened and puckered in reaction, and Mindy's breathing ratcheted up a notch. She blew air softly in and out, and her body writhed and arched the tiniest bit, revealing her yearning for more of what he offered.

So he cradled her full round globe in his hand, kneading and squeezing, then running his thumb across and around her ever-tightening nipple. His erection grew harder, longer, as his body throbbed in familiar reaction to her obvious need and desire. Turning her on had always fed his own desire.

But this—what he felt right now—was a level of longing he'd never before experienced. Not even when they were horny teenagers, searching for a place where they could be alone together.

"How—how does it feel?" he asked with trepidation. "To be pregnant?"

Mindy put her hand on top of his. It had always awed her how much bigger his hand was than hers. "It's really strange. Different every day."

She looked at the man who'd created this baby with her. He was so scared. She could read the fear in his face. Over the years she'd known him, she'd watched him forge himself into a warrior. He'd taught himself not to be afraid of anything. Yet this small, helpless life within her terrified him.

"He feels like you," she whispered, her voice catching. "It's like I have a part of you inside me all the time."

She'd known that, deep inside, but she'd never said

the words, not even to herself. Now she understood the erotic dreams that woke her deep in the night. Now the indescribable longings she'd never acknowledged in daylight had a source. And the source was Deke.

He made a deep, throaty sound, and a shudder rumbled through him. His erection pulsed against her thigh.

Instantly, her body tightened in desire and in the deepest, most intimate part of her, a sweet familiar throbbing began.

Deke continued caressing the tip of her breast as he lifted his head. He leaned forward until his mouth brushed hers.

Then he kissed her. A desperate, deep, soul-searching kiss. As his mouth took hers, she whimpered in uncontrollable response.

He froze.

She moaned in frustration as he pulled away.

"What's wrong?" she whispered.

"I'm hurting you."

"Deke, believe me, you're not." Mindy's breasts, her center, burned with frustration. "Please." She wrapped her hand around the nape of his neck and pulled his head toward her. "Don't stop."

And he didn't. He kissed her over and over, tasting her as if it were the first time. She was as sexy to him as she'd always been. Maybe more so. Something, whether it was her pregnancy or just the fact that it had been so long, had him so turned on that he was afraid he might explode like a horny kid. He pulled back, trying to control himself, but Mindy moaned in protest. She caught his hand and brought it to the apex of her thighs.

He felt her heat, even beneath the wool pants she wore. And when he pressed his palm against her, her already labored breathing sped up.

"Deke," she whispered, then gasped again. "Oh!" Her hand covered his, and she pressed down against his palm.

He listened to her shallow, rhythmic breaths, her small cries. And clenched his teeth to keep from following her climax with his own.

"Deke," she finally breathed. "Don't run away. Let me—" She reached for his pants zipper.

"No. This isn't a good idea."

"Why?" She clasped his hand in hers and brought his palm to her lips. She chuckled, still feeling the small aftershocks of her climax. "It's not like you can get me *more* pregnant."

As soon as the words were out of her mouth, she knew she'd screwed up. Royally.

Deke pushed away and sat up. "Nope," he rasped, as he pushed his fingers through his shaggy hair. "Apparently that was one time I managed to deliver maximum damage on the first try."

"Deke, wait. I'm sorry."

"For what? Getting pregnant? That wasn't your fault." He rubbed his eyes, then swiped a hand across his face. "It was your mother's funeral. I took advantage of your grief."

"You did not! It just happened. In fact, if I hadn't kissed you, you'd have been out of there like a cat with its tail on fire." She smiled briefly. "Trust me, Deke. I do not regret being pregnant."

"I do."

She flinched and her eyes pricked with tears at his

quick, simple declaration. But she had known this was how he would feel. From the first moment she'd realized that she was pregnant, there had been no question in her mind.

She'd wanted the baby, whether Deke did or not.

Gingerly, as if he were a skittish colt, she took his hand and pressed it against her tummy.

"Can you regret this? He's your son, Deke. A part of you and me. If we're lucky, the best parts."

"And if we're not lucky?" He was thinking of his father.

"Trust me. In this we're lucky."

"Good to know," he muttered. "When we get out of here, remind me to buy a lottery ticket." He stared at his hand where it rested on her stomach. He still seemed awestruck—and terrified—by her pregnancy.

"Don't make fun of me. You have no idea how beautiful, how sexy you make me feel. I haven't felt either for months. Come back and lie down with me," she said. "I'm cold."

He scooted back over and reclined against the warm dirt wall, positioning himself so that she leaned against his left side.

She pressed her hand against his chest and tucked her head into the snug, sweet place between his neck and shoulder.

"This feels good," she whispered. "Like home."

Deke grimaced at her sleepy words and tightened his arm around her shoulders.

"Deke?" she whispered.

"Yeah, sugar?"

"What time do you think it is? And what day?"

It was a good question. He'd tried his best to keep

up with the time. "It's dark. I'd guess it might be around midnight. Best I can figure, it's Thursday night. Or Friday morning."

He bent his head and pressed a kiss against her hair. "Sleep, Min. I'll keep you safe." He leaned his head back against the hard dirt wall and stared at the starlit sky through the opening high above their heads. He felt her breasts rise and fall with her breaths, heard them slow and even out as she dozed.

The immediacy and strength of Mindy's response to him awed him—and terrified him.

He hadn't meant to lose control of himself, or get caught up in her growing reaction to his caresses.

All he'd wanted to do was taste, just for a moment, the sweetness of her kisses, feel the lovely soft firmness of her skin.

He hadn't meant to turn her on.

The thought sent a shudder of erotic thrill through him. He grimaced and shifted uncomfortably. He could easily and quickly take care of his discomfort, but he'd promised Mindy he'd keep her safe. He wasn't going to take the slightest risk of being distracted, not even for a moment.

Besides, from the very first time he'd touched her, when they'd both been innocent teens, he'd never known anything that fueled his own desire as much as stoking the fires of hers did.

She'd thanked him, but in truth she'd turned herself on. In doing so she'd turned him on, too. He'd gotten as much—well, almost as much—satisfaction as she had.

His eyes slowly closed, and his thoughts began to wander. He clamped his jaw. He couldn't sleep. He needed to keep lookout.

He couldn't do anything about the signs they'd left at the campfire. Probably didn't matter, anyway. Novus knew they were here. He'd probably arranged for the kindling and candles.

Deke snorted. If there hadn't been any fish in the spring, he'd have probably arranged for them, too.

He looked down at the top of Mindy's head. She was asleep in his arms, trusting him to keep her safe.

Anger, hot as a flash fire, whooshed through him. It took every ounce of his strength to stay still.

Why don't you just come and get me? he wanted to stand up and shout. *Come on, Novus. Show your face. Fight it out, fair and square, like a man.*

He doubted they'd managed to wire the entire mine, so he'd probably be yelling to deaf ears, but it would sure make him feel better.

I know why you won't face me, you scumbag. You're no man. You're a coward. Just like your wormy outlaw brother. Frank James. Give me a break! Covering up your weaselly face with a mask! Just like his boss Novus.

"I'll be damned—!" *Just like Novus.* The significance of his comparison slammed him in the gut. He clamped his jaw and took long, even breaths, trying to slow his suddenly racing heart. Trying not to disturb Mindy.

Could that be it? Could this guy, obviously American, actually be the brother of Novus Ordo? Deke knew from Rook's description and the forensic artist's rendering he'd seen that the terrorist was medium height and skinny with a narrow face and beady eyes. And Rook had sworn that Novus, whose messages were always delivered on CD in a heavy, Middle Eastern accent, was actually American.

It would explain everything. Novus's obsessive need to hide his face. Frank James affecting that ridiculous bandanna. It might be a leap, but it made sense.

Why else would James hide his face? Deke knew the weasel didn't intend to let either Mindy or himself get out of there alive.

Deke cursed silently. He had information that could bring Novus down, and he had no way to get a message out.

Rook, you sonofabitch! I need you, man. More than I ever have before. Between us, we'd figure out who Novus is and bring him and his brother down.

"Deke?" Mindy lifted her head. "What's the matter?"

Damn it, he'd woken her. "Nothing, sugar. Go to sleep."

She shifted. "Did you hear something?"

He shook his head and cradled the back of her head in his palm. "Nope. Just thinking."

She laid her hand on his chest. "Must have been some kind of thinking, to send your heart racing like that. What were you thinking about?"

"Novus," he said reluctantly. He didn't want her to know his fears. On the other hand, he owed her the truth. He'd gotten her into this. He probably should tell her exactly what and who they were battling.

"How we ended up here. It started out innocently enough. Irina's accountant gave her final warning. He'd apparently talked with her a few times before about her depleted funds. But this time he warned her that if she continued the same level of spending for another three to four months, she'd be bankrupt. Irina had to make a decision. Shut down BHSAR or stop spending a fortune searching for Rook. She made the only decision she could."

"I still don't understand why she gave up. They were more in love than any two people I've ever met. If I were Irina, the only way I'd ever give up is if I saw the body."

Deke tried to suppress the thought that sprang to the front of his mind.

So your definition of giving up doesn't include divorce?

He bit his tongue until the urge to lash out at her for leaving him went away. Hell, he knew he'd been an ass and had hurt her in too many ways to count, but it still hurt that she'd done the very thing he'd expected her— that he'd pushed her—to do.

He clenched his jaw and continued his explanation. "When Rook left the air force, he still had his burning desire to rescue the innocent. Black Hills Search and Rescue was his baby. Irina knew that Rook would never want to give up his dream. So she made the choice he'd have wanted her to make."

He felt Mindy's shoulder quiver and heard her swallow a sob. "Min? You okay?"

She nodded against his shoulder. "It's just so sad."

"Yeah. Apparently, as soon as Irina stopped searching, rumors started circulating that she'd found him. The first indication we got was from Homeland Security, reporting on the increased international chatter. Especially in the regions around the corridor that joins Pakistan, China and Afghanistan. A small province called Mahjidastan."

"Where you were shot down."

He nodded. "Novus Ordo's headquarters."

Mindy pushed herself up to a sitting position, groaning with the effort. Deke moved to help her. "So Novus found out that Irina had stopped the search."

"Matt left Mahjidastan within six hours after Irina called him—on the first flight he could get. He was followed. Then as soon as he got back, Aimee Vick's baby was kidnapped. That means that Novus knew what Irina had done *before* the chatter started."

"But how—"

"Only one way. We've got a traitor inside BHSAR."

"Oh my God, Deke. Who? Don't you know everyone?"

"I know the BHSAR team. I've met the rest of the staff. Don't know much about them. But the traitor has to be someone who knows everything that goes on. The specialists, Irina's personal assistant, her lawyer—"

"That's—what? Five people."

"Six, if I don't count Matt. Aaron Gold, Brock O'Neill, Rafe Jackson, Pam Jameison, Richards the lawyer, and maybe her accountant."

"I forgot about Rafe Jackson. I've never met him. Which one could do something like this?"

Deke shook his head. "Before all this started, I'd have said none of them. But now—everybody on the team, especially Irina, is in danger because I didn't identify a traitor in our midst. Think about it. They've already sabotaged my bird. Almost cost Matt and Aimee and her baby their lives."

Mindy considered the few times she'd met the other members of the team. "Brock's awfully secretive."

"Yeah, but can you see him betraying his country?"

"Maybe he doesn't consider it his country. He's Sioux, right? We destroyed *his* country."

Deke frowned at her.

"Or Aaron Gold? I only met him a couple of times."

"His dad was in the air force with Rook. He died a hero. Aaron was thrilled to be asked to join the BHSAR team."

"And Rafe Jackson?"

Deke didn't speak for a moment. "Rafe was born in England, but he went to a lot of trouble to become an American citizen."

"He's British?"

"Actually, his mother is from Saudi Arabia. His name is Rafiq."

"Wow. Any one of them could be the traitor."

Deke shook his head. "I guess you're right."

"What did you tell them about coming here to rescue me? I mean, if one of them is working with Novus, they know what's going on here."

"Let's just say I took precautions."

"What kind of precautions? What could you do to be sure the terrorist didn't find out vital information?"

"I'd rather not say."

"Really? Here, too?" Mindy craned her neck to look around.

"I have no idea. I just don't want to take any chances."

"So all this—it's because Novus is trying to find Rook, when he doesn't even know if he's alive? I guess whoever shot Rook didn't have the luxury of hanging around to make sure he died."

Deke sighed. "Guess not."

"Why don't they just go after you? Or Irina?"

"He can't get to us directly, and he knows that. There's too much security at the ranch. And it's the same reason he didn't just grab Matt. One of *us* disappearing would create an international incident, just like Rook's disappearance did. Since we're still connected with the military."

"So instead, he's grabbing those close to you."

Deke squeezed his eyes shut and rubbed his temple. "Something like that."

"Why? What's he after?"

"He's doing everything he can to be sure Rook can't identify him. You've seen the mask that Novus Ordo always wears?"

"Sure. I've seen the pictures they've shown on the news shows. It looks like those green and white disposable surgical masks you can buy in any drugstore." She uttered a short laugh. "He looks pretty ridiculous."

"Yeah, well, they've been effective. For several years, he's been the most famous and most dangerous terrorist on the planet. The mask fascinates people. It makes him look mysterious."

"And nobody's ever seen his face?"

"That's the word. No one except his most trusted inner circle. And Rook." Deke's gut twisted at his friend's name. Rook had taken Deke under his wing on the first day of first grade. He was only a few months older, but he'd always been the stronger one, the more courageous one, the leader. Rook had been born to lead, and Deke had been perfectly happy to be his sidekick.

"He saw him when he rescued you."

He looked at her, surprised.

"Rook told me. He said you saved Travis Ronson's life."

He'd never wanted her to know about that. Perversely, he would rather have her believe he didn't love her anymore.

The truth, that his helicopter had been shot down, which provided the means for Rook's team to find Novus, painted him in a sympathetic light that he didn't deserve.

"I only found out all that afterwards. The way Rook tells it, he and his team hit their camp at night while most of Novus's men were sleeping. He found the camp by using the GPS locator in my shoulder."

"In your shoulder? Is it still there?"

"No." He reached with his right hand to touch the little bump where the small chip was located, but the movement made his inflamed wound sting so he stopped. "The battery only lasts about a year. Still itches, though."

"So Rook rescued you."

"The team did. While they were transporting me to the helicopter, Rook took out a couple of guards with a silenced handgun, and found himself face-to-face with Novus, mask and all. Then a gust of wind ripped the mask right off him. Rook said he got an extreme close-up view before Novus covered his face with his arm."

"Oh my God! He saw Novus Ordo's face."

"Then two more guards tackled him. He almost didn't get away. One of them grabbed his dog tags and tried to choke him. About that time Brock O'Neill took out the other one with a machine gun. They got to the helicopter just as it was lifting off. Another few seconds and one of Novus's machine guns or flamethrowers could have grounded it. Then everybody would be dead." He wiped a hand down his face. "Truth is, it's my fault Novus targeted Rook."

Mindy shuddered. "What did Rook say about Novus? What did he look like?"

Deke laid his head back against the dirt wall. His mouth lifted at one corner. "That's classified."

"Right. Classified. Does Irina know?"

He frowned. "Probably."

"Do you think she's more trustworthy than me?"

"No. But—"

"Then tell me. You've always said how important it is to know your enemy. Well, I need to know my enemy, too."

He sent her a pensive look. "Okay. The latest, greatest, most infamous terrorist on the planet is American."

Chapter Eight

"Novus Ordo is American? No way!" Mindy stared at Deke, stunned. His head still rested against the wall behind him. He swallowed, and his Adam's apple moved up and down. The tendons in his neck and the muscles that joined his neck and shoulder stood out as sharp shadows. Dear heavens, there was nothing about him that wasn't sexy. Even his neck. Even his Adam's apple.

Deke smiled and her heart gave a little leap at the curve of his lips. "Way."

"Is— Was Rook sure? What did he tell you he looked like?"

"Rook said he was kind of ordinary looking, maybe of Irish or Scottish or British ancestry. But get this. He heard him curse, in a very American accent."

"Deke, this is unbelievable. Why would an American—?" She stopped. It was a silly and useless question. There had been other Americans who'd turned against their country. "But the audio recordings he's sent to the media have all been heavily accented English."

"Right. You notice he's never sent a video. Homeland Security's theory is that one of his inner circle makes the recordings for him. Plus Rook worked with a computer facial recognition analyst for the CIA. For the past two years the CIA and Homeland Security have been trying to find a match to fit his description."

"Have you seen it? The sketch?"

Deke nodded. "Average-looking guy. Medium height. Bordering on skinny. Long nose, close-set eyes, sharp chin."

Disturbingly similar to Frank James. The cowboy outfit and bandanna mask couldn't hide James's slender build, his beady eyes or his narrow face. With every passing minute, Deke was more convinced that James was Novus's brother, since, based on the sketch, he was too old to be his son.

Deke wasn't naive enough to think that Novus would be here carrying out this witch hunt himself, but he could easily believe that Novus's brother would do it. Hell, the sketch could be of Frank James himself.

He wondered what their real names were, and if they were born and reared in this part of the country or had located here because of Rook.

At least he had information that Novus didn't know he had, and he would guard that information with his life. It might be a way to bring Novus down.

"Deke?"

Mindy had asked him a question. "What?"

"What did Rook say about Novus's hair color? Was he dark or fair?"

"Rook couldn't see his hair because of his shemagh, but he said the CGI expert did a great job on the face."

"Shemagh?"

"That's the traditional Arabian headdress. Novus wears it on his head, but doesn't use it to cover his face. He uses the surgical mask for that."

"So none of you recognized the sketch? You'd never seen him before?"

"Nope."

"And the CIA has no idea who he is?"

He shook his head. "They've been going over all reports of missing Caucasian males from the past ten or so years, starting with the first known reports of Novus Ordo's involvement in terrorism."

Mindy felt like she'd woken up in the middle of a movie—a thriller. She couldn't keep up with everything Deke was telling her. She was still processing his astonishing statement: *Novus Ordo is American.*

More specifically, she was processing the realization that Deke knew so much about international terrorist activities, Novus Ordo and what sounded like classified government secrets.

He hadn't been kidding when he'd said *it's classified.* He had just told her a secret of global importance.

A sudden sense of overwhelming responsibility weighed on her shoulders. It was crushing. Suffocating. She put a hand to her breastbone as her pulse hammered in her ears. "Oh."

"Mindy? Is it the baby?"

She shook her head. "It's just—I almost wish you hadn't told me."

"I know what you mean. But after everything I've put you through, I figured you deserved to know. I can trust you not to tell anyone, can't I?"

"Of course you can. Deke, is *this* what you do? What you've been doing since you got back from Mahjidastan? You're a—a secret government agent? Some kind of covert operative?"

He laughed, but he sounded more ironic than

amused. "No. BHSAR isn't a secret government agency. It's what Rook wanted it to be. A private search-and-rescue company that does as many volunteer rescues as paid jobs, if not more."

"A private company. So, what were you doing over there spying on Novus Ordo?"

"That was supposed to be a one-time thing. A personal favor asked of him by—" he paused and drew in a long breath "—by a friend."

A very high-placed, influential friend. Mindy had no doubt those were the words Deke hadn't said.

"If I hadn't gotten shot down…if Rook hadn't seen Novus's face…" He shrugged. "Once all this is over, we should be able to do what we thought we'd done years ago. Be private citizens who just happen to run a local search-and-rescue operation."

"With an occasional favor for a special friend or two."

Deke just shrugged and quirked up the corner of his mouth.

"I don't know how you've managed to stay sane."

Another harsh laugh. "Maybe I haven't."

"Oh, I think you're much stronger than you realize." Mindy lay back against the softness of Deke's shearling jacket.

"Yeah? Have you decided I'm not broken?"

The question sounded ironic, but Mindy heard an undertone that she'd never heard in his voice before—an anxiousness, as if the answer she gave to that question was very important to him.

"Hmm. I think most of your life you've looked at strength in the wrong way. You equate strength with rigidity. And that's dangerous. You don't need to be too strong to break. If you're rigid, then you can't bend. And if you can't bend, you're doomed to break." She yawned. "Or something like that…"

"And bending. How is that a good thing? Isn't it like bowing down?"

She opened one eye and squinted at him. "No. It means you're resilient. You can take punishment without breaking. You'll be beaten down, but you'll spring back again."

A deep laugh rumbled through his chest. "You're exhausted. You need to get some sleep," Deke murmured.

"I'm not sure if I'll ever sleep again…" Her words faded.

"Oh, I think you will." He leaned over and pressed a kiss against her forehead. "I'm going to get up and take a look around, okay?"

"You need to sleep, too." She was already drifting off. *Sprout, don't you dare decide to be born until we get out of here. You can hold off another day or so, right?*

"I'll wait. I've gone without sleep for longer than this and survived. If you need me, call me."

"My hero," she whispered.

Deke slid carefully away from Mindy just as a deep rumble echoed through the cavern.

Mindy jerked and Deke stiffened.

That was an explosion. What the hell?

"What was that?" Mindy asked, worry lacing her voice.

"Thunder." Deke winced at his lie. "Go back to sleep. Even if it rains, we're protected here."

He rose to his feet and looked down at her. She'd already drifted back to sleep. She was so pretty, so young, so trusting, looking with her eyes closed and her face relaxed in sleep. Her silky-smooth hair fell across her cheek like chocolate-colored velvet.

God, I know I don't deserve to have a prayer answered, but don't make her suffer for my screwups. Please don't let her die.

What had gone so wrong? How had he let her get caught up in the train wreck that was his life? She didn't deserve this. She deserved a safe, stable home with all the special things that came with it: a husband who loved her and put her safety above everything else; beautiful, smart children she could be proud of; a life free of fear and danger.

The kind of life he could never give her.

His fists clenched as he turned away. It hurt his heart too much to look at her for very long. Especially like she was now. Innocent, vulnerable, trusting enough to sleep peacefully. It didn't seem to bother her that she had no one but him to protect her.

He should have brought backup. Rafe had been available, as had Aaron. But even if he'd trusted them enough, it would have been a fatal mistake. Novus had demanded that he come alone. He'd given him no choice. Out here on this lonely stretch of prairie, a second car or a second body would have been immediately noticeable. They could have been killed.

He fingered the bump on his shoulder. He hadn't told Mindy a complete lie. His scar did itch, partly because of the previous transmitter, but partly because of the new one. Who knew if it would prove useful, especially if they stayed underground. But he was glad he had it. He only wished he had some sort of two-way communication device.

If he stood directly under the ventilation shaft at exactly the right time, there might be a chance that one of the specialists would pick up on the chip's location. He needed to let someone know that Mindy was eight months pregnant. But he had no way to get the information out.

He should have hidden a two-way transmitter somewhere on him. But hell, they'd searched him. He was damn lucky they didn't get around to checking his boots.

Why hadn't he taken steps to protect Mindy from Novus like he had Irina?

Because he'd been clinging to the hope that after two years she was no longer close enough to him to be in danger. It was a stupid assumption.

Deke stood under the ventilation shaft as he argued with himself. And then argued with himself about the futility of arguing with himself. Finally, he stopped at the far end of the lagoon and stared at the coal-car rails that plummeted down the steep incline.

They couldn't go that way. He could make it on foot if he were alone, but Mindy would never be able to stay on her feet. The incline was about twenty degrees, which didn't sound like much, but in her condition she had enough trouble walking on level ground.

It amazed him that the heavily loaded coal cars had managed to stay on the tracks, especially if the tracks curved.

He did an about-face, just as another rumble shook the ground. Again, he held his breath. But nothing else happened. After another few seconds, the rumble faded.

He swallowed heavily. Those were explosions, not

thunder. And he'd bet money he knew what was being blown up.

The mine tunnels. James was trapping them in here. And there were only two reasons he would do that. Either he was ensuring that the only way out was back through the hotel, or— Deke did not want to think about the second reason. But he had to.

Or James was sealing them inside the mine before he killed them.

But why do that when he could just man the exits?

Good question. Maybe Novus didn't have as many men at his disposal as Deke had assumed he had. Maybe James was blowing up the tunnels because he couldn't guard them all at once.

If that was the case, then maybe Deke could get the upper hand after all. He figured he could handle two-to-one odds—maybe even three to one.

He turned to stare at the other end of the tracks, wondering if one of the explosions had caved in that tunnel. With a shrug, he continued his analysis of the best way to proceed. It was something to do at least.

The upper incline was much shallower—nearly level. If he were Novus, he'd discard that incline and the branch tunnel that led back to the hotel. Those were the easy choices.

But then, if Deke was thinking about taking the most difficult tunnel, even with a pregnant woman in tow, then Novus would also think about it.

He sighed and rubbed his temples. His thoughts were whirling out of control. Probably the result of too little food and sleep, and too many zaps with James's fancy Taser. At least the racing thoughts had distracted him from his other problem—his frustrated libido. He dropped to his haunches and winced at the pressure of the denim on his not-quite-deflated erection. Okay, he wasn't totally distracted.

He dipped his hands into the cold spring and splashed water on his face. Then, sitting back on his heels, he let his gaze wander around the large room. The only sounds that reached his ears were the soft trilling of the spring and an almost inaudible whistle of wind from the ventilation shaft high above.

He massaged the back of his neck. Much as he would have liked to catch a few winks of sleep, he needed to search the area for anything he could use as a weapon.

With a tired groan, he rose to his feet and went searching. The first thing he wanted to do was check out that blanket on the man car. If it wasn't too filthy, Mindy could cover up with it. He was sure that she was going to get cold before the night was over.

He crossed the shallow spring and approached the vehicle. A quick inspection told him that not only was the wool blanket filthy and moth-eaten, it was mildewed, as well. It wouldn't be healthy for Mindy to wrap up in it.

Gingerly, he pulled the thing off the car and peered over the sides, holding the lantern high in the air.

He froze.

Dynamite. Old dynamite. Several bundles of it. And from the little he knew about it, old meant dangerous. Carefully, holding his breath, he lowered the lantern enough to get a good look at the sticks without letting the lantern's heat come close to it.

The first thing he noticed once the vehicles floor was illuminated was a tangle of blasting caps. Dozens of them. The second thing he noticed was the bright spots on the surface of the sticks.

Crystals. Ah, hell. Those crystals were pure nitroglycerine. A bump—even a slight movement, could cause them to explode.

Hardly daring to breathe, he backed away from the car. Was that dynamite set to explode? He held the lantern up, searching to see if there was a fuse running from the car. But he didn't see anything.

So he crouched down, checking underneath, and walked all the way around, but he didn't see a fuse there, either. He did, however, find a crowbar leaning against the wall behind the car. Grabbing it, he straightened, blowing his breath out in a sigh. Maybe the dynamite hadn't been rigged by James. Maybe it had just been stored there for the past fifty or so years.

Still, the question remained. Did James know it was here?

It hardly mattered. They couldn't go near that car. They couldn't even breathe on it, or the nitroglycerine might blow. He headed back toward the alcove, testing the crowbar in his hands.

He crouched at the spring and scooped another couple of handfuls of water into his mouth, then sat back under the shaft and took his first deep breath since discovering the dynamite. He knew one thing for certain. They had to get out of here as soon as possible. In the meantime, on the minuscule chance that a satellite was in range and anyone might be monitoring transmissions, he'd stay under the opening as long as he could.

DEKE WOKE UP. HE'D HEARD something besides the quiet sound of burbling water.

There it was again. A quiet moan.

Mindy!

He vaulted to his feet, swaying a little as the blood rushed away from his head, and ran to the alcove.

She was sitting up, her hands pressed against her stomach.

"Min? What is it?"

"I don't kn—" Her whole body stiffened, and a sharp gasp cut off her words. "There's something—wrong."

Deke sat and took her hands in his. "What can I do?"

She shook her head. Even in the dim light of dawn seeping in through the ventilation shaft, he could see how pale her face was.

"Hey," he said, keeping his voice as calm as he could. He squeezed her fingers gently. "I'm pretty sure you're supposed to breathe."

She looked up at him. "So now you know all about pregnancy?" Her voice was strained, belying the lightness of her words.

"I took a course."

"Nice to know."

She pushed a breath out through pursed lips. Then drew in another. Taking them long and slow.

"That's good. Good, Min." He brought her hands to his mouth and kissed her knuckles, buying some time as he racked his brain. He *had* taken a course years ago, during his air force training. It had included an overview of delivering a baby. A *brief* overview.

Dear God, please don't let this baby come now. There was no way he could keep a newborn infant safe. No way he could take care of Mindy.

Focus. What were the signs of labor? *Contractions,* he answered himself.

"Are you hurting?" he asked.

She shook her head. "Not now."

He nodded. "So that wasn't a contraction?"

Mindy closed her eyes and flattened her lips. "No. It was a contraction, all right. And I don't think it was the first one."

Deke's training was coming back to him. Beads of sweat prickled his forehead and the nape of his neck. "How—how far apart are they?"

"I don't know. They started in my sleep. I was having a little back pain. And once or twice I felt a cramp. I palpated my abdomen. The uterus is definitely contracting."

"I didn't understand most of that, but you're the nurse, so I'll take your word for it."

She sent him a wan smile. "Thanks."

"Is this—" he made a vague gesture toward her tummy "—is this it? Are you having the baby?"

"No." Mindy lifted her chin. "No. It's too early. And—look where we are. No. My baby will *not* be born here." She cradled her tummy. "Did you hear me, Sprout? Stay in there. We'll be home soon."

My baby. Those two words echoed in his ears. She'd told him that the baby was his. She'd even referred to him as *our baby* a few times. He was surprised how much it hurt to hear her say *my* instead of *our* right now.

He cleared his throat. "What can I do to help?"

Her olive-green eyes met his gaze. "Go find a way out of here, get help and come back and rescue me."

"Forget that. I'm not leaving you here. Especially if you're having the baby." And especially since he knew they were practically sitting on enough dynamite to blow the entire mine.

She glared at him. "I am not having the baby."

Despite the seriousness of their situation, her determination made him smile. "What? You're going to stop him from being born with your steely resolve?"

"Damn straight I will." She stuck her chin out pugnaciously.

"And you call me stubborn," he muttered under his breath.

"I heard tha— Oh!"

"Min?" He took her hand and squeezed it reassuringly. Her fingers tightened around his with surprising strength. "Breathe, sugar."

She kept a stranglehold on his fingers until the contraction was over. He spent the time watching her, and estimating how long it had been between contractions.

"I think it's been ten minutes since the first contraction," he said, as she pushed herself back against the dirt wall.

She nodded. "That's what I thought. Ten minutes apart. I'm in premature labor."

"Is that some kind of labor that comes before real labor?" he asked hopefully. He had a sinking feeling that the answer to that question was no.

Sure enough, she shook her head. His heart sank and his pulse sped up.

"It's real labor, but it'll go away. Like I told you, it's too early. He's not due to make his appearance for six more weeks." She pushed herself up a little more. "Can you bring me some water?"

Deke fetched her a bucket of water. She drank several swallows.

"I've got to lie down," she told him. "The recommendation for slowing or stopping premature contractions is to lie still for a couple of hours and drink lots of water. That's the best chance I have to stop them."

"Okay, so we'll wait for two hours, then we'll both get out of here."

Mindy shook her head. "I don't think I'll be able to walk. Not in two hours. I'd just go back into labor." She put her hand on his. "Deke, you've got to find the way out."

"No. I'm not leaving you."

She maneuvered herself into a reclining position and turned onto her left side.

"This is no time to start being sentimental," she said. "I need you to do what you do best. What would you do if I were an injured man? Or a female innocent you were sent in to rescue?"

He scowled at her. "You're not."

She scowled right back at him.

He relented. "I'd leave the man with a weapon to defend himself while I scouted the best way out. I'd probably carry the female out with me."

"You can't. You're injured, and I'm not only too heavy, I can't walk."

"I can't leave you here, alone and helpless."

"It's the only way. Now give me the knife and go find us a way out."

He silently handed the knife over to her.

"I know you've already figured out what Novus is doing," she said.

He nodded. "He's got all the exits manned, and he's figured out what he thinks I'm going to do. I'm telling you, he's got a time frame he's working within. As soon as he can figure out a way to get to Irina—" He stopped. He didn't want to tell her that Novus's timeline included killing the two of them as soon as he got his hands on Irina Castle.

"He's having fun trying to anticipate my next move. His favorite thing to do is toy with people."

"Like a cat with a mouse."

"And like that cat, he knows exactly when and how he's going to go in for the kill."

EVERYTHING WAS ABOUT CHOICE.

Deke had to give Novus credit. James had said Novus's goal was to wear him down. And as bad as he hated to admit it, Novus was accomplishing his goal. Because right now, Deke was just about at the end of his rope.

He was tired. He was weak and nauseated from loss of blood and the fever brought on by his wound. And he hadn't slept more than an hour in the last twenty-four.

Now, he'd literally come to the end of the line. He sat on his haunches and stared at the pile of rock and broken timbers in front of him. Dark shadows danced in the lantern's light, and the burbling of the spring mocked him. Every few seconds, a silvery reflection in the water caught his eye. The little fish, battling their way through the rocks to swim downstream.

Toward Mindy.

He thought about her, back in that alcove alone where he'd left her over an hour ago. That had been a bad choice. The fact that it was the only choice didn't make it good.

And now he was staring at the result of the rumbling he'd heard, the rumbling he'd told her was thunder. He knew the cave-in he was staring at had been caused by the explosion, because here and there, wisps of smoke still rose from the debris, and the hot smell of explosive and ozone permeated the air.

He'd tried to dig through the debris in a couple of places using the crowbar, but he hadn't gotten very far. All he'd managed to do was start a couple of small rock slides and stir up a fog of hot, choking smoke and dust. He couldn't take the chance of tumbling the whole wall of rocks and timbers down on his head.

So he had no choice here, either. He had to go back.

But what was he going back to? Another dead end and the choice of lying to Mindy or telling her the truth, that they were trapped in the mine?

Because if James had blown this tunnel then he'd blown the downhill one, too. It confirmed his suspicion that James didn't have enough men to guard every exit.

One thing in their favor. Maybe.

He cupped his left hand and scooped up water to drink, then bent down and splashed some on his face. After swiping the water from his eyes, he picked up the lantern and the crowbar and turned on his heel.

MINDY JERKED AWAKE. She'd heard something.

Dear God, let it be Deke.

She winced as her little Sprout kicked her, reminding her that he'd been asleep, too.

Holding her breath, she listened. There it was again. The noise that had woken her. And this time she knew what it was.

The crunch of footsteps on dirt and gravel.

Not Deke. Her pulse skittered, stealing her breath. Deke would have already called out to her.

As quietly as she could, she scooted farther back

against the farthest wall of the alcove, pulling the knife from her bra.

She stared at the dim glow that outlined the alcove's opening, doing her best to keep her breathing steady. The knife's handle was warm from her body heat, and although she'd seen the damage it could do, right now it felt pitifully small.

Then the light at the entrance changed, brightened.

Her breath hitched. Whoever it was had a flashlight. The beam was too concentrated to be a lantern.

Just then a contraction hit her. She gasped and bit her lip, working to stay quiet.

Deke? Where are you?

The footsteps grew louder and the flashlight's beam flitted across the alcove's entrance.

Her breath caught. Had they missed it?

It snapped back.

Her mouth went dry. She drew her feet up, trying to make herself as small as possible while the flashlight penetrated the darkness in front of her.

Then the pale blue moonlight was blocked by shadows—two shadows, and the beam swept back and forth, back and forth, as it crawled toward her along the dirt floor.

It touched the toes of her shoes. The sensation was almost physical.

She couldn't get a breath. Her left hand instinctively cradled her tummy as the circle of light climbed up her leg.

It was almost a relief when the beam finally blinded her.

"Hello, Mrs. Cunningham." The voice was unmistakable. Frank James. "Shame on your husband for leaving you alone."

AN HOUR LATER, HE FELT cool air on his heated face. In the next instant, his eyes detected a difference in the total blackness before him.

It was the end of the tunnel. He slowed, using his instincts and his honed senses to assess any danger, before he burst out into the open.

What if Novus had blown those tunnels, not because he didn't have enough men, but to separate Deke and Mindy? If he guessed that Deke would leave Mindy to investigate the explosions, this would be the perfect time to have James capture her.

Flattening himself against the tunnel opening, he scanned the open area.

Nothing.

As much as he wanted to believe that nothing was a good thing, his natural caution told him otherwise. He longed to rush over to the alcove and take Mindy into his arms, but he had to proceed as if he were infiltrating enemy lines.

Sweat trickled down the side of his face. He wiped it away, and felt the heat radiating from his skin.

He had a fever. That meant his damn arm was infected. He laid his palm on the bandage covering his wound. Sure enough, it was hot, too. And the pressure of his hand was excruciating.

Judging by the way his head kept threatening to spin and by the blackness encroaching on his vision, he was close to passing out. He swallowed.

Damn close.

He took a deep breath and eased out into the open. Hugging the wall, he slid around to the edge of the alcove, scanning the room the whole time, alert to any slight movement or sound.

He set the lantern down and lit it awkwardly. He held it in his right hand and brandished the crowbar in his left.

His pulse drummed in his ears and his heartbeat shot sky-high. He wished it was merely the anticipation of seeing Mindy safe and sound, but he knew it was an adrenaline response, readying him to attack.

Rocking to the balls of his feet, he angled around the alcove opening.

No Mindy. Even though he'd expected it, his heart sank. She wasn't where he'd left her.

At that moment, a movement in the shadows at the back caught his eye.

"Mindy?" Even as the word formed on his lips, the shadow lunged toward him. Mindy couldn't stand up by herself, much less lunge.

He swung the crowbar with all his might, following it with the lantern. The arc of flame revealed a glimpse of a grimacing black mask of a face with bared teeth gleaming.

Then a huge weight sent him plummeting backward. His skull slammed into the dirt floor—hard. Pain blinded him. A dreadful growling filled his ears.

He tried to roll away, but the monster rolled with him, trailed by a strange orange light. He blinked. It was a man—a very big black man with his hair on fire.

The man shook his head, flinging drops of hot oil onto Deke's face, and propelled himself toward the spring. He dunked his head, frantically trying to douse the flames.

Deke retrieved his crowbar and followed him. Awkwardly, he gripped the crowbar, wishing he was left-handed, and drew his arm back.

When the man lifted his head, Deke leaped, swinging. The crowbar connected with a loud crack.

The man dropped like a stone, and Deke's momentum carried him right over him. He landed sideways on his injured arm. He clamped his jaw and hissed.

Breathing hard, he got his feet under him and crouched over the unconscious man. He patted him down and hit pay dirt. A portable Taser—dripping wet.

Deke grabbed it. Just looking at it tightened his muscles in involuntary reaction. He shook it and dried it on his pants, then examined it. He started to turn it on, but on second though he decided to give it time to dry out.

Pocketing it, he dropped to his haunches. He needed a couple of minutes to rest before he headed back toward the hotel.

After a few deep breaths and a swallow of water, he headed across the spring. He eyed the tunnels for a moment, then turned and looked at the rusted car that held the dynamite.

A sense of inevitability settled on his shoulders. As dangerous as it was, he had to carry the old, unstable explosive back to the hotel. He had to blow the two remaining entrances to the mine. He couldn't take the chance that James might escape through them, or force Mindy back into this dark abyss.

He swayed and had to steady himself against the wall. He clenched his teeth, refusing to give in to the fever that was trying to take him down. He couldn't. He had to keep going.

This time, if he failed, Mindy would die, and so would his son.

Chapter Nine

The pitch-black tunnel seemed endless. Deke trudged along, carefully balancing the dynamite and blasting caps in the crude sling he'd made from the musty blanket, and using the crowbar as a walking stick. It was a sobering thought that he was carrying his own mode of destruction. He was literally a walking, ticking bomb.

But the dynamite wasn't his biggest worry. His biggest worry was that he wouldn't make it. He was having a hard time putting one foot in front of the other. And he felt cold and hot at the same time.

In a part of his brain he was trying to ignore, he knew what was wrong. His arm was bleeding again. The knife wound ached with a stomach-churning pain that turned the edge of his vision black. When he'd looked at it, he'd seen the red line running up his arm. It was an artery, and it was infected. If that line got much closer to his heart, he'd be in real danger of dying.

He'd tried Mindy's home remedy for stanching the bleeding. He'd gathered up spiderwebs and pressed them into the oozing gash on his arm. Then he'd rebandaged it. Not surprisingly, they'd helped for a while.

And if he'd been able to immobilize his arm, they probably would have stopped the bleeding entirely, just like Mindy had said they would.

He'd stopped trying to use his arm, working hard to keep it still. He'd draped it over the dynamite-filled blanket, and occasionally he felt the faint tickle of a drop of blood running down his wrist to drip slowly off his fingers.

He stumbled over a rock, catching himself just in time, cringing as he had to adjust the blanket containing the dynamite. The misstep jarred his arm and turned the darkness in front of his eyes into a bright fireworks show. He ducked his head and braced himself against the wall. He needed to shut his eyes for just a few moments, until the fireworks went away.

WHEN HE OPENED HIS EYES AGAIN, he was crouched against the wall. He'd fallen asleep—or passed out, for no telling how long. At least the blanket was still in place, slung over his shoulder.

Breathing through his mouth, trying to settle his racing heart, he lifted his head and blinked.

Was he still woozy, or was that a real light in front of him? It didn't dance around, and it wasn't the same bright yellow as his internal fireworks show.

This light was dim and pale and vaguely rectangular. A lump of relief closed the back of his throat and stung his eyes.

It was the end of the tunnel. Where Mindy was. Just a few yards farther. He covered half the remaining distance before he had to stop.

He pressed his back to the wall and rested his head against it for a moment. With his eyes closed, he pictured the small anteroom that connected the tunnels with the hotel basement. He'd returned the way he'd gone, back through the south tunnel—had it just been yesterday?

He was less than two yards from the anteroom. He had to work fast. He carefully placed the blanket-covered dynamite on the floor just inside the tunnel entrance. He'd already attached one of the blasting caps and a length of fuse to the sticks. So all he had to do was unroll the fuse and light it.

He started working, but he kept losing focus. What the hell was the matter with him? His legs were heavy and slow. Sweat rolled down his face, chilling his skin. He shuddered and concentrated on making it to the south wall. He slid along it, keeping to the shadows until he reached the framed doorway. Then he stopped and listened.

Nothing.

To the east was the trapdoor, and on the north wall was the massive wooden door through which James had disappeared.

Before he positioned the fuse, he had something he wanted to check out. After listening again and hearing nothing, he moved from the dirt wall to the timbers that framed the tunnel opening. He angled around quickly, sweeping the room quickly with his gaze, then ducked back behind the timbers.

He looked at the trapdoor through which he'd crawled earlier. He'd discarded it because Mindy would never be able to crawl through the small opening.

But the thing that had puzzled him ever since he first knocked on that wood still held his interest. Sixty years ago, this alcove had obviously provided a passage from the hotel and the building to the north into the mine from the two buildings. That trapdoor must have once been a full-size doorway.

Deke gripped the crowbar in his hand and examined the wooden planks carefully. Whereas the other side looked like a door, this side appeared to be a rough-hewn planked wall, except that the planks above the trapdoor looked newer than the rest.

There *was* a door there. Relief stung his throat and turned the back of his neck clammy. With the noise he was about to make, he figured he had two minutes at the most before one of James's men saw or heard him.

He attached the fuse to the dynamite and ran it along the wall to the north door. There was barely enough to reach. He didn't know much about detonation. That was Brock's specialty. But he knew that fuse burned rapidly, so he figured he had about enough to last five minutes.

Five minutes to get Mindy outside to safety. If she was in there. Through the haze in his brain, Deke tried to remember why he was sure that was where Frank was holding her. He couldn't. But it hardly mattered. It could be their only chance.

He set the end of the fuse down at the edge of the inner door, praying he'd be able to come back and light it. He patted his jeans pocket, where the disposable lighter was.

That much dynamite would blow this whole basement area to smithereens, if the fuse stayed lit.

Then he turned to the door. He had maybe three minutes before the noise of prying the planks away from the door alerted James.

Here goes. He started with the planks at knee level,

just above the top of the trapdoor. The nails screeched and the wood creaked. But within thirty seconds he had two of the twelve-inch-wide planks off and had started on a third.

Sure enough, the wood behind the cross-nailed planks was just like the wood he'd kicked in to get through the trapdoor. He figured with one or two well-placed kicks he could have an opening that was thirty inches wide and about three and a half to four feet tall. Plenty of room for Mindy to get through. If he had the strength to kick the boards away.

By the time the third plank let go, he was reeling from exhaustion. Fever from loss of blood, he was sure. He gulped in a lungful of air, hoping it would fortify him for another few seconds. He reared back and kicked the door. Wood splintered loudly.

At that moment, the north door opened and two soldiers in desert camo grabbed him, jerking the crowbar out of his hands and wrenching his arms behind his back. He groaned out loud at the screaming pain in his right arm.

Somehow, the pain heightened his senses. Suddenly, he was hyperaware of everything around him. The bright light from the open door. The air that swirled about him, evaporating the sweat and cooling his skin. The loud, sawing breathing of the two guards.

They shoved him through the door into a narrow foyer. He directed all his strength toward staying aware of everything around him. There were three doors in the tiny foyer. Besides the one they'd pushed him through, there was a door to his left and one directly in front of him. He was about to find out where at least one of those doors led.

A guard pushed open the door in front of him.

Across a short expanse of rough flooring, lit by a single bare bulb, he saw Mindy. Tied up and gagged.

His heart slammed against his chest with a ferocity that left him breathless.

"Mindy," he rasped. His throat closed up and his eyes stung with relief. He hadn't let himself even think of the possibility that she wasn't behind the door. But now, seeing her, he knew he'd feared just that.

She shook her head violently. He nodded slightly, hoping to send her the message that he knew James was waiting for him. That he was prepared.

By the look in her wide, frightened eyes he knew he wasn't fooling her. With one quick glance, she saw how sick he was. How weak.

She knew that he wasn't prepared. That he wasn't even sure how much longer he could stay upright.

Her gaze dropped to his right hand and back to meet his eyes. She knew how long it had been since James had cut his arm. He could see in her eyes that she was calculating the amount of blood he'd lost and how far along the infection was. She shook her head again.

He sent her what he hoped was an encouraging smile and took a step forward.

With a *whoosh* of noise, spotlights flared, blinding him. Immediately, the sound of weapons being raised hit his ears. And slowly, as the red spots from the lights faded, the outlines of three men coalesced. They were dressed in military fatigues and boots, and were aiming their weapons at his head.

The smallest man slung his rifle over his shoulder and stepped over to Mindy's side. He extracted a 9 mm handgun from a side holster and pointed it at the side of her head.

"Nice of you to join us. What were you doing out there, tearing through the wall? Trying to get away and leave your pretty girl behind? That's cold."

Deke's gaze snapped to the speaker. The accompanying movement of his head made the edges of his vision turn dark again.

Still, there was no mistaking who the speaker was. It was Frank James—without his bandanna. No question. As he thought, the face was so close to the sketch of Novus as to almost be identical.

Deke blinked to clear his vision and studied James's face. Somehow, without the bandanna covering his lower face, his eyes seemed more pronounced.

And familiar.

"Hey, Min. You feeling better?" he said casually, inwardly wincing at the sound of his voice. It wouldn't fool an infant, much less a roomful of trained combatants.

Mindy nodded, but her face was still drawn and pale, and she looked exhausted. Worse, if he could judge by the look in her eyes, she was worried about *him*.

"She's doing just fine, Cunningham. When we found her where you'd abandoned her, she was in a lot of pain. But thanks to some friends of ours, we were able to figure out what was wrong and correct it."

Correct it? Bile churned in Deke's stomach. "I swear to God," he said hoarsely, "if you hurt her, or—"

"Calm down, Cunningham. The drug we gave her is a medication that's commonly used for preterm labor. Ask your wife."

"You've got a gun to her head. What do you think she's going to say?" He met Mindy's gaze, and saw that James was telling the truth. *If* he could still read her as well as he once could.

"You'll see that she's no longer in labor. And she's feeling fine, which is more than I can say for you right now."

Deke shook his head and concentrated on the pipsqueak's words. He was well aware of the blood slowly oozing out of his wounded arm, and the clammy sweat prickling his forehead and neck. It infuriated him that he was letting a little knife wound affect him.

"Don't worry about me," he growled.

"I'm not. Trust me." James grinned, and the thing that had been bothering Deke ever since the first time he'd seen the fake cowboy suddenly came clear.

Of course Frank James was Novus Ordo's brother. But looking at him, Deke realized something else. Those eyes had looked at him from behind the shemagh every day while he was held prisoner by Novus.

It was Novus himself who'd held the gun to Deke's head, who'd grinned at him when he'd ordered him to rise to his knees. His eyes were older and more sinister than James's, but they were the same eyes.

James nodded his head. The three guards stepped toward Deke in unison, their weapons still raised.

Deke noticed that they were—to a man—Middle Eastern in appearance. Novus's men who'd infiltrated the United States. A chill ran through him. The implications were ominous.

On a few days' notice, Novus Ordo had brought together a half dozen armed and trained zealots to carry out a plan he was creating on the fly.

At least a half dozen. Probably more.

"What do you want from me, James?"

"Okay, Cunningham. Time to do a little business."

"You've heard my offer. It hasn't changed."

"Sure. I know your offer. I let your wife—'scuse me, *ex*-wife—go, and you'll answer all my questions. And I'm sure you're telling the truth—you'll answer my questions. But all your answers will be lies." He shook his head, laughing. "Now I'm sure that you've practiced 'em until they sound just as good as the truth—even while you're being tortured."

"Nnh," Mindy moaned and struggled, and shook her head. "Nnnh—nhh."

He knew exactly what she was saying. *Tell them.* He loved her for caring whether they hurt him. But there was far more at stake here than the lives of two people.

"I'll tell you the truth," he said quietly.

Mindy couldn't take her eyes off Deke. She was so glad he was here. And so worried about him.

Spots of color stained his cheeks, standing out against his pale skin and pinched mouth. His right hand hung useless at his side, and a drop of blood shimmered on the end of one finger. Also, one end of the bandage she'd made out of his shirt dangled from the sleeve of his shearling jacket. It, too, looked soaked with blood.

Mindy's stomach churned. It had been doing flip-flops ever since the nurse had given her the injection of magnesium sulfate.

Deke must have lost at least a pint of blood, maybe more. She wondered how long the wound had been actively bleeding. She'd wrapped it as well as she could, but she'd known it would eventually come loose and separate the edges of the cut. She'd intended to be there to rewrap it.

No, truthfully, she'd hoped they would be out of here safe and sound by now, and he'd have a stitched-up arm and a course of antibiotics for the infection.

Acrid saliva filled her mouth. She swallowed and focused all her strength on not giving in to the nausea. Magnesium sulfate was excellent for slowing premature labor, but it was also excellent for causing nausea. She clenched her teeth against the queasiness, praying that she wouldn't throw up while her mouth was gagged.

At least these terrorists had a health professional in their group. Although the idea that they had soldiers and nurses and God only knew who else available inside the United States was a sobering one.

"Just let Mindy go," Deke muttered. His words sounded slurred.

Frank James laughed.

As calmly as she could, Mindy assessed their situation. Not good.

Judging by the lack of color in his face and the way he was swaying, it was a miracle that he was still upright.

A miracle and a testament to his strength of will and his determination. He needed lots of fluids, and probably a blood transfusion.

His skin looked tight and drawn across his cheekbones. His mouth was compressed into a thin line, and his nostrils and the corners of his lips were white and pinched. Sweat glistened on his forehead and neck.

Stay with me, Deke. Don't quit now, she wanted to say. But that wasn't fair. He was the strongest man she'd ever met. He would die for an innocent. She knew he'd endure anything for his son. But he'd pushed himself further than any normal human being could have. He'd pushed himself past his body's limits, and it was shutting down.

The idea that he was mortal, that there was a point beyond which even his steely resolve couldn't push, sent a soul-deep terror searing through her like a spark touching a line of gasoline. The terror manifested itself physically as paralyzing nausea.

Her throat was too dry to swallow, so she squeezed her eyes shut and waited until the red haze of intense queasiness passed.

At that instant, Sprout kicked her, as if to remind her that everything she did, everything she felt, affected him, too.

For the moment, the mag sulfate had done its job. But every few moments, she felt little aftershocks of contractions.

At eight-plus months, Sprout was capable of surviving on his own. With her knowledge and experience, she'd bet money that Deke's son would be born within the next twenty-four hours.

She did not want him born in an underground mine, held hostage by terrorists. And she certainly did not want him born an orphan.

She had to come up with a plan.

"You sound sincere, Cunningham. But then you always do. Even with a gun at *your* head, you still lie."

The gun barrel pressed against Mindy's head dug into her flesh. She couldn't see James, but she could see Deke.

His pallor had taken on a gray tinge, and his eyes weren't focused on anything. He took a stumbling step forward.

A soldier stepped in front of him and swung the butt of his gun at his head. The impact sounded like a gunshot.

Deke slumped to the ground.

"No!" Mindy screamed through her gag.

"Get up!" the guard growled in a heavy accent. He raised the gun butt again.

"Stop!" she cried desperately.

"Hold it," James snapped. "Careful. He's no good to us dead. Pull his head up. I want him to see this."

The guard grabbed a handful of Deke's hair and jerked his head up.

Deke rose to his knees, swaying. He squeezed his eyes shut, then blinked several times. The guard's blow hadn't broken the skin, but he was going to have a black eye and one hell of a headache.

Don't fight them, she begged silently.

"Let's see if you can lie while there's a gun at your wife's head. Is it loaded? Is it not?" He cocked the hammer of the .45. Mindy closed her eyes.

"What do you think, Mrs. Cunningham?" He jerked the bandanna away from her mouth.

She winced, and felt Sprout move in reaction to her pain. She licked her dry, chapped lips.

He wasn't going to kill her. He couldn't. If James killed her, he'd never get anything out of Deke. Somehow, her argument didn't make her feel better, considering the gun barrel pressed to her temple.

Deke's jaw clenched and his chin ratcheted up a notch. His face was pale as death. "Wait—" he muttered.

"Deke, no," she gasped. "He won't do it. He needs me."

"You think so?" James mumbled, easing the pressure of the barrel against her temple.

Mindy held her breath.

"I don't know whether Rook is alive—"

James pushed the gun's barrel against her head again.

"I don't know," Deke said quickly, "but I know the most likely place he'd be."

"You know where he might be if he were alive, which you don't know." James barked a short derisive laugh. "Sorry, I just don't buy it. You're not quite ready to tell the truth." He squeezed the trigger, and the hammer clicked—a hollow sound that seemed to hover in the air.

Mindy's chest was tight with tension. She struggled for breath, as Sprout moved restlessly inside her. Fine tremors rippled through her limbs.

James made a gesture that she could barely see out of the corner of her eye. Two guards rushed toward Deke and jerked him upright. He didn't speak. Mindy had no idea if it was stoicism or pain and exhaustion.

His head lolled on his neck. He could hardly stand on his own.

"All right, Cunningham. Let's see how much stamina you've got. Every hour on the hour I'm gonna stick one live round into this gun, spin the chamber and put it against your wife's head and—bam!" He grinned. "Or not. Every hour on the half hour, I'm gonna break one of your fingers. So don't count on being able to handle a weapon." He nodded to the guards.

The two men pulled Deke to his feet and began to half drag him to a door in the back of the room.

"By the way, Cunningham. There's only one thing we want to know. You lead us to Castle, and we'll make sure your wife and baby are safe."

Deke muttered a curse aimed at James.

The fake cowboy just chuckled.

Mindy hoped that in his dazed and injured state, Deke knew what she knew.

Frank James had shown his face to them. There was no way he was going to let them live.

Chapter Ten

There was a clock on the wall, put there on purpose, Mindy was sure, so she could watch the minute hand go around. So she could anticipate, minute by minute, second by second, the instant when the guards would break one of Deke's fingers.

Then she'd have to watch the crawling hand for another half hour as she waited for James to come in, stand in front of her and load the single bullet into the revolver. Then he'd spin the chamber, press the barrel to her head and pull the trigger.

A twinge—like a miniature contraction, tightened her abdominal muscles for an instant.

Settle down, Sprout. You stay put. Mommy needs time to figure out a way to save your daddy.

There had to be a trick to it. Didn't there? As long as Novus believed Deke had the information he needed, he wouldn't kill her. Nor would he leave her life or death—or anything else he could control—to chance. So the bullet in the spinning chamber had to be a fake.

The minute hand bumped forward. Her heart bumped against her chest. It was eleven twenty-nine. One minute until they broke Deke's finger.

She opened her mouth and screamed. She didn't know why James had removed the gag, but she was thankful that he had.

"Don't do it!" she yelled. "Stop! I'll make him talk! I swear! Just don't hurt him!"

She stopped, holding her breath, but the only thing she heard was the silence.

"Don't hurt him!" Her eyes were glued to the clock.

The minute hand quivered.

"Please!" she whispered in desperation, as tears welled in her eyes.

It jerked forward. And centered on the six.

"No!" she screamed as the tears streamed down her face. "No! Please!"

The door behind her opened.

She twisted, straining to see who'd entered the room. "Who is it? Is that you, James?"

The man who called himself Frank James stepped into her field of vision. "What are you yelling about?" he asked in an impatient tone.

"Where's Deke? Is he all right? Did you—"

James held up his hand. "Slow down. Try to stay calm. Now what are you saying?"

Mindy glared at the man who held Deke's well-being and the fate of her child in his hands. "Please bring Deke back in here, or take me to him. I'll make him tell you the truth."

James assessed her. "Has he told you the truth?"

She did her best not to look away from his staring eyes, but she couldn't stop herself from blinking.

"So he has. Well, the truth is the truth, no matter who delivers it. Why don't you tell me what he told you?"

She dropped her gaze then, wondering what Deke would want her to say.

He took a step toward her. "Mrs. Cunningham?"

"He told me he doesn't know where Rook is." She looked up at the fake cowboy.

James's beady eyes studied her face for a long moment. She could see the little wheels in his little brain turning, and hear what he was thinking. He had to decide if he believed her.

She tried to keep her expression bland, even as her mind raced. Ever since James had captured her she'd known this moment would come. But she still hadn't figured out what she was going to tell him.

She knew one thing though. If she admitted to James that Deke had no idea where Rook was, then James would come to the same conclusion she had. *They'd be of no more use to him.*

Finally he spoke. "Do you believe him?"

Slowly, deliberately, she met Frank James's gaze. "No," she said.

James's eyes twinkled and his mouth twitched. For the life of her Mindy couldn't figure out if he was amused by her or pleased that he'd gotten her to tell the truth.

"Why should I believe you?"

"Men care about country. About honor. About freedom. They will die for any of those things." She took a long breath. "But I'm a woman. There are only two things I would die for," she said evenly, as she cradled her stomach. "My child and Deke. And I don't want to die."

James laughed. "Well said, Mrs. Cunningham."

"So you'll bring Deke to me?"

"I'll let you know." James turned and left through the door.

"Wait!" she cried. "You're underestimating me. I can make him tell. Please wait!"

But the door closed with an unmistakable finality. James wasn't coming back. Not anytime soon.

DEKE RAISED HIS HEAD, wondering if he'd been asleep or if he'd passed out. Either way, his head felt heavy and swollen, and his eyes stung with the clammy sweat that poured off his forehead.

For a couple of seconds, he wasn't sure where he was. He tried to lift a hand to wipe his face, and found out he couldn't. He was tied up—again.

The memories came back. He and Mindy were prisoners of a ridiculous costumed cowboy who called himself Frank James, and who so far hadn't admitted that he was working for Novus Ordo. He was, though. Deke was sure of it.

He almost laughed. Were these knots going to be as easy to undo as the others were? Not a chance. As weak and sick as he felt, he wouldn't be able to untie a birthday bow.

He was sitting in a hard wooden chair behind a desk. He looked down and saw that his left hand was tied to the chair's arm.

He glanced at his right hand, which was lashed to the opposite chair arm. It was red with blood from the slash on his forearm. He stared at the bandaged wound.

How had that happened? He had a vague recollection of a hand slashing through the air and burning pain, but that was all. No face. No name.

He did remember the bandage. It was his shirt—a

brand-new white dress shirt. Mindy had torn it apart to fashion the makeshift bandage.

It had served fairly well. The material still partially covered the wound, but here and there, where the blood-soaked strips had slipped, he could see the jagged, inflamed edges of the wound.

He blinked, trying to clear the stinging sweat from his eyes, and noticed that his fingers were moving. Was he doing that? He really didn't know.

He looked up, seeking the source of light in the room. It was a lamp, with only one bare bulb in it, sitting on the scarred wooden desk. It provided very little light—just enough for him to make out what was around him.

The big desk, of course, which sat directly across the room from the door. And the lamp, an old-fashioned leather desk blotter that held a 1959 calendar from Sundance Printing Company, and a pen stand with a wooden fountain pen. There were several ink stains on the polished surface of the desk.

Heavy, dark curtains covered the windows behind him, so he assumed he was aboveground. Probably the mine foreman's office, or maybe the office of the hotel manager.

On either side of the door were ancient, dusty barrister bookcases stuffed full of old books, folders and stacks of paper. Mindy would have a fit. She loved old books.

His mouth turned up in a wry smile. Mindy. He'd have to tell her about the bookcases, once they were safe.

All at once, the significance of those last words hit him. *Once they were safe.* That meant they weren't— Mindy wasn't.

Now he remembered, and all his scattered thoughts began to coalesce. He'd come here to rescue Mindy. They'd been trapped in an abandoned mine, and Frank James had cut him with his own knife.

More memories assaulted his brain. He'd gone looking for a way out of the mine, but he'd run into a cave-in. Then when he got back to where he'd left Mindy, she was gone, captured again by Frank James.

The sound of the hammer clicking against metal rang in his ears. The sound of one more day.

No. Not one more day. One more *hour.*

He didn't have a day because within a few minutes someone was going to walk in here with a heavy hammer and smash one of his fingers.

Then a half hour after that, they were going to play Russian roulette with Mindy again.

He wished he knew how long he'd been here. If he hadn't passed out, maybe he could have figured out a plan to get out of here and save Mindy.

Mindy didn't deserve any of this. She was innocent. As innocent as a newborn baby.

Baby. Deke blinked slowly and felt himself drifting off to sleep again.

If he could just wipe his eyes. They stung and itched like fire, until he couldn't think of anything else.

He lifted his hand and rediscovered that it wouldn't lift. He wiggled his fingers, idly wondering which one they'd break first. He shuddered with anticipated pain.

It hardly mattered. He just wished they'd come and get it over with. Then he could stop worrying about it and think about rescuing Mindy.

He drummed his fingers, one at a time, on the wooden desk and sleepily chanted, "One, two, three four five. Once I caught a fish alive." He started over. "Six, seven, eight nine ten. Then I let him go again. One, two—"

He heard something and froze, with his third, fourth and fifth fingers in the air.

He didn't move for a long time, but nothing else happened. It must have been the wooden beams creaking, or a clod of dirt falling.

One, two, three four five—

He shook his head. He had to get that annoying nursery rhyme out of his head.

Maybe he should search the room for hidden cameras. He wasn't sure what good finding them would do him, but at least he'd be doing something, rather than drifting off into unconsciousness.

While they were in the air force, Matt Parker had developed a foolproof visual search grid for assessing the danger points in a specified terrain. Maybe he could use the same principle to search this room for a camera.

He quelled the voice in his head that kept trying to chant the nursery rhyme and concentrated on the grid. He was almost done when he heard the doorknob rattle.

The wooden door swung open with a loud creak.

It was Frank James. And one of the soldiers was with him. The soldier held a hammer.

"Here we are, Cunningham. Ready to make good on our promise." James grinned, showing crooked teeth. "Got anything to say? Or should we just get to it."

"By all means, go ahead," Deke said hoarsely. "I've got nothing to say."

James nodded at the other man, who stepped up to the chair. He was holding a small sledgehammer—

probably six pounds. Enough to make mush out of his fingers.

The soldier took a balanced stance, then reared back like a baseball player, holding the hammer in both hands, and prepared to swing.

Deke wanted more than anything in the world to look James in the eye as the hammer came down on his hand, but he couldn't stop himself from cringing.

He closed his eyes and clenched his jaw so he wouldn't scream.

"Wait!"

Deke jerked at the single explosive word. Sweat rolled off his forehead and into his eyes.

James had stopped the soldier.

A painful spasm of reaction shrieked through his arm, from the shoulder all the way down to his fingers.

"Sorry about that, Cunningham, I almost forgot something." James smiled. "How would you like to see your wife?"

Deke swallowed bile and opened his eyes to a slit. "What are you talking about?" he asked, his stomach churning with worry. What was James up to now?

"I'm asking you a simple question. Your wife begged me not to break your fingers. Begged me to let her see you. She said she had something to say to you."

There was no way Deke was going to trust James. "What did you do to her?" He sat up as straight as he could and clenched his teeth against the dizziness that threatened to spin his head right off.

"Do to her? Me? Nothing. I told you my plan. You know exactly what I planned to do. But Mrs. Cunningham is so sweet and lovely, I couldn't deny her request."

"Great. I want to see her, too." Deke spoke in a tone-less, measured voice. He wasn't sure what James was up to, but whatever it was, he knew it was designed to get him to waver.

And it had probably been planned by Novus.

Rather than ask James more questions, Deke closed his eyes. "I'm not feeling too good, so whatever you've got planned, can you hurry up? I'm pretty sure I'm in danger of bleeding to death, and I would definitely like to see my wife before I die."

"Your ex-wife," James corrected him. He nodded at the soldier who set the sledgehammer down and left the room.

"I've got a message for you to give Novus," Deke said, as soon as the man left.

James waved a hand dismissively. "I have no idea what you're talking about, but fine. Give me the mes-sage. I'm sure it'll be funny."

"You tell Novus Ordo he made a mistake when he targeted my friends and my wife. He's dealt with me before and he knows I mean what I say. Tell him if it's the last thing I do on this earth, I'm coming to get him."

James chuckled. "That is funny. You're talking about Novus Ordo, the international terrorist? That's some imagination you've got."

James bent down until he was mere inches away from Deke's face. "Now let me give you a message. You think you're so smart? You don't know anything. Treating me like I'm nobody? You'll soon find out just who I am, and when you do, I'm going to be right here, in your face. And I'll make you sorry you didn't respect me."

Through the haze that kept drifting in front of his

eyes, Deke stared at James's thin, weaselly face and dark, beady eyes.

He closed his eyes, trying to give James the impression that he was totally bored with his threat while he drew on his memory, conjuring up the likeness of Novus Ordo that Rook had described to the facial recognition artist for the CIA.

James had to be related to Novus. Deke could believe he *was* Novus, except that Novus was too smart to place himself smack in the middle of a terrorist plot in the U.S.

He squeezed his eyes shut tighter, and a splash of reddish stars appeared before his closed eyelids. He squinted open one eye and saw that James had straightened and was watching him with a vicious hatred.

He drew a deep breath, then another, trying to ward off the loss of consciousness with an overload of oxygen. It helped a little.

The doorknob turned, and the soldier was back with Mindy in tow. Her hands were still tied behind her back.

When she saw Deke, her face turned white and she swayed. The soldier tightened his hold on her arm.

"Deke. Did he—?" Her eyes flew to his bound hands, then to his face. As soon as she looked into his eyes, she relaxed. "Oh, thank God."

James gestured to a straight-backed chair on the other side of the desk. "Here you are, Mrs. Cunningham."

"For heaven's sake, give my husband some water," Mindy cried. "He's about to pass out. He's lost too much blood. He needs fluids. Where's that nurse of yours?"

James nodded at the soldier, who turned and left the room.

"Are you okay?" Deke asked her.

"For now," she said. "The medication they gave me did stop the contractions, at least so far."

The man dressed in desert camo was back almost immediately with a big jar of water. James took it from him and held it to Deke's lips. He wasn't careful, and a lot of the liquid spilled down Deke's bare chest and torso, but Deke managed to gulp down at least a pint's worth.

He did feel better immediately. It washed the haze from his brain and the heaviness from his eyelids and limbs.

"Now that we've provided *room service,* take her and tie her to that straight-backed chair," James instructed his sidekick.

"Please don't," she begged him. "I'm so sick. If the contractions start again, I'll need to lie down. Tie my hands in front of me, but please don't tie me to that chair. If I go into labor, I have to be able to move or—" Her eyes filled with tears. "Or," she sobbed. "I'm going to lose my baby."

James rolled his eyes. "Fine. You'll have your hands tied in front and you won't be tied down. So let me save you some trouble, Mrs. Cunningham. There's no need for you to go exploring around the room. It's been completely cleaned out. There's nothing in here you can use as a weapon. Nothing that you can cut your ropes with. I'd hate for anything to happen to your kid. I've only got so much patience. If you or Cunningham try anything, I'll go back to my original plan—with one change."

He looked at Deke, then at her. "Instead of breaking his fingers, I think I'll just go ahead and cut 'em off. I've got a cigar cutter that ought to do the trick just fine."

Mindy swayed. Only the man's hand on her arm kept her from falling.

"For God's sake, James. What did you bring her here for? There's no reason she has to go through this."

"I'll let her tell you why she's here." He turned to his sidekick. "Tie her hands in front of her."

"Not tie to the chair?" the man asked in broken English.

"No." James half turned toward the door. "Goodbye, Mrs. Cunningham. I'll be looking forward to talking with you. I'll see both of you in one hour."

The door closed quietly behind them as they left.

Mindy opened her mouth to speak, but Deke shook his head.

"Wait," he mouthed.

She nodded.

Deke waited a full five minutes—probably more. He counted to sixty five times, then added another sixty for a buffer, in case he'd counted too fast.

Meeting Mindy's gaze, he motioned with his head for her to come over to his chair.

She slowly pushed herself up out of the straight-backed chair and walked over to stand in front of him.

"Lean down," he whispered.

As soon as he smelled her tangerine scent and felt her hair soft and tickly against his lips, he whispered, "I've grid-searched the room. I'm pretty sure there are no cameras, but there could be recording devices. So play along with the things I say out loud, and whisper to answer my whispers. Do you still have the knife?"

She nodded, pointing to her breasts where she'd hidden it before.

"Good girl." Then he said aloud, "Why did James say he'd let you tell me why he brought you here?"

"Deke, please," Mindy answered, as she worked to retrieve the knife with her bound hands. "I was so worried about you. I was afraid they'd broken your fingers. Tell him what he wants to know. He'll let us go."

She finally had the knife in her hands. She pushed the button that snicked the blade into place.

Deke indicated his hands with a nod. "I *was* telling the truth. Are you saying you don't believe me?"

Mindy quickly cut the ropes binding his hands to the chair. He flexed his left hand, then his right.

"How can I believe you? You've lied to me over and over again." Mindy's eyes filled with tears and she shook her head.

Deke knew she was apologizing for saying those things to him, but he also knew he deserved them. He hadn't lied overtly to her, but he'd lied by omission, time and time again.

"I'm sorry, Min. I never meant to hurt you."

She blinked and the tears fell down her cheeks.

Taking the knife, he slipped it between her hands and cut the ropes binding her.

"Deke, tell me what you know. I know you haven't been truthful with James. Why would you, after what he's done to us?"

"You think I know something about Rook? Hell, Mindy. He was my best friend, and Novus had him killed. Even if I did know anything, I wouldn't tell that slimy terrorist."

She leaned closer. "What now?" she whispered.

"Do you know what time it is?" he whispered back to her.

She looked at him in surprise. "About three-thirty. Why?"

He shook his head. He wasn't about to tell her what he had planned. "And today is Saturday?"

She nodded in answer. "But Deke," she said out loud, "if Novus had Rook killed, why is he doing this? Why does he think Rook might still be alive?"

"The same reason Irina couldn't give up. Because they never recovered a body. Novus must not trust his sniper's aim. Besides, don't you think if Rook were still alive, he'd have contacted Irina? Do you think he'd have let her believe he was dead all this time?"

Mindy stared at Deke. She'd never thought about that before. What if Rook were alive? "He could have been horribly wounded and didn't want her to see him. Or maybe he has amnesia."

Deke frowned at her, but made a sound like a laugh. "All right, Mindy. Back off the romancing."

But her brain was racing. If Novus's man had killed Rook, wouldn't he have known it? Wouldn't the body have surfaced eventually? "Maybe Rook *is* hiding. Maybe he's alive, but he wants Novus to think he's dead. Maybe he's out there searching for Novus."

Deke pulled his right arm into his side and sent a scowl her way. "What was in that medicine they gave you? You're getting ridiculous. Rook is dead, and Novus holding a gun to my head or yours isn't going to change that."

Chapter Eleven

"Okay, it's done. I've worked out a way to get past security and into the house. It's going to be very tricky, though, so we probably ought to use it as a last resort."

"Last resort? What good is a last resort if we don't have a first resort?"

"That's just it. I'm working on something else. It'll be much cleaner and less risky. Tomorrow is Irina's regular monthly visit to the Children's Burn Center. She never misses going when she's in town. She'll probably get one of the specialists to drive her. I'm sure that's how Cunningham told her to handle it."

"So what's your big plan?"

"Shoot the specialist—wound him—just enough to put him in the hospital for a day or two. That buys us another couple of days. If one of her employees is in the hospital, she'll be there every day."

"That's your big plan? There are holes big enough to drive a semitrailer through."

"Yeah? You have a better idea?"

The voice on the other end of the line was silent for a few seconds. "You think I've got sharpshooters sitting around waiting for something to do? Keep working on *a way to get past security. That spread is huge. There's got to be a few feet that are undefended."*

"What about Cunningham?"

The man on the phone cursed in Arabic. *"He's still swearing that Rook is dead. Even when he's alone with his wife."*

"You think Cunningham doesn't suspect that you have every corner of every room bugged? Stop fooling with them. Stop just threatening the wife. Do some real damage."

A frustrated growl echoed through the phone. *"I'm not sure Elliott has the stomach for that."*

He sympathized with the man on the phone. He understood family loyalty, too, all too well. But it was sounding more and more like Elliott was a coward.

"Maybe you should have somebody in there that does have the stomach."

Sudden silence crackled across the miles. He sat there, watching his hand shake. Had he gone too far? He'd just given one of the most dangerous men on the planet a surefire plan to assassinate him—or one of his teammates.

"You just deliver Irina Castle to me. I'll take care of Cunningham."

"Don't make the mistake of underestimating him. Whatever else he is, I can guarantee you he's not stupid."

"WHAT ARE WE GOING TO DO, Deke?" Mindy whispered. "He's coming back, and when he does, he's going to cut—" she shuddered as nausea swelled inside her "—cut off—" She couldn't say it. "I can't let them do that. What can you tell them that will satisfy them?"

Deke took her hand and put his lips to her ear. "Listen to me, Mindy. I swear I'd rather die myself than scare you, but you've got to understand what's going on here. There's *nothing* I can say that they'll be satisfied with. Nothing. Whatever I say, the end result is going to be the same."

Mindy's heart leapt into her throat. "End result?" she whispered brokenly. "What do you mean?"

He shook his head. "You know what I mean. Can you act like you're sleepy? We can't keep up this talking for their benefit. I've got something I need to do."

Mindy sat up straight and spoke aloud. "I guess all this is catching up to me. I'm so tired, and I'm feeing some minor contractions."

"Contractions?" Deke said. "You're not going into labor, are you?"

"The drug is still working, but I do need to rest. Do you think it's okay if I sit down in the chair and try to sleep a little?"

He nodded, then quirked his mouth. "Sure, hon," he drawled. "You've got about forty minutes to nap until they come back to cut off my finger."

Even though she knew he was talking for whoever was listening, the words still made her wince.

"Deke, I didn't—"

"Drag the chair over here," he said. "You won't be able to sleep sitting straight up in that chair. At least over here you can lean against me."

"That's very nice of you," she said stiffly. "I'll do that. And just so you know, I really don't want them to hurt you."

"Hmph. Good to know. Thanks."

She made a face at him and dragged the chair, slowly and loudly, over beside his desk chair, which was just opposite the door, and made a production of sitting down in it.

"Oh," she sighed. "I am so tired. You're sweet to let me lean on you."

Once she was settled in the chair, Deke whispered, "Did they bring you in here through that foyer?"

She nodded.

"So this room is the third door?"

"Yes, why?"

"I may have a way for us to escape."

Mindy's hand flew to her mouth. She couldn't help it. She'd tried hard not to think about their fate, but when she heard Deke's words, she realized that a large part of her had actually believed that they wouldn't live through this.

He put his hand on top of hers and shook his head. "Not foolproof. It's extremely dangerous. We could die."

And there it was. The one thing she'd counted on was Deke's strength and confidence. But if he thought they could die—

She felt the blood drain from her face, felt a hideous chill run down her spine. "Okay," she whispered.

"I'll do everything I can to make sure you're safe."

"*We're* safe."

He nodded, but he didn't look at her.

"So what do I need to do?"

"Go into labor."

A short, sharp laugh escaped her lips.

He held up a warning hand. "Mindy, you okay?" he said aloud.

"Oh," she responded. "What? I was asleep."

"You were dreaming. Go back to sleep."

"Go into labor?" she mouthed. Had she heard him right? He was whispering so softly she couldn't be sure.

He nodded. "I need a distraction so I can get the drop on them when they come into the room."

"Deke, you're injured and weak as a kitten. I doubt you could get the drop on a mouse."

His turn to make a face. "Well, I'm your only hope."

"Tell me what your plan is." She waited while he scrutinized her.

"I'm going to blow up the tunnel."

This time she clamped both hands over her mouth and stared at him over her fingers.

He put his hand over hers and held it there. "Dynamite," he mouthed.

She started to speak, but he shook his head. "Don't even ask. Just do what I say."

"But if you blow it up—" Her brain was filled with visions of smoke and rocks and dirt and body parts.

"And don't tell me you can't run. When I say run, you run. Your job is to save your—our—Sprout there."

Her hands flew to her tummy.

"They'll be in any minute." He scooped up the cut ropes they'd used to bind her hands. "Sit. Put your hands in your lap."

She did as he instructed, and within a few seconds he had the ropes arranged so she looked like she was still tied up.

Then he leaned back down and whispered in her ear. "There. That'll fool them on first glance. Once I take them down, we'll have about thirty seconds. Now, start faking labor."

She turned her head until her mouth was next to his ear. As much as she wanted to lay her cheek against his, just for a second, she knew she had to stay strong. "What are you going to do?"

"Hide behind the door."

"And do what? Slam it on them?"

Deke shook his head. "I've got the knife and a Taser. As soon as I take them down, you run out the south door into the foyer. I pried some boards off the trap door before they heard me and stopped me. Then get up the stairs and out. Remember what I said about my car?"

She nodded, feeling stunned. As far as she was concerned, he was telling her a fairy tale. There was no way she could climb through the trap door, run up the basement stairs and out to his car—not in her condition. But she'd try. She'd die trying, if that was her only chance.

As long as Deke didn't give up, she wasn't going to.

"Remember what I told you? If Irina's men aren't there yet, there's a cell phone under the driver's seat with the keys. Press Call for Irina's number, then turn the car around and drive away from the house as fast as you can."

"What about you?"

"I can take care of myself." Deke turned and placed himself behind the door, so that when it swung open, he'd be in the perfect position to get the drop on their attackers. He held the portable Taser in his weaker right hand and the knife in his left.

As she watched, he adjusted the dial on the Taser down and held it against his hand. He hit the switch. His fingers contracted.

He looked up with a small smile on his face. "It works."

She gave him a thumbs-up.

He twisted the dial up to maximum, then paused and sighed. He raised his gaze. "Mindy—" His whisper carried across the distance between them. "Don't—give up on me, okay?"

Her eyes filled with tears that spilled down her cheeks. "I never have. I never would," she whispered.

"Okay, ready?" he asked.

"Should I talk out loud?"

He shrugged. "Whatever you think will convince them."

Mindy started moaning, as if in her sleep.

Deke stood behind the door, balanced on the balls of his feet in attack mode. He watched Mindy in admiration. She scrunched her face up, as if in pain, and began blowing air out through her mouth. She was acting just like she had when she'd gone into premature labor down in the mine.

A chill slid down his spine. What if she really went into labor? He had no idea what a woman in labor could or couldn't do, but he was pretty sure climbing stairs and running was way down on the list.

She groaned louder and started pushing air through her mouth in little bursts.

Deke waited. He wished he knew what time it was, and how long it would be before James burst in. He normally had a good sense of time, but there were too many factors working against him here.

He was weak and shaky from blood loss and infection, and for the first time in his life he was questioning his own judgment. He had no idea whether he could hold his own against James and his soldiers.

And then there was Mindy. He looked over at her.

Her hair was tangled and stringy. Her eyes had deep shadows underneath them. The skin of her face was tight and drawn across her cheekbones. She was still the most beautiful thing he'd ever laid eyes on.

She was as brave as any soldier he'd fought along-side, but bravery alone didn't win battles. He knew she would push to the ends of her endurance to save the baby she cradled within her, but he was desperately afraid that wouldn't be enough. And he was terrified that he was asking too much of her.

He wasn't sure if he could survive if something happened to her or to his son.

His son. He had a son to fight for. A piece of him. His own flesh and blood.

He straightened his back and tightened his fists around the Taser and the knife. He had one chance to prove himself worthy of being a father. He would win, or he'd go down fighting for his wife and child.

"Deke? I'm getting worried. My contractions are getting stronger." She spoke aloud.

"Try to hang in there. Do you need to lie down?"

"I—may in a few—minutes," she gasped.

"Hey! James!" he shouted at the ceiling. "My wife's in labor. Help!"

He rocked up to the balls of his feet and readied himself. He knew James wouldn't come in here alone, and he fully expected that he and whoever came with him would be armed.

Glancing over at Mindy as she simulated the sounds and actions of a woman in labor, he saw his fear reflected in her eyes. He quirked his mouth in a smile, hoping to reassure her.

She wasn't fooled.

Then he heard footsteps outside the door. He caught her gaze and gestured toward the door with his head. "Here they are," he mouthed. He tensed, ready to spring—not on the first man. That would be suicide. He had to wait for the second, and hope there were only two.

The door slammed open and he flattened himself against the wall so it wouldn't hit him. Frank James walked in, followed by a soldier with a rifle cradled casually in his arms. The soldier had barely cleared the edge of the door by the time James realized that Deke wasn't in the desk chair.

"What's going on—?" he started.

The soldier reacted almost as fast. He raised the rifle.

As he did, Deke reached out and looped his left arm through the rifle's sling and jerked as hard as he could. He jabbed the Taser into the soldier's solar plexus and zapped him with a whopping dose of electric current.

The soldier shrieked and collapsed.

Deke jerked the rifle out of the soldier's limp hands and, in a single sweeping motion, swung it in an arc, slamming the butt into James's shoulder and knocking him aside.

He saw the flash of silver as James tumbled and immediately righted himself. He held a revolver.

"Get out, Mindy!" he yelled, as he lunged toward the gun. If James was still playing his game of Russian roulette, Deke might be able to overpower the fake cowboy before he could fire enough times to get to the live round. Or he might go down on the first pull of the trigger.

"Deke!" Mindy cried.

"Go, damn it."

He couldn't afford two seconds to turn his head and make sure she made it safely out the door. He got a good grip on the rifle and pushed the barrel into James's chest.

"I'll blow your heart right out of your chest, you sadistic bastard."

James's eyes widened in terror, but his shaky hand pulled the trigger on the revolver.

Even as Deke cringed, waiting for the hollow click of the hammer or the impact of the bullet, he bent down and Tasered James in the neck. As the hammer clicked impotently, James's body arched then went limp.

Deke grabbed the revolver.

He whirled and headed toward the door. As he stepped over the soldier, the man reached out and grabbed his boot.

He almost stumbled, but recovered himself and kicked backward, dislodging the soldier's hand.

Damn, with the dose of current he'd used, he'd have thought both of them would have been out of commission for several minutes at least.

The soldier tried to push himself up, but his arms collapsed. He screamed in a language Deke didn't understand, but the meaning was clear.

He was calling for help. Any second now, his buddies would burst in.

Deke had to get out of there.

He zapped the soldier again, but from the sound and the soldier's diminished reaction, he knew the Taser was almost out of juice. So he rammed the butt of the rifle into the man's head. At this point Deke didn't care whether any of them survived or not. They were terrorists.

Enemies of the United States. And they'd tried to hurt Mindy.

Still carrying both the revolver and the automatic rifle, Deke rushed through the door.

He didn't see Mindy anywhere. "Mindy!" he called. *Nothing.* Dear God, he hoped she'd gotten out and up the stairs. "Min!" he yelled. "Run!"

He slammed the door into the foyer, wishing he had something to block it with. But there was no time for wishes.

He ran to the abandoned tunnel, carefully scooped up a double handful of blasting caps and slid them across the dirt floor to the foyer door. He ducked back into the tunnel as they clattered against the door. None of them went off from the impact.

Leaning back against the wall, he gulped in a huge breath, hoping it would clear his head. His arm burned, and he felt so sleepy. If he could just close his eyes for a couple of minutes…

No! Closing his eyes was giving up. Whatever strength he had left in him would go to making sure Mindy got to safety. He hadn't told her, but he was afraid Frank's men might have found his car, or that Irina might not have been able to zero in on his shoulder chip.

That car was her only chance. He needed her to trust that it was safe.

Digging in his pocket, he pulled out the disposable lighter and flicked it with his thumb. Spark but no flame.

Not now! He flicked it again, and again. *Light, damn it! I did not use all the butane!*

Finally a weak flame appeared. He paused. Had Mindy made it out of the building?

Please, God.

He waited a few more seconds—as long as he dared, before lighting the fuse, holding his breath with apprehension until it caught.

Then he rushed for the trapdoor.

Shouts and thundering footsteps filled his ears. He dove through the opening into the hotel's basement and right into the path of two soldiers careering down the stairs.

One of them grabbed him by the collar, and the other pointed a combat rifle at him and shouted something in a foreign language.

Deke raised his hands. The soldier holding his collar kicked him behind the knees and he fell to the ground.

"Dynamite!" he yelled. "Back there."

Whoever was in the foyer was banging on the door, trying to get through.

The soldier holding him yelled a warning at him and prodded his back with the rifle.

Deke didn't have to know the language to understand what the guy was saying.

Shut up or die.

"Back there!" he shouted again. "Boom boom!" Wasn't *boom* the same in every language?

The sound of splintering wood told him that the soldiers had broken through the door to the foyer. He held his breath, and squeezed his eyes shut, trying not to think about what all those blasting caps would do when stepped on.

Sure enough, explosions like the sounds of giant firecrackers filled the air, followed by screams and shouts and the smell of gunpowder and burned metal.

In the next second, the hand on his collar let go, and both soldiers hit the ground.

Deke used their surprise and fear to push himself forward, toward the stairs. The dynamite was going to blow soon. He had to get out. If one of the soldiers recovered his wits and shot him, then so be it.

At least he'd die believing that Mindy had made it to safety.

He hit the stairs running, but with every step he climbed, his legs got heavier and slower.

A soldier yelled, and Deke instinctively flattened himself against the stairs. A bullet took a huge chunk out of the step near his head. He knew the man's next shot would be on target.

"Boom!" he yelled desperately. "Much more booms! Run!" Enveloped in a haze of drowsiness, he pulled together the last frayed threads of his strength and threw himself up the remaining steps.

A volley of bullets followed him. He stumbled through the door and spotted a patch of sunlight to his left. Was that the back door he'd told Mindy to look for? Or was just the flashing lights in his head signaling that he was about to pass out?

Didn't matter. Whatever the light was, it was his only hope for survival, because he heard heavy footsteps on the stairs behind him.

He staggered toward the light, noticing that it got brighter and dimmer at the same time. He shook his head, hoping he wasn't hallucinating, and grabbed at what looked like a door facing.

The light was bright and hot. And out in the distance, he saw two large uniformed men with a small figure in tow.

Mindy! They'd captured her.

He propelled himself forward just as a huge rumbling noise rose behind him and a blast of hot air slammed against his back, burning his skin.

It was over.

Tell Mindy I'm sorry.

Chapter Twelve

"Mindy, I'm sorry," Deke whispered brokenly through lips that wouldn't move. His mouth felt stuffed with cotton, and his head felt like it was made of lead. Helpless tears filled his eyes.

He hadn't wanted it to end like this. He would have gladly given his life for Mindy and their baby, but he had hoped he could have seen his son before he died.

"Mr. Cunningham?" A voice he didn't recognize was speaking very close to his ear. "Mr. Cunningham, are you awake? You need to wake up."

He wanted to swat at the annoying voice and sink back into oblivion, but he couldn't move his arm.

"We can't let you leave recovery until you wake up. Can you talk to me?"

Whoever was bothering him wasn't going to give up. He opened bleary eyes and then closed them immediately. The light was too bright. "Where's Mindy?"

"Mr. Cunningham, I need you to talk to *me*."

"Leave me alone."

He heard a soft chuckle. "Well, that's something, I guess. Now open your eyes. Do you know where you are?"

Deke growled under his breath. If he couldn't see Mindy, he wanted to be left alone. He felt helpless— and feeling helpless pissed him off.

"In hell?" he muttered.

Another chuckle. "Not quite. You're in the recovery room, but now that I've got your attention, I'll make arrangements for you to be taken to your room. See this?"

He forced his eyes open and saw a blue plastic container that looked like it was made to hold a kidney. "I'm setting it right here beside you. If you feel sick, use it."

Whatever the woman was talking about, it didn't interest Deke in the least. All he cared about was finding Mindy. He sat up—or tried to. As soon as he raised his head, his vision went black.

Mindy! he screamed, but nobody answered.

DEKE OPENED HIS EYES. The last thing he remembered was the blast of exploding dynamite against his back.

No. There was something else he remembered—an annoying voice, but he couldn't place it.

He took a careful breath and was surprised at what he smelled. No heat, no burning cloth or wood—or flesh.

He smelled bleach, and something fresh and medicinal. He opened his eyes to a narrow slit. Everything was a muted green color.

Hospital! He was in a hospital. Suddenly he was wide-awake. That meant he hadn't been blown up when the dynamite exploded. And that meant—

Did that mean that Mindy was all right? And the baby?

He looked at himself. His left arm was bandaged

from elbow to wrist. There was a blood pressure cuff
on his right upper arm and a needle sticking out of his
wrist.

But not for long. He'd put in an IV port before, in
the field. He could take one out.

And he did, with a little difficulty, hampered by the
bandage on his right arm. The stick point bled a little,
but he'd seen worse. Hell, he'd bled worse.

He slipped his arm out of the blood pressure cuff and
sat up on the side of the bed—and discovered he had
nothing on but the flimsy, open-backed hospital gown.
He stood slowly, careful to give himself time to make
sure his head was clear, then checked the closet and
drawers. His clothes weren't there—not surprising.
They'd been tattered and filthy. With a little digging,
he found a set of scrubs—probably for him to wear
when they discharged him.

He yanked off the gown and pulled on the scrub
pants, stopping a time or two when his head began to
spin.

By the time he got the pants on and the drawstring
tied he was out of breath again. He took a long drink
from a plastic water jug, letting a little of it drizzle
down over his neck and chest. After rubbing it into his
skin, he poured some in his hand and splashed his face.

Fortified by the water, he left his hospital room and
headed down the hall to the nurse's station.

By the time he got there he was out of breath.

The ward clerk looked up from the orders she was
transcribing. "Yes?" she said. "What room?"

"Where's my wife?" he demanded.

The clerk sighed. "What's your name and date of
birth, please?"

"My room's right back there."

The clerk glanced past him. Deke turned and saw a security officer coming toward him.

"Take me to Mindy Cunningham," he demanded.

"Now Mr. Cunningham, I've been directed to see that you stay in your room. We need to make sure—"

"I need to make sure my *wife* is all right. Take me to her."

The guard held up his hands. "Now settle down—"

"No, you settle!" Deke's head was spinning again, but he took a step forward and got in the guard's face. "My wife was in labor. She'd better be here some-where." He lowered his head and glared at the security guard from under his brows. "Take me to her—now!"

The guard nodded past him at the ward clerk.

The clerk typed a few keystrokes on a computer. "Room 410," she said.

"Where are the elevators?" Deke put a hand out to the wall to steady himself.

"Hold it. The only way you're going to leave this floor is in a wheelchair pushed by me. I have my orders."

"From who?"

The guard gestured at a nurse, who pushed a wheel-chair up behind Deke. The guard put a hand on Deke's chest. Deke sank into the chair without a protest.

"From Irina Castle."

That shut Deke up for a few seconds. As the guard pushed him into the elevator, he finally found his voice. "Irina told you to make me use a wheelchair?" he asked suspiciously.

The security guard didn't answer him directly. He leaned forward and punched the button labeled 4. "She warned me that you'd be stubborn and difficult."

Deke watched the display as it showed 2, then 3 and finally 4. "Here we are."

"Stay put. You don't get to walk."

As the guard pushed Deke out onto the fourth floor, he realized it was the maternity ward. The sight of yellow ducks and pink and blue elephants on the walls and the smell of baby powder rendered him speechless and paralyzed with fear.

Had Mindy had her baby? His baby?

Their baby?

The halls were filled with hospital employees dressed in pink and yellow and blue printed scrubs, carrying stacks of snowy-white linens, armfuls of tubing, pushing medication carts—he even saw one carrying an infant.

Then he saw the rooms and the numbers on the doors.

"Stop!"

The guard kept pushing the chair.

"Stop!" Deke put his bare foot out to try and stop the chair. He groped along the side until he found the lever that threw the brake.

"Hey!" the guard said.

"There's room 410," Deke snapped.

"Right. That's where we're headed."

Deke turned his head and looked up at the guard from under his brows. "I'm not going in there in a wheelchair. She will *not* see me in a wheelchair, do you understand?"

He saw the guard's Adam's apple bob as he swallowed. "Yes."

Deke stood. He had on nothing but green cotton pants and a bandage on his right arm, but at least he was standing on his own two feet.

It took him a couple of seconds to be sure he was steady enough to walk. The guard reached out a hand, but he shook his head.

A nurse walked up. "Are you Mr. Cunningham?" she asked.

He nodded. "Is my— Is Mindy—?"

The nurse smiled. "She just got back to her room."

"And the—"

"The baby is just fine. We'll be bringing him to her in a few minutes."

Deke's throat closed up.

The nurse patted his arm. "You can go on in."

He nodded.

The guard clasped him on the shoulder. "Congratulations, son."

Deke frowned at him for a second, then nodded. He waited until the nurse and the guard left before he stepped up to the closed door.

He put out his hand, but stopped short of pushing the door open. It wasn't fair to her to barge in on her without her permission.

Nothing had changed. Not really.

Mindy had never deserved what he'd put her through. His life was and always had been a train wreck, and she'd been dragged along with him for far too long.

She deserved to have the safe, normal life she'd always wanted.

He drew his hand back and wiped his face. One thing had changed. Him. At least now he could see how bad he was for her. What kind of danger she was in because of him.

Hell, if he had any courage at all, he'd turn and walk away.

THE OBSTETRICIAN HAD been very clear.

Relax! I want you to sleep at least twelve hours a day if not more. Every time your baby sleeps, you sleep.

Easy for you to say, she'd responded. She was too tired—and too tense to sleep. After three days of unrelenting fear and tension as she and Deke ran from terrorists, she'd barely had enough strength to assist in her Sprout's birth.

The doctor had threatened several times to do a Caesarian, but she'd refused every time.

"I'm fine," she'd puffed in the middle of her contractions. "I want to have him naturally. I want to see him the very instant he comes out, and I can*not* be confined to bed."

The doctor hadn't been happy, but Mindy had won. She'd told the doctor the truth, but not the whole truth. There was no way she'd let the doctor cut on her because as soon as she was able, she was going to find Deke.

In fact, she was just about to get up now. She took a deep breath that turned into a jaw-cracking yawn. She closed her eyes. After a couple of minutes of rest, she was definitely going to go searching for Deke.

The last glimpse she'd had of him was when he'd stumbled out the back door of the old hotel. In the very next instant, he'd disappeared in a cloud of black smoke as the building behind him had exploded.

She'd screamed and tried to run toward the burning building, but men in black secret service jackets had forced her into their SUV and rushed her with sirens wailing to Crook County Hospital's Maternity Ward. She'd screamed in protest until one of them made a call and verified for her that Deke was alive and on the way to the same hospital.

By the time Sprout had made his appearance, Mindy had made such a pest of herself that one of the labor and delivery nurses had checked with hospital admissions and found that he'd been admitted and rushed into surgery.

And that was all she'd been able to find out. Everyone seemed much more concerned with her resting and getting plenty of IV fluids.

She knew the nurses were going to be bringing little Sprout in to her within the hour, and her arms and heart ached to hold him. But she *knew* her baby was fine. She'd seen him briefly, and the doctor had reassured her that he had all the requisite fingers and toes.

She had no idea how Deke was. She had to find out if he was all right.

Dear God, please let him be all right. Let him be whole and well. And don't scar him any more than you have to, God.

Tears seeped out from underneath her closed lids. She knew scars wouldn't matter to him. She could hear him now. He'd say that the scars on the outside were a good match for the scars inside.

He'd endured so much. Been through so many trials, and kept his sanity and his goodness. If anybody in the world had earned the right to be happy, he had.

But his childhood had left such a mark on him. He was so afraid that he wasn't worthy of being a father. So afraid of being like his own father.

She wished she could convince him that he was nothing like Jim Cunningham. Deke's father had been a sick, lonely old man who'd wallowed in his own misery. He might have been a good man once, but he'd let drink and bitterness overwhelm him until he was consumed by self-hatred.

Deke had never let anything—not alcohol, not torture, not even heartbreak, overwhelm him. His innate goodness, combined with the love and trust of his friends, had kept him from veering onto the path his father had taken.

She just wished he believed in himself as much as everyone believed in him. Deke was a hero. He just didn't know it.

Mindy let her head recline back on the pillow, not caring that tears slid down her cheeks and neck. She'd never been able to break through the armor he'd built around his heart. Never been able to convince him of the kind of man he was. What made her think that she could now? It broke her heart that he might never accept that he deserved to be a part of his son's life or, more important, how much his son needed and deserved to have him as a father.

"You're a hero, Deke. Your son needs you, and so do I."

The door to her room eased open with a small squeak.

It was the nurse bringing her baby. Mindy smiled and pushed herself up in the bed.

"Come in," she called. "I've been wait—"

The hand that grasped the edge of the door was not a nurse's hand. It was big and long-fingered, with ragged nails, scraped knuckles and a specks of dried blood coating its back.

Mindy couldn't breathe as the door swung open and Deke stepped into the room.

He had on nothing but green scrub pants that hung low on his lean hips. His right arm was bandaged and the cut on his forehead was striped with sterile strips. His torso was an abstract painting in blues and purples and greens.

He looked exhausted and sick and scared. His blue eyes glittered in contrast to his pale face.

To Mindy, he'd always been larger than life. At over six feet, he towered over her five feet seven inches. But the physical difference between them had paled in comparison to his *presence*.

Now, however, standing half-naked in front of her, with all his hurts exposed, he seemed smaller, thinner. He looked human and breakable.

And she loved him so much that the mere sight of him stole her breath and hurt her heart.

She held out her hand. "Deke."

Deke stared at Mindy, unable to move. Hardly able to breathe. To his hazy brain, she looked like an angel, lying in the glow of the dim light that shone down from over the head of her bed. Her hair lay against the pale green sheets like dark angel wings.

He swallowed. "Can I—come in?" he said hoarsely.

She stared at him for a few seconds. Then her tongue flicked out to moisten her lips and his heart skipped a beat.

She nodded, still holding out her hand.

He stepped over to the side of the bed and took her hand in his. This close he could see the purple shadows under her eyes and the drawn translucence of her skin.

"Where's Sprout? I mean, have you—?"

She nodded. "They'll be bringing him in here in a few minutes."

A hot flash of pure panic ripped through him. "I should go."

Mindy's hand tightened on his. "Oh, no, you don't," she said. "You're not getting away that easily. Sit down here and tell me what happened."

He nodded. Sitting down would be a good idea right now. He gingerly perched on the edge of the bed, wincing as the movement made his bandaged arm ache.

"How's your arm?"

"I think it's going to be okay. I was supposed to wait for the doctor to come talk to me, but I needed to find you."

Mindy's eyes turned bright with tears. "That's funny. I was just about to go looking for you," she whispered. Her fingers slid back and forth across his knuckles. "The hotel blew up."

"Dynamite."

"What about James, and—?"

He shook his head, his lips flattened into a straight grim line. "I don't know."

Her hand squeezed his. "It had to be done, Deke."

"I know." He looked down at their hands. "Min, I'm glad you're okay. You and the baby." He paused, almost overwhelmed by all the emotions swirling through him. Love, fear, relief, sadness. "Really glad."

"I'm glad you're okay, too. I was so afraid—"

He nodded. "Do you remember how we got to the hospital?"

"Your car was surrounded by black SUVs when I got outside. I was terrified, but the men said they were Secret Service. I had no choice but to believe them. I got the feeling they would have gotten me into one of the vehicles one way or another."

"Secret Service. Aaron must have given them my

location. Or maybe Rafe tracked me by the chip." He rubbed his shoulder.

"Chip?" Mindy's eyes widened. "You told me—"

A sharp rap at the door made them both jump.

"Hi, Mindy," a cheerful voice said. "You've got a little visitor." The overhead light came on, chasing every last shadow from the room.

Deke's chest tightened. He had an overwhelming desire to bolt; to run as fast as he could somewhere— anywhere—as long as it was far away from the tiny baby that he was about to see.

He vaulted to his feet and backed away from the bed.

"Oh, hello." The nurse said. "You must be Mr. Cunningham. Congratulations."

All Deke could manage was a brief nod. He was too busy staring at the tiny baby the nurse was placing in Mindy's arms.

How could such a little thing cause so much of a stir? The whole room was alive with its presence. Mindy was glowing like a real angel. Her face was filled with a love and serenity he'd never seen before. He almost had to turn away from her beauty and happiness.

The nurse glanced from Deke to Mindy. She cleared her throat. "Well, why don't I come back in about a half hour? I can help you get started nursing him." She backed out of the room, turning off the glaring overhead light as she left.

Mindy smiled at her little Sprout. She'd held him for a few minutes in the delivery room, but there had been doctors and nurses all around, rattling instruments, cleaning and talking, and obviously impatient to clear the room and bring in the next delivery.

Now it was just him and her—and Deke. She touched

the little nose, the impossibly soft cheek. She held a finger for him to wrap his tiny fist around.

"Deke, look at his little fingernails." She kissed his fingers and rubbed her nose on his brand-new little arm. "He's so soft. So perfect."

She looked up at her ex-husband, and her heart twisted painfully in her chest. He'd been pale before, but now he looked positively ashen. If this were a sitcom, the audience would be laughing, she thought. But it wasn't a sitcom. This was real life, and Deke Cunningham had finally met his match.

"Come look at him," she coaxed, sending him a smile.

But he seemed to be frozen in place. His throat moved as he swallowed. His eyes looked huge and terrified.

Just moments before, Mindy had been worried about how he would react to their baby. But now that he was standing here in front of her, enveloped in paralyzing fear that not even the threat of death—not even the threat of *her* death—had raised in him, she was furious.

"Is this it, then?" she whispered fiercely, trying not to disturb the baby. "With everything that you've faced, the great, brave Deke Cunningham is going to be taken down by a six-pound newborn?"

She pressed her cheek against the top of her son's head for an instant, reassuring him.

Deke didn't move. He just stared at her.

"You're a coward. If you don't know by now what a wonderful father you'd make, then maybe you don't deserve him. Look at him. How could a bad person produce such a beautiful baby?"

"My father—" he started, but she cut him off.

"You know what? I know your dad hurt you, physically and emotionally. But my guess is he did the best he could. He just wasn't as strong as you. Maybe you got your strength from your mother. Or maybe something broke inside him." She took a shaky breath to try and calm her racing heart.

"I'm not excusing him, but maybe he couldn't handle life alone after your mother left. I don't know. What I do know is you are not your father. You are a hero, and the bravest man I've ever known. But if you can't face fatherhood, then I guess you're not as brave as I thought you were."

Had she gone too far? Too late now. She lifted her chin and met Deke's gaze. He either believed in himself or he didn't. the next few seconds might decide the rest of their lives.

He swallowed again and glanced down at the baby cradled in her arms, then looked back up to meet her gaze. "What—what do I do?"

"Come over here and sit down." Her scalp burned with relief, and her hands shook. But she wasn't about to show him how worried she'd been that he'd turn and bolt. She sat up a little straighter.

Deke looked like he was taking the last two steps to the gallows. But he finally sat down on the edge of the bed.

"Here," she said. "Take him in your left arm. Tuck his head right in the bend of your elbow."

Deke took the baby in the crook of his arm. His head was bowed and his hair covered his face. All she could tell was that he was looking at their son.

"He's little," he whispered.

"Thank goodness," Mindy said.

She heard him chuckle. Then he bent his head and pressed a kiss to his son's temple.

"You're almost as beautiful as your mother," he whispered. "I love you, Sprout."

Mindy's heart melted. He'd told his son he loved him, and the hitch in his voice let Mindy know that he'd never meant anything so much in his life.

He was going to be okay.

She watched him staring at his son. She could make it without Deke now. Now that she knew there was one person who'd broken through the wall around his heart. Knowing how much he loved their son was enough—almost.

LESS THAN TWELVE HOURS LATER, Deke sat in a borrowed conference room at the hospital, facing Mike Taylor, the new Secret Service agent in charge of the security detail assigned to Castle Ranch. He'd arrived just after Aimee Vick's baby was kidnapped.

He'd tried his damnedest to get discharged, but the nurses had told him he couldn't leave for another twenty-four hours.

In the chair next to Deke, looking as if she'd seen a ghost, sat Irina. On her left was Brock O'Neill. His carefully stiff demeanor, combined with the Bluetooth device in his ear, made him look more like a Secret Service agent than the casually dressed Taylor. On the other hand, the black patch over one eye made him look like a pirate.

But it was Taylor who had just dropped the bombshell. He'd just told Deke in his soft, careful voice that someone had tried to kill Irina.

"Tried?" Deke echoed. He reached out and touched

Irina's arm. "Are you okay?" he asked her while at the same time looking over her shoulder at Brock O'Neill.

She nodded, but he could feel the fine tremors that shook her body.

Brock's black gaze flickered. He had something to say, and he wanted to say it to Deke alone.

"What happened—and when?"

"I'm okay," she said quietly. "As soon as I heard that they'd found you and Mindy, I wanted to come and see you—"

"Thirty-five minutes ago," Taylor said. "Bastard was bold enough. It happened in the parking lot of the hospital."

Deke sat up, cradling his bandaged arm. "Here? I didn't hear anything."

"You wouldn't. Nobody did. It was a sniper, from who knows how far away. I've got men out searching for his nest, but—" Taylor shook his head.

Deke understood perfectly. He knew the range of the weapons he'd shot, and it was expansive. "Can you estimate the trajectory? The height? I can help—"

"Deke," Irina said, laying a hand on his left arm. "That's not all."

Her voice was tight. He met her gaze and saw tears.

"What? Who was shot?"

She shook her head. "Brock tried to talk me out of coming, but Rafe told me he'd come with me. So Brock told Rafe and Aaron both to bring me."

Deke met Brock's gaze again and knew he'd been right to trust the ex-navy SEAL. Brock knew what Deke knew. Either Aaron or Rafe was Novus's mole.

"What happened?" He directed that question at Mike.

"Rafiq Jackson was shot. The shooter got off three

rounds, then disappeared. Got Jackson in the meaty part of his thigh. Missed the artery. Damn lucky."

Damn good shot, Deke thought. "What about Aaron?" he asked.

"Narrow miss. The bullet grazed the skin right behind his temple. Both Gold and Jackson handled things well. The third round ricocheted off the top of Mrs. Castle's car. Your specialists both stated that a fifth of a second sooner and she'd have been hit between the eyes." Mike sent Irina a quick apologetic glance. "Sorry, Mrs. Castle."

She shook her head.

"Where's Rafe? And Aaron?"

"Jackson was rushed right up to surgery. Gold is in the emergency room. I'm about to go down there and debrief him."

Deke looked at Irina. "Would you like to go see Mindy and the baby for a few minutes?"

Irina's eyes darkened and she started to say something. But within a split second, she changed her mind and decided to do what Deke asked.

"I'll talk to you later," she said pointedly.

Deke nodded, suppressing a small smile. She was as gutsy as she'd always been.

He waited until she was out of the room.

"What the hell?" he asked Brock. "Which one?"

Taylor stayed quiet, but he was all ears.

Brock shook his head a fraction of an inch in each direction. "They're both spooked. Jackson was sure his femoral artery had been sliced. Gold knows he was about two millimeters from being toast."

"I know there are some sharpshooters out there, but you think those two shots were on target?"

Brock snorted.

Deke sent the Secret Service agent a sidelong glance.

"What?" Taylor demanded.

"This man could have nicked Jackson's femoral and given Gold a pierced ear," Brock said.

Taylor's mouth turned up slightly. "I heard you were good, Cunningham. I get the message. How do you want to handle it?"

"How many men can you put on my specialists while they're here at the hospital?" Deke asked.

Mike opened his mouth, but he waved his hand. "Figure it out, and figure out how many more you can place on the ranch. Novus is getting desperate and careless. He's failed twice—first Matt and now me. This sniper attack is showing us that he's willing to go to any lengths to get Irina." Deke paused. He didn't want to say anything more out loud. There was no telling who might be listening.

"Get Irina back to the ranch, and put every man you've got available on security. I'll be out to talk to you later today."

Taylor shifted uncomfortably. "I say we take Mrs. Castle to Washington, where we can ensure her safety."

Brock folded his arms across his chest.

Deke shook his head. "We'll lose Novus if we do that. She's got to be here."

"You're using her as *bait?*"

Deke couldn't explain the real reason he needed to keep Irina close. So he nodded. "Find where the sniper's nest was. As soon as I get out of here I want to see it. I might be able to tell you who it was."

He turned to Brock. "Will you wait here until Rafe's out of surgery?"

Brock nodded and left the room.

Taylor watched him until the door closed behind him, then he turned to Deke. "I'd sure like to know why you're able to command this much manpower from this high up in the government."

Deke didn't acknowledge his question. "Don't let Irina out of your sight, please. And I mean *your* sight, until she's safely back at the ranch. I'll be out of here this afternoon. I'll want to talk to you after dark."

Taylor gave Deke a brief nod and left the room.

Deke looked around the room. On a side table in the far corner of the large room was a telephone. For an instant, Deke considered using it. But it would be too dangerous.

He left the conference room and stepped over to a receptionist's desk. "Are there still pay phones anywhere around here?"

The young woman looked up and smiled. "Yes, sir," she said. "In the elevator lobby." She nodded toward her right.

The telephone kiosks were hardly private, but that was okay. All he was going to do was listen. He entered a memorized phone card number, then entered the number he wanted to call.

After six rings, he heard a click.

One message.

Deke's heart rate sped up. He entered a six-digit PIN. After a few more clicks, he heard the message.

He pushed his breath out in a huge whooshing sigh. Then he entered the code for Repeat and listened again.

Then pressed Delete and hung up.

For a second, he closed his eyes and leaned against the tiny metal frame around the phone. Then he wiped a hand down his face and punched the elevator call button.

Irina was coming out of Mindy's room when he got there. She had tears in her eyes.

"You are so blessed," she said, her voice a mixture of joy and tears. "Don't you dare mess this up."

He pulled back, not wanting to look her in the eye, but knowing she'd be suspicious if he didn't. "Yes, ma'am." He smiled.

But it didn't fool her for a second. Her brows drew down in a frown. "What's the matter? Is Rafe all right?"

"He's fine." Dear God, he wanted to tell her what he'd just found out. But he couldn't. No way. Even with everything that had happened, the worst still wasn't over.

In fact, the real battle hadn't even started, although it was about to.

Irina held his gaze for a beat, then nodded. "Good. Now get in there with your wife and son."

As Irina walked away, he rapped lightly on the open door, then stepped inside.

And stopped dead in his tracks.

Mindy was holding their son—nursing him.

"I'll— I can come back later," he stammered, awed and intimidated by the sight before him.

Mindy looked up and smiled. "Our little boy was very hungry."

He swallowed hard.

She laughed softly. "He's almost done. Want to hold him?"

Deke meant to shake his head no, but somehow it bobbed up and down instead.

"Come sit here."

He sat on the edge of the bed. "I don't know—"

"Don't worry. He's less fragile than he looks. I'm

going to put one hand under his head and one under his body. You take him the same way."

Deke did, amazed at how tiny and perfect he was. "Six pounds?" he whispered, staring at the tiny, scrunched-up face.

"And three ounces. He looks like you."

"How can you tell?"

"Oh, I can tell."

When Deke looked at her, his heart swelled so much he was sure it would burst out of his chest. "You are so beautiful."

"Liar." She touched her hair and smiled sheepishly.

"No," he said solemnly. "I've always thought you were the most beautiful thing I'd ever seen, although you may have a rival here." He nodded toward the precious baby he held. "But I don't think you've ever been as beautiful to me as you are right now. Min, I've broken too many promises. And God knows I don't deserve another chance, but—"

Mindy's eyes grew wide, but she didn't say anything.

"I want to *be* your husband. His father. Can we at least talk about it?"

For a long time she didn't say anything.

That's it then, he thought, bracing himself. He held Sprout closer to his chest.

"There's nothing to talk about," she whispered breathlessly.

Fear and dread certainty hit him like a blow. "There's not?"

She shook her head. "You *are* my husband. You *are* his father. You are my hero."

While Deke was still processing what she'd said, she

lay her palm against his stubbled cheek and raised her head to kiss him.

He kissed her back, holding their brand-new son between them.

* * * * *

FURY CALLS

BY
CARIDAD PIÑEIRO

Caridad Piñeiro is a bestselling author of twenty novels. In 2007, she was selected as the 2007 Golden Apple Author of the Year by the New York City Romance Writers. Caridad's novels have won many awards, including Best Short Contemporary Romance of 2001 in the New Jersey Romance Writers Golden Leaf Contest and Top Fantasy Book of 2005 and 2006 from *Catalina* magazine. Caridad's books have also received award nominations for RIO Reviewers and SingleTitles. com for Top Contemporary Romance. A tech- and promo-savvy author, Caridad has appeared on various television shows, such as the FOX News early edition in New York. In addition, articles featuring her novels have been published in several leading newspapers and magazines, such as the *New York Daily News, Latina* and the *Star-Ledger.* For more information on Caridad, please visit www.caridad.com or www. thecallingvampirenovels.com.

To my wonderful editor, Stacy Boyd, who has always
believed in and supported this series of my heart.
I am eternally grateful for all that you do for me.

Prologue

Her deadly kiss was near, but he welcomed it.

He buried his fangs deep in her breast and she held him, the way a mother might cradle a child, while he fed on milk-spiced blood. But then she gently eased his head back, enough to expose the rising pulse beating at his neck. Bending her head, she sank her fangs through the fragile barrier of his skin.

Blood rushed, hot and sweet, awakening the kind of passion that only vampires could share. The little love drug he had added to their drinks earlier that night ramped up the passion surging through their bodies. As his partner murmured a growly complaint that she was still hungry, he said, "It's the juice. It'll pass once you sip a little more."

And once *he* had a little more, he thought, as he tried

to sate his need from her sweet breast. When they finally ripped away from each other their bodies were super-charged—sexually and violently. Their fangs, stained crimson from their feast, retracted as they surged together for a kiss, bodies naked and heated from the torrent of immortal blood rushing through their veins and the potent chemical mix of the drug.

Over and over they kissed, licking the last remnants of blood from their lips, but soon that wasn't enough.

He pulled away from her, unseeing of anything other than the perfection of her body as he trailed his hands across her warm skin, flush with the life bestowed by his blood. He kissed the tip of her breast where he had been feeding just moments earlier.

There wasn't even a hint of his bite there, since she had already healed.

He suckled the tip and she moaned, reached down and unerringly found the head of his erection and stroked it, pulling a needy groan from him.

Their passion was too great for prolonged foreplay, he knew. Besides, his blood seemed to be sizzling in his veins from the demand to devour every part of her in every possible way.

He dragged her beneath him and onto the plush cushions of the settee in their private dining room, and without further delay he drove into her, seeking sat-isfaction.

His thrusts grew stronger, more violent, yanking a strangled gasp from her as the craving to feed rose again, potent and more demanding than anything he had ever experienced. For a fleeting moment, he wondered how long it would take for the kick of the love drug they had ingested earlier to subside.

He shook his head, nearly light-headed from the strength of his lust. He felt that if he didn't taste her life's blood again, he would die from the want of it.

As his gaze met hers, he realized she was feeling the same overwhelming pull of hunger.

Surging toward each other, they bared their fangs once again and attacked, fury replacing any other wants, driving them to the darkest corners known to their immortal kind.

Chapter 1

Meghan Thomas was just adding some cream to her porcini mushroom sauce when she sensed it.

Meghan didn't really know what "it" was, but her vampire powers told her that something was very wrong. The other vamps in the kitchen sensed it as well. From the bus boys to the other chef a few stations down, they were all aware of something odd. It had to be something powerfully wrong for vampires of all ages, even someone as new to the undead world as she was, to feel "it."

She took the pan off the flame and put it to the side just as Diego Rivera, part owner of the restaurant and her mentor of sorts, pushed through the door into the kitchen. Diego looked around and then he faced her.

"Is everything okay in here, Meghan?"

Wiping her hands on the towel tucked into her apron,

she walked up to him and said, "Yes, but you feel some-thing as well, don't you?"

At his abrupt nod, she laid a hand on the sleeve of his expensive silk suit jacket and asked, "What was it?"

She had hoped that with his greater vampire age and therefore stronger powers, he would have identified the sensation they had experienced, but the look on his face told her otherwise.

"I'll find out," Diego said, worry stamped on his fine features. A deep furrow was etched between his brows as he pivoted on one heel and walked out of the kitchen, Meghan right behind him.

When he realized she was following, he stopped. "There's no need for you to come with me."

She searched his features and realized he was just trying to protect her as he had for almost four years now. Although she had appreciated that assistance before she had resigned herself to her new immortal life, it was time for her to be a help rather than a hindrance. "I can watch your back if need be. I'm not a newbie anymore."

For a moment Diego appeared ready to protest, but then he turned and strode through the restaurant's main floor. As she followed, she took a quick look around.

Most of the diners were intent on their meals, but several heads turned her way. She recognized some familiar vampire faces. They too had sensed the distur-bance. But they'd remained in their seats, not wanting to reveal their undead status to the human partners at their tables. At least, not yet, Meghan thought.

They entered the hallway that led to the private dining rooms, but she detected nothing unusual as they walked past the pair of doors. At the end of the hall, Diego vaulted up the stairs to the next floor.

The feeling grew stronger here, but Diego didn't pause, as if he already knew the answer to their question rested on the uppermost floor of the building, where the last two private dining rooms were located. As young as she was in vampire years, even Meghan felt the pull of that weird something dragging them ever upward.

When they stepped from the stairs into the hallway on the top floor, the smell of blood assaulted them.

Meghan felt a burst of heat in the center of her body. Before she could control the reaction, the heat traveled through her like fast-moving lava, summoning the vampire she hated and had struggled for so long to learn to control. Her fangs burst from her gums, her vamp senses went into overdrive. They registered every little nuance that a human couldn't, things she couldn't have detected before being turned years earlier. Fury rose inside of her, much as it did every time she was reminded of what she no longer was. Her anger was fueled by the violence of the vampire that now controlled her, thanks to the strong smell of blood.

Diego shot a concerned look at her, his brows still furrowed over crystal blue eyes that were bleeding out to the strange neon-green of the undead. But nothing else gave away what he was. He was mastering his transformation, and as he noted that she hadn't—and maybe even picked up on her anger—he said, "*Niña*, you need to collect yourself. There are others around."

Others meaning humans, she realized. Others not like her anymore.

The doors to the private dining rooms were closed, and she was certain that if there had been any vampires there—any live vampires—they would be out in the hallway investigating the source of the disturbance and the overwhelming aroma of blood.

With a deep breath, she gathered herself and forced back her fury and bloodlust, summoning the human to return. But even after resuming control, the scent of death and the frisson of fear still lingered.

Diego strode to the door of one private dining room, seemingly sure that this was where they would find an answer.

Meghan knew he was right since the sanguine smell was redolent here as was the unusual feeling, almost like an out-of-rhythm vibration buffeting her vampire senses. Once again the heat pooled in her center, but this time she quickly battled the demon back and took a spot beside Diego, waiting for whatever would happen next, prepared to help her mentor if it became necessary.

He rapped his knuckles against the thick wood of the ornately carved door, but no response came from within.

He knocked again, stronger this time. Silence greeted them yet again.

Diego grasped the doorknob, turned it and slowly opened the door.

As he did so, she peered within and then wished she hadn't.

It was hard to tell where one vampire began and the other ended. Their bloody, naked bodies were wrapped around each other in a tangle of pale limbs. Vamp bites were visible at dozens of places along their torsos, a testament to how often they had fed from each other and how weak they were.

The bites weren't healing, but they were still alive.

She sensed the power of the vampires' life energy, but it was fading quickly. The entwined couple writhing on the floor were still feeding from each other, their fangs buried deep in each other's necks. A sickly, slurpy sound escaped one of them and she wanted to cover her ears to avoid the noise.

Instead, she slipped beneath Diego's arm, intent on doing something to help the two struggling vampires, but he snared her arm and held her back.

"We cannot do anything now. They are too far gone."

She didn't doubt it. Blood oozed from the many bites and as she looked around, she noted the large smears of blood along the floor and couch. Against one wall and part of a window, a spray marked the spot where one of the vamps had likely torn open an artery.

Before them, the movements of the vampire couple quickly stilled and as they did, the preternatural sensation that had called Meghan and Diego to that room slowly fled. When the bodies gave one final twitch, calm returned.

But when Meghan peered up at Diego's face, she sensed the present calm would be short-lived.

As she glanced once again at the blood and death before her, it reminded her of the world into which she had been thrust so many years earlier.

A world of destruction and loneliness.

A world she hated almost as much as she hated the demon she had become.

* * *

Blake Richards shuffled the empty glass from one hand to the other across the pitted surface of the bar.

The remnants of cheap beef's blood clung to the sides of the glass, painting it with thick fingers of red-violet. A vintage libation fresh from one of the Blood Bank's regular human contributors would have left far less proof of the nature of the grisly beverage.

But then again, no self-respecting vampire would leave behind a drop of something so fine as fresh human blood.

Something so fine which was relatively lacking tonight, Blake thought, as he glanced around the bar. In recent weeks there had been a decided decline in the number of vampires frequenting the bar, and that had resulted in a slowly decreasing stream of humans seeking the more dangerous fun and games for which the Blood Bank was known in Manhattan's undead underworld.

Rumor had it that a goodly number of his fellow vamps had taken their business to Otro Mundo, the new hangout that Ryder Latimer and Diego Rivera had opened adjacent to Diego's art gallery in SoHo.

Otro Mundo provided fine dining and the possibility for other adventures in the kinds of decadent surroundings that the two older vampires had experienced over the course of their long lives.

Apparently the two human wannabes had struck a chord with a growing contingent of the undead, providing them and their human consorts with such opulence that the Blood Bank no longer held any interest. Not that he would know much about such opulence, he thought, recalling the hungry days of his youth in Wales.

After his father had been killed in a coal-mining accident, his family had been forced to live off whatever they could grow on their small plot of land. Not nearly enough for the brood of six. At times food had been so scarce that he would make a thin soup from whatever greens he could gather in the woods so that he could leave what little food they had for his mother and younger siblings.

Until he had found a way to earn some money. He considered now that starving might have been better.

Shoving those painful recollections away, Blake scoped out the occupants of the bar, needing to satisfy the hunger that the inexpensive beef's blood had failed to quench.

As his gaze swept over the dance floor, he noticed the attractive blonde moving to the hard beats of the music spewing from the Blood Bank's stereo system. Foley, the owner of the Blood Bank, was too cheap to hire live musicians.

When she turned in his direction as she danced, her gaze briefly skimmed across his.

He thought he detected a glimmer of interest there and so he rose, added a bit of swagger to his walk as he approached the dance floor. He weaved through the crowd of dancers until he was just an arm's length from the blonde.

No doubt remained about her interest, since she shot a knowing grin his way. He joined her in the dance, her luscious young body plastered to his, her sweet, firm buttocks caressing his front. Even as he did so, he knew the attractive chit could only fulfill one need—his thirst for blood.

Satisfaction of an emotional kind had eluded him for too long, and as for the physical…

His recent interlude with a vampire elder had taught him a thing or two about physical satisfaction. Despite how good it had been with the beautiful and powerful Stacia, it had occurred to him too quickly in the relationship that there was something lacking.

Something he hadn't experienced since…

He drove thoughts of *her* away as the young woman eased up onto her toes, slipped an arm around his neck and drew his head near. She whispered into his ear, "Would you like to go somewhere more private?"

She inclined her head in the direction of the Blood Bank's back rooms and he knew just what she wanted— a quick tryst and maybe even some painful play with the toys Foley kept in the rooms for his more daring clientele.

He smiled, slipped his hand into hers and quickly strode toward the private rooms, intending to fulfill the young woman's needs and his own.

But even as he did so, memories sprang up of the last young blonde he had taken into that area. Of the joy and pain that tryst had brought.

He cursed beneath his breath as all desire fled.

Chapter 2

He had been reduced to a stalker guy, Blake thought as he hid in the shadows of the alley behind Otro Mundo, waiting for her to emerge.

He had been visiting that spot for nearly two months now, ever since the human wannabes had opened their posh restaurant.

He refused to admit that inside of him lurked a little of the wannabe, especially as he rubbed his full belly. The blonde earlier that evening had been a splendid dining experience, but he still needed more.

Far more than what he would find in the fancy-ass restaurant Diego and Ryder had opened. A part of him resented them—his two kind-of-friends. "Kind-of-friends" because he was only included in their circle when they needed something.

Nothing new. He had been an outsider most of his life. He should have been used to being on the fringe, and yet it gnawed at his gut, as did their philosophy of striving to maintain their humanity rather than giving in to their demons.

As he stood behind the restaurant, he reminded himself that he was a vampire and damned proud of it. He had no need of humanity with all the attendant emotions, especially love.

Love only complicated the whole undead-demon gig.

He told himself that over and over again, until she emerged from the back door of the restaurant and sat on the first step of the landing leading down into the alley.

Meghan's blond hair glistened beneath the light of a bright new moon. She wrapped her arms around herself, as if to ward off the chill of the early spring night. Not that vamps like them really felt the cold. The gesture was probably a lingering human habit.

Meghan had been a vamp for only about four years now. Actually three years, eleven months and ten days, but who was counting? Blake realized that besides Meghan, he would be the one to know.

He had turned her, after all.

Because of that, the connection between them told him that she was deeply troubled. Her hands had been shaking as she had wrapped them around the flesh of her upper arms, and from within her, disquiet radiated out to him, beating against his vampire senses, strumming the bond between a sire and the one he had turned.

Meghan picked up her head and stared his way, finally registering his presence. The unease that had bathed her soul moments earlier vanished and was replaced by her typical anger toward him. He had wondered more than once if she could ever forgive him for siring her, but her continued rage made him doubt that anything other than discord was possible between them.

Straightening from where he was leaning against the brick wall, he jerked on his black leather jacket and told himself to stop pining after the young chit.

The forever-young chit, thanks to him.

Guilt tore into him before he firmly shoved it aside.

For one and half centuries he had survived alone, and there was no reason he couldn't do the same for the next one and half centuries.

As he stepped away from the shadows, the chains on his jacket scraped across the rough brick, the noise loud in the otherwise quiet night.

Meghan rose from the stoop as he made himself visible, her body tense and seemingly poised for flight. But he wasn't about to let her run away.

Blake stood at the mouth of the service alley for the restaurant, resplendent in all his punk glory. His black leather jacket strained against the broad width of his shoulders. Beneath the jacket, a black shirt encased the lean muscles of his upper body while wickedly tight jeans hugged the perfection of his long muscled legs.

He wasn't tall, but he had amazing legs. Come to

think of it, most of him was fairly magnificent, which was what had gotten her into trouble in the first place.

She had fallen for the sexy, dimpled grin and the crystalline blue gaze. Not to mention all that perfectly defined muscle.

Plus, he had made her laugh with his insolent charm and self-confidence. That had been her ultimate downfall—that he could make her laugh. If she had learned one thing from her parents, it was that laughter lasted long after the passion of youth had fled.

But not even Blake could make her laugh tonight, Meghan thought, as she looked up to the window of the private dining room that held the grisly remains of the two dead vampires.

Smeared blood marred what had once been the pristine glass of the window. In her mind flashed the sight of their bodies writhing together and the sound of the sick sucking noises they had made before death forever stilled them.

Blake tracked her gaze and as he noted the sight, worry slipped into his normally cocky features. He took a step toward her but then stopped, clearly unsure of his reception, as well he should be.

She'd had more than a taste of Blake and was sure she didn't want yet another.

For all his charm, he wasn't trustworthy.

She had learned that the hard way and had no intention of dealing with him yet again. She rose from the step and walked toward him, her pace brisk.

Blake watched as Meghan approached, anger evident in every short and determined stride.

He could tell that much. She was not only upset by whatever had happened up in that room with the blood-smeared window, she was mad. He didn't need to ask if she was pissed off at him.

She was always pissed off at him.

"What are you doing here?" She stopped sharply before him and jammed her hands onto her hips. The motion strained the fabric of the white chef's jacket covering her ample breasts.

"Out for a stroll. And you, love?" He jerked his head in the direction of the bloodied window. "Having a bit of fun?"

She slapped him hard, rocking his head back with the strength of the blow, surprising him with the force of her vehemence.

"Don't you respect anything?"

He rubbed his jaw and snorted. "'Course I do, love. Motherhood, apple pie and Chevrolet."

Meghan whipped her hand forward to strike him again, but he snagged it midslap.

"Don't," he said, then immediately added in a softer tone, "I'm sorry. I didn't mean to start off on the wrong foot."

"Wrong is all we ever do, Blake. Don't you get that by now?" She jerked her wrist out of his grasp and rubbed it, as if to wipe away something dirty.

Irritation flared up in him, but he tamped it down. There had already been too much violence and hostility between them, although there had been other things as well. Good things.

"We managed to do some things right."

She sighed roughly and smoothed back a strand of hair that had escaped her French braid. "Why are you here, Blake? Why tonight?"

He didn't want to admit that the cute blond chit earlier that night had satisfied one hunger but whetted another. With a negligent shrug, he said, "Heard a rumor that Diego and Ryder were still hiring."

"As if you know what it is to earn an honest day's wage."

He arched a brow and disdainfully raked his gaze over the chef's attire she wore. "Want to make a little wager, love?"

She snorted and crossed her arms again. Leaning forward slightly in challenge, she said, "A wager? With you?"

"'Fraid you're wrong about me? 'Fraid I might prove I'm not the kind of man you think I am?" He stepped close to her, raised his hand and was about to cup her cheek when she took a step back out of his reach.

It might have hurt less if she had hit him again.

"Chicken," he taunted, and sauntered away.

Chapter 3

The Blood Bank, New York City
Three years, eleven months and ten days earlier

Meghan and her friends had heard about the Goth bar rumored to have the kinds of men and pleasures in which good little Midwestern farm girls didn't get involved.

All the more reason for her to check out the place, she'd thought, when one of her more world-weary college classmates had dared her to go to the hangout. After having spent the last four years in New York City as a good girl, she knew this was her last opportunity for a walk on the wild side before she headed home.

Her Midwestern parents expected her to do as they

had done—a nine-to-five job, marriage by twenty-five, followed by kids and a nice home in the suburbs. The only problem with that American dream was that it wasn't her own.

Meghan loved the whole Manhattan vibe and could easily imagine herself staying here, continuing to explore the kinds of things only Manhattan could offer.

Like this supposedly dangerous Goth bar.

It had taken the better part of the day to prepare for the senior dare.

She and her NYU friends had spent the morning searching a variety of vintage stores near Washington Square, rounding up accessories for their Goth getups. Two of her friends had even bought temporary black hair dye to make the look complete.

Meghan, however, had opted to keep her blond locks, thinking that her black clothes would be more than enough.

As she walked through the door of the Blood Bank, she reassessed that thought.

Black was definitely the one and only theme.

Everything and everyone in the bar was swathed in darkness.

The floors and walls were black, as were the surfaces of all the tables and booths scattered throughout the club. The dark color swallowed up the overhead spotlights that panned the sea of bodies on the dance floor and at the tables.

As the light swept the far end of the bar, however, she caught sight of one glaring platinum-blond head. The daring of that one brave individual brought a grin to her face before she forced it away and tried to adopt a serious glare in response to the threatening looks being sent her way by the patrons.

She slipped into a gap at the bar area, close to the spot where she had noticed the man with nearly white hair. After she and her friends had squeezed their way to the edge of the bar, they all ordered shots of Cuervo.

The punky, peroxide-headed Goth down at the end of the long wooden bar wasn't drinking. Instead he shuffled an empty glass from one hand to the other. He had big hands with long, nicely shaped fingers. His hands were sure as he repeated the shuffle of the glass back and forth, obviously bored by all the goings-on around him.

When he finally picked up his head, their gazes connected.

He had amazing ice-blue eyes, and when he smiled, a sexy grin dragged a dimple out on the right side of his handsome face.

She smiled back, picked up her glass of tequila and downed it in one gulp, wincing at the strength of the straight liquor.

Mr. Platinum Punk clearly seemed amused by her as he chuckled and shook his head. The longer strands of hair at the top of his head shifted with the motion. He picked up his empty glass and motioned to it with an index finger. She noticed as he did so that he wore a steel ring with some kind of ornate design on his thumb and some thin black bracelets on his wrist.

He definitely had the whole Bad Boy thing down pat.

She didn't need any further prompting, determined

to live out the dare that had been made earlier in the day. The dare that said she not only had to visit the hangout but hook up with at least one bar denizen before leaving for the night. While she wasn't into one-night stands, a makeout session with someone as sexy as the man at the end of the bar wouldn't be so bad.

She shoved two fingers into the air and waved them to get the barkeep's attention. When he brought the shots over, she reached into her jeans, pulled out a twenty and tossed it on the counter. Ignoring her friends' excited squeals as they realized her intent, she sashayed the few feet to the handsome punk, smiling as his gaze drifted down her body to where her hips were encased in snug black jeans, then shifted back upward across her breasts and finally settled on her face.

Slipping onto the cracked plastic pad of the empty bar stool beside his, she slammed the shot onto the bar.

"This is what you wanted, right?" she said.

Blake's gaze slipped from her attractive face to linger on her body, admiring all the lush curves. Her full breasts strained over the edge of the cotton tank top she wore beneath a leather jacket that was a bit too big, almost as if she had borrowed it for the night.

She shifted the glass closer to him and a hint of black lace peeked out from the neckline of the tank top as she said, "Well? Cat got your tongue?"

"No would be the answer to both of those questions, love." He pitched the tone of his voice low, striving for that sexy rasp women seemed to find so enticing.

"Brit?" she asked before downing the contents of her

shot glass. As she had done before, she winced after the drink went down.

"New to this, love?" he teased.

He picked up his own glass and tossed back the drink, the strong liquor dragging a grimace from him, too. His preferred beverage—blood—generally went down smoother and had a far different kick.

She chuckled at his reaction and shook her head. "Seems you're new to this as well."

The liquor warmed his belly, but not as much as the thought of taking a nip out of her luscious flesh. Scooting to the edge of his bar stool, he leaned toward her, brushed aside her shoulder-length hair and whispered in her ear, "Cat definitely doesn't have *my* tongue."

To prove it, he licked the shell of her ear, and she couldn't control the shiver that traveled over her body before she moved away from him.

"Fast, aren't you?" she said, but her words lacked sting. An amused expression slipped across her cute Girl-Next-Door features before she resumed the scowl she had worn when he had first noticed her.

"That makes two of us, doesn't it?"

She arched a perfectly waxed brow. "So you think you and I are alike somehow?"

He eyeballed her from head to toe again before signaling the bartender for another round. The man sneered and ignored his request until Blake reached into his jacket pocket and tossed a hard-earned twenty onto the bar. After that, the bartender deposited the shots with little finesse and snagged the payment quickly.

Blake raised his glass and slugged down the drink, as did his companion. After mutual grimaces, he motioned to her with the empty tumbler. "I think that getup you're wearing is borrowed and the shots are for courage, love. I think you might even be a cheerleader in another life. Am I wrong?"

Meghan crinkled her nose in response.

"A cheerleader?" she said, but damn, did she resent that he had nailed it on the head. Deciding a little payback was in order, she pointed at his getup with a perfectly manicured finger sporting blush pink polish. "That look is so carbon-dated. Besides, a cheerleader beats a bad Billy Idol clone any day."

To her surprise, he threw back his head and laughed. When he faced her again, that damned sexy grin and dimple were back, flushing her body with a warmth that had nothing to do with the liquor.

"Care to test that theory, love?"

"Test?"

He leaned close once again. The sharp scent of tequila wafted around him as he nuzzled her cheek with his nose and said, "You asked what I wanted before."

"The tequila, right?"

"Wrong."

He closed his mouth over hers, his lips surprisingly tender as he moved them against hers, inviting her to understand just what he wanted.

Possibly what she wanted as well, she thought, as she opened her mouth and accepted the sweet slide of his tongue. She shivered as he slipped his hand to the nape of her neck and cradled her close.

"Get a room, Blake."

She jumped away from him at the abrupt command coming from beside them. A lean rail of a man, with skin so translucent and pale that he almost seemed like a ghost, slipped his hand between them and slapped it on the bar.

The specter jerked his head in the direction of the barkeep, and the shoulder-length strands of his nearly white hair barely shifted, hanging lankly around a thin, long face. "If he hasn't got the cash, get him out of here so a paying customer can sit."

"He's flush tonight, boss. So's his girl," the bartender responded.

"Is there a problem?" Meghan snared the sleeve of the boss man's suit and daintily pulled his arm out of the way.

The man's cold gray eyes searched her face before he turned that condemning gaze on her companion.

"Take your little adventures to one of the back rooms, Blake."

Blake. The name suited him somehow. Short and to the point, but a little pretentious, much like his punk getup.

Annoyed by the man's attitude, and recalling that earlier sweet kiss that he had interrupted, she laid her hand on Blake's thigh and said, "Let's go somewhere more private."

Her touch on his thigh, a combination of natural innocence and practiced seduction, burned through the denim.

"Are you sure, love?" he asked, not quite believing his luck.

"Chicken?" She eased from the bar stool and held out her hand.

He slipped his hand into hers. Her warm, silky skin awakened imaginings of how the rest of her would feel pressed against him. He suspected that tonight he would finally satisfy both the demon and the human.

Eagerly he followed her to where Foley's vampire guard blocked the hall leading to the back rooms.

The vamp barely glanced at him while he rubbed together his thumb and index finger. Blake didn't hesitate to reach into his pocket for his last twenty. He handed it to the man, who shot him an annoyed look and grunted, "Last one on the left."

The smallest of the rooms, Blake knew, but it would hopefully do for whatever was going to happen with Little Miss Cheerleader.

She led the way, the sharp staccato of her high-heeled boots setting a rhythm as they walked to the farthest room on the left and paused before the door. He detected her hesitation then, in the slight hitch her breath gave and the waver of her hand in his.

"Nervous?" He cradled her cheek, his touch meant to soothe, but as his gaze met hers, he sensed her sudden reluctance.

Her eyes were an amazing emerald green and as her gaze swept over his face, she said, "I have a confession to make."

"Kind of cliché at this moment, don't you think?"

A hint of bravado flared to life in her eyes, bringing a plucky twinkle there. "Actually, the confession is that I'm kind of glad I accepted my friend's dare."

"A dare? Is that what I am, love?"

She shocked him by rising a bit on her tiptoes and

kissing him. Her lips were warm and alive as she swept them across his mouth, then she cradled his cheek with her hand. When she finally broke away, she trailed her thumb across the slick wetness her lips had left behind on his, bringing to life an intense desire with that seductive touch.

It had been way too long since a woman had been able to reach that part of him.

"What do you think?" she said and with a wink, she opened the door, but stopped short at the sight of an assortment of whips, chains and cuffs tacked to the far wall.

He slipped in behind her and laid his hands at her waist. Bending, he whispered in her ear, "I don't think we'll have need of those."

"At least not tonight," she said, striving for a bravado that she wasn't feeling. This definitely was not the kind of thing she had expected to encounter.

Nervously Meghan placed her hands over his as they rested at her waist. His hands were chilled. With the same reticence she was suddenly experiencing? she wondered.

"Having second thoughts?" she asked, as she faced him.

Wordlessly he moved his hands to cradle her back. His movements were sure and yet surprisingly tender as he swept them up to her shoulders. With a deft touch, he slipped her jacket off and let it fall to the ground.

"That's better," he said.

He ran his hands across the skin of her bare arms and the exposed expanse of her shoulders. Stroking her softly, the palms of his hands felt slightly rough against her skin. They felt like hands of someone who did physical work for a living.

"You're so warm. Smooth," he said.

His gentle touch roused her and drove away her earlier hesitation. From the rough look of him, she had expected that he wouldn't be much for preliminaries, but she had been wrong. He caressed her skin before bending to kiss her.

The kiss started with a soft whisper of his lips against hers as he explored the shape of her mouth before he finally covered her mouth with his. Tentative at first, the kiss deepened by degrees until she was finally straining against him, her hands fisted in the soft leather of his jacket, pulling herself closer to him.

He took the next step then, easing his jacket off. It fell to the floor with a jangle of chains.

Beneath the jacket he wore a black T-shirt that hugged every hard line of his lean body. Meghan found that she was suddenly impatient to see more.

She grabbed the hem of his shirt and pulled it up and over his head, exposing a body that looked to be sculpted from the palest alabaster.

He wasn't a tall man, barely inches over her own five-foot-seven height, but what there was of him was magnificently formed male. Broad shoulders, big enough to bear any burden, were thick with hard muscles that felt smooth beneath the palms of her hands. She measured the strength in them before trailing her fingers down his well-defined chest to his abdomen and then back up. She ran her fingers through the pale whorls of hair on his chest, which matched the arrogant color on his head.

"You really are a blond," she teased, and stroked her index finger over the hard nub of his nipple.

"Are you?" he asked, and picked up his hand, trailed the rough pads of his fingers along the swell of her breasts exposed by the low neckline of the tank top and the push-up bra she wore. His actions got an immediate response as her nipples tightened in anticipation of his touch.

She looked up at him and curved her lips in what she hoped was a seductive smile. "You may have to wait a bit to find out."

Blake laughed, her bravado stirring something deep within him. Something that couldn't wait a second longer to take their little interlude to the next step.

He reached for the neckline of her tank top and slipped his fingers beneath, pulling away both shirt and bra with a quick tug. He heard the snap of the bra strap and felt the give as her breasts slipped free of all the fabric.

Her creamy skin was a sharp contrast to her black clothing. A flush worked over her flesh at his perusal, tempting him to feel the warmth of it against his palm.

He cupped her, and the heat of her nipple seemed to burn a hole into his palm. Still, he didn't pull back. Instead he stroked her nipple between his thumb and forefinger.

The action dragged a soft moan from her and she copied his actions, tweaking his hard male nipple with her fingers, jerking his erection to painful life.

Her gaze slipped there for but a moment before she leaned forward and closed her mouth over his nipple.

He shut his eyes against the sensation that rocketed through his body and focused on the feel of her breast in his hand, all warm and creamy. Her pulsebeat was loud in his ears and vibrated against his hand as it rested inches away from her heart, reminding him of what he was not.

Alive. Alive. Alive, drummed loudly in his head in the same beat as her pulse.

"You're cold," she said, In response, he called forth a bit of his demon, driving away the chill in his body to allay her concern.

"Blake?" she asked, and he realized that he didn't even know her name.

"That's my name, and you're…"

"Meghan," she said in a husky whisper, as he bent his head and took her hard nipple in his mouth.

She cradled him close, her hand snaking through his hair to keep him near as she arched her back.

Not that he was going anywhere, he thought. He sucked on her nipple and relished the soft mewl of pleasure that came from her.

He shifted his other hand upward, tugged down the rest of her shirt and bra so that he could pleasure her other breast with his mouth until it wasn't enough.

"Touch me, Meghan," he almost begged. When she ran her hands across the width of his shoulders, he surged upward, wrapping his arms around her waist and crushing her tight to his body.

"Blake, what—"

He silenced her with a kiss and walked with her to the edge of the bed, but then he slowly eased her down his body, the smooth hard tips of her breasts brushing along him, awakening fire wherever she touched. The sensation elicited a shiver from him.

"Has it been that long?" Meghan asked, surprising him with her sensitivity.

He shocked himself by admitting, "Since I felt something like this? Too long, love."

"Why?" she wondered aloud, even as she tenderly ran her hands across his shoulders and then let them dip down to cover the muscles of his chest with one hand while she placed the other flat over his heart.

Her touch reached deep within him, to emotions he thought he had suppressed long ago. Covering her hand with his, he said, "Let's not go there tonight."

He didn't think it was possible that the green of her eyes could get any darker, but with his words, her pupils deepened to almost black with emotion. Reaching up, she cradled his cheek, tracing the sharp line of it.

"Where would you like to go tonight?"

"To heaven," he said, as he bent his head and took her lips with his once again.

"Heaven it is, then," Meghan murmured as she accepted the gentle pass of his lips over hers. His touch was tentative, almost pleading. The emotions it roused sank its hooks deep into her heart, scaring her with their intensity.

She laid her hands on his shoulders as he effortlessly picked her up and placed her on the bed. When he joined her there, he lay beside her fully. Their bodies barely brushed, but it was enough to make her want more.

She cupped the swell of his pectoral muscle and ran

her thumb across the hard nub. A small shudder racked his body, emboldening her.

"Ah, love. That feels good." He looked down at her hand where she continued to strum his tight nipple.

She smiled, filled with a bravado she hadn't known she possessed. In a playful tone she said, "Well, if it feels good for you, I imagine that it might feel good for me, too."

He chuckled and met her gaze, amusement glittering in his crystal-blue eyes. With a cocky grin on his face, he passed the back of his hand across her breast, dragging a rough sigh from her at the pleasure that simple touch created in her core.

"Is that the sound of good, luv?"

"Yes," she said with a sigh, then took his nipple between her fingers, rotated it gently. At their hips, where their bodies were closest, she felt the jump of his erection, a reaction that was echoed in the sympathetic pull between her legs. She twined her legs with his and he pushed his thigh upward, tight against the growing pulse at her center.

As she rode him, trying to assuage her need, he took her hard nipple between his thumb and forefinger. He pulled on it gently then gave it a playful twist, which yanked a moan from her.

He immediately seized on that sound of desire.

"So was that the sound of…even better?" he teased, even as he was bending his head and she was arching her back, offering herself up to him.

His lips closed over her nipple. He sucked the tip before circling the hard nub with his tongue and then teething it into an even tighter point. She cradled his head close and as he suckled her she thrust her hips against his.

He responded by increasing the pull of his mouth and insinuating his thigh ever tighter against her.

She rode him with growing need, but recalling his earlier playfulness and wanting to join in it, she said, "And this is the sound of un-freakin'-believable," and finally released the low, long moan that had built within her at his actions.

Her words pulled a rough laugh from him and made his already full erection swell to painful proportions. He wanted nothing more than to bury himself in her. Nothing except possibly a taste of her humanity.

A bite of the life held tight against him.

Her heart beat furiously against his ear as he once again brought his mouth to her breast and suckled. The warmth of her—her mortal warmth—bathed his upper body with heat. The smell of her—all musky femininity—covered by the tight jeans that she wore brought sweet temptation.

The bit of vampire he had released earlier to warm her became a pool of heat at the center of him, growing ever stronger with each touch and taste of her. As she slipped her hand downward and covered his erection, a shudder ripped through him and the fire of the vampire flared across his body, breaking free and wanting dominion.

He fought the demon's control, fearing the strength of the emotion she had called forth. He feared it even as he acknowledged that he had never experienced anything like it in either of his lives.

She must have sensed the difference in him, since she urged him up from her breast and rubbed her lips against his. "I'm afraid too, Blake. I'm afraid of how much I like the way I feel with you."

Her confession undid the last dregs of his humanity and released the demon.

"Forgive me, love," he said as he gently eased her head to the side and bit down.

Pain seared through her neck, but immediately after came intense desire that made her entire body throb for fulfillment.

Meghan held him close, moaning and riding his thigh as desire gripped her hard, refusing to let go much like he seemed unable to release her. The pulse of her need beat through her body and seemed to echo from his, but little by little that beat grew weaker and erratic. Somehow she realized that the fading rhythm was that of her heart, failing slowly as Blake continued to suck at her neck until only a negligible thrum remained.

Cold enveloped her body. Weakness. Her extremities became numb and useless.

As Blake finally pulled away, she caught a glimpse of his face. Long, blood-stained fangs extended well beyond his upper lip. The ice blue of his eyes burned with almost phosphorescent brightness and called to her as her eyesight dimmed.

"Sweet Jesus, Meghan. I'm sorry, love. So sorry," he said, but his words were growing distant, as if she was fading away. Maybe she was.

A part of her brain understood that she was dying and struggled to hold on. To not let go of what little life remained. That consciousness latched onto the feel of him cradling her. Of the wetness of tears on her face and then the saltiness of something warm against her lips.

"Drink, Meghan," she heard, and knew that he was

offering her life. She didn't know how she knew it, she just did, as if something deep in her subconscious had elemental knowledge of what he offered.

All she knew at that moment was that she didn't want to die.

She was only twenty-one and she wasn't ready to die.

She opened her mouth and placed it against the flesh he offered. She drank of the warmth of his life's blood. With each pull of her mouth and each sip, strength grew in her body. She felt strength infusing each cell until she was able to force herself away from him.

With a brutal shove she drove him from her. As he rose from the floor beside the bed where he had fallen, he gazed down at her with eyes filled with tears, but they created no emotion in her other than hatred. Within her, fury rose with the realization that he had irrevocably changed her life.

She sat up and grabbed at her clothes, and when he would have reached for her, she slapped away his hands.

"Don't touch me. Don't ever touch me again."

"Ever is a long time now, luv," he said sadly.

"It *is* forever now, isn't it? You made me something other than human."

At his nod, she said, "I'll hate you forever."

He morphed back to his human form then and despite her statement, emotion rose up in her at the sadness in his eyes and at the words he uttered next.

"No need to waste your emotion, Meghan. I'll hate myself on your behalf."

Chapter 4

The Blood Bank, present day

Even before the knock on the door, Foley knew trouble had landed on his doorstep.

Not that he was unused to trouble. Running the Blood Bank included dealing with an underworld of both humans and vampires who thought trouble was just another word for fun. A night didn't go by when there wasn't violence of some kind in the club, not that he minded. A good fight with spilt blood always satisfied the darker aspects of his persona.

Amazingly, it was usually the vampires who were the easier ones to control during any kind of disagreement. They knew the rules and that the penalties for breaking

them would be swiftly enforced. Justice delayed was
justice denied, he thought, as with a last suck he reluctantly pulled himself away from that night's plaything.

She fell away limply, her eyes unfocused from the
blood loss. The bite mark on her neck was vivid against
the flush on her skin.

Rising from the bed in the back room, Foley swept
his gaze over the young woman's prone body. It was
made for pleasure, he thought. He itched to join her once
again and finish both feeding and loving, but another
knock came at the door, more insistent than the one
before.

That wasn't what got him moving away from his
beautiful dinner companion.

He is here, Foley thought, suddenly sensing the other
vampire's presence and the growing anger. The last
thing Foley wanted to do was to piss him off.

In a blur of vampire speed, he dressed and raced out
the door to the small office he kept beyond the Blood
Bank's well-known back rooms and beside a larger
meeting space, where the vampires sometimes joined
into a council to dispense their sure brand of justice.

Foley paused at the door and drew in a breath to steady
his nerves. It had been nearly three years since the last
time the Blood Bank's real owner had made his presence
known. His visit today could only mean one thing.

Trouble.

Immediately upon entering the room, Foley felt the
strength of the other vampire's power take hold of him.
It roughly forced him down to his knees as the vampire
said, "I don't like to be kept waiting."

"I'm sorry, Sun Tze. I was—"

"Feeding. I can smell her blood. Come here," he said, raising his hand and, with that movement, pulling Foley back up from his knees as if he were no more than a puppet on a string.

Fear so strong he almost wet himself slammed into Foley's gut as he obeyed and approached the other vampire. As he did so, he examined Sun Tze Lee, thinking that little had changed about him in the century since they had first crossed paths.

Lee's dark, almond-shaped eyes glittered with amusement at his dread, and a smile split his full lips, displaying perfect white teeth with a hint of fang that refused to go away. Lee had spent too much time in his vampire state for them to ever be normal again. The broad plains of Lee's ruthlessly handsome face had a telltale flush of color.

He had fed recently, Foley realized, but he also knew Lee intended to feast on him. Lee's dining would have nothing to do with satisfying his hunger. It would be all about reasserting the control he had claimed over Foley when they had run into each other during the Boxer Rebellion.

On a lark, Foley had headed to Beijing, then known as Peking, tired of the pickings in Dublin and intrigued by the talk of all the exotic delights he might find in China. He had arrived at the outbreak of the rebellion and realized that the time would be good for feeding and satisfying the demands of his body.

Sun Tze Lee had been there with a horde of fellow Chinese vampires—*kiang-shi*, as they were called—to drive away the foreigners exerting too much influence on their homeland and to sate their bloodlust in the course of the battle.

The fighting in Beijing hadn't lasted too long—fifty-five days, to be exact. But in that time, Lee and the other kiang-shi had decimated not only the foreign civilians and soldiers in the area, but also thousands of Chinese Christians in the city and in provinces like Shandong.

Lee had come upon him as he was draining a beautiful Chinese girl just beyond the steps of the Catholic church to which she had been trying to flee. He supposed now, as he took the final step that brought him close to Lee, that he had been lucky in a way. Instead of ripping his throat out for being a foreigner, Lee had decided to feed from him and make him his slave.

For over a hundred years, Foley had done whatever Lee ordered, and so when he'd entered the office and Lee had said, "On your knees," Foley had immediately complied.

The Chinese vampire now smiled and cupped Foley's face in his hands. With an almost tender touch he stroked his jaw with long, graceful fingers, urging Foley to bare his neck.

Foley did as he was bid, closing his eyes as a wave of desire skittered across his body, awakening unwanted passion. With a chuckle, Lee softly said, "Do not fear. We will get to that later."

Which was just what Foley was afraid of. He whimpered and finally did wet himself as he recalled the last time Lee had taken him. The Asian vampire had been brutal and uncaring of how much damage he had done.

Dreading a repeat of that performance, Foley said, "Master—"

"Sssh, Daniel," Lee began, using his given name the way one might a lover's, only Lee knew nothing of love. Only conquest and pain, Foley thought.

"You will enjoy it, Daniel. You always do," Lee said, beginning to transform. The black of his eyes literally bled out and became glowing embers of red. The black of his hair receded, replaced by the palest strands of glistening white, making him look almost albino.

But it was his fangs that snared and held Foley's attention.

From the small buds he had noticed earlier burst shiny white and lethally long fangs that extended well beyond the lower jaw. Needle-sharp, they could easily pierce the toughest of hides, but what Lee clearly wanted tonight was him.

Before he could protest, Lee forced aside Foley's head and perforated the skin at his neck to sink his teeth deep into an artery.

The pain of the kiang-shi's bite seared along Foley's nerves and exploded in the center of his brain like a supernova. The explosion continued outward, tearing into every sensitive synapse in its path, creating fiery agony in each cell of his body.

Foley screamed, his harsh guttural cry resounding in the confines of his small office.

Against his neck, Lee's throaty laughter erupted. In his brain came Lee's insistent command.

Scream some more. I love it when you scream.

Blake noticed the way Diego's nose wrinkled in apparent disgust and how Ryder Latimer, the other co-

owner of Otro Mundo, eyeballed him the way a father
might a virgin daughter's first date.

"What is that smell?" Diego said.

The debonair vampire, chic in a charcoal gray suit
that probably cost more than Blake had ever made in
both his lifetimes combined, walked from around his
large desk and stood beside him. Diego bent from his
greater height, took another sniff and said, "Moth-
balls?"

"Is that getup for real?" Ryder asked. He motioned
with his finger to the rather dated, dark blue polyester suit
Blake had lifted from the Goodwill store earlier in the day.

Blake tugged at the lapels of the jacket and inched his
head up defiantly. "Didn't think the chains and leather
would make a good impression during an interview."

"An interview?" Diego said with a sneer. He sat on
the edge of his desk and across the way from Ryder, who
lounged lazily in the chair beside where Blake stood.

Blake fought the urge to fidget beneath the probing
glances of both vampires. With his head tilted upward
at a defiant angle, he said, "Heard you were still hiring. Thought it was about time I had some gainful em-
ployment."

"What you really mean is that you want to stalk
Meghan up close and personal." Diego crossed his
arms, straining the fabric of the suit across his powerful shoulders.

"It's not a good idea, Blake," Ryder added, his tone
a trifle more friendly, but tinged with concern.

"Look, I know the little chit probably wants nothing
to do with me—"

"'Probably' being a major understatement," Ryder said with a chuckle. Then he grew more serious and continued. "If I recall correctly, she spent the first year of her undead life trying to rip your throat out."

"Or put a stake through your heart," Diego added.

It was hard to argue with them when they were right, Blake thought. "Things have changed since then."

"That's right, amigo. Things changed when you betrayed me to the man who killed Esperanza." Diego rose from the desk and came to stand nose to nose with him, his posture more challenging than it had been before. "You do remember that you nearly cost us all our lives during that little escapade."

Meeting Diego's gaze, he noted the telltale blossoming of neon green in his eyes that said the other vampire was battling to rein in his anger. Blake had no desire for Diego to lose that control. He was no match physically for Diego—or even Ryder, for that matter. But that didn't mean he would give up so easily or tuck his tail in like a whipped dog.

Rising on tiptoe until he nearly bumped noses with Diego, he said, "I saved your life and the little chit's."

Turning to Ryder, he pointed to him and said, "And I've helped you and yours out of more than one scrape."

Ryder surged from his seat, all earlier traces of friendliness gone, and came to stand beside Diego. "Which makes you an Eagle Scout all of a sudden?"

"All I want is a job."

"And a chance to see Meghan every day," Diego pressed.

True, not that he would admit it. "I won't bother her."

"Why do I find that so hard to believe?" Ryder said, before plopping back down in his chair.

"Maybe because in the same circumstances, you wouldn't leave her alone, either," Blake said, earning a chuckle from Ryder, who also acknowledged the statement with a nod. He pressed on, "Look, mates. I've had your backs and it seems to me you could use a few more friends to watch out for you, considering what happened the other night."

With a surge of speed and power, Diego had him by the throat, his feet dangling off the ground. "What do you know about that?"

"Just what I saw from the alley afterward, but there's all kinds of rumors floating around about what happened to those two vamps," he replied in a choked voice, all he could muster thanks to the force of Diego's grip on his throat.

Diego tossed him away and leaned on the edge of the desk.

Ryder faced him and in a calm voice asked, "What kinds of rumors?"

"Suicide pact. Murder. Humans wanting revenge. You name it." With a nonchalant shrug, Blake continued. "So what really happened?"

Diego and Ryder exchanged a look, as if considering whether or not to answer, but then Ryder admitted, "We don't know."

"You don't know? Isn't your little FBI friend—"

"Diana's out of this, Blake," Ryder said, the tone of his voice growing harsh.

"Lover's spat?" he tossed out without a thought, but was sorry he did so at Ryder's reaction.

Ryder bowed his head and took a deep breath. His body grew frighteningly still the way the air turned dead before a storm. Diego reached out, laid a hand on Ryder's shoulder and asked, "Amigo, are you okay?"

Ryder nodded and then faced Blake once again, his eyes glittering with the harsh bright color of the vampire. A low rumble filled Ryder's voice and a hint of fang became visible as he spoke. "You want us to think you're honorable? That you understand friendship and respect—"

"I'm sorry, Ryder. I didn't mean anything about Diana."

"We'll give you a job, Blake." Ryder rose slowly from the chair, his hands clenched at his sides. He stood before Blake, his troubled gaze boring into him and his face fully transformed to that of the vampire. Considering that Ryder kept the vampire in check more often than any of them, Blake knew it was not a good sign. Ryder made his demands. When he was finished he added, "And we'll expect you to respect us and do as you're told. Understood?"

Blake hated the feeling of unworthiness that both men brought out in him, but he was determined to get this job and prove them wrong. He wanted to show all of them he was reliable and trustworthy. He wanted to prove to Meghan that he wasn't the no-account she thought him to be.

"Understood, mate."

Chapter 5

The knife slipped, nipping the pad of her index finger.

Meghan cursed as a small droplet of blood welled before immortal healing took over and the wound quickly closed.

"You've been decidedly clumsy the past two weeks," Diego said from behind her, causing Meghan to jump. "And antsy."

"It's just the pace of things. There's been a lot of work lately." She didn't meet his gaze as she walked over to one of the sinks and carefully washed the knife and her hands. Not that such a little bit of blood would cause problems to any humans. She just didn't want the health department on her case if they paid a surprise visit.

Diego stepped in her path, blocking the way back to

her workstation. "Has he been bothering you?" he asked in tones low enough that only she could hear.

To emphasize the question, he cocked his head in the direction of the back of the kitchen, where Blake was hard at work removing trash-filled bags from the garbage cans. As he hefted the bag, his muscles flexed. The hairs on his arm were golden in the light cast by the backdoor bulb.

She remembered the feel of all that muscle and the soft hair quite well, but drove those distracting thoughts from her mind. She had been having too many of those kinds of thoughts lately.

"No, he hasn't. Just hello and goodbye," she replied, almost slightly irked by Blake's decided lack of attention.

A chuckle escaped Diego as she brushed past him and back to her workstation, her mentor following close behind her.

"I have to confess. I didn't expect him to last a day, much less two weeks."

As she resumed chopping the vegetables for a mirepoix, she nodded. "I didn't, either. Especially since you've given him every crap job in the book."

"Man's on a mission," Diego proclaimed, before he sauntered away, hands tucked into the pockets of a designer suit that screamed old money. *Way* old money, Meghan thought; there was still much of the wealthy Spanish lord in Diego's attitude and attire.

Much like there was still much of the punk in Blake.

She glanced in Blake's direction, but he had already headed out to the alley. She resumed her work, but her mind was half on Blake, and when he returned, she watched him work out of the corner of her eye.

He did every menial task he had been assigned. Even when the other vampire chef intentionally spilled a pan of sauce across Blake's apron and the floor, he minded himself and did just what he should, although inside of her, she perceived the heat of his anger thanks to the special sire bond that they shared.

She hated that bond, a constant reminder of what he had done. Of the life to which she had been condemned by a man who still managed to intrigue her on some level. A man who had, as Diego noted, gone on a mission to prove that he could be good.

So far, all he had managed to prove was that he was determined, she thought.

After cleaning up the spill, Blake returned to the back of the kitchen where he ripped off the apron, stuffed it into the laundry bin and escaped into the alley.

She wondered if he would return or if that had been the final straw, but after a quarter of an hour, he stormed back in and snagged a clean apron from a stack of fresh laundry in the pantry. Then he resumed work.

Meghan did the same, turning her attention to the osso bucco she was preparing and then the next. The pace was grueling; the restaurant had developed a regular human clientele as well as a vampire following that kept on coming back, even with the deadly incident two weeks earlier.

The disturbing event in the private dining room had created a buzz in their community for days, but beyond that nothing else had happened. No one had a clue as to why the two vampires had decided to feed to their deaths. No one even seemed bothered by it. Why should they when their worlds were regularly filled with blood and violence?

But it bothered *her*.

She could still recall the sight of their naked, bloody bodies. The awful slurping sound as they had fed to the death rang in her ears time and time again.

Forcing those troubling recollections away, she finished up the last of the orders and then started on a few dishes for the kitchen staff that would take care of cleaning and closing up for the night. It had become a ritual for them to share a meal and some conversation before completing their chores.

She was laying out the food on the table with the help of one of the busboys when she noticed Blake at the door to the alley. Another of the helpers—one of the dishwashers that Blake regularly assisted—had stopped Blake by the door.

"*Vamos, mano*. Stay. She makes a great spread and we could use your help to clean up," the man said in cajoling tones and placed a few friendly claps on Blake's back.

Blake hesitated, looking from her to the man and then back to her again, well aware that Diego had put her in charge of the kitchen and that if she wanted him to go, he would be dismissed.

"We could use the help tonight. There's a lot to clean," she heard herself saying. She wondered what had possessed her to issue the invite. By now she knew that anything involving Blake didn't end well, but in the past two weeks, she had sensed a difference in him. A determined difference that she now felt compelled to acknowledge.

He smiled at her invite, but it wasn't his cocky self-satisfied grin. Warmth filled his features and reached up to his ice-blue eyes, which glittered with relief. Inside of her, the connection between them flared to life once again and she experienced his emotion. She almost physically felt the loneliness slip from him as he walked to her workstation, grabbed some of the food she had waiting there and walked the plates over to the table.

She wiped her hands on her apron and returned to her station, and then Blake was immediately behind her, helping her pick up the rest of the food she had made and serve it to the crew waiting to finish up for the night. With the long day behind them and the late night still ahead, the food disappeared quickly amid snatches of conversation, sating the human's hunger.

As for herself, Blake and one other vampire, an older immortal who was their sommelier, they would have to quench their thirst for blood somewhere else. But the experience of sitting with the others, like she might have with her family back home, made her forget about the needs that the food wouldn't satisfy.

She wondered whether Blake felt the same and watched as he ate some of the roast chicken she had rubbed with thyme. He must have noticed her interest since he picked up his head from the plate and said, "Tasty, love. Better than me mum used to make."

His mum. She wondered what his mother had been like. What she might have thought about a son…

Who drained an innocent young woman until she was dead.

Who had only just gotten his first paying job in a couple hundred years.

"It's not what you think," he said, earning the curious glances of those seated around the table who had picked up on the vibes between the two of them.

"Is something up, Meghan?" the vampire sommelier asked, more attuned to their connection than the humans at the table.

"No, Bruce. Everything's just fine," she lied, but the meal had been ruined for her.

She remained quiet, as did Blake, while the others finished up their dinners, but she sensed he still had more to say to her. To his credit, he chose to keep silent as they cleared off the table and proceeded to finish up for the night.

Since Diego had entrusted her with the kitchen and because of all that he had done and continued to do for her, she always made a point of making sure everything was perfectly in order.

Satisfied, she told everyone to call it a night, and the few remaining people straggled out the door, Blake included, leaving her alone in the kitchen.

She took a few minutes to glance lovingly at the space—her space—pleased by the current state of her life, vampness notwithstanding. If there was one blemish on what might be her idea of Happy Ending it was her immortal status. She hadn't quite had that on her list of what to do before she died.

Of course, thanks to Blake she hadn't even hit item

number one on her list of what to do before she died. Normally anger would rise at him and at her situation, but tonight a mix of sadness and satisfaction came instead.

She had to acknowledge that if not for the whole undead thing, she would be back in the Midwest doing something other than what she wanted to be doing. If it hadn't been for Blake she wouldn't have trained to be a chef and she wouldn't have started to receive some notice of her skills from the local papers.

The door to the alley opened and Blake walked back in.

He stopped short as he saw her standing there. "Sorry, love. I didn't mean to intrude. I just needed to clean up before I left."

"Go right ahead."

As Blake walked to the sinks by the pantry, she did as well, pulling off her dirty apron and chef's jacket and tossing them into the laundry bin.

From the corner of his eye, Blake admired all her curves beneath the loose checkerboard chef's pants and the small black tank top she wore, reminiscent of what she had worn on the day they had first met. Desire rose and he soaped up and scrubbed his arms and then splashed bracing cold water over his face, hoping to quell the need she would not appreciate.

He was about to reach for a towel, but she was there, handing him one, challenging his control.

"Thanks."

As he toweled down, he noticed that she had slipped on a tight-fitting denim jacket and loosened her blond hair from the French braid she usually wore while she

cooked. She looked so young. A pang of guilt rose up—
thanks to him, she would always be that young.

Some women might have liked that, but not Meghan.
In the last four years he had come to know that much
about her—she feared little. He suspected that was why
after her initial reaction to being a vampire, she had
settled into immortal life.

With the damp towel, he motioned to the kitchen.
"This seems to suit you."

She crossed her arms and the action plumped up her
already generous breasts, dragging his gaze there.
Aware of his interest, she immediately changed her
pose and said, "It wasn't quite what I had planned for
my life, but I like it."

He tossed his dirty towel into the laundry bin. "What
had you planned on, love?"

"You mean what had my parents planned for me,"
she said. Before he could respond, she continued,
"Going back home after college. A nine-to-five job
somewhere with the requisite husband, house and a few
kids."

"Can you say 'boring much'?"

Blake hadn't expected that she would reply, but he
sensed her pique as he walked to the pantry, snagged
his black leather jacket from a hook on the wall and
slipped it on. When he turned, she was so close, he
nearly knocked her down.

He took a step back to give her some space, but she
advanced on him and poked him in the chest. "So I
suppose you had so much more planned for your life.
Tell me, Blake. What did you want from life?"

She probably wouldn't understand, but he gave it a
shot. With a long heartfelt sigh, he said, "Just to survive,
love. Just to survive."

Chapter 6

Blake's pockets hung heavy with the new potatoes he had pilfered from the abandoned farm up the road from the meager cottage he shared with his mother and five brothers and sisters. The smallish potatoes were all he had managed to round up that day to feed his family.

With the latest accident closing the coal mine, there had been too many young men like him in town, looking for either jobs or handouts. It was possibly harder now than it had been when his da had passed in an accident nearly a dozen years earlier. At least back then he had found a way to put food on the table.

A chill sweat erupted through his body at the memory of what he had done for the coins for that food. Of the old man's cold touch and the press of the papery dry lips against his. The slide of a gnarled hand into Blake's pants. Pants made loose from weeks of hunger.

He had survived those weeks by finding greens in the forest and boiling them with water to make a thin soup that somehow managed to sustain him. Whatever food he had been able to scrounge back then, or buy with the coins the old man gave him in exchange for the liberties he took, he had left for his family.

Luckily the mine had reopened several weeks after the accident that killed his da. With the mine short-handed due to the men that had been lost, Blake had secured a job going down into the pit in place of his da and labored there for over a dozen years. His young boy's body had become a man's, filled out with thick, hard muscle from the arduous labor and the food he had been finally able to put on the table.

But then another, much larger accident a month ago had forced the closure of the mine. The main shaft had been too badly damaged to repair, and the mine had nearly been tapped out anyway. With only one other mine left in town, many men had lost their livelihood, Blake included.

As he approached their small homestead, guilt assaulted him that all he had to show his family was a few handfuls of stolen potatoes. At least it would be enough to take the edge off their hunger, he thought.

To Blake's surprise, the smell of something rich and

earthy filled the room when he entered the cottage, making his stomach rumble and clench. He approached his mother as she stirred the pot at the stove, laid a hand on the small of her back as he had watched his da do for so many years. He leaned over her petite body and glanced at the thick, meat-filled stew simmering on the stove.

"Ma, that looks wonderful. Where did you—"

"Bryan caught a pair of rabbits in his snares this morning. Managed to find a patch of wild carrots as well," his mother replied. But her anxious glance told him she didn't quite believe Bryan's explanation for the sudden bounty.

Neither did he, judging from the thick diameter of the carrot pieces floating in the stew. No wild carrot he'd ever seen was that plump, not to mention that the wild rabbits had been scarce that spring, a by-product of the many snares that had been set to catch them.

"I'll talk to him, Ma," he said, and emptied his pockets onto the work-rough surface of the kitchen table.

His mother picked up one of the potatoes. "These will make a nice addition to the stew. You're a good son, Blake."

He took hold of her hand and squeezed it tenderly. "Don't worry about Bryan, Ma. I'll see to it that he stays out of trouble."

His mother shot him a grateful glance and a nod of approval. "I know you will, son."

With that, he walked out of the cottage and toward the ramshackle shed where they kept a few scraggly chickens that occasionally provided them some eggs, and sometimes a meal when a hen became barren. As he did so, he waved at two of his sisters as they tended the tiny plot of vegetables that somehow managed to grow in the rocky soil.

By the shed he ran into Bryan, who was tossing a handful of seed to the scrawny chickens within.

Crossing his arms, he asked, "Where's William and Edward?"

"Snuck off to try and catch some fish," Bryan answered, as he put down the nearly empty seed pail.

"Figured they were going to get as lucky as you and hook a few fat bass for us to eat?"

Bryan tensed, and when he looked, Blake's worst suspicions were confirmed.

"You went to ol' man Winchcombe, didn't you?"

His brother's head dropped down as he took a step to walk past him, but Blake snared his arm and roughly pulled him close.

"You're not to go back there, Bryan." For good measure, he jerked on his brother's arm to bring the point home.

Bryan ripped from his grasp. "What if I did go to him? What does it matter—"

"It matters, Bryan. You don't need to do this. I'll find a way—"

"Like you did last time, Blake? Winchcombe told me. He told me—"

Blake struck out, punching his brother in the mouth and sending him sprawling onto the ground, but that wasn't enough to stop Bryan. His brother sat up, bracing himself on arms too thin for a thirteen-year-old. Tears mingled with the blood from the cut on his lip as Bryan said, "He said he liked that I looked like you. That you had known how to please him."

Fear and rage filled his gut. Jabbing a finger at his brother, he warned, "Don't go back there again, Bryan."

He whirled on his heel, away from his brother and back in the direction of town, his long legs eating up ground quickly as he hurried along. Bryan *was* too much like him, both physically and mentally. His younger brother would go back to Winchcombe if he thought that would put food on their table, much like he himself had done a dozen years earlier.

Blake wasn't about to let that happen to Bryan again.

The Winchcombe mansion hadn't changed in over a dozen years.

Why should it have? Blake thought. The blood and sweat of hundreds of men down in the mines provided ol' man Winchcombe with the money he needed.

The hunger of the miners' young sons provided Winchcombe with the prurient pleasures he needed to satisfy his physical needs.

But no longer, Blake thought, as he pounded on the door of the mansion, rattling the thick wood against the door hinges with the force of his blows.

Winchcombe's retainer slowly opened the door, seemingly unfazed by Blake's angry summons.

Michael Dillon was a large forty-something man who had once worked belowground as a miner. Much like the house, Dillon didn't seem to have aged at all in the dozen years since Blake had last come to earn some coins. He was still a strapping man, thick across the chest, and at least a foot taller than Blake, making him an imposing figure as he stood in the doorway.

"Is he here, Dillon?"

"Didn't fancy seeing you here again," Dillon said, and crossed his arms, obstructing the entry with his immense size. But Blake wasn't about to be dissuaded. He viciously shoved past the larger man and stormed into the house, calling out Winchcombe's name as he did so.

"Come out, you old pervert!" he called out, as he walked into the front parlor. Dillon grabbed him from behind.

"You don't want to do this." Dillon jerked him back toward the front door, but Blake planted his feet. With the muscles developed in the mine, and some knowledge of fighting from an occasional Friday night brawl at the pub, he tossed the big man up and over himself.

Dillon landed with a thick thud and appeared stunned for a moment before slowly rising to his feet, his ham-hock-sized hands fisted at his side. "You're strong for a puny man."

"Tell Winchcombe—"

"Why don't you tell me yourself?" a cultured voice asked from above.

Winchcombe appeared on the second-floor landing. He took a step forward and seemed to float down the stairs, freezing Blake in his place.

Blake took a step forward, the need to please the older man almost ingrained in him from the many years he had answered Winchcombe's call. But he was no longer that scared and hungry young boy, and he didn't intend for his brother to take his place. He battled back the fear within him and fury rose in its place.

"Do not go near Bryan again," he warned, his voice low and filled not with threat, but promise. He clenched his hands at his sides, ready to fight both Dillon and Winchcombe if need be.

Dillon chuckled and was about to advance on him when Winchcombe laid a pale thin hand on the other man's broad chest. "I'll see to this myself."

Blake braced himself since the old man still seemed quite capable of causing injury. In fact, Winchcombe seemed not a day older than when Blake had first come to his door.

"Stay away from Bryan," he threatened yet again.

With a burst of speed, Winchcombe was suddenly standing in front of him, a broad smile across his face.

"Do you plan on taking his place, Blake?" Winchcombe caressed his jaw, and as much as Blake wanted to retreat from the embrace, his feet seemed rooted in place.

Winchcombe moved his hand downward to Blake's chest, where he ran it across the lean, corded muscle there. The smile on the old man's face tightened with seeming displeasure.

"You're no longer a fine young lad, but you'll do," Winchcombe said. He grabbed Blake's shoulder, imprisoning him in a surprisingly strong grip. His long, bony fingers dug painfully into Blake's shoulder.

Then Winchcombe slowly transformed before Blake's eyes, stunning Blake into nonaction. Winchcombe's rheumy brown eyes brightened, becoming a startling shade of glowing green-blue unlike anything he had ever seen before. When the smile on his face broadened, Blake saw his teeth turn to fangs, which extended beyond the old man's lower lip.

His knees weakened at the sight, but Blake forced himself upright. "You can't scare me, ol' man," he said, grabbing the man's wrist and trying to break the nearly intractable grip Winchcombe had on his shoulder. He noticed then how thin the other man's wrist was. How cold and dry the skin felt beneath his fingers.

Winchcombe laughed, and an odd growl tinged his mirth.

"I like spirit in a man, Blake. So much so that I think I'll keep you around for a while."

Before Blake could protest, Winchcombe had him in a powerful embrace, but Blake rocked from side to side, trying to free himself. As he glanced up at the demon the old man had become, he said, "You'll never get my spirit, ol' man."

Winchcombe roared with laughter and then bit down on Blake's neck even as he continued his defiant struggles.

Pain erupted through Blake's skull, followed by need so great that he soon found himself clutching the old man close, welcoming his virulent embrace. The pain slowly fled, but the desire remained, only it wasn't human desire.

This need was bathed in violence, filled with a fury unlike any he had ever experienced in his life. It called to him for fulfillment. It called to him for vengeance. The need that grew was so strong that Blake soon found himself able to deflect whatever power the old man had on him.

Yanking Winchcombe away from his neck, he held the old man at arm's length, emboldened by whatever was growing within him, taking hold of him body and soul. Strong and uncontrollable, it demanded satisfaction.

Winchcombe hung from his grasp, an astonished look on his face as blood dripped from his fangs.

His blood.

At the sight heat coalesced in Blake's center and suddenly erupted throughout his body, staggering him with its force. He battled back the sensation, but it struck him again until the heat fully enveloped him and everything around him grew brighter and more vibrant.

Beneath his fingers was the papery feel of Winchcombe's cold skin and the fragility of his throat as he held him and raised him high above the floor. He reveled in the sight of the old man dangling weakly from his hand and Dillon backing away from them, as if sensing that control had turned. Fear filled the big man's face as he beheld what was happening before his eyes.

Blake breathed in deeply and the smell of the blood on the old man's breath saturated the air.

His blood, he thought again. His blood and that of his father and brother and dozens of other men. Blood that would continue to be shed unless…

He knew what was needed next and with that realization, his own fangs erupted from his mouth.

Winchcombe shivered in his grasp as he brought him close and bared his neck. He begged and pleaded much as Blake had done years earlier. Cried out loud with fear much as Blake had when Winchcombe had satisfied himself on his young boy's body.

Now he would be satisfied.

As he brought his mouth to the old thin skin beneath which there was a barely perceptible pulse, the old man implored him once more for mercy.

Blake just smiled and said, "You will never lay a hand on my family again."

Chapter 7

"Blake…" Meghan cradled his face, pulling him back into the now, but he reared away at her touch, feeling dirty from the memories. Feeling unworthy and angry.

"I don't want your pity."

She snatched her hand back and tension crept into the lines of her body. Narrowing her eyes, she examined him sharply, her gaze now filled with hostility at his rebuff. It beat the sympathy he had seen there just moments before. He needed no one's sympathy to lift his shame.

"What do you want, Blake?"

To make amends, he thought. Since the day he had sired her he had known that he had to make it up to her, but at first her rage at him had been so great that none of his actions had reached her. When they had all been taken captive two years ago by a mad scientist, he had protected her even at the risk of his own life. That had defused her anger somewhat, but he had known that it wouldn't be enough to put things right between them.

As he took note of the tight lines of her body and the disapproval stamped on her face, for the first time it occurred to him that he might not ever be able to square things between them.

"What do you want?" she pressed again, but he wasn't ready to answer her. Not when he was so unsure of the reception his confession would receive.

"It's late. I'll see you home," he said. As he turned and walked out into the night, he thought he caught sight of something at the far end of the service alley.

"Did you see that?" he asked, as Meghan walked out beside him.

As she peered over the edge of the metal railing, he noticed a flash of something large and white-haired hopping away from the Dumpsters.

"Well, did you?" he repeated, but Meghan shook her head.

"I didn't see a thing."

Blake bounded down the steps and hurried to the end of the alley. He stopped short at the sight of the feet poking out from between two of the smaller garbage cans. Meghan bumped him from behind, caught unaware by his abrupt stop. As she saw the feet, she mumbled a curse beneath her breath.

"Stay here," he ordered.

But she immediately countered with, "Where you go, I go."

"How I wish that were true, love," he mumbled, too low for her to hear before hesitantly edging to the garbage cans and shifting them aside to fully reveal the body lying on the ground.

"Sweet Jesus," he said, peering down at the remains of the male vampire. His throat had been ripped out so savagely, Blake could see the vertebrae of his neck, gleaming a sickly pink white in the light of the moon.

"Not again," Meghan whispered, and covered her mouth with her hand.

Blake shot a look at her. "Seen this before, have you?" He bent closer to inspect the body, but as he did so, the smell of the blood pulled at his demon to come out and feed.

He heard a growl from behind him and looked up. Meghan was also transforming.

"Control it, love. There's nothing here for us tonight," he said, calling back his own demon. Judging from the lack of blood on the ground beside the corpse, this vampire had been drained dry.

"We need to get Ryder and Diego," she said as she raced back toward the restaurant.

"That's right. Call in the cavalry, 'cause there's no hero here," he muttered to no one. Then he rose and searched out the area around the garbage cans.

The slightest scent, like some kind of spice, teased his nose as he walked away from the garbage cans and toward where the alley opened onto the street. At that opening, he sniffed deeply, smelling the scent again, but he couldn't recognize the aroma.

Peering from one end of the street to the other, he

searched for anything out of the ordinary or the source of that aroma, but there was nothing in sight. Whatever had savaged the dead vampire was obviously long gone.

He headed back toward the restaurant, sparing but a glance at the body as he passed.

Whatever had done this killing had been one major nasty, he decided.

"So you say you saw—"

"Something big and white-haired hopping away," Blake finished. "Hippity hop, like the Easter Bunny."

Diego glared at him and then glanced at Meghan.

She shrugged. "I didn't see it."

"Did you hear or feel anything out of the ordinary?" Ryder asked, laying a hand on her shoulder in order to comfort her.

Meghan hadn't been able to forget the feeling from the night the two vampires had killed each other. That preternatural pulse that had beat against her vampire senses had indelibly registered in her brain. She hadn't felt anything like that energy until they had been right on top of the body. Then there had been the remnant of…evil. Slimy, like an oil slick against a pristine shore.

"I felt…something wicked, but not supernatural wicked, I don't think. Mortal malevolence maybe, but that doesn't make sense, does it? This was a vampire attack, right?"

Ryder dropped his hand from her shoulder, paced back and forth for a moment before facing Blake. "Neither of you fed from this vampire?"

"Not a drop left in the poor sod."

Diego shook his head. It was clear he had been ripped from either rest or something more pleasurable. His shirt was wrinkled and didn't quite match the pants he wore. Diego was always sartorially splendid, and Meghan suspected that he and his lover, Ramona, had been otherwise engaged when she had called him.

"Diego?" she prompted now, growing concerned that neither of the older vampires nor Blake seemed to have a clue as to what had happened to the dead vampire in the alley.

Blake clearly sensed her upset. He had taken no action to calm her, sensing she might rebuff any overture he made. He had been standing across the way from her, sandwiched between the two other men, almost as if they wanted to keep him from her. He finally stepped from between them and came to her side. Touching her forearm tentatively, he said, "Don't worry, love. We'll figure out what nasty did this."

Meghan thought about the rumors that another, stronger demon had been responsible for causing the earlier deaths. "Could it have been the same demon that made those two vamps feed to death?" she asked.

"Unlikely," he said, and Ryder and Diego echoed those sentiments.

"This killing is distinct, Meghan," Diego offered.

Ryder jumped in with "Different M.O."

Blake chuckled. "Little woman is rubbing off on you, Ryder. Maybe you could get her to give us some FBI assistance."

Hesitation crept into Ryder's features and his body

grew taut with irritation. Meghan wondered at his anger, but then Blake quickly added, "No joke, Ryder. Diana has the kind of experience we need around here."

Diego surged forward and got right into Blake's face. "There is no 'we' around here. It's us and you."

"Right. Sorry, mate. Forgot I'm just the hired help, but thanks for setting me straight. Seeing that you don't need me anymore…" He shot her a quick, pained look before sauntering off with a cocky bounce in his step, but she recognized he was forcing it for the benefit of the two older vampires.

As he neared the door, he tossed out over his shoulder, "I'm feeling a might peckish. I'm going to go grab a bite somewhere that understands our kind."

With that he surged out the door and was gone from sight even before the door could close behind him.

Meghan advanced on Diego as soon as Blake had vanished into the night. She didn't much care for Blake, but she also didn't like to see anyone abused. "That was mean."

He arched one tawny brow. "Mean? He's lucky I didn't rip his throat out when—"

"He gave up Esperanza to that scientist creep? You seem to forget that *I* was the one who gave that creep the info about your lair and that *Blake* was the one who helped save us."

Shoving her hands onto her hips, she pivoted to face Ryder. "And what's so crazy about his suggestion that Diana help us? She is Little Miss Save the World, isn't she?"

Ryder's stance grew even more rigid. Nearly every

muscle in his body tightened and from the slight bleed of neon vamp color into his eyes, she realized he was royally pissed off. With a low growl in his voice from the emerging vampire, he said, "Diana is… She doesn't need the pressure of this right now."

Did he think that she couldn't physically handle the strain? Meghan thought.

Facing the two men, arms still akimbo, she asked, "So we've got three dead vampires and an Evil Energizer Bunny running around, according to Blake. What do you suppose we should do about that?"

Diego quickly answered, "Ryder and I will consider what we should do next."

She was being dismissed. It didn't sit any better with her than it had with Blake. "I understand, Diego. It's you and then it's just me."

She didn't wait for his reply. She was a mite peckish too, she thought with a chuckle, and sped out the door into the night.

Chapter 8

Normally Meghan would feed once she got back to the posh Upper West Side apartment Diego had loaned her after he had moved to his lover's downtown digs. While under his protection in her early vampire years, Meghan had lived in one of his guest rooms, but with his absence, he had given her full run of the place and was generous enough to still occasionally stock the fridge there with a fresh supply of blood bags.

She had no desire to feed alone tonight.

The sense of satisfaction she had felt in the kitchen earlier had fled, giving rise to the sadness that had lurked there as well.

Sadness about the undead state of her life and the loneliness that came with it. Vampires didn't normally form many close relationships. She was lucky to have fallen in with those who did, although even then the friendships were inevitably tinged with power struggles. It was just a vampire's way.

Much like it was a vampire's way to hunt and feed.

She didn't much care for it. Hated it, in fact. So instead she chose to visit the Blood Bank for a nip of something fresher, as she suspected Blake had done.

As she flashed some fang to the bouncer at the door and strolled into the club, she realized that little had changed in the years since her last visit. She then realized Blake was sitting at the same spot where she had first seen him: at the end of the bar, his blond hair a glaring anomaly amongst the darkness in the club. It dragged up painful memories and anger, but she forced down those emotions.

She had been angry for so long. Maybe far too long, she considered, feeling the weight of loneliness pressing down on her. She sensed that if only for a moment, the man sitting at the end of the bar could bring a smile.

She approached where he sat, shuffling an empty glass from hand to hand, much as he had been doing almost four years earlier when he had first caught her eye.

With barely a glance in her direction, he mumbled, "Slumming it, princess?"

"I'm sorry about what happened before." She plopped herself down on the empty bar stool beside him.

"No reason for you to apologize. You didn't do anything." He picked up his hand and motioned for the bartender, who glared at him until Blake reached into his pocket and tossed some cash on the counter.

Some things never change, she thought, but then quickly regretted the thought. Blake had changed, or at least he was trying to, as much as she didn't want to acknowledge that. It would be easier to keep on hating him if she didn't.

"Maybe not doing anything is enough to apologize for," she said as she grabbed Blake's money and handed it back to him. Reaching into the pocket of the denim jacket she wore, she pulled out some cash and laid a twenty on the bar. "My treat."

"There's no treat in drinking alone," he challenged, and as the bartender came over, he took the liberty of ordering. "Two O negs. Freshest that you have."

Meghan didn't particularly like satisfying her hunger in public, but the last thing she wanted was to go into one of the back rooms to feed. She was sure she couldn't handle that. Even returning to the club had been difficult.

As they waited for the bartender, Blake swiveled toward her on his bar stool. "If there's anywhere we might get information on the roadkill we found earlier tonight, this is the place."

"So it wasn't just 'cause you were peckish," she teased.

When the bartender brought over the tumblers filled with warm blood, Blake picked up his glass and took a sip, showing a reserve she couldn't muster. She was just too hungry. With a large gulp, she sucked down a good amount of the blood and immediately experienced the rush of its power through her body.

"Easy, love. This is heady stuff. You don't want to lose control," Blake said in low tones intended for only her ears.

Meghan sucked in a breath and mustered the composure necessary to suppress the demon that wanted to escape now that she'd had a taste of the blood.

Blake smiled and nodded his approval. He could feel her demon calling to his, rousing his desire to share their demons' passion. Shoving away his own vampire, he motioned to a spot across the way where Foley was chatting with a stranger in a too-familiar way. As the stranger—an extremely attractive Asian man—passed a hand across Foley's face in a gesture more common to lovers, he said, "Seems like our Foley is playing both sides of the field."

Meghan tracked his gaze. Her eyebrows narrowed as she considered the two men and their intimate pose. "Foley never set off my gaydar."

"Mine either, which makes me wonder who that is."

He drained his glass and slammed it on the counter. Then he jumped off the bar stool and quickly strode across the length of the room, weaving his way through those on the dance floor, Meghan close behind him. When he neared the two men, he sensed the thrum of undead power, but it was an unfamiliar kind of energy. Off somehow. Threatening just by virtue of its oddity.

Instead of proceeding closer, he stopped, quickly turned and slipped his arm around Meghan's waist, surprising her although she seemed to know better than to make a scene. He urged her into a slow dance, one hand braced against the small of her back.

"What are you doing?" she hissed in his ear, her body tight against his until he relaxed his hold and she put a little distance between them.

"There's something not right about Foley's Asian friend," he said, shifting to get a better view as they danced.

"I don't feel—"

"Close your eyes and release your vampire, but only a little," he urged and surprisingly, she did as he asked.

She closed her eyes and the power of her vampire grew, enveloping him in its force due to their proximity. As the spill of her energy intensified, he eased her closer until their bodies were pressed together and their energies merged thanks to his blood flowing in her veins.

At the press of his body against hers, Meghan moaned and opened her eyes. The deep emerald color had disappeared, and they now glowed with the brilliant brightness of the vampire.

"Blake, I don't want this," she protested, a rumble from low in her throat tightening his body with desire.

"Do you think I want to feel this way about someone who hates me?" he said, but despite his words, he pressed one hand against the small of her back. Laying the side of his face on hers, he cradled her head, his movements as gentle as he could make them, aware that her feelings for him were always on the edge of anger and a wrong move could doom the moment.

With the music still slow and beating, with a bass sound that vibrated through their bodies, he invited her into the dance, shifting his feet. His hips joined to hers, urging her to move in time. He took care in the way his hands slowly relaxed their hold and the way a stroke against her back became a caress against the damp skin where her shirt had ridden upward.

The rumble came again from deep within her, and she bent her head to his neck. He felt the graze of her teeth there, and a ripple of longing shot through his body before she slowly pulled away.

"This is crazy," she said, clearly battling her own need.

"Is it, love? Don't you remember how good it was?"

"Was it? Hard to remember since I ended up dead," she said, and ripped from his arms. She raced off before he could stop her, but he knew one thing even as she did so.

She remembered just how good and bad it had been.

Chapter 9

Meghan hadn't known what to expect of Blake the morning after their brief encounter at the Blood Bank. A part of her wanted to lash out at him and vent her rage and frustration so that she could drive from her mind just how good it had felt to be in his arms. How she had wanted so much more but had also wanted to take a bite out of him as payback. The desire only served to remind her that after nearly four years, her emotions about Blake were as confused as they ever had been.

Luckily, Blake chose to keep his distance, although she was certain that he wasn't ignoring her. With every move she made in the kitchen she sensed his attention on her even as he completed the assortment of tasks he had been given that night. An assortment of crap tasks that indicated Diego and Ryder were still not pleased with him.

The day passed slowly, filled as it was with confusion about Blake but also with concern about what had been happening at Otro Mundo lately. Three dead vamps in just over two weeks was not a good thing. As she occasionally connected with one of the other vampires working in the kitchen, she sensed their discomfort, as well. Word was getting around about the incidents, and she worried how that was going to affect the restaurant.

Diego had also been preoccupied that afternoon, but not just about the business. After catching a series of looks between her and Blake, he had come over to warn her against him. Although she appreciated Diego's protection and concern, whatever happened between her and Blake was none of his business.

The drag of emotion during the course of the long day tired her, making her grateful for the last seating of the night. She had finished her final order and was getting ready to fix the food for the closing staff when Diego entered the kitchen, an even more troubled look on his face.

"Is something wrong?" she asked, as he approached her.

"There's a patron out front who would like to compliment you on his meal."

Never a bad thing in the cooking world, which didn't quite mesh with Diego's appearance. "Why so glum, then? Unless of course he's the owner of a competing restaurant and wants to spirit me away."

Diego laughed as she had intended, but then grew serious once again. "I don't think he is, but what he is… He's undead, although I've never met any of his kind before."

"His kind?" She wiped her hands on her soiled apron before removing it to reveal the pristine white chef's jacket beneath. It was important to make a good appearance before the public—even the undead ones.

"A Chinese vampire—a kiang-shi," he explained, even as he was placing a hand at the small of her back and walking with her out to the main floor of the restaurant. As she entered, she experienced the slimy odd energy from the night before as well as a very strong pulse of immortal power.

Looking toward the source of that energy, she noticed Stacia at one of the tables beside a human who, judging from her engaging posture, was going to be Stacia's dessert. As their gazes collided, the vampire elder smiled at her, lips full and painted a deep red that just made her pale skin even more pronounced. As was her bent, Stacia was dressed from head to toe in form-fitting black, which just accentuated the pallor of her skin and the lethal curves of her body.

Meghan had met the vampire elder two years ago, but didn't much care for her. Stacia seemed to take whatever she wanted whenever she wanted—including an assortment of men.

Rumor had it that Blake had recently been added to her list of conquests—a rumor Meghan tried avoiding, lest she experience any more jealousy about a vampire whom she regularly wished was dead.

The meal was excellent came into her head, and she

acknowledged Stacia's unspoken compliment with a nod as she continued walking.

Diego guided her toward a table at the opposite side of the restaurant. The force of the odd power grew more potent as they neared a table of four, one of whom she recognized as the Asian man from the night before. He was surrounded by a trio of women, each one as different as the next.

A statuesque African-American woman sat beside a petite and doll-like blonde. They leaned toward one another, exchanged a comment and laughed in unison with a disturbing trill. To the other side of the handsome Asian was an Asian woman, beautiful but with a distant expression on her face that left her looking cold. Almost vacant.

His harem, she thought, but forced a smile to her face as he met her gaze.

He was stunning, she would give him that. The planes of his face were broad, but it served to highlight his intense, brown, almond-shaped eyes and the fullness of his lips. When he rose as she approached, she sucked in a breath at the height and strength of him. He was easily six foot two or three, with thick, powerful shoulders and lean hips. The elegant silk suit he wore emphasized his physique, and the almond color of his shirt warmed the color of his skin to a luscious vanilla-cream hue. Dark, thick hair was raked ruthlessly back from that exotic face.

He smiled sexily as he caught her appraisal and held out his hand. His long, almost feminine fingers seemed to caress the air before she took his hand. Immediately upon contact with his skin she sensed the rush of power into her body.

She quickly jerked her hand away, fearing its spread. It had been dark power, nasty and filled with vileness. Not to mention that his hand had been cold and slightly oily. As she rubbed at her hand, a whiff of a cloying scent rose up. Cardamom? she thought. But then the scent disappeared, leaving her to wonder if she had only imagined it.

But she hadn't imagined the darkness of the power that his beautiful face and form couldn't disguise.

The smile on his face tightened with displeasure at her actions, but his features revealed nothing else as he said, "I just wanted to offer my compliments on such an extraordinary repast."

"Thank you." Normally she would have said that she hoped they would return again for another meal, but she couldn't bring the lie to her lips. His one touch had her hoping she would never lay eyes on him again.

"Not much for words, are you? I'm Sun Tze Lee," he said, and returned to his seat, where the two closest women immediately draped themselves on him while the tall black beauty blasted a hostile glare in her direction, as if affronted on Mr. Lee's behalf.

"It was our pleasure to serve you, Mr. Lee. I hope you'll come again," Diego offered. At the slight press of his hand at her back, Meghan immediately chimed in with the most truthful statement she could muster:

"I'm glad you enjoyed the meal."

Lee nodded and fixed his gaze on the neck of the woman closest to him before he turned his attention to her. "I suspect I'll enjoy dessert even more."

Disgusting, she thought as she whirled and walked away, but as she did so, she caught sight of Blake busing one of the nearby tables. The features of his face were tight with disapproval. For her or for Mr. Lee? she wondered, but then continued onward to the kitchen, determined to finish the night and go home.

Committed as she was to that goal, she made the meals for the staff quickly and hurried them along until, like the night before, only she and Blake remained. She was about to protest his presence, only he said, "I didn't right much like the way he looked at you. Like you were going to be the end to the meal. Figured you could use an escort home."

She didn't argue. She didn't much like Lee's comment nor the residue his power had left behind. No matter how many times she had washed her hands, she still felt as if something of him remained, and every now and then, that whiff of cardamom would rise up, as if to remind her of their brief encounter.

Normally she would grab a subway uptown. If she was running very late, she would try to snag a cab. She felt like neither tonight, and Blake must have sensed it.

"Need to flex the demon, do you?"

She didn't know why she needed to release the vampire, but she did. Maybe the demon inside of her realized that freeing her own power might obliterate the residue of Lee's touch.

"Do you mind?" she asked.

He grinned, a sexy grin that lit up his blue eyes with pleasure and dragged out the dimple that caused a flip-flop within her chest. "Lead the way, luv."

She morphed, releasing the vampire and its power. The heat of it spread through every part of her body, bringing the night to life. Only a sliver of a moon lit the night sky, but with her vamp eyesight, everything became brighter and more alive. A footstep behind her sounded like a gunshot and as she whirled, she realized that it was just Blake, coming to stand at her back, waiting for her to take off.

She did, accelerating to the speed that made them nearly impervious to human eyes. She could understand the myths about vampires seeming to fly as she and Blake leaped from building to building, blurs against the moonlight. The damp chill of the early spring night felt stronger as their speed rushed air against their bodies.

When they reached Fifty-ninth Street, she chose to shift downward to the ground and head through the park.

As they zipped past one hansom cab waiting for a last late fare, the horse whinnied with disapproval at their presence, but the driver remained unaware of them. They rushed into a stand of trees by the low stone wall surrounding the park.

Feeling the need to brush away Lee's lingering presence and his scent, she slalomed through the pines and other trees in their path, letting their soft branches brush her as she passed. Blake joined in, slipping in front and beside her, turning it into a daring game of follow-the-leader.

By the time she reached the upper Sixties and the West Side, she was breathless from the sheer joy of the superpowered antics that had driven away the miasma of Lee's touch. Stopping at the edge of the park, she paused to catch her breath. As Blake came up behind her and put his arms around her, she laughed, feeling a lightness of spirit that she hadn't in a long time.

"That was fun," he said.

"Yes, it was. Just what I needed to forget Mr. Ol' Kiang-shi."

Blake turned her to face him. "Kiang-shi? That was his name?"

She shook her head. "Lee's his name. Kiang-shi is what he is—a Chinese vampire."

"That explains the weirdness from the other night," he said. She glanced down at his hands on her waist, and he released her, although clearly reluctantly.

She shivered. "What we felt at the Blood Bank is nothing like what I experienced tonight."

"That bad, was it?" he asked.

She nodded and wrapped her arms around herself. "Mad odd. Dark, like if you stayed close for too long it would swallow you up."

With another shudder, she motioned to the apartment building across the way. "Time I went in. Thanks for walking me home."

He made a move toward her, as if for a good-night kiss, and she took a step toward him as well, but then thought better of it and pulled back as he did also. Suddenly awkward, shoved his hands into his pockets, obviously uncertain of what to do.

"Anytime," he finally said when too much time passed. They both just stood there, uncertain of the next step in their dance. Inclining his head in the direction of her building, he finished with, "I'll just stay here until I know that you're safely inside."

She nodded and walked to the sidewalk, her pace mortal and easygoing. As she neared the building, the doorman opened the door, but something made her stop and look back across the street.

Blake was still standing there as he had promised, and that made her feel…safe. An odd thing to be feeling about the man who had stolen her life.

Driving away that perplexing emotion, she waved goodbye.

Blake waved back and shot her an easy grin, although he was feeling anything but.

He didn't like what Meghan had had to say about the Asian vamp, nor what she had felt.

The fact that he had never met a kiang-shi was the likely reason he didn't feel quite right about the vampire. But he also had to admit to himself that he hadn't liked the way Lee had been touching Foley last night. Not that he was a homophobe, but he knew fear when he saw it. He'd experienced it often enough himself as a young boy when Winchcombe had used him. He had seen the same kind of fear in Foley's eyes, and Foley wasn't easily intimidated.

Then there had been the way the Asian vampire had been looking at Meghan tonight—as if she was going to be the fortune cookie to finish his meal.

He had gotten that odd pulse of undead energy from Lee last night and again tonight, but his gut warned him that Lee had been masking his power. That the Asian vampire had strength he wasn't revealing. Possibly even more strength than one of their elders, like Stacia.

Stacia. She had been at the restaurant tonight. With her nearly two thousand years of age, he was certain she would know something about the Asian immortal. He was also fairly sure that she would come to him if he asked nicely.

Unlike Meghan, who might not come even if he begged.

With one last glance at the apartment building, he sped off, heading downtown and back to the East Side. As he raced along, he focused on the fragment of Stacia's power nestled within him. You didn't share time and blood with an elder and not have a piece of them left in you.

The focus on that power grew until she finally connected with him, an exasperated tone coloring her response.

What do you want, Blake?

Annoying an elder was never a good thing, but Blake pressed on, channeling a part of his vampire power into reaching back out to her.

I need a favor.

Husky laughter was her response, and it awakened desire in him so strong that it made him lose his concentration midleap. He almost didn't make it to the next rooftop and had to grab the ledge of the building to keep from falling to the ground below. Just a few stories and a big ouch for a vampire, nothing life-threatening.

He closed his eyes and focused on Stacia. The desire returned, stronger than before, and he knew then what she would want in payment for the favor he was requesting.

Was he willing to pay the price to keep Meghan safe?

He knew the answer was a resounding yes. He would do whatever he could to protect Meghan. To make things right with her.

I'll be waiting for you, the elder said. Blake released the bond and devoted his energy and attention to the race home.

He knew Stacia would be at his apartment when he arrived so that he could fulfill his part of the bargain.

Chapter 10

Blake landed on the rooftop of his building, which was directly across from Gramercy Park. In the early spring night, the sliver of moon illuminated the branches of the trees with their burgeoning growth of bright green buds. The sight brought a sense of joy to him. Chalk it up to rebirth, new life and all that other spring claptrap that brought the promise of untold possibilities.

Possibilities like those he had imagined growing between him and Meghan as they had awkwardly stood on the curb outside her building.

He glanced around the rooftop to the wrought-iron chairs and table, as well as the assorted pots for plants. They were empty now, but in another week or so he intended to plant some flowers and vegetables, much as his mother might have back in Wales. The feel of the soil in his hands grounded him, reminding him of what he had once been. Almost mocking him with the reminder that there was still a touch of humanity left within him despite his having embraced his vampire self. That humanity lately hungered for more than his vampire existence provided despite all his protestations to the contrary.

He headed to the French doors at the far end of the patio. He had picked up the doors from a nearby demolition site and installed them to give him access to the roof.

Once he was inside, he placed his hands on his hips and looked all around, sensing her presence. He searched for her amidst the collection of castoffs in his cozy rooftop room.

Thick oriental rugs covered the floor. They had been in better shape years earlier, but he kept them ruthlessly clean and their former quality still showed through in the intricate patterns and colors that time hadn't faded all that much. Rich mahogany furniture was scattered about, from the small tables carefully placed here and there, which held an assortment of candles, to the crowning glory of the room—a large four-poster bed piled high with a sumptuous collection of linens.

In the midst of those linens, completely naked, was Stacia.

Her skin was creamy white against the maroon and gold of the bed linens, her nearly seal-black hair and dark eyes a sharp contrast to the paleness of her body.

As her gaze settled on him, he knew exactly what she wanted and with each step he took, he removed a piece of clothing.

By the time he climbed into bed beside her, he was naked and painfully erect.

He lay on his side and propped his head up on one arm, placed his hand in the middle of her flat belly and ran it down her skin. With his index finger, he traced a circle around her navel and then flicked the gold ring there, bending close to her to say, "Do you want this first or can I get my favor?"

In response, she turned to him. The deep, coral-colored tips of her breasts brushed against his chest. Her flat stomach caressed his erection a second before she reached down with her hand and encircled him.

"What do you think?" she asked, and laid her lips against his collarbone. A moment later came the brush of her fangs, tantalizing and deadly if he should disfavor her.

He shivered, her elder's power creating a dizzying rush of passion through his body. Passion that wouldn't wait to be abated.

But it was passion without love. Without the life he had experienced with Meghan.

Meghan was all he could think about as he paid Stacia her due, and he hoped that the price would be worth the information he received.

He lay beside Stacia and stroked her body, calming her with his hands. She was still wired from their passion and feeding, but he had no desire for a repeat performance, and she must have realized it. It worried him for a moment that she would be angry with him, until he sensed the serene aura surrounding her and that she was well pleased with him…for the moment.

"You wish to push me from your bed so soon?" She laid her hand on his chest and ran her thumb across his nipple, attempting to awaken desire once again.

"Not so soon," he said, anxious not to annoy her before he got the information he needed to keep Meghan safe.

Stacia wasn't fooled by his actions, but she had obviously decided to play along with him. "You had a favor to ask of me."

He gazed into her eyes, almond-shaped and dark like Lee's but glittering with life and desire.

"Know anything about the kiang-shi?"

Her body tensed, but nothing in her gaze gave away any concern. "The kiang-shi are corpses condemned to live forever because of the evil they did during their mortal existence."

"Living corpses? How's that possible?" he asked, but then immediately laughed at himself. "Stupid question coming from a vampire, huh?"

Stacia shrugged, laid a hand on his shoulder and stroked the muscle there. "Vampires never really die if you think about it. At that moment when we are at death's door, the blood of our sire saves us, keeps us alive."

"But not the kiang-shi?"

"The kiang-shi die. No breath, no pulse, no living flesh. Before they're buried, they are reanimated by evil, either a spark that remains within them or the wrongful actions of someone else."

"So what could someone else do that would make a kiang-shi?" he asked.

"Refuse to bury them. Dishonor their name or body in some other fashion. Asian concepts of honor and face are quite extreme, much like a kiang-shi. All that evil…"

She shuddered, surprising him. There was little that could scare an elder, especially one as old and powerful as Stacia.

"So all that evil lingers after death. But if they're corpses—"

"Why don't they rot? Some use oils, herbs and certain spices to keep their flesh intact. Others feed on vampires like us and become hybrids." She settled her head on his chest and laid a hand on his waist in a relaxed way.

Feed on vampires like us.

Blake immediately thought of Foley and the dread on his face. He had no doubt Lee was feeding from the owner of the Blood Bank. Since Foley was normally a badass, it made him wonder just how much worse Lee could be to instill such terror in him.

He decided that he didn't want to find out—although if Lee made any kind of overture toward Meghan, he might not have a choice. Which made him wonder out loud, "Do you think you could take a kiang-shi?"

Stacia shifted away from him enough to be able to read his face. "Take as in—"

"Kick his undead immortal ass."

"If he's old and has fed from one of us, I'm not sure that trying to kick his ass would be such a good idea for a vampire of your age."

As she rose from the bed, he suspected she was right, but decided he wouldn't back away if it became necessary.

* * *

"There was a blond chef at Otro Mundo tonight. Do you know who she is?" Lee asked the other man, who was kneeling, head bowed low, nearly scraping the ground.

"If she was a vampire, her name is Meghan Thomas. She's under the protection of Diego and Ryder," Foley said, wiping his hands against his naked thighs, but never deviating from his subservient pose.

Lee could almost taste Foley's fear. Fear had an intoxicating odor. He had always been able to smell it in his opponents during battle. He had smelled it in himself a second before the thrust of the sword that had snuffed out his life.

He hadn't experienced any worry of his own in quite a long time. While some thought that good, living without fear meant there was nothing left to lose in life. That made for a long and boring existence.

Except for moments like this, when the terror of others brought a morsel of joy.

He undid the sash on the robe he wore, exposing his erection to the other vampire. Placing a hand beneath Foley's chin, he exerted gentle pressure to urge him upward and forward.

Foley understood what he wanted. But for a moment Lee saw a flicker of defiance in the other man's steel-gray eyes. A hint of spirit that he thought he had drummed out of Foley with over a century of punishment and enslavement.

"Do you challenge me?" Lee slowly roused his demon, made powerful by both the evil energy of the kiang-shi and the blood of the many vampires he had drained.

With an abrupt shake of his head, Foley closed his eyes and brought his mouth between Lee's legs. Hesitantly at first, he took the erection into his mouth, but then Lee grasped the back of Foley's skull and applied slightly stronger pressure. He forced the man's mouth down onto him, guided Foley in what he demanded.

Foley pleasured him until the need built within Lee, requiring greater satisfaction than just the caress of a skillful tongue and mouth. Foley must have felt the change in Lee for he fell back on his heels, attempting to get away, but Lee was quickly upon him, forcing him onto his knees.

Lee imprisoned Foley's hips in his strong grasp and drove into him without preliminaries. Without preparation or caring. The other vampire screamed and tried to buck him off, finally showing some spirit.

Lee liked spirit. It only increased his pleasure, he thought, riding Foley as he might a temperamental mare, trying to break her. He delighted in the push and shove of his hips against the other man's body until he was at the edge and needed just one last thing to take him to his release.

He grabbed hold of Foley's long, nearly white hair and jerked his head back, exposing the long line of his neck. With one last strong thrust that had the other vampire whimpering with pain, Lee sank his fangs deep into Foley's neck.

The blood from the other vampire surged through his body, reanimating the dying cells of the kiang-shi with the force of its life energy. He grew nearly light-headed from the rush, consuming Foley until he was dizzy. Only then did he withdraw from the other vampire, tossing him away as he might a piece of trash.

Foley collapsed on the ground, his body bloodied and bruised from the dual possession.

Lee watched as Foley curled into the fetal position, wrapping his arms around his legs, curling tight as if to protect himself.

Not that he could, Lee thought, but then his gaze locked with Foley's. The spirit was there, but surprisingly not subdued after his taking of the man. If anything the determination in Foley's gaze seemed to have grown stronger, reminding Lee that he couldn't underestimate the other vampire.

He would have to keep a close watch on Foley in the future, especially as he executed the next step in his little plan.

Although Foley didn't have a clue, Lee hadn't just come back to New York on a lark. Business had been down at the Blood Bank recently and he had wanted to find out for himself why that had been the case.

He had discovered the reason a few weeks ago—Otro Mundo, and its calling to those vampires who fancied themselves as still having some humanity. It disgusted him to think about those wannabes, so eager to deny their essential being and consort with the humans as if the mortals were more than just a handy meal.

Pity them, he thought. They were deluding themselves with such nonsense, and his current visit was intended to show them just how foolish they were being.

He had already set the first steps in his plan into motion. When the rest of the plan fell into place…

Pity the vampire who didn't understand the true nature of their kind.

Chapter 11

Meghan didn't want to admit that something had changed since the night of her game of follow-the-leader with Blake.

She didn't want to admit it, but she also couldn't muster the will to deny it.

Something had changed.

For the last few days she had once again watched as Blake dutifully worked, assisting anyone who needed a helping hand and earning the friendship of the kitchen staff, even the vampire chef who had originally gone out of his way to harass him.

He had kept his distance from her, however, respecting the wishes she had made known to him time and time again, except...

Something had changed.

Or maybe it had been happening all along and she had only allowed herself to experience it the other night.

She had reveled in the gifts the demon brought as they raced through the city and played in the park. She had forgotten for a moment all that she had lost from her mortal world and for once sampled joy in what she now possessed.

Much like she had experienced satisfaction as she surveyed her kitchen, standing there on the edge of the park with Blake, she had felt…

She shook her head as if arguing with herself, but as she did so, she caught a glimpse of him as he prepped a tray to bus tables. He had been recruited for that job when one of the busboys had failed to show up for work.

Promoted by the kitchen staff, a sure sign of their growing respect for him.

She hadn't objected and as he had met her gaze he nodded in acknowledgment.

That she hadn't objected confirmed that change had indeed occurred. It was a scary change because it exposed her heart, and if she took the next step and put aside her anger, she would be embracing her new life.

Her demon life.

She paused, the blade of her knife immobile against the shallots she had been chopping.

Glancing up once again, she took note of the other vampires in the kitchen. Vampires who had already accepted their fates and made new lives for themselves.

Vampires like Diego and Ryder…and Blake.

She searched for him but he was gone, probably out in the restaurant, doing his job.

A job he had taken to prove something to her.

She wondered whether that demanded something of her, and if it did, whether she was prepared to give it.

Days had gone by since the kiang-shi's visit and Blake's dalliance with Stacia. Both were still causing him a bit of discomfort.

The first because there was something about the Asian vampire that continued to rub him the wrong way. Besides the whole Foley thing, there was the way he had stared at Meghan during their meeting in the restaurant nights earlier. Lee's gaze had been hungry, but also filled with distaste, as if he was a man used to filet mignon and a hot dog had just been served to him.

Meghan might be your All-American cheerleader type, but she was anything but pedestrian, Blake thought. He snuck a peek at her as she busily chopped some shallots, her hands capably handling the knife then sheathing it at her side, like a gunfighter returning his weapon to the holster.

He imagined that she might skillfully use that knife on a certain part of his anatomy if she found out about his brief tryst with Stacia, but then again, such action would require jealousy. To be jealous, one had to care at least a whit and, sadly, he didn't believe that was the case.

Despite his attempts to prove himself a changed man, Meghan seemed reluctant to acknowledge it. Although she hadn't objected to his becoming a busboy for the night.

Such a job elevation probably wouldn't seem like much to most people, but it had meant a lot to him.

Before turning her, he had been a loner, not even

engaging in relationships with other vampires. Her new vampire existence and associations with the human wannabes had forced him to take part in their world time and time again. Each time he had tried to protect her or help them, he'd become a hanger-on to their crowd so that she might see who he really was.

And now he was at it again, but maybe he was finally making some headway. He was slowly becoming one of them, Blake thought, as he strode out of the kitchen with a serving tray for one of the tables.

It wasn't a bad gig, considering that since leaving Wales so long ago, he had drifted from one temporary job to another. When the jobs were over and money was scarce, he would take what he needed despite the shame that filled him at his thievery.

He knew his mother wouldn't have been proud of the man he had been for so long. A man without friends. Without honor. Without love.

Since meeting Meghan, he had been trying to change all that. To become the man he had once been. One who cared about the people in his life. Who understood right from wrong. Who knew he was loved.

Someday, he told himself as he worked.

With it being midweek, Otro Mundo wasn't all that busy. Just a few couples remained in the dining room, finishing up their meals.

Stacia was at one table with a handsome mortal man. As Blake approached she winked at him, and he shot her a quick smile before placing their coffees on the table along with the desserts he had grabbed back in the kitchen.

Finished with that task, he returned to the back to

pick up the items for the last table he had to serve. It was in one of the private dining rooms on the main level, where one vampire couple had arrived just in time for the final seating. Imagining what they planned to do after their meal, he suspected it might be a late night while the staff waited for the couple to finish.

Meghan had just plated the vampires' meals when he walked to her workstation. "Looks good," he said, as he placed the dishes onto a serving tray.

A tired smile swept across her lips, and she tucked back a wisp of hair that had escaped her French braid. "Thanks. I'm going to get to work on the meals for the staff. Craving anything tonight?"

He almost dropped the tray he had been putting up to his shoulder.

She was asking if he was craving anything? As if she cared?

Not wanting her to have to work so hard since she seemed drained tonight, he shrugged and said, "I'm a meat-and-potatoes kind of man. Anything simple will do."

She nodded and he went off to deliver the meals, his strides deliberate as he walked through the main dining room and to the hallway to the private rooms. The one door was closed and he rapped on the wood and waited for an invitation before entering.

The young vampire couple had clearly been engaged in naughtiness. Their clothes were disheveled and the barest whiff of blood greeted his senses when he neared them. Someone had taken a nip before the meal, he thought, as he laid the dishes down on the coffee table before the sofa where the two vampires reclined.

As he glanced at them, something else caught his eye besides the slight hint of blood on the otherwise pristine white collar of the male vampire's shirt. The young female vamp had a wild gleam in her eyes—a feral, intensely needy look that Blake didn't quite like. Even if he hadn't seen the blood on the male vamp's neck, he would have known that she had been the one doing the biting from that savage glimmer in her gaze.

He faced the young male vampire, a recently turned yuppie if he was any judge of age. "Mind the little chit, mate. She seems a bit too hungry for you to handle," he said, but the newbie vampire merely laughed, making Blake feel like a doddering old fool as he left the room.

Maybe he *was* doddering, he thought, recalling how in his youth he might have enjoyed a roughhouse tryst with an eager vampiress in her prime.

With a sniff of prideful indignation, he tucked the tray under his arm and returned to the kitchen, intending to help out Meghan and maybe walk her home again.

Maybe even take another step toward convincing her that he was changing for the better.

He had just finished laying out the last of the plates Meghan had prepared for the staff when he felt an odd vibration beating against his vampire senses.

A plate crashed to the floor a few feet away. Meghan had dropped one of the meals she had prepared. He realized she felt the sensation as well, given the pale greenish cast to her skin and the way her eyes widened with fear.

He rushed over and laid his hand on her arm. "Meghan, what's wrong?"

A second later Diego and Ryder came running into the kitchen.

"Who's left in the building?" Ryder asked, looking around, his gaze lingering on the vampires in the kitchen area.

Blake answered first. "Stacia, possibly. A young couple in a private room—"

Diego and Ryder tore out of the kitchen and Meghan raced after them. He joined in and realized that they were headed to the dining room he had left just moments earlier.

As they neared the door, the out-of-sync vibration intensified, growing so strong that it called forth the demon in each of them.

Ryder tossed open the door and they all spilled into the private room.

The willing vampiress from before had the male vampire pinned to the ground. She had torn open the yuppie vamp's throat and a regular spray of blood splattered against her face, but she seemed to not notice as she continued to feed noisily from his ravaged neck.

Ryder launched himself at her, dislodging her from the prone body of the vampire. She bit and clawed at him, and Diego had to join Ryder to keep a hold on the young hellcat.

"Bloody hell," Blake muttered, pulled off the small towel that Meghan always kept tucked into her apron strings and raced to the bleeding vampire.

As Blake applied pressure with the towel to staunch the flow of blood, he said, "Meghan, could you go shut and lock that door? We don't want prying eyes seeing what's happening."

She raced back to the entrance. A few of the staff were headed toward the room, and rather than cause a scene she shut the door and locked it behind her.

Walking to the staff, she smiled at them and waved off their fears. "Just someone who had a little too much to drink. The men are taking care of getting the young couple a cab."

Her acting must have been enough to convince the mortals, but the undead employees recognized her lie and were probably already guessing at what had happened…again.

She shooed everyone into the kitchen so that they could finish up, but as she did so, she shot a look back at the locked door and worried about exactly what was going on within.

Blake stared at the young vampire's eyes. They were glazing over, losing the sheen of life. His skin was damp and growing colder with each passing second.

Definitely not good.

The pressure he was applying at the vampire's ravaged throat had slowed the flow of blood. Vamp healing had started to close the wound, but the youngster had lost way too much blood. He needed to feed if he was to survive the wounds.

Blake would have suggested a quick nip from his female friend, but she was crazy mad and had already done a bit of damage to both Ryder and Diego. Each of the men bore an assortment of scratches and bite marks and were still struggling to subdue the young female. She was kicking mightily and keening in a strange unnatural way in protest to the way the two men had her pinned to the ground.

Which left him only one option for getting some blood into the dying yuppie.

He brought his wrist to the other vamp's mouth, but the young vamp was too disoriented to understand.

"Stupid shit," he said, and slapped the vampire to rouse him.

The young man jerked to consciousness and finally focused. Seeing Blake's wrist before his lips, he sank his teeth into the flesh and began to feed.

"Not too much, mind you," he admonished, and for good measure added, "maybe next time you'll listen when someone warns you."

With another sharp pull that dug the newbie's fangs deeper into his wrist, Blake decided he was done playing nursemaid. After a quick look at the vampire's neck, which had healed enough to almost stop bleeding, he grabbed the vamp's hand and brought it up to the makeshift bandage he had fashioned from Meghan's kitchen towel.

"Keep up the pressure." He broke the vampire's bite on his wrist and rose from his spot to find Diego and Ryder putting the finishing touches to the bindings holding the young female vamp to the legs of the sofa. Still wild with hunger, she snapped and lunged at them like a sideshow crocodile after a piece of meat on a trainer's rope.

Her face still bore the splatter from her earlier attacks on the men. When she failed to sink her teeth into Diego, she turned to licking those remnants off her skin, her tongue working furiously to swipe off each seemingly precious smear.

Ryder stood up beside him. "What did you warn them about?"

Blake shook his head and pointed at the injured vampire. "Not them. The yuppie over there. This one here…" He motioned to the bound vampiress, who strained to reach him and bared and gnashed her teeth in frustration when the bindings held her back.

"She's crazy. When I was serving them dinner, she had already taken a nip out of him. I sensed something wrong. She had this wild look in her eyes."

Diego rubbed at his wrist and the action drew Blake's attention to the blood staining the cuff of his shirt and the long, ragged tears in Diego's suit jacket.

"Got you good, didn't she?"

The older vamp glared at him and then considered Ryder at length. "This is one too many incidents for my taste, amigo." He held a hand out toward the vampiress, ignoring the way she snapped at him, and said, "I can feel the disturbance in her energy, can't you?"

Come to think of it, a push of power, unsteady but forceful, registered more cleanly against his vamp senses, Blake thought. He had been too occupied with saving the other vampire's life to pay much mind to it before. But now that he had…

"What is that and why did we all come running when we felt it?" Well, most of us, he thought, recalling that Stacia had been in the dining room but had yet to make an appearance.

I was busy, he heard in his head, followed immediately by, *Come open the door.*

All three of them turned and took a step toward the

entry in deference to Stacia's bidding. Blake had known that Stacia and Diego had sometimes shared blood with each other, but Ryder…

"Blimey, mate. I thought you and your little law enforcement chit—"

"Shut it, Blake," Ryder warned, and strode to the entrance to the room, his steps clipped and urgent.

He swung open the ornately carved door. Stacia sauntered in but stopped short as the blood-crazed vampiress strapped down to the love seat grew even more hostile. She yanked at the ties on her wrists and ankles, and the legs of the love seat groaned from the pressure she exerted in her quest for freedom.

When she saw Stacia, a wild guttural cry spilled from her lips and was immediately followed by the snap of her jaw, over and over again as if she was anticipating feeding from the elder.

"This is not good," Stacia said. She slowly walked closer to the young woman, then stopped and kept her distance, pacing back and forth as she considered the vampiress and her actions. Stacia raised her hands and closed her eyes as if to experience the primordial beat of her vampire energy that they had all previously sensed.

The young woman stilled for a moment, but then renewed her attempts to escape, her actions even more frenzied than before until it seemed as if she was having a seizure.

Ryder and Diego flew to her side to keep her down as the love seat started to buck from the force of her wild movements. After a minute of the nearly panicked seizures, the vampiress arched her back off the love seat, her body spasming into a tight knot before she fell back against the cushions, her body limp.

She was dead.

The raw and unbalanced power they had sensed earlier instantly evaporated.

Stacia finally neared the dead woman, her earlier reticence gone. With one finger she tilted up the dead vampire's head and urged it back onto the edge of the love seat. That position exposed the blood oozing from her eyes, nose, mouth and ears. As Stacia gingerly pried open the lids of one eye, it uncovered the shining neon glow of the vampire's iris swimming in a sea of blood. Nothing remained of the white of her eye.

"Creepy," Blake said, as he shivered, unnerved by the sight. He had never seen anything like it before—and judging from the looks on Ryder's and Diego's faces, neither had they.

"Dangerous," Stacia replied, and shifted her gaze up to Diego and Ryder. "I haven't seen this in nearly two millennia."

"Seen what?" Diego pressed, sliding his hand beneath Stacia's to close the one damning eye of the dead vampiress.

"*Sanguinarium coitus prohibitum.* It's the equivalent of vampire Ecstasy, but the drug's effects are deadly and uncontrollable. It's why the sanguinarium drug was outlawed by the vampire elders close to a millennium ago. The entire supply was supposedly destroyed at that time," she explained.

"So how did she get an outlawed thousand-year-old drug?" Ryder asked, as he bent and started to undo the bindings.

Stacia stayed his hand. "I wouldn't rush it just yet. Some vampires have been known to revive and try to satisfy their bloodlust."

"So what do we do?" Ryder asked, moving away from the body.

Blake chuckled harshly. "First thing is we make sure the chit is dead. Second thing is for you find out who's got a beef with you."

Diego shook his head, frustration and concern on his features. "Why would you think someone has a beef with us?"

Once again, Blake let out a rough laugh. "You've got three dead vamps in less than a month and Bloodzilla here. Seems to me that's too many things to be just coincidence."

In unison both Diego and Ryder glanced at Stacia, who slipped her arm through Blake's and said, "For once I think he's right."

"Is he now?" he heard from behind him and turned to see Meghan walking into the room. When she looked up from their entwined arms to meet his gaze, the chill in her emerald green eyes was foreboding. Her lips thinned into a tight line and a small part of him was pleased that she seemed just the tiniest bit jealous.

Another part of him worried that Meghan in a fury was probably worse than Bloodzilla had ever been that night. He braced himself for what she would do next.

Chapter 12

"So nice to see you again, Meghan," Stacia said, disengaging her arm from Blake's and strolling sexily to her, her graceful hand extended in greeting.

Meghan peered down at Stacia's hand. An assortment of finely wrought gold rings graced her slender, elegant fingers. It was impossible not to imagine those fingers touching Blake, since her vampire powers were picking up on the connection between them. The connection that confirmed they had shared their bodies and their blood. Worse yet, the sharing had been recent.

The bite of jealousy roughly sank its teeth into her gut, sharper and more painful than any vampire's kiss.

She took hold of Stacia's hand in a no-nonsense grip that made it clear she wouldn't be intimidated.

The vampire elder grinned in challenge and tight-ened her hold in response until the designs on some of the rings began to painfully dig into Meghan's skin and were followed by the ache of bone grinding on bone.

Meghan directly met Stacia's dark-eyed gaze. A smirk played across Stacia's face, as if she was enjoying Meghan's discomfort, but Meghan didn't flinch or pull away. Instead, she increased the pressure of her grasp, letting the other woman know that she refused to be cowed.

Blake walked over and stood to the side of them, rocking back and forth on his heels, obviously amused. Damn him.

"Ladies. While this display is rather gratifying—"

"Don't flatter yourself, luv," Meghan mimicked, and ripped her hand out of Stacia's. Although she knew she was bleeding and possibly bruised, she didn't look down nor rub her hand.

"Later," Stacia nearly purred. She caressed Blake's cheek before flipping a dismissive wave in Meghan's direction. But then Meghan heard in her head, loudly and with a bit of annoyance, *He called your name as he came.*

The knowledge did little to assuage an anger Meghan knew she shouldn't be feeling. There was nothing between her and Blake. If she had any sense at all, there never would be.

Contrary to her earlier thoughts, nothing had changed.

Blake had turned her. He had disappointed her more than once despite all the good things he had done in the past. Even lately, when he seemed to be almost a good guy, she always seemed to be waiting for him to screw things up—like his apparent tryst with Stacia.

He just wasn't a trustworthy guy, she reminded herself. She glared at Blake, who started to apologize, but then Ryder and Diego walked over, preventing any kind of private discussion.

Diego motioned toward the kitchen and inclined his head in her direction. "Please hurry everyone along so we can deal with this."

Ryder added, "I'm going to call Diana."

"It's about time," Blake said, with a snort of disgust.

Diego jerked his hand up and pointed a finger in Meghan's direction. "Go with Meghan. Help her out and then leave."

"I don't need him helping me," she said and strode away. But Blake ignored her comment and followed anyway. As they quickly moved toward the kitchen, he leaned close and said, "It's not what you think."

She stopped and turned without warning, and Blake ran into her. He was forced to grab hold of her arms to keep her from being bowled over.

"Not what I think?" she hissed from between clenched teeth.

"I'm sorry, Meghan."

"You know what?" She jabbed him in the chest with one finger. "There's nothing to be sorry about, Blake. There's nothing between us."

"Liar. We both know there's feelings between us," he urged, rubbing his hands up and down her arms. A shiver of desire danced over her, but she forced it down, wanting to regain her anger as a defense.

She shook off his touch and started walking again. "The only feelings between us are hard feelings."

"Meghan—"

She held up her hand to silence him, and without even looking at him said, "Go home, Blake. You're not wanted here."

"Bollocks," he mumbled, and immediately thereafter, she felt his absence as he left. The satisfaction of his departure was soon tempered by the disappointment that he hadn't put up a fight to stay. Damn him anyway, she thought, as she headed into the kitchen to do as Diego asked.

At her workstation, she finally looked down at the palm of her hand. The cuts from Stacia's rings were nearly healed over and a yellowish tinge remained from a bruise. Pain lingered there, however.

She rubbed her hand, trying to drive away the ache. Trying to ignore the concern that the pain she was feeling was other than physical.

She refused to acknowledge that anything Blake had done with Stacia bothered her. But then Stacia's words replayed in her head.

He called your name as he came.

And with that came some small sense of satisfaction along with dread. She didn't want to admit that Blake stirred any emotions in her other than anger.

To do so would surely cause her nothing but grief.

Blake didn't take kindly to being dismissed. Not by Meghan and not by Ryder and Diego.

As he paced back and forth in the alley behind Otro

Mundo, he considered leaving as Meghan had commanded, but his pride dictated that he go back in and tell her a thing or two.

With a determined swagger in his step, he returned to the restaurant and nearly ran over Meghan once again.

She stopped abruptly, clearly surprised that he had come back. Her chef's jacket hung open as it usually did when she had finished working, revealing the tight black tank top she wore beneath. He looked around. Everyone else in the kitchen was gone.

"What are you doing back?" she asked.

He took the last step necessary to bring them face-to-face. "Whether any of you like it or not, I'm as involved in this as you are."

She crossed her arms and arched a manicured brow. "Really? What makes you think that?"

He pushed back the one sleeve on his jacket and shirt, revealing the healing bite mark from where he had fed the injured vampire. "This."

Her stance softened and she laid her hand on the pink skin over the twin bites of teeth. Her fingers trembled against his flesh. "What's this?"

"Fed the bloke. Couldn't let him expire and make it five dead vamps." He shrugged, trying to seem nonchalant, but Meghan didn't seem to buy his act.

"Why does any of this matter to you, Blake?"

He turned his hand and took hold of her fingers, battling between denying the reason for his interest and telling her the truth. The first would salvage his pride while the second would risk his heart.

Either choice could bring loss, but only one could bring satisfaction.

He closed the distance between them and braced himself for rejection. "It matters to me because I know how much this place matters to you."

At the spot where he held her fingers came tension, followed by a quaking release that traveled from her fingers up her body.

"Damn you, Blake. Why do you have to make this so hard?" she said, and lowered her head. She had released her shoulder-length hair from the French braid, and now it spilled forward, hiding her face from him.

He placed his thumb beneath her chin and applied gentle pressure. When she met his gaze, tears shimmered in her deep green eyes. Once again, she asked, "Why, damn you?"

"I just want a chance to prove to you—"

"That you're a good man? Technically, you're not a man anymore and thanks to you, I'm not the woman I used to be," she reminded him. A tear escaped and slipped down her cheek.

He wiped it away with the pads of his fingers and said, "I'm not a man, but I am good. All I want is a chance."

She sighed roughly and dragged her fingers through her hair. "Did you prove you're a better man by sleeping with Stacia? Is screwing an elder some kind of notch on your vampire belt?"

She had him dead to rights on the screwing-Stacia part, so he didn't try to deny that. "We have a history."

"When you're as old as dirt I would imagine there's lots of history," she said, irritation apparent in her voice.

"I slept with her because I needed a favor," he admitted, wanting no secrets between them.

Meghan pulled away from him and wrapped her arms around herself again before facing him. "Do you value yourself so little that you would trade your body for a favor?"

Her words ripped into his soul, reopening old wounds. Reminding him of how he had once sacrificed himself for his family. Chastising him for so willingly giving himself to Stacia on Meghan's behalf. Despite that, he knew there was only one answer to her question. Only one reason why he had done what he had done.

"It's not that I value myself so little, love," he said, and approached her. When he stood barely an inch away from her, he softly said, "It's that I value you more. I did it because I wanted to keep you safe."

"Damn you," she said, and buried her face in her hands.

He closed the final distance and wrapped his arms around her. He held her tentatively at first, allowing her the tears born of her confusion and, he hoped, her acceptance of the truth of his statement.

Her body was tight at first, but as it gradually relaxed he strengthened his hold on her, drawing her close until their bodies were flush against each other.

Meghan reluctantly dropped her arms and then slipped them around his waist. As she did so, she raised her face up, and he cradled her cheeks and wiped away her tears.

"Forever could be a lot less lonely if we take this risk, Meghan."

At her slow nod, he brought his lips to hers and

tenderly sampled them, accepting her reluctant acquiescence. He didn't press, aware that if he did, it might shatter the moment.

He rubbed his lips across hers and then placed a kiss at the edge of her mouth. Slowly he shifted his lips along hers and she finally responded, meeting his lips in a kiss.

Her breath spilled against his mouth a second before she tasted him. He accepted the hesitant slide of her tongue along the seam of his lips and opened his mouth.

She slipped the tip of her tongue in and he met it with his, danced his tongue with hers and along her lips. A breathy sigh escaped her, and she deepened the kiss and pressed against him.

He eased his hands down to her waist and beneath her open jacket. Grasping the trim line of her waist with one hand, he splayed the other along the small of her back as they continued kissing.

Meghan grabbed hold of his shoulders, her hands shaky as she accepted the thrust of his tongue. He pulled her closer and she noticed how every lean line of his body perfectly matched every curve and hollow of hers. She shivered as passion roused.

"Easy, Meghan. Let's take this slow," he urged against her lips, seemingly content to just keep on kissing her.

Not that she would complain. He was a marvelous kisser, enticing her to respond with a gentle nip of her lower lip that he salved with the soft swipe of his tongue. As she met his tongue with hers, he playfully sucked it in before slipping away to kiss the contours of her mouth, exploring every valley and arch.

It almost became a game of tag as he sampled each millimeter of her lips, inviting her to meet him there with the play of her tongue and mouth before moving on to another spot.

She chuckled and slipped her hand to the back of his head, cradling it and keeping him close. As he teased her, nipping the edge of her bottom lip, she applied soft pressure and deepened the kiss. She slid her tongue into his mouth and urged her hips against his. The hard ridge of his erection pressed into the softness of her belly. She rubbed her hips across him, and at the small of her back the pressure of his hand increased to press her ever closer.

Between her legs came the pull of need and the memory of the satisfaction she had once experienced in his arms. With that memory, however, came hesitation. Once again she questioned the wisdom of giving in to the desire between them.

"Blake," she said with a breathy sigh. She broke the kiss but couldn't stop touching him. She moved her hand from cradling his head to stroking the strong line of his jaw.

"I understand, Meghan. I'm a patient man," he said. He bent his head for a last kiss, but a deliberately loud cough broke the magic of the moment.

They stepped away from each other, although Blake slipped his hand into hers as they turned in unison to face Diego.

He stood at the mouth of the hall leading to the office, his face all hard planes and surfaces. A chill in his eyes made them the color of glacial ice.

"Diana has arrived" was all he said, the tone of his

voice formal and clipped, before he pivoted in the direction of the office.

"Hail, hail the gang's all here," Meghan quipped, and took a step, but Blake tugged her hand to keep her from advancing. She shot him a quizzical look, puzzled by his actions.

"Are you sure about this?" he asked.

She didn't know if he was referring to their little interlude or to whatever they would need to do to find out why Otro Mundo had suddenly become a vamp killing ground. Uncertainty clouded both issues, but as he gazed at her, his emotions openly displayed on his face, she knew what he wanted to hear. Confused by all that was happening, however, she was unprepared to take it further at that moment.

She slipped her hand from his and she said, "I'm not sure of anything, but I would like to know I can count on you to watch my back."

A glimmer of disappointment flickered across his features before he teased, "I'll be watching your back, not to mention your front and all other sides of you."

The patented boyish grin that followed tugged a hesitant smile to her lips.

"I think you were a rake in another life." With that she turned and walked in the direction of Diego's office. Blake followed behind her.

Chapter 13

"I never got to thank you before, but I appreciate what you did for my partner," Diana Reyes said, hugging Blake and then Meghan as they walked into the office.

He dipped his head in acknowledgment, and as a puzzled look swept over Meghan's face, he said, "Diego and I got her partner out of a bind. Is he better?"

Diana forced a smile to her lips, but the smile stopped there while her eyes remained dark and troubled by the discussion. "David is…recovering."

Much like she must be, Blake thought. The FBI agent seemed a bit too pale and had felt decidedly too frail as he had returned her hug. When she sat on the sofa, Ryder took a spot on the arm of the couch, hovering protectively.

He and Meghan took the chairs opposite the couple

while Diego stood to the side of them, his hands jammed into his pants pockets.

Diana's gaze focused on the gashes and scratches on Diego and then shot quickly up to those on Ryder's face. "Ryder said you'd had a problem tonight, but I'm finding it hard to believe that one young vampire did all this damage," she said.

Blake held up his wrist. "Actually, this is from the newbie that's still alive. I had to feed him," he explained with a casual shrug.

"Where is the injured vamp?" she asked.

Diego answered, "He's on his way home with a supply of blood bags and a promise to keep quiet for now."

"Did he have anything to say?" she asked, but both Ryder and Diego shook their heads. She returned her attention to Blake.

"Ryder mentioned that you noticed something was wrong with her?"

"She seemed a might bloodthirsty for my tastes. I tried to tell the male vamp to watch himself, but he wouldn't listen," he explained.

"And the dead vamp? What's with her?" She rose as she said it, leaving no doubt that she intended to survey the scene of the attack and the now-deceased vampiress.

Diego led the way. Meghan and Blake hung back, allowing the others to precede them into the private dining room, where the blood-crazed young woman remained bound to the small sofa. He stopped by the door and urged Meghan to stay with him as Diana walked around the corpse, the scene, before she pulled latex gloves from her jacket pocket along with some small bags and tweezers.

She slipped on the gloves and began to process the body of the vampiress, searching for clues as to what had happened.

Blake had watched enough crime shows on a cast-off television to know she was looking for evidence. The FBI agent carefully inspected the body, placing what he assumed were hairs and other fibers in the bags.

The vampiress was wearing a tight-fitting bustier and equally body-hugging leather pants. Diana recovered little from those items of clothing, but dangling from the vamp's neck was a long gold necklace with a pendant that had been resting in her cleavage.

Diana pulled it off her neck and held it up for all of them to view. The pendant consisted of an intricately woven web of gold that held a small glass vial. She peered into the vial, but it appeared to be empty.

"Any idea what was in here?" Diana slipped the necklace and pendant into one of the evidence bags.

"Maybe some of the banned drug Stacia told us about," Blake replied, keeping an eye on Meghan for any reaction to the mention of the vampire elder.

Diana jiggled the bag in midair for emphasis, but then asked, "A drug that none of you knew anything about?"

"Stacia claims it was banned nearly a thousand years ago. None of us are old enough to have known," Diego said.

"So we can keep the list of possible suspects to vampire elders?" Diana suggested.

"Now that's a right scary thought," Blake said, imagining that none of the elders, except possibly Stacia, would be all that keen to talk to a mortal—or even one of them—about a supposedly banned drug.

Before anyone could answer, Meghan asked, "Just how many elders are there?"

"Dozens worldwide who flit from one city to the other," Diego began. He paced back and forth for a moment, lost in thought, then said, "Stacia's in town. I'd have to see if she knows which other elders have come in. As for elders who reside in Manhattan, there's Hadrian and Maximillian."

"Maximillian the designer?" Diana asked. At Diego's nod, she chuckled and added, "That explains his *outré* taste."

Diana slipped the bag with the vial into her jacket pocket then withdrew test tubes with swabs. With deliberate care she took several different blood samples and specimens from the dead vampire's mouth and throat.

"Do we know whether this drug is ingested, snorted or shot up?" she asked.

"We'll have to question Stacia," Ryder said, but Diana shook her head.

"Not we. Me," she said, the tone of her voice rife with jealousy at the thought of Ryder going anywhere near Stacia.

"Ditto that," Meghan mumbled, both pleasing and surprising Blake with the comment.

Diana stepped back to walk around the room, seemingly on the lookout for anything unusual. She examined the coffee table area, making note of what had been on its surface. Motioning to the remnants of the food, she said, "Are we sure that nothing was put in the meal?"

"I made it myself," Meghan said.

Blake quickly added, "And I brought it straight here. No one else touched it."

With a nod, Diana resumed her inspection of the room, but clearly found nothing of interest. When she returned to stand beside Ryder, she said, "Who knows Hadrian and Maximillian well enough to approach them?"

"I do," Diego immediately confirmed.

"Try to do it as soon as you can while I get these samples processed," she instructed, and Diego nodded.

Blake felt useless just standing there. While Diana's FBI geeks were working on processing the evidence, the delay might bring yet more dead vampires. "While the FBI lab works on the samples—"

"I'm not taking these to the FBI lab," Diana said. Her gaze locked with Ryder's as she continued. "I'm on leave right now. Besides, I think Melissa Danvers is a better candidate to help us. She's a hematologist. Plus, she knows our secrets and how to keep them."

Our secrets, Blake thought, wondering at Diana's choice of words as well as the reason for why the agent was on leave. Although he was intensely curious about both, he kept his silence, well aware that to press would elicit Ryder's anger. For now, he wanted to stay on the good side of everyone involved.

"What can we do in the meantime?" he asked.

"The other incidents were very different, weren't

they?" Diana pulled out a small notebook to record the details of the earlier attacks.

"The first time, we found two vampires feeding to the death from each other," Meghan offered, with a shiver that he felt rattle her body as she stood beside him.

"And the second?" Diana questioned, arching one dark brow in emphasis.

"We saw something in the alley by the garbage cans. Found the body when we went back there," Blake said. "Something with white hair that did a bunny hop away from the corpse right after I spotted it."

Diana jotted down something in her notebook. "What about this one?"

Blake shot an uneasy glance at the dead young woman again. "This vamp had a wild look in her eye when I came to serve the meal. She'd already taken a bite from her dinner companion."

"Dinner taking on a whole new meaning in the context of this setting," Diana quipped morbidly, and smiled. The smile transformed her face, eliminating some of the tired lines and bringing the barest hint of color to her wan cheeks.

"We don't just wait now, do we?" Diego inquired, pacing back and forth once more. His concern and frustration were evident in every line of his body.

"We don't just wait. Like I said, I'll get the samples processed. You'll reach out to Hadrian and Maximillian."

"What about Stacia?" Ryder asked, earning another disgruntled glare from Diana.

"We'll ask her in for some questions once we know

a little more." Diana faced Blake and Meghan. "The Blood Bank should be good for some kind of information. Do you think—"

"Been there, done that," he advised. "The only new thing is that this Asian vamp—"

"An Asian vampire?" Diana questioned.

Out of the corner of his eye, he shot a glimpse at Meghan. "A kiang-shi, according to what I got out of Stacia."

"That girl does get around," Diana murmured, seemingly aware of how he had gotten that information. "You've met this…kiang-shi?"

"The other night. He dined in the restaurant and wanted to meet me," Meghan said. She picked up her hand and rubbed it, once again experiencing the oily feeling of malevolence she'd gotten from Lee. "I didn't like him. I felt his evil," she admitted.

Blake snorted in agreement. "Totally evil, according to Stacia, although Foley would probably know best."

"Why Foley?" Diego asked, approaching them as they waited at the door to the room.

"They seemed to be friends. *Very* good friends," Meghan said, recalling the way Lee had touched Foley.

"Not friends," Blake corrected. "It was more like he had control over Foley. Like Foley was afraid."

Diana was taken aback by the statement. "Foley afraid? Now that's something I never expected to hear."

"Just my opinion, mind you," Blake added.

Meghan quickly chimed in with, "Something was really off about them."

Diana considered their statements, then said, "I'll see

what I can find out about the kiang-shi. In the meantime, if you and Blake could somehow talk to Foley about him…"

"Will do," Blake confirmed straightaway.

"Good. Seems like we've all got our work cut out for us."

Ryder rose and stood behind Diana. He laid a hand on her shoulder, the gesture protective, Meghan thought, though the look on his face seemed filled with sadness.

"Certainly seems like we do," Ryder said.

"I guess we're off to the Blood Bank." Blake glanced in her direction, obviously wondering whether she would agree to go with him.

Recalling their earlier encounter in the kitchen, going to the Blood Bank brought concern that something would go on besides questioning Foley. The allure of the back rooms and another intimate session with Blake might just prove too tempting, and yet…

"The Blood Bank it is," she confirmed.

Meghan and Blake leapt down from the rooftop to the mouth of the small cobblestoned street leading to the Blood Bank. A Friday night, there was a line of patrons waiting to enter the nondescript building. The Blood Bank needed no fancy signs or other trappings to attract the clientele to its door. Word of mouth had kept it going for decades.

The door was guarded by a large, muscular bouncer. As Blake approached, the man made a menacing motion in his direction until Blake flashed a bit of fang.

The bouncer then stepped back and held open the door for them.

Inside, the place was far more crowded than it had been the other night. Definitely more vampires present, Blake thought, the vibration of vamp power wafting to him from those immortals mingling with the humans.

He searched the crowd for any sign of Foley, but he was nowhere to be found. Leading Meghan to the bar, he inched between two lesser vampires and, with a quick rumbling growl and hint of fang, warned them away from their spots.

Meghan slipped into the space he had created and, after they got their drinks, downed her tumbler filled with blood. When she finished and met his gaze, the bright glow of vampire sight had replaced the deeper emerald color of her eyes.

He cupped her cheek, leaned close to her lips and whispered, "Can I have a taste?"

She hesitated for a moment, but then she slowly closed the distance between them and he covered her mouth with his, licking at the remnants of her feeding. As he passed his tongue along her lips, the slight bit of fang she had released nicked it. The barest hint of his blood escaped, but she quickly licked it away.

He felt the rush through her body from the sip of his blood, vamp blood being supercharged to another immortal. When she pressed against him, he somehow managed some control. Easing away slightly, he whispered, "Later, love. Control yourself for now."

Meghan moaned in frustration, needy from the rush of desire his blood had created and disgusted with herself at her lack of composure. She reminded herself where that had gotten her last time and that during this go-round with Blake—if that was where all this was leading—she would need to rein in her reactions to him.

She pulled away from him and reached for her glass, but it was empty. Blake offered up his. She took a small sip and then returned the tumbler. He made a point of turning the glass to the spot where her lips had left their mark. As he drank, she imagined his mouth on hers again. On other parts of her that were throbbing and vibrating with the pull of their undead connection.

"Now this is something I didn't quite expect to see," Foley said, as he sauntered up to them, having apparently taken note of them at the bar. He leaned close to her and sniffed. "Deliciously ripe, Blake. She's more than ready for you…unless of course you'd rather I had a go first."

Blake opened his mouth to answer, but she shot up her hand to silence him.

"First of all, I decide who I 'have a go with,' Foley, and secondly—" she mimicked his actions, bending near and inhaling deeply "—what is that smell? Not ripe, more like…decay, with a hint of…cardamom."

A surprised look flashed across Blake's features before he, too, took a whiff. Although he kept silent, she knew that the smell had triggered some recollection in him. Instead, he goaded Foley, clearly hoping to get a rise out of him.

"Your better half was in the restaurant the other night, only he was playing the other side of the field. Must be rough—"

Blake didn't get to finish as Foley snared him by the neck and yanked him to his feet. "You can't even begin to understand what rough is to someone like Lee."

In a choked voice, Blake said, "Try me."

Foley tossed him back against the edge of the bar. Blake's side bore the brunt of the impact. "Bollocks, mate. That hurt like a bitch."

"Speaking of bitches…she stays here," Foley said, but Meghan shook her head and looped her arm through Blake's.

"Where he goes—"

"This is man talk, love. Stay here and I'll be back in a few," Blake said. Before she could stop him, he sauntered off with Foley, leaving her alone.

As she snagged the tumbler with the remains of Blake's drink, she turned and scoped out the crowd.

Bingo, she thought, spotting Lee across the way with the same harem who had been with him at the restaurant. They were piled into one of the booths at the back of the club, pressed tightly together in the small space. The women were busy vying for Lee's attention, and when he favored one, the other two passed the time by pleasuring each other.

Disgust rose sharply in her at their wantonness, but she forced it away. Taking a final fortifying brace of the drink, she walked across the bar, intending to find out for herself why Lee had suddenly turned up in town.

Chapter 14

"Bugger, mate. Why haven't you said anything before now?" Blake asked as he sipped the very fine vintage Foley had served up—an AB-positive NYU coed stolen earlier that day from a blood donation drive.

"I had handled it up until now, but lately…there's something crazier about him. Something even scarier than before," Foley said. He put his glass down on his desktop and laid his hands on either side of it, his long fingers splayed on the surface of the desk. His knuckles were almost translucent from the pressure he was exerting, and a fine network of veins bulged along the tops of his hands.

"Why is Lee here?" Blake pressed.

Foley shook his head, and his long white hair swung loose around his lean face. "He owns the damn place.

He comes every couple of years to make sure I'm doing things right."

"But besides checking the books—"

"Stop," Foley said with an angry slash of his hand. He obviously did not want to continue with a discussion of what else Lee did when he came for a visit.

"Why don't you stop him? You're one of the strongest—"

"I'm strong only because *he* makes me strong. He fed from me and made me his slave, but his bite… It gave me strength I didn't have, and now…"

He didn't need to finish for Blake to understand. Every time Lee fed from Foley he empowered him, only…

"Is it worth the power, Foley? Is it worth what he takes from you?"

Foley glanced up and met his gaze. "I am what I am because of him."

Blake was torn between pity for the other vampire and anger. Pity because he knew all too well what it was to be at the mercy of someone more powerful. Anger because he had found the strength to overcome that cycle of abuse and he didn't abide those who couldn't muster the same courage.

Foley clearly remained at the mercy of Lee and needed to find the inner strength to break away from him. Maybe with their help he could.

"You're not alone, Foley. Maybe you'll realize that in time."

But as he walked out of Foley's office, it occurred to him that he and Foley weren't all that different. It also

occurred to him that he was just one degree of separa-
tion away from being alone.

When he entered the main space of the club, trying
to locate the one being that kept him from loneliness,
he realized Meghan was across the way, talking to none
other than Lee himself.

He opened himself up to feel Meghan's power,
hoping to get a sense of whether she was uneasy with
Lee, but she was too far away. Judging from her body
language, though, she seemed in charge of the situation.

Time to sit back and watch the show, he thought, and
took a spot at the bar.

"Do you plan on standing there all night or would
you care to join me?" Lee motioned to the women
sitting beside him in the booth fawning over his every
move.

"You mean 'join us,' don't you?" she said, arching a
brow in question.

He snapped his fingers and the three women with
him rose from their chairs and hurried away. "No, I mean
me."

Meghan shook her head in disbelief and disgust. She
didn't care for subservient women. "Do you always get
what you want, Mr. Lee?"

"Sun Tze, please," he said, and gestured to the chair,
the sweep of his hand gracefully elegant. The movement
shifted the cuff of his red silk shirt to reveal a rather thick
and expensive gold watch. Everything about him
screamed wealth, but none of that could change the dirt
deep within him that she had sensed at his touch.

"Do you always get what you want, Mr. Lee?" she pressed again. A second later, a strong pull erupted in her center, jerking her forward and into the chair beside him.

"I guess you do," she said, starting to experience a bit of fear at the magnitude of his power, but determined not to show it.

He waved at a passing waiter, who quickly brought them two wineglasses filled with a deep burgundy liquid—a rich blend of wine and blood with an assortment of mulling spices, including the cardamom that she associated with him.

"Why are you here?" he asked, as he picked up one of the glasses, took a sip and then propped an elbow on the table. He leaned his head on his hand and examined her as he waited for her response.

"Came for a drink after work and when I saw you, I wanted to apologize," she lied.

Lee smirked, well aware of her prevarication. "Try again, Miss Thomas."

"So you know my name. Why?" She took a small sip of the drink and found it deliciously different, but she demurred from taking another taste. If Lee was involved in whatever was going on, she didn't trust that the unusual mix didn't contain some of the sanguinarium drug Stacia had alerted them about.

"Because I never got my dessert the other night," he said. He shifted closer and brushed aside her hair with one hand, exposing the column of her neck. With the motion of his hand, the strong scent of cardamom wafted around him and insinuated itself in her nostrils, so potent it started an ache in her head.

She pinched the bridge of her nose and shifted away from him on the seat of the booth. "Sorry to disappoint you, Mr. Lee, but I don't do dessert."

"Liar," he said, and stroked one long finger along the side of her cheek. The pad of his finger was slightly oily, his skin ice cold, dragging a shiver from her.

"Ready to go, luv?" Blake asked, as he took a spot before them, his arms crossed against his chest, his shoulders pulled back as if to make himself appear larger.

Lee chuckled, made a shooing motion with his one hand, and said, "Ah, the insolent bantam rooster has come after his hen. Go away, little man."

Blake experienced the push of Lee's hand as strongly as if the other man had actually touched him. The strength of the energy was much like the force of an elder, making Blake wonder again just how powerful the kiang-shi was in comparison. He summoned what power remained from his interlude with Stacia and shoved back.

A flicker of surprise flitted across Lee's eyes before they narrowed as he examined him. "So the cock is not just all crow?"

"Never underestimate an opponent," Blake said. He held out his hand to Meghan, who scooted from the booth and slipped her hand into his.

"Opponent? An interesting choice in words. I thought *suitor* might have been a more appropriate one, but at least now I know where we stand." Lee held up his hand and the entourage of women who had been with him earlier returned, bringing with them three rather brawny males.

Undead males, Blake realized, as their energy brushed against him when the trio took up positions behind Lee. The energy had that strange force he had picked up from Lee, so he suspected they were kiang-shi as well. He decided to confirm it to be sure.

"Kiang-shi like you, I suppose."

Lee laughed out loud, a broad smile on his face that displayed an ever present hint of fang. As his mirth died down, a hint of a glow entered his eyes. The irises slowly became an intense red and seemed to dance like the flames in a fire. When he spoke, his voice echoed with a low rumble, like thunder before an impending storm.

"You will find that there are few like me, little man."

As if to prove his point, a wave of energy flew away from Lee, forceful enough to drive both him and Meghan back a step. A cloying and disturbing residue of disquiet settled over him.

"Let's go, luv," he said.

He heard her whisper, "I so totally agree."

They hurried out to the street and away from the crowd still lingering at the door. As he gazed at her, he understood she wanted to throw off the sensation Lee's power had left on them. A quick race through the night would do it, he thought, but he was loathe to take her home and end their interlude.

She must have picked up on his feelings since she said, "You're place isn't far from here, is it?"

"Not far at all," he admitted with a smile.

"Good," she said, and raced off into the night with him hot on her tail.

* * *

They landed on the small patio adjacent to his apartment.

Not that it was really an apartment, Blake thought. He suddenly felt inadequate about what was little more than a large storage area he had converted into living space. He had finagled the rental of the space from the building superintendent who appreciated the decline in crime that Blake's presence had seemingly wrought—along with the assorted chores and two hundred dollars in off-the-books cash that Blake paid out every month.

To someone used to an apartment that took up a floor on Central Park West, this was slumming.

He took hold of her hand as she took a step toward the French doors and said, "Maybe I should take you home."

"No, not at all," she said, and dropped his hand. She walked to the neatly organized pots along the edge of the patio. The soil was ready for planting, and he had started some spring lettuce and swiss chard in a few of the pots. She lovingly ran her hands over the plants and said, "My father's already planting the early spring greens at home."

He clasped his hands before him and shifted on his heels as she approached him once again.

"Do you see them often?" he asked.

"Not since…" She was aware that any explanation for her lack of contact with her parents might spoil the moment, yet she needed for him to know. To understand. Maybe with that understanding the healing would continue.

"They visit infrequently. That makes it easier to hide what I am."

"I'm sorry I made it so hard for you."

With a shrug, she said, "Part of the problem is that they're not really city people, but being a vampire… makes it difficult to travel home. I talk to them a lot on the phone. Makes me not miss them as much."

He sighed his relief. "It's nice you still have them in your life."

She placed her hand over the one holding his wrist and pulled him toward the edge so they could peer down at Gramercy Park below them.

"It's wonderful to have the park so close."

With a shrug, he said, "This place is tiny compared to Central Park. I bet you go there often."

Nodding, she faced him and picked up her hand, laid it in the center of his chest. "I liked our game of follow-the-leader the other night."

He covered her hand, gently rubbed his palm across it. "We could manage a little chase through the park tonight if you'd like."

The spring night was clear and crisp, bordering on chilly. Meghan thought about the chase, but realized their games might be leading them to something that would be dangerous to her heart.

"You know I'm not sure—"

"You don't need to be sure right now, love. You just need to believe in the possibilities," he said, and gave her hand a reassuring squeeze.

The possibilities… She thought about all that had happened between them and the transformation she had seen in him recently. She couldn't deny that he had been trying to be different. To be a better man just for her.

Could anyone ask for more?

Wrapping her arms around him, she snuggled tight to him and said, "I'm sure of one thing. I'd like to relax a bit. It's been a long day."

"I imagine it must be tiring to be on your feet for so long." Blake started a gentle massage of her shoulders and she shivered with pleasure.

"That feels good."

"You feel good," he said, and dipped his head to touch his cheek to hers. He rubbed his face against hers, and the soft bristle of his beard tickled her. She scrunched up her neck in protest.

"Stop that."

"Really?" he said, but tickled her again. When she tilted her head to the side once more, he kissed his way down to the crook of her neck and playfully bit her.

"Yes, really. As good as it feels..." She sucked in a breath as he bit down again and then licked the spot.

"Feels that good, does it?" he teased, before raising his face to meet her gaze.

Meghan cradled his cheek and swiped her thumb across his lips. "You'd like me to admit that, but I don't want to give you a swelled head."

With a sexy grin and the press of his hips against hers, he said, "Too late."

She chuckled and shook her head. "This is what got me in trouble the last time, so why don't we try something different this time?"

Blake shifted away from her, a puzzled look on his face. "Like what?"

"How about just talking?" she said, stepping away from him and wrapping her arms around herself.

"Just talking? As in our lips moving but not doing anything else with them?"

"Yes. As in we move our lips and words come out. We listen to those words—"

He placed his index finger on her mouth to silence her. "And after we put our lips to better use?" he teased,

"Possibly," she admitted with a smile, unable to resist his charm.

At that he grinned, took hold of her hand and led her into his apartment.

Lee watched Foley as he made his nightly rounds at the Blood Bank. He had to give Foley credit for his efficiency and inventiveness. When he had won the run-down building in the early sixties during a mah-jongg game in Chinatown, he hadn't known what to do with the space. It had been Foley who had perceived the need for a place where humans clamoring for a walk on the wild side could go. It had been an added benefit that those drugged-up, sex-crazed humans were perfect prey for the vampires.

In the nearly forty years since then, Foley had kept the place profitable. Lee had to say that this new Goth crowd was just as easy to ensnare as the hippies and yuppies before them. The vampires appreciated their easy availability, and up until recently all had been good.

It occurred to Lee, as he watched one vampire corral

and lead a human to one of the back rooms, that it was only a small group of vampires who were giving them problems. Wannabes, he thought, recalling the exchange earlier that night with Meghan and her friend. They seemed to have no fear of him or if they did, they hid it well.

He didn't like their spirit or the human way they seemed to care for each other. So unlike the immortal credo he ascribed to of taking what he wanted when he wanted.

Of course, that had been his credo all his life, not just during his undead existence. It was why as he lay dying on the battlefield, he had been cursed by his opponents and paraded around for all to see his defeat. Their hatred of him was why they had chosen to further dishonor him by refusing to bury him.

Even his own family had not claimed his body, ashamed as they were of the reputation he had built with his merciless attacks and slow punishment of those who had defied him. As his corpse lay rotting and alone, the evil within him had sprung back within his body, intending to seek vengeance on all who had defied him.

He would not be defied in this life, either, he thought. His hand clenched on the tabletop as he considered how he might punish Meghan and her little man. Chastise the circle of friends and the followers who disdained the vampire way for the stench of humanity. The more he thought about all that they believed in and cherished, all the goodness he had despised all his life, the greater his anger grew, until he had devised just the plan for his revenge.

A plan that would deliver his message to the human wannabes who had been busily spreading their sickening sweetness through the Manhattan underworld.

For now, however, he would have to satisfy his anger with someone else. As Foley came into view again, Lee smiled and rose.

He knew just the thing to bring some contentment to his soul.

Chapter 15

"So your pom-poms were purple?" Blake teased her and rubbed his hand up and down her arm, which was resting against his chest.

They were sprawled together on some kind of lounger, long and with a slight dip in the center. He had covered whatever was beneath with a chenille bedspread in a deep maroon hue that complemented the colors in the rest of the space. The lounger was surprisingly comfortable as they'd lain there for hours, talking and finding out all kinds of things about one another.

Like the color of her pom-poms in her past life.

"Not purple. Violet. And it's 'G-o-o Bobcats!'" she said, mimicking one of the cheers she'd had to perform as a cheerleader at NYU.

He didn't say anything else; he just kept up the slow

caress on her arm. After long minutes had passed, she said, "It's getting very late."

He nodded. "Dawn is in a couple of hours. I can feel it coming."

As she could. It was one of those weird vampire traits that served as an early warning system, like being able to sense Lee's peculiar power or Stacia's elder strength.

"I guess I should be going." She made a halfhearted motion to rise and immediately regretted the loss of contact with him. "Or maybe not," she said, and plopped back down next to him.

"It's okay if you stay. We never did get to the part about doing something else with our lips."

She looked up at him. That sexy grin that caused her heart to do something funky in the middle of her chest was back, along with a wickedly inviting gleam in his crystal-blue eyes.

"You seem fixated on the lip thing."

His grin broadened. He placed his index finger beneath her chin, then applied gentle pressure to urge her upward until their lips were nearly touching.

"I guess that's what you would call an oral fixation?" He brought his lips to hers and rubbed them back and forth, inviting her to respond, reminding her that she had a choice about what would happen next.

Only Meghan suspected she had made that choice long before this moment.

She closed the distance between them and sampled his mouth, placing kiss after kiss along his top lip and then moving downward to the fullness of his lower lip.

He gently snagged her bottom lip with his teeth and playfully tugged on it before soothing that spot with a lick.

Heat flared within her as she imagined him licking elsewhere. As she remembered the feel of that sexy mouth on other parts of her body. With a shaky sigh, she snuggled closer to him, throwing her thigh over his lower body and feeling the hard jut of his erection against her inner thigh.

She suddenly wanted more and shifted her body until she was covering him, the hard ridge of him nestled between her legs as she straddled him. Leaning over him, she braced her hands on either side of his shoulders as she brought her mouth back to his and dragged herself across his erection. He groaned into her mouth and it vibrated throughout her body, spreading need through every cell of her being.

"Blake, I know this is crazy…" she whispered against his lips, not wanting to lose contact with them for even a moment.

"Crazy, but right," he murmured, and grasped her hips with his hands, stilling the motion of them.

Meghan didn't know if it was right or wrong. All she knew was that he stirred something inside of her that she hadn't been able to forget in nearly four years, try as she might. Maybe it was time to finally explore that feeling and find out if it was one meant to last or if it was truly the worst mistake of both her mortal and undead lives.

"Touch me, Blake," she said urging her lips upward, but Blake was clearly in no hurry. He slowly trailed his hands up her sides, caressing each inch he traveled until he arrived at her breasts.

She sighed as he finally cupped them and began a gentle caress, squeezing tenderly before running his thumbs over their hardened tips.

He raised himself off the bed, bringing his mouth to her breast. He grasped the tip in his mouth through the thin fabric of her top and teethed it until she ached for more. She yanked the tank top up and over her head while he made quick work of her bra.

When she was bared to his gaze, he once again resumed his tarried loving, caressing her breasts, playing with her nipples, until with a bump of her hips against his she once again urged him to taste her.

Blake thought he would explode from the sensations buffeting his body. The feel of her along the length of him. The silk of her skin, soft to the palms of his hands. The hard tips of her breasts, a caramel color against the peach of her skin.

When she urged him on with the grind of her hips, he rose off the lounger once again, eager for a taste. Closing his mouth over one tight nub, he suckled the tip, and she held his head close and urged him on with a soft cry. He shifted his mouth to the other breast but continued the sure caress of his fingers on the breast he had just left. The tip was wet and slick from his mouth.

In response to his ministrations, she dragged herself across his length again in invitation. Considering how long he had been waiting, he wasn't about to refuse.

With tender pressure, he reversed their positions until she was the one lying on the surface of the lounger, her upper body bare to his gaze to just below her navel, thanks to her low-riding jeans. He just loved those jeans, he thought, as he dipped his head down and planted a kiss right on the sweet indentation of her navel before placing a string of kisses along the softness of her skin above the waistband.

As she had before, she cupped the back of his head and lifted her hips, wanting more.

Blake wasn't about to disappoint.

He undid the snap on her jeans and dragged the zipper open, kissing each bit of flesh that he exposed. When the jeans were fully undone, he eased them off, revealing the darker blonde whorls at her center and her long, toned legs.

He shot only a quick glance at her, hesitant until she parted her legs, making her desire clear.

But he wasn't about to rush the moment he had been anticipating for such a long time.

Leaning against the edge of the lounger, he began with a kiss and nibble on the inside of her ankle, discovering the tattoo of a small heart with an intricate scrollwork of barbed wire.

It suited her, he thought. Meghan had shut off her heart to him for way too long. It had made any of his overtures at apology fall painfully short of reaching her until recently.

He slowly moved upward, trailing his lips and tongue along the inside of her calf, up to her knees. He paused there to glance at her once again and realized she was watching him, her gaze expectant but conflicted. The emerald of her eyes had darkened, reminding him of the shadows in the pine trees behind the cottage of his old home in Wales.

It occurred to him then that there were so many things about her that brought the comforting memories of home. He only hoped that whatever he could offer would bring such solace to her. That it would be enough to fend off the anger she'd felt.

But even as she lay before him, he could see that she was still reluctant, that the barbed wire still guarded her heart. Her hands were at her sides, clenched into tight fists, as if to keep from reaching for him and finally giving herself over to what was happening.

He intended to break through that reserve. To find a way past the barriers she had put up around her heart.

With greater caution he moved upward, past the tender flesh of her inner thighs and to the center of her. The musky smell of her arousal called to the demon who wanted a taste as well, but Blake drove him back. The demon had already had his fill of Meghan on more than one occasion.

This time the human wanted his share.

He nudged the curls at her center with his nose before finding the nub beneath with the tip of his tongue.

She bucked up then, clearly surprised by the feel of his mouth there, but then he deepened his caress, kissing that swollen nub, licking until she surged off the lounger again.

"Easy, Meghan," he urged. "I won't leave you wanting."

He tugged at her again with his mouth before bringing his thumb to the nub and applying gentle pressure. While he did so, he dipped his head a fraction lower, licked along her nether lips, moist with desire and blushed with the sweet blood that the demon wanted to sample, but which he ignored.

Easing his tongue into her, he mimicked how he intended to love her and then brought his mouth back to her nub while he drew her to the edge with his fingers.

Meghan moved her hips upward, straining, her body awake to every caress. To every movement he made, only she needed more from him. She wanted to feel all of him and share the pleasure he was bringing her with the wonderful touch of his mouth and hands.

Grabbing hold of his shoulders, she sat up and he took advantage of that short break in their connection to rip off the black T-shirt he had been wearing.

When he stepped back within the vee of her legs, his sculpted midsection was directly in front of her face and she laid her lips along the ridges of muscle there. As she worked on freeing him of his jeans, she trailed her mouth down to his navel and licked it, causing a shiver to dance across his body.

She chuckled wantonly and he groaned, bent and tossed away his jeans, leaving him naked before her.

Her insides clenched at the sight of him, magnificent as he was with all the hard muscle and the long, thick length of him that would fill her fully while he caressed her with his able hands and brought a smile to her face with his sinful charm.

As she met his gaze, he seemed to realize she didn't want another second to go by before his possession, and so she made the final invitation.

Lying down, she inched her hips along the lounger until he was poised at her entrance. He lingered there, the head of his penis just barely making contact, and her body responded, growing wet and vibrating with demand for his entry.

He forced a smile. She could see he was near the end of his control, but somehow he managed some semblance of restraint and entered her slowly until he was completely sheathed within her. Contractions she couldn't control milked him, but he surprised her by remaining immobile, gritting his teeth as if his control was paining him.

"Blake?" she asked, and wrapped her legs around his hips, almost fearing that he would leave her now when they had finally made the first step in this dance.

He sucked in a shaky breath and grasped her hands with his to keep her from any motion. "I've no need for heaven now, Meghan. I've found it here with you."

The burden of such a confession was almost too great for her to bear until she met his gaze and realized that maybe she had found a part of heaven here as well. She placed her hands over his and gently urged them from her waist and to her breasts.

"Make me believe heaven is possible for us, Blake."

Whatever fragile control Blake had mustered disappeared like dew beneath the morning sun.

He caressed her breasts, tweaking the taut tips with his fingers before soothing them with his mouth. All the while, however, he remained immobile inside of her, savoring the motion of her muscles and the slickness surrounding him. Only when she arched into him, demanding a fulfillment that he couldn't refuse, did he finally allow himself to move. He shifted in and out of her slowly at first, but then lost any and all restraint as her soft cries and the clutch of her hands on his shoulders drove him on.

She came loudly, calling his name in a soft scream. He followed her, murmuring her name and dropping down onto her, his body depleted of strength.

Somehow he shifted them upward on the lounger while remaining inside of her long after pleasure had sated them and the holding and joining had become about more.

As he cuddled her close, still buried deep within, she slowly relaxed and eventually fell asleep.

But he was awake long after. As he finally softened and slipped from her body, he worried that it might be just as easy to slip from her life again unless he made good on his promise to be a better man.

As he lay next to her, their bodies close, Blake worried and planned for what he would do next. For what it would take to fully recapture the trust he had lost the night he had turned her.

He worried about whether when the time came, he could be the man she needed. If he failed her this time, he suspected that her fury would return with even greater vigor and drive him from her life forever.

Forever without Meghan would be an existence he didn't want to contemplate.

Meghan didn't know how she came to be the one brokering a meeting between two scary women— Stacia and Diana.

She suspected that it was because none of the men wanted to risk the wrath of either of the two and hoped Meghan would be a calming influence.

Not that she was feeling calm. She was feeling dazed ever since her interlude with Blake days ago. And confused because she had found comfort in his arms. Not to mention jealous when faced with the prospect of talking to Stacia.

She didn't want to be jealous because that implied she cared for Blake. He had asked her to believe in possibilities, only she wasn't ready to consider that possibility right now.

Diana was the first to arrive. Even in jeans instead of her requisite suit, she was all business. She stepped into the apartment and scoped out the room, clearly expecting to encounter the vampire elder.

"She's not here yet."

Diana chuckled. "She has to make her appearance."

Holding out her hand, Meghan invited Diana into the living room, where she had laid out some wine and glasses. She hoped to keep things friendly, and Diana must have picked up on that, since she said, "Worried that Stacia and I won't play nice?"

"Actually, I'm not sure how I'll handle being with her."

Diana chuckled once again and shook her head. "So the rumor about Stacia and Blake is true?"

She shrugged. "Heard you and Stacia have some history as well."

"Much the same history that you have with her. I don't like anyone messing with my man." Anger finally colored the other woman's words as she took a spot on the sofa.

Meghan understood. "Blake and I... I'm not quite certain he's... That we're..." She tossed her hands up, fumbling for the words.

"Being in love with a vampire..." Diana shrugged, apparently also at a loss. "It's confusing, and Stacia's involvement with the men—all of them, it seems—just complicates things. Let's hope she'll be able to provide some information tonight to make up for it."

A harsh laugh escaped Meghan. "Maybe the supernatural slut will have something worthwhile to spill."

A knock came, but not at the door.

Meghan rose and approached the window where another impatient rap sounded sharply against the glass.

Perched on the ledge, Stacia was a dark silhouette against the night sky.

Meghan opened the window and Stacia seemed to float into the apartment. A sheer black wrap, which covered a wealth of black leather, billowed behind her with an unseen wind. As she drifted by, Stacia patted her cheek the way a maiden aunt might a child's and smiled indulgently.

"So nice to see you again, little one."

Hostility rose up in her at Stacia's dismissal and the vampire elder must have sensed it since she shot Meghan a vexed look.

"Getting bold, are we?" Stacia asked, her gaze darkening, but then Diana rose from the sofa. Stacia's features filled with yearning, and inside of Meghan came the pull of need that Stacia's elder power was casting off.

Meghan shook off the sensation and walked to where

Stacia and Diana stood, staring at each other across the coffee table. Diana stood with her arms crossed, legs braced about a foot apart, as if she might need to spring into action at any second. A harsh glare had settled onto her features, leaving no doubt about her feelings toward the vampire elder.

Stacia seemed to have copied Diana's pose, but a bemused smile tempered the earlier ferocity of her look, masking her yearning as well. As Meghan approached them, Stacia addressed Diana.

"*Mia amica.* It's been too long since we've been together."

Been together? Meghan wondered at the odd choice of words.

"In your dreams, Stacia," Diana rejoined.

Stacia laughed huskily and, as she gracefully settled herself in a nearby chair, she said, "And in yours, Diana. Do you not realize it is only a matter of time before you come to me?"

Meghan had obviously stepped into something that went well beyond Stacia's dalliances with most of the male vampires in Manhattan. At the thought of Stacia and Blake together, confusion and outrage reemerged. As she neared to pour them some wine, her feelings drew Stacia's attention once more.

"Jealous, little one? Do you want a taste of my passion for yourself?"

She almost purred as she stroked Meghan's cheek.

"Get over yourself. I've no interest in sloppy seconds." Meghan needed to deny her interest in Blake as a matter of self-preservation against the vampire elder. She knew Stacia would gladly jump on any sign of weakness.

"Nor am I," Diana said. To Meghan's relief, Stacia seemed amused by their comments. She merely shook her head with mirth while Diana resumed her seat on the opposite side of the coffee table.

Meghan poured the wine and offered each of the women a glass. She filled her own to the brim, suspecting she would need the additional fortification before the night was out.

When they were seated, Diana skipped the preliminaries and went straight to the core of their problem. "Heard tell that you know about this drug that seems to be responsible for what's been going on at Otro Mundo."

Stacia shrugged and shifted in her chair, eased one leg over the arm. The pose was both casual and sensual, making Meghan think of her lying on a settee while she waited to be served. "A thousand years ago, sanguinarium became all the rage in more ways than one."

"The drug makes a vampire's bloodlust uncontrollable?" Diana asked.

With a husky laugh, Stacia said, "It was never about the bloodlust, *mia amica*. That was just a nasty side effect."

Diana leaned forward, her elbows braced on her knees as she loosely held the glass of wine in her hands. "So what was it about the drug that made it so popular?"

"The desire," Stacia immediately answered. "Think of it as Viagra for vamps. Just a few drops and a vampire's body would be sexually supercharged. Filled with immense need."

"And intense satisfaction," Diana said.

Stacia slowly slung her leg over the edge of the chair and rose. The air in the room seemed to grow thick, and within her, Meghan suddenly felt a deep throb that grew in intensity in achingly slow moments. She sucked in a breath, battling the urge and heard Diana's sharp gasp.

"Imagine this, *cara*," Stacia said, clearly in control of both her and Diana. "Imagine this feeling for hours on end. Imagine that every touch, every caress, brings infinite satisfaction. Release beyond anything you can imagine."

With those words and a careless flick of her hand, the vampire elder released them from her control.

Diana immediately shot up from her seat, her body shaking with anger. "Don't ever use your vamp energy on me again, Stacia."

"Or what, *cara?* You'll cuff me? That might be fun," Stacia said with a wicked laugh as she curled back into her seat like a pleased cat.

Diana hesitated, clearly battling with herself before she finally said, "Pray that you never push me that far."

Stacia waved her hand dismissively and took a sip of her wine. "Do you need to know anything else?"

Diana handled Stacia blowing her off more gracefully than Meghan had expected. Maybe it was because the agent was used to uncooperative suspects. With a bracing breath, Diana continued her questioning. "So if none of the men knew about the drug—"

"All of the men are too young. Sanguinarium was outlawed hundreds of years before they were turned," Stacia said.

"So only the elders would know about it. But where would someone get their hands on it?" Meghan asked, needing to do more than just sit there.

Stacia quirked a brow at her. "When the drug was outlawed, any stashes of it were destroyed. Anyone caught selling or using the drug was put to death."

"Death seems like a pretty extreme punishment."

"You've seen what it can do, little one. The blood-lust that comes with the passion is nearly impossible to control, and if the lust isn't sated, the vamp may expire from the want. Dead vampires and humans started turning up everywhere, their bodies ravaged as the sanguinarium user tried to satisfy their hunger."

"And too many bodies around is never good, is it, *amiga?*" Diana offered as explanation.

Stacia's mood sombered. She turned in her seat and, with her eyes downcast, said, "Vampires used to live peacefully in Rome, and then the troubles started. We were rounded up. Destroyed by the hundreds. To survive, we had to go underground."

She raised her face then and no doubt remained about her anguish. "We managed to stay peacefully in our own underworld until the bodies began to show up again. People started hunting down all of our kind once more, threatening our existence."

Diana nodded. "I understand."

"There's not an elder I know that would risk another slaughter like the many we've managed to survive," Stacia said, slowly rising from her chair.

Diana did the same, only this time there was something different in her stance, Meghan realized. Unexpectedly, Diana rounded the coffee table, walked up to Stacia and wrapped her arms around the vampire elder.

Stacia was stiff in her arms for a moment before she freed her emotions and embraced the other woman.

They were so alike, physically and spiritually, that it was almost like seeing double, Meghan realized, until the two women pulled apart and the moment of connection between them snapped.

"If you hear anything about this—"

"I'll be sure to call," Stacia said. With the same kind of theatrics she used to make her entrance, she made her exit, her sheer, black chiffon wrap trailing behind her, seemingly waving them goodbye as she leapt out the window.

"That is one piece of work," Meghan said.

"One of a kind," Diana agreed, shaking her head. She walked back to the sofa, picked up her glass and took a bracing sip of wine.

Meghan fiddled with her glass, considering Stacia's words. "So if none of the elders she knows would do this, who is it?"

"It may be someone new in town. Anyone you can think of?"

One person came to mind immediately. "That new vampire at the Blood Bank—Sun Tze Lee—the kiangshi. He's nasty."

"Have you and Blake been able to get any more info on him?"

She shook her head. "Not really. All I can tell you is that he creeps me out."

Diana chuckled. "It's always good to go with your gut, Meghan. It never fails you."

"Unlike your heart," Meghan surprised herself by saying.

A melancholy cast slipped over Diana's features. "Your heart can sometimes lead you places that can only bring you a world of hurt."

She met the other woman's gaze. Sorrow had taken hold there, darkening the brown of her eyes until they were almost black. "You regret what you have with Ryder?"

A flicker of pain passed across Diana's features. "I regret how little time I'll have with him."

As Meghan considered her, she realized that Diana possibly wasn't referring to the whole "I'll grow old and die and you won't" part of loving a vampire. Before she could say anything, Diana asked, "What's up with you and Blake?"

Meghan wished she could say what was up, but her feelings were too uncertain. "We've hooked up, only… it's hard to forget the past. How he stole my life."

"Your mortal life. But now you've got another life— an eternal one that he's already saved," Diana said, reminding her of how Blake had helped her years earlier when she had been kidnapped.

"Do you think that's a fair trade? Losing my fairly happy humanity for an eternally lonely existence?"

The FBI agent smiled, but the smile didn't reach those now nearly fathomless eyes. Eyes that clearly had seen more than their share of anguish in the course of Diana's relatively young life.

"The rest of your undead life doesn't have to be lonely. Look at Ryder and me," she said, only Meghan recognized the lie in her words. Diana didn't believe in happily-ever-after, and neither could she.

With the kind of world both of them had been thrust into, nothing could ever end happily, she thought, which made her reconsider what she was doing with Blake.

Whether she was only opening herself up to a whole new world of loss.

Better she guard her heart once again because an eternal life of loneliness beat one filled with endless heartache.

Chapter 16

Two days later, time seemed to pass slowly in the Otro Mundo kitchen as Meghan worked. Anticipating the upcoming meeting with Ryder, Diana and Diego made every action seem long and drawn out. She hoped they'd been able to learn more than she had about the killings. And adding to her edginess was her reticence about Blake, which made every interaction with him awkward.

When the last of the workers had been fed and the kitchen was spotless, it was nearly midnight. Blake and she reunited at the door to the alley.

"Is everything all right, love? You seemed distant tonight," he said, laying a hand on her shoulder.

She shrugged off his touch and stepped away from him, earning Blake's perplexed look. "Meghan?"

"I'm just worried, that's all. Stacia—"

"Don't let her get to you," he urged, and reached for her again.

"Like she got to you?" she challenged, but then shook her head. "Sorry. I know why you did it."

"And it won't happen again, love. I promise," he said. At her nod, they walked together to the meeting in the office where Diego, Ryder and Diana were already seated.

The three were having some brandy and, when they entered, offered them a drink. Blake quickly accepted, but she demurred. She had never been much of a drinker, and she blamed Mr. Cuervo in part for her decision to go to the back rooms with Blake that long ago night.

The civility of the drinks and the genteel sipping that ensued seemed at odds with the reason for their gathering. Since she was eager for news, she pressed forward after she and Blake sat down on the sofa.

"Have you found out anything, Diana?"

Diana was sitting at Diego's desk in one of the chairs that had been turned to face the sofa. Diego and Ryder stood on either side of her, looking like the muscle in a movie star's entourage. Diana took a sip of her brandy and nodded before beginning. "In studying vampire blood, Melissa discovered that in addition to the typical human blood cells, there are two vampire cell strains."

"Why was she playing with vampire blood?" Blake asked, earning a glare from Ryder and a sharp command for silence from Diego.

"Sorry. Forgot that I'm just the hired help here," he said, as he leaned back and took a sip from his snifter.

"The second of the vampire cell strains," Diana continued, "is rather fragile and survives just a short time after the blood is drawn from the vampire."

It was apparently Diego's turn to be impatient. "What does this have to do with the outlawed sanguinarium drug?"

"Melissa confirmed that the dead vamp's blood contained similar trace elements to those left in the vial, so the vamp had clearly used the drug. She also found that there was an abnormally large amount of the one strain and the total absence of the more fragile cells in the dead vamp's blood."

Meghan spoke up. "So this vampire crack causes one kind of cell to go crazy and destroys the second?"

Diana nodded. "Apparently it's the fragile strain that keeps control. Without them the bigger cells, which seem to deal with healing and vamp power, go wild and create—"

"Horny, demented, throat-slashing bloodsuckers," Blake chimed in. "So how do we stop a vamp who's stoned on this stuff?"

Ryder shrugged and crossed his arms. "Melissa is still working on an antidote. What have you been able to find out?"

Blake squirmed in his chair and uneasily glanced at Meghan from the corner of his eye. "I talked to Foley at the Blood Bank. Seems he's not the owner of the club."

"Really? That's news. So who is?" Diego asked, clearly surprised by Blake's revelation.

Meghan replied at once. "The kiang-shi. Lee has been behind the scenes from the very beginning."

This earned a questioning look from Blake. "Found that out while you were having your little tête-à-tête with the Chinaman, did you?" A hint of jealousy filled his voice.

"I did. So what else did you learn during your little *mano a mano* with Foley?"

Blake shifted to avoid the glances of the others and slugged down a healthy gulp of the brandy. "Nothing that's pertinent to this discussion."

"And you've made that determination because you're suddenly an expert on criminal investigations?" Diana asked, arching one brow in challenge.

"What Foley and I discussed is private and personal. Nothing else to say about it." He fidgeted in his seat once more and Diana must have decided that there was no sense pressing him. Looking up at Diego, she said, "So what happened with Maximillian and Hadrian?"

Diego leaned back against the edge of the desk and looked downward, his discomfort clear. "Hadrian has too much to lose right now to be involved in this."

"Too much to lose? Like what?" Ryder pressed.

From across the room Meghan sensed Diego's reticence to answer. Whatever he had to tell them was going to be a bombshell, she suspected, but she wasn't prepared for what Diego said next.

"His new wife is pregnant."

A stunned stillness settled over the room. Involuntarily Meghan's hand fluttered upward to rest over her abdomen. "Pregnant? And she's a—"

"Vampire. He sired her after she'd been mortally wounded during a robbery. That siring produced—"

"A baby," Diana said with such a heartfelt sigh that

Meghan felt her own heart clutch with pain. Diana's head jerked to Ryder and then to Diego.

"How is that possible?" she asked in whispered disbelief.

"It's rare, but…" Diego laid a hand on Diana's shoulder. "If a woman is fertile at the time of siring and mating occurs, there's a very small chance that a child can be conceived."

Meghan rubbed her hand over her barren belly. It hadn't struck her until that moment that there might have been one glimmer of humanity still possible in her undead life. Clearly Diana felt the same way, judging from the wistful look that came to her face, only…

Diana was still mortal, she thought. Making a baby with Ryder was therefore a possibility. It was a possibility Meghan had been robbed of thanks to…

Blake.

Thanks to him, there was nothing left of a normal life anymore. No husband. No kids.

No happily-ever-after.

Pain filled her at that thought and must have communicated itself to Blake from the special connection they shared.

He reached out and laid a hand over hers, stilled the nervous motion of it against her empty womb.

"I'm sorry, Meghan. Truly I am."

His words could never make up for not only her barren womb, but for the stark eternal life she had envisioned one time too many.

Emotion swelled over her, so overwhelming that she ran from the room and back to the pantry. She laid her arms against the wall and buried her head against them, fought a losing battle with the tears and sobs that rattled the bones of her body.

A second later she felt his touch on her arm, but she didn't turn, didn't release herself to the comfort he offered.

Instead, Blake wrapped his arms around her waist. Leaning his head close to her ear, he said, "I wish I could take it all back, but I can't."

No, he couldn't, she thought. But the bigger question left to be answered was whether he could be the one to change her future. To possibly give her the hope that life eternal could hold some joy and not just loneliness.

He held her for long moments, gentling her with his presence, as if trying to convince her that her current undead state didn't need to amount to endless solitude. Look at Diego and Ramona, she told herself. And Hadrian and his pregnant wife.

She drove away the thoughts of all she had lost, sucked in a long, settling breath and gathered herself. Turning, she said, "We need to go back in so we can find out what they want us to do next."

"If that's what you want to do." He cupped her cheeks and wiped away the trails of tears with his thumbs.

"It's what we need to do," she said and moved away from him, but he was quick to act.

"Don't run away from me, Meghan. I know all of this is unexpected—"

"That's an understatement," she confessed.

He leaned his forehead against hers and dropped a quick kiss on her lips. "Trust in this, love. Give it the time it needs to develop."

"I guess time is one thing we have plenty of, isn't it?"

He recognized the bitterness of her words and backed away. "I'll take you home after this, if you'd rather."

Meghan thought of the large, empty apartment awaiting her if she took him up on his offer. She had been rattling around the rooms for months, almost lost. As luxurious as it was, it didn't feel like home.

She had to admit to herself that the apartment didn't provide her the kind of comfort she had experienced since setting foot in Blake's unusual apartment.

With a quick hitch of her shoulders, she said, "Your place is…cozier."

Blake chuckled, clearly trying to keep the tone of their talk light. "*Cozy* being a right proper euphemism for *small*."

She smiled reluctantly. "Nope. *Cozy* being another word for *homey*. Comfortable," she added at the last minute, surprising even herself with the confession.

Blake made her feel comfortable. She had never expected to feel that way about the man who had irrevocably changed the course of her life, but she did. As baffled as she was by all that she was feeling, she had taken the time to consider Diana's words of the other day and her fears about future heartache. She had realized that in the years since he turned her, Blake had been there to protect her time and time again. That he had made himself a part of her circle of friends, always there to lend a hand. Always there without being asked or even appreciated.

He had been proving himself for years, only she had

never been willing to accept it or him. Even now, she feared to believe as he asked, but maybe if she did…

Maybe some things were possible.

He slipped his hand into hers without saying anything as if he knew that by speaking he would splinter the fragile trust she had bestowed with her earlier words.

She accepted that silence and followed him back to the office. All eyes were on them as they reentered and took their places again. As they sat, she slowly pulled her hand from his, wanting to guard what was happening between them for the moment. It was still too new, too fragile and too uncertain for her to shout out about it with any public displays of affection.

"What do we do next?" she asked, wanting to return to the reason for the meeting.

Ryder spoke first. "Melissa is going to try and isolate the active ingredient in the drug that causes the imbalance between the two cell strains. If she can do that, she may be able to create an antidote that will neutralize the drug's effects and end the bloodlust."

Diana immediately jumped in and added, "You two should head to the Blood Bank again. See if there's anything that appears like drug dealing going on with the vampires. Find out more about this kiang-shi. See if he's old enough to know about the drug."

"And boss man here?" Blake questioned, motioning to Diego.

"I'm going to keep an eye out around here. Talk to Stacia and see if there's some way she can help us find out where the drug is coming from," Diego replied.

"Sounds like a plan," Blake said, and rose from the couch. "We've got to go. Late night. Need to rest up for work tomorrow," he said, and faked a yawn.

"This isn't a joking matter," Ryder said.

In a fatherly tone, Diego added, "You two need to take this seriously."

Meghan met Blake's gaze and it was intense. His bright-blue eyes were alive with life and humor. With a crooked grin, he said, "Oh, I believe we are quite serious this time. Right, Meghan?"

Once again it was difficult for her to deal publicly with whatever was happening between them, but she couldn't hurt him and so she tried to make her response as neutral as she could.

"We are serious, Diego. We understand the consequences of what may happen." As she said the words, however, she realized they were about much more than the investigation, as did Blake.

His smile wavered for a moment, but then he added, "Totally understood. Some things are too important to risk."

When he slipped his hand into hers this time, she couldn't deny him, sensing she would jeopardize whatever was happening between them. Sensing that whatever was happening could make a huge difference for the future.

Maybe a future filled with something other than heartache and desolation.

Lee had selected the three women not just for their beauty but, more important, for their decided susceptibility to suggestion. A thought implanted here and there, coupled with the pull of his undead power, was enough to guarantee him both bedmates and a meal.

Tonight he had all three women pleasing him physically. That he could order them to do anything he wished only increased the gratification he took from his debaucheries.

"Baobei," he said to the Chinese girl on her knees before him.

A shy smile came to her face, and she bent her head obediently. "This treasure would like to please you, Sun Tze."

At his curt nod, she encircled his flaccid penis and from behind him he heard, "May I pleasure you as well?"

He glanced over his shoulder at the tall African-American girl, and something cold slithered down his back. As he spied what was missing from the wall of the back room, he grinned and said, "Why of course, my pet."

The third woman—the young blonde who reminded him too much of the feisty chef—took a place at his side. With a sexy pout, she rubbed her naked breasts against his arm. "What? No room for me?"

"Do not worry. There is enough of me for all of you," he said, but a rough gasp was torn from his throat as the woman behind him finally penetrated him and the woman on her knees took him into her mouth.

Not to be left out, the blonde beside him reached down and cupped his balls. With practiced caresses she squeezed and fondled him, stroking the sensitive gap between his balls as the two other women continued with their ministrations as well, building his passion.

The blonde sensed his growing arousal and leaned ever closer to him, knowingly caressing him with her hands and with the sweep of her breasts. The demon that he was forgot all about the pleasures of the flesh as the smell of her skin infused him, as warmth of her life pressed against him. As the beat of her heart registered strong and steady beside him.

He slipped his arm around the blonde's waist and bent his head to inhale her freshness. He imagined that her blood would be as clean and crisp.

Just as refreshing as he imagined Meghan Thomas might be if he were to sample her. He envisioned taking the independent chef, violating her while he drank his fill…

But he was saving her for something else. Something very special that would show all the human wannabes what being a vampire was all about.

As he imagined that bloodbath the demon erupted, long fangs bursting forth from his mouth to pierce the long line of the blonde's neck. His eyes became solid orbs of crimson, coloring everything in his world in hues of blood.

The blonde managed a short scream as he fed, but he drained her so quickly that he was already grabbing the other two women when her limp body fell away and they realized what was happening.

He continued his feasting on the tall African-American girl, savoring the strength that surged through his veins with her blood. As she, too, dropped away, slack from the blood loss, he finally turned his attention to the young Asian girl, who cowered before him, crying in fear. "Kiang-shi. Kiang-shi."

Laughing, he hauled her up and with his greater strength, lifted her so that he could impale himself in her body while he fed, violating her not once but twice. As he did so, he called out to his kiang-shi bodyguards to come and share in the feast. To come and finish granting him his pleasure.

The first kiang-shi through the door immediately took the place of the African-American girl, driving deep and finally releasing Lee's climax into the girl he still held in his arms.

When he freed her, he motioned to the other two kiang-shi bodyguards, offering them his leftovers. What remained of the women's blood would keep their bodies from decomposing for the next few days. Since he had forbidden them from exchanging blood with any of their European cousins, they were not filled with the strength and powers of the vampire elders as he was.

As for the vampire who had rushed in to satisfy him, Lee urged him around so that they were facing. Leaning close, he whispered a kiss across the other man's lips before raising his wrist to reward him with a taste of his elder blood. Spiced as it was with the life of Foley's blood, it was more potent and would sustain his kiang-shi guard for days longer than anything human.

The glow began in his bodyguard's eyes, a dull red like that of a lunar eclipse, but as his fangs elongated, the gleam intensified until only bright-red orbs remained.

The kiang-shi pierced the skin at Lee's wrist and drank thirstily. Each pull and suck of his mouth roused Lee's passion yet again. When the kiang-shi was nearly done feeding, Lee pulled him off his wrist, whirled him around and plunged himself deep into the other man.

The startled cry of pain only intensified the bliss surging through Lee's veins. As the other man grappled with him to be set free, Lee sank his fangs deep into the thick muscle at the man's shoulder, punishing him for his desire to escape.

The shaken kiang-shi stilled and with a soft moan of acquiescence, accepted the violation.

When Lee was done sating himself, he tossed the kiang-shi away and to the floor, where the two others were finishing up their meals.

It was then, as the limp body of the blonde snared his gaze again, that he reminded himself of the unfinished business to be settled.

He had to find a way to foment discord amongst the cadre of vamps at Otro Mundo and their other human haunts. Once they were busy distrusting one another, he would take Meghan and unleash hell upon them.

If any of them managed to survive, he and his kiang-shi would be there to finish them off.

Chapter 17

Blake had skipped the closing get-together at the restaurant that night in favor of scoping out the Blood Bank again. There was just too much about Lee that he didn't like, and he figured that the Asian vampire had to have something to do with all the problems going down lately at Otro Mundo. Not that Foley had mentioned anything about that during their talk. So far, all he could pin on Lee was his abuse of Foley and the too-lewd looks he had bestowed on Meghan on various occasions.

That made him a sodomizer and a lecher, but not necessarily a murderer.

Blake intended to find out if he was the latter.

As he had on a multitude of other nights, he hung around the bar drinking blood, only this time he was listening for anything out of the ordinary. Unfortunately, it seemed like just another night at the Blood Bank. A few shoving matches out on the dance floor. A dozen or so couples heading into the back rooms for some naughty games.

Wickedly naughty, he thought, watching one particularly amorous couple groping each other while waiting for the vampire guard to finish with another twosome in the back rooms. A spark of passion flared to life as he imagined what he and Meghan might do later that night.

That is, he thought, if she wanted to go home with him again tonight. Maybe he was presuming too much to think that she would want to.

It had been damn good last night and not just sexually. When he lay in her arms the harsh reality of their world fell away, and he could imagine in those moments that they were regular people living everyday lives and not demons.

He understood better now how Diego and Ryder must feel. How the desire to be normal once again could overcome the demands of the vampire. How it could hold at bay that world of death and destruction that had been his existence for so long.

"She must be pretty special," Foley said, as he plopped down in the stool next to Blake and crooked his finger. The bartender immediately arrived with a glass of blood for Foley, but he pushed it in Blake's direction and signaled the bartender to bring another.

"Feeling generous, mate? Rather rare for you, isn't it?" Blake picked up the glass and raised it in a toast once Foley had his own drink.

"Feeling decidedly relieved." Foley took a sip. His gaze skipped to the back rooms for a moment before he leaned close and said, "Lee's found someone else to satisfy him tonight."

"Lucky you," he said, and surprisingly he meant it. He and Foley had never been the best of friends, but the past week had altered their relationship. Maybe because they were two of a kind in some ways.

"You'd do well to stay clear of him. You and your special little woman," Foley said.

Blake smiled and drained the blood from the tumbler. "Rattled him, did we?"

"Major-league pissed him off." Foley finished his drink and once again signaled the bartender for another.

"Must be a sight to see when he's angry," Blake said offhandedly, hoping to find out more about the kiang-shi's behavior.

"Scarier than your everyday vamp for sure," Foley confirmed. "Teeth are needle-thin and long as can be. Hurts like a bitch when he gets you."

Intrigued despite his concern for Foley, he said, "Any other creepiness I should beware of?"

"Red eyes like the flames of hell," Foley replied, voice growing lower and more dismayed. He leaned conspiratorially close as he added, "And that damn black hair goes white. Pure white against those gleaming fired-up eyes."

Foley shuddered, clearly put off by the idea, but Blake was anything but. "White, you say? And I suppose he hops hops hops like the Easter Bunny when he's in that form?"

With a shrug, Foley said, "Who knows? When he's got his fangs in me, all I can think about is the pain."

Blake nodded. "I'll try to remember that, mate."

They landed on the patio of his apartment noise-lessly, stirring not even the new green leaves of the plants he had potted. As she stood there with him, her hand in his, that potently appealing sense of comfort and welcome washed over her.

It had been so long since she had experienced that feeling of homecoming. She took a moment to fully embrace it. At her hesitation, Blake playfully tugged on her hand.

"Having second thoughts?" The cocky grin and gleam in his eyes had left his handsome face. The all-too-serious features that had replaced it were stamped with doubt.

She suspected much of his life had been filled with doubt. From the uncertainty of his family's survival to his becoming a vampire, instability had been the only thing he could call his own. She realized now that it was the reason for the persona he had opted to present to the world. The brash, don't-give-a-shit personality that she had somehow seen past on that night so many years ago.

In its place now was a new man. The honorable man he had struggled to display to her time and time again, but she had refused to see because of her anger.

The weird thing was, he hadn't stirred her anger in some time. Not since the night in the alley when he had announced he was going to take a job at Otro Mundo. She hadn't believed him back then. Hadn't thought he could do as he promised, but he had.

He had shown her a man filled with determination. A man who could love with all his heart. A man who would respect her. By doing so, he had reined in the fury she had felt toward him.

Cradling the hard line of his jaw with one hand, she leaned forward and brushed a kiss across his lips. "Having penny kinds of thoughts," she explained, wanting to remove his anxiety.

Beneath her lips she felt the shift of his smile as his lips curled beneath hers. He chuckled and drew her near. "Only a penny for your thoughts? They seemed to be much more valuable than that."

She kissed him again before murmuring, "They were. There were naughty thoughts as well."

Blake chuckled and sensed that she was holding back, but gave himself over to her kiss anyway. He sensed that whatever valuable thoughts she'd had might be too new and too special to share with him. Much as what he had been feeling about her was also possibly too untried to share. He wanted to hoard up all the feelings she brought to his heart until the time was right and he could give them to her without fear.

So for now, he just gave as much as she did, kissing her until she was breathless and clinging to him beneath the crescent of moon that bathed the patio in shades of silver and blue. When she murmured a protest, demanding more, he tugged on her lower lip in mock punishment and said, "Let's head in, love. I imagine the bed is a might more comfortable than staying out here."

She laughed lightly and followed him into his apartment. As they entered, it occurred to him that for nearly a dozen years he had been carefully piecing together this place. Everything in it, old as it was, he had chosen. Those things that had been battered or a bit bruised he had repaired as best he could.

Much like he had tried to repair his life, he realized.

Much like he was trying to mend the damage that he had done to Meghan.

He faced her. She was gazing at him intently as she asked, "I know those thoughts were downright serious. I can feel it here." She laid a hand over her heart and within him, he felt that touch as if she were laying her hand on his heart.

It was that freaky vampire connection. The one that stretched between them, thanks to the shared blood pulsing through their veins. Forcing a bright smile to his face, he laid a hand on her waist and eased her close. "What I'm damn serious about, Meghan, is that I'm going to love you tonight as if there's no tomorrow."

Because he wasn't sure that she wouldn't change her mind. That the past and all that had happened between them wouldn't rise up and stoke her anger again, he thought sadly as he brought his lips to hers and cherished them.

He slipped off her clothes, worshipping every inch of her that he exposed. Leaving the reminder of his hands and lips on her body so that she would never forget how he could make her feel.

So that no other man who had come before or would come after would be free of that memory.

As they fell to the bed and he eased within her, he shook from the force of the union, knowing that he, too, would never be free of her. That she had imprisoned his heart forever.

She rose up then and encircled him in her arms, held him to her and whispered, "I want to believe in forever, Blake."

The release slammed through them then. Physical. Mental. Emotional.

Still shaking from the force of it, he eased her to the center of the bed and wrapped his arms around her. He twined his legs with hers until they were so tightly bound together, it was as if they were one.

It was the way they were supposed to be, Blake thought, as he began loving her once more.

Blake heaved the trash bag up and over the landing and to the ground below. It was easier than navigating the narrow steps with the oversized bag. After he did so, however, he noticed motion at the end of the alley, close to the spot where he and Meghan had discovered the dead vampire weeks ago.

They said lightning never struck twice in the same place, but he knew better. High on a hilltop by his old home was a gnarled old oak that had been repeatedly stricken until one last blast had toppled it.

Walking down the steps, he held the bag in one hand, light as it was with his vamp strength. He slowly headed for the nearby Dumpsters and tossed in the bag, all the time peering down the alley for any sign of action once again.

He was rewarded for his patience with the sight of two persons standing at the mouth of the alley. They were handing over money and a quick exchange followed, but all he saw of the one person was hands. Pale hands with long, effeminate nails.

Before he could act on it, the two must have detected his presence. In a blur of speed, they left.

Vamp speed, Blake decided. He put on his own burst of speed to reach the mouth of the alley, intending to give pursuit, but by the time he got there both vampires were long out of sight.

Two vampires and money exchanging hands was the kind of thing to cause him worry. He looked upward at the rooftops and considered where they might have gone. For a second he thought he detected a glimmer of red from one rooftop, but he blinked and it was gone.

But what wasn't gone was a cloying scent. Spicy and aromatic. He sniffed deeply, realizing it was the same aroma he had noted when they had found the dead vampire here weeks ago. He took another deep inhale, sure that the scent was the odor of whoever was involved in what was going on.

He was convinced that he had smelled that aroma around Foley recently.

Returning down the alley, he bounded back up the steps of the landing and into the restaurant, determined to share this bit of information with Meghan and the others when they met later.

Chapter 18

Blake sensed anger the moment he stepped into the office of Otro Mundo for another meeting. So much anger that he was almost fearful of hearing what Diana Reyes had to say, and so he decided to hold his bit of news for later.

The FBI agent had been pacing back and forth in the room when he and Meghan entered, her strides clipped, tension gripping every line of her body. At his entry, she faced him and jammed her hands onto her hips.

"Do you have something to share?" Diana held his gaze for too long a moment, making him even more uncomfortable.

He shook his head and shot an anxious glance at Meghan, who in turn presented him with a puzzled look. She was as baffled as he by Diana's apparent animosity.

"Nothing to report," he said.

"Really?" Diana challenged.

Ryder came to stand at her side and Diego on the other, the three of them clearly united against him.

"Did Melissa find out anything else about the drug?" Meghan asked, apparently trying to deflect their attention.

"The drug's a doozy," Diana said, as Ryder placed his hand on Diana's shoulder to restrain her. "Melissa is still trying to find a way to keep the sanguinarium drug from causing the one cell strain to multiply out of control."

"But she thinks she can find a way to stop it, right?" Meghan asked. In an almost surprising manifest show of unity, she slipped her hand onto Blake's as they sat side by side on the couch.

"Massive feeding from another vampire will supply enough of the delicate cell strain to absorb the drug in the vampire's system. It's why those vamps drained each other dry. The drug created the demand for the one thing that would neutralize its action."

Blake considered what Diana had said and shook his head. "So human blood—"

"Won't bond with the drug and offset it. Turn a vamp on the drug loose in a crowd of humans and he could drain them dry but never find release from the effects of the drug," Diego explained.

"Which brings us to you, Blake. What do you have to tell us?" Diana asked.

He didn't like the way the three of them were looking at him. He had faced those kinds of looks before and they generally didn't bode well. "We didn't learn a thing at the Blood Bank during the last few days."

"Nothing," Meghan confirmed, and anxiously squeezed his hand.

"Really?" Diana slipped from Ryder's grasp and began to pace once again, before whirling to face them. "Okay, let's start with this. Where were you on the night the first vampire couple fed to the death?"

He shrugged carelessly. "I was at the Blood Bank for the better part of the night."

"And then in the alley. We met in the alley that night," Meghan added.

He nodded in agreement, glad that Meghan had supported his alibi and wondering why he suddenly felt as if he needed one. He pressed on with his defense, however. "That's right. I came by—"

He stopped, not about to give up his real reasons for dropping in. "I just came by to see how things were going."

Ryder laughed harshly. "And they were going much as you expected them to be."

His comment was totally not good, Blake thought. He grew even more worried when Diana said, "You were the one who noticed the dead vampire in the alleyway a few days later."

"I was putting out the trash and saw something move." He glanced at Meghan, urging her to confirm his statement.

She immediately responded with, "When we walked to the end of the alley, we found the body."

"But *you* didn't see anything or hear anything before that?" Diego insisted, directing his attention to Meghan.

"Nothing," Meghan answered. Her hand twitched in his, filling him with unease. Their relationship was still fragile. The trust that had developed between them untested.

Until now, he suspected and worried that it was too new to hold fast.

Ryder narrowed his eyes as he observed them and asked, "The night the young vampiress attacked her dining companion, you brought them their food and drink, didn't you?"

So totally not good, he thought.

Meghan pulled her hand from Blake's as she, no doubt, realized where the others were going with their line of questioning. She met his gaze, and he could see her searching his features for any signs of deception.

There were none, of course, but he still felt her unease.

"I have nothing to do with what's been happening," Blake urged. He raised his hands and emphasized the point with a slash of his hands. "Nothing."

"You said you saw something funky in the vampiress. How did you see that?" Meghan asked, hoping he would have a reasonable explanation to dispel the apprehension growing within her.

"Meghan, I didn't do anything wrong," he insisted, but she just repeated her question.

"How did you know?"

He shrugged and shook his head, so forcefully it sent strands of his hair shifting forward onto his forehead. "I just knew. She had a crazy look in her eye. One I didn't like, kind of like I'm not liking the way all of you are looking at me right now."

Diana stepped in front of him. She counted down on her fingers as she said, "There have been three incidents,

Blake. Surprisingly, you've been present at all three. While I don't want to believe you had a role in them—"

"I don't." He rose from the sofa and faced Meghan, wordlessly asking her to believe in the man he had shown her the past few weeks.

But from the way her gaze had grown cold, Blake knew his plea might have gone unheard. He repeated yet again, his voice softer as the futility of his plea registered, "I have nothing to do with what's happened. It's just coincidence."

"Coincidence, huh?" Diana pulled a plastic bag from the pocket of her loose-fitting jeans and held it up for all to see.

"Is this coincidence also?" she challenged as she jiggled the evidence bag in his face.

He snagged it from her grasp and examined the contents. Three glass vials wrapped in intricate golden webwork, much like the vial they had found on the out-of-control vampiress, were sealed in the bag.

"Where did you get these?" he asked, as he returned them to the FBI agent.

"You were out in the alley tonight?" Diego asked, but Blake scoffed at the question.

"Of course I was. You've had me hauling your sorry garbage for weeks now. Where did you think I would take it?"

Diego was on him in a flash, grabbing him by the throat and lifting him as if he weighed nothing. The force of his grip was punishing and cut off his air. Blake yanked at Diego's hand with his, fighting to be free, but Diego didn't relent until Meghan laid her hand on him and gently said, "Let him go, Diego. Please."

At her request, Diego thrust Blake aside with so much force that he couldn't stop his fall.

Blake picked himself up from the floor, rubbing his throat as he looked at Diana and said with a rasp, "Where did you get those?"

"Don't play stupid," Ryder replied, ready to go at him as well, only Diana stepped in front of him, blocking his path. Surprisingly strong for a human, Blake thought for only a second before concern for his own ass came to the forefront.

"Why don't you tell us where you got these?" Diana said, once again holding up the bag.

"I don't know what you're talking about. You have to believe me, Meghan." He took a step toward her, but she backed away from him and toward the other vampires. She might as well have staked him through the heart, the pain was so great.

"One of the vampire busboys saw you at the end of the alley. They thought you were with someone else," Diego offered up as explanation.

"I saw something going on. Money exchanged hands between two vamps, but by the time I got there, they were long gone—only I smelled something familiar. Something I smelled the night we found the dead vampire in the alley." He dragged a hand through his hair in frustration, wishing he could put a name to the scent, but he couldn't. His mum had never been one for fancy fare like Meghan prepared.

Meghan, he thought. If anyone could identify the scent, it would be her. Pleading once more, he said, "You smelled it, didn't you? That night in the alley."

"I smelled blood and garbage. Nothing else," she said. The tone of her voice sounded sad, and the grim set of her lips damned him as a liar.

Something died inside of him. More dead than the demon within. More painful than anything he had ever experienced. Meghan believed the evidence the others had found. It had called to her doubt, the doubt that lay just below the surface, waiting for him to screw up once again. It was the excuse she needed to push him away.

Although it was a useless protest, he repeated, "I don't know anything about those vials."

"Then why were they in your locker?" Ryder asked.

"My locker? What about the Fourth Amendment and all that? Or is it the Fifth? You law-enforcement types must know you can't just look in someone's locker."

"Is that why you had them there? Because you thought we wouldn't look there? Because you thought we would trust you?" Meghan asked. Anger sparked in her eyes as she confronted him. Her hands were clenched at her sides, her knuckles white from the pressure of her grip.

"After everything we've shared, how can you believe the worst of me so quickly?" he said testily. At the same time, he realized that only a guilty man would start quoting legalities.

Her stance softened then, but only a bit. Lifting her glittering gaze to his, she said, "Why won't you tell us anything that would make us think otherwise?"

He shook his head and gave a harsh laugh. Meeting her gaze directly, he said, "Because I thought that all I've done for you would speak louder than words."

Then he shifted his gaze to the other three. "I don't know how the drugs got in my locker. But I have my suspicions about who might be involved."

Surprisingly, Diana slackened her attack at his words and with that, the others seemed to lose some of their aggressiveness as well. She glanced at him and said, "Who do you think is involved?"

"I suspect Foley might have a connection to whoever is doing this. Whatever that odor is, I've smelled it around Foley," he explained.

Diego shook his head. "Foley isn't old enough to know about the drug."

"But he's got all kinds of badass vamps hanging out at the Blood Bank," he offered. "We've become friends, Foley and I. Give me a chance to talk to him and find out what he knows."

Diana looked to Ryder and Diego before nodding. "One chance, Blake. Convince us that we're wrong to doubt you."

One chance, he thought, but as he met Meghan's gaze and she looked away, he realized that she had already given him his one chance and found him lacking.

Regardless, he intended to prove his innocence. To show her how wrong she had been to lose her faith in him so easily.

Meghan watched as with a burst of vampire speed, Blake escaped from the office. After he did so, Diego came up to her and consoled her with a reassuring squeeze on her shoulder. "I'm sorry, *niña.*"

She shrugged off his touch and faced the others.

"What if he was telling the truth?" she asked, confusion and guilt tumbling together within her. She wanted to doubt him as much as she wanted to believe that Blake hadn't been lying. He had no reason to cause them such problems, after all. No motive to want to harm them.

"I want to give him the benefit of the doubt because of all that he's done for us in the past," Diana began, a chill tone coloring her words. "But if he is involved in this, he may lead us to whoever provided him with the drug. It's why we let him go."

"And if he's innocent, whoever is behind this may cap his ass if he gets too close to them," she shot back.

"You can still care for him even thinking that he might be behind this?" Diego asked, disdain filling his voice.

Did she still care? Meghan wondered. Could she still feel something for him, even with the damning evidence they had discovered?

Her confusion evaporated as she dejectedly realized the answer might be yes. Despite everything, a part of her continued to believe in him. At that, her shame rose even more sharply. When he had asked for her support, she had failed to provide it. Instead she had given in to her fears and jumped on the first thing she could to drive him away.

"We can't just use him as chum and hope that somehow he can survive to prove his innocence."

Surprisingly, it was Diana who approached her and gently laid a hand on her shoulder. "You're worried he can't handle whatever happens?"

Meghan shook her head and inhaled deeply. "Foley has a lot of backup. I'm not sure Blake… I hope he can…"

She didn't say it, but as her gaze met the other woman's, Diana knew. They both wanted to believe that love could make anything possible.

With a nod, Diana said, "We'll be ready in case anything happens."

"So where do we go from here?" Meghan asked.

Chapter 19

Disillusionment over Meghan's lack of faith sent Blake on a wild ride over the rooftops of Manhattan. He vaulted from building to building, climbing ever higher before plummeting downward. More than once he misjudged the distance and ended up sprawled ignominiously on the ground, his body smarting from the fall. Each time he erred, he picked himself up and pushed onward until he finally set down on the patio of his apartment.

He had thought that he had exhausted the emotion that had forced him out into the night.

He was wrong.

Fury sank its vicious teeth into his belly and drove him to further violence.

He kicked at the pots with the plants he had carefully cultivated. Soil and foliage went flying. He stomped through the tender leaves and roots on his way to the French doors of his apartment.

He nearly unhinged the doors from the frame as he tore them open and stalked inside. For years he had painstakingly gathered these things, trying to make the small space a home. Trying to delude himself that he could have what others had. That the poor coal miner's son might not have a lot of money but still have things he could call his own.

Old things, he thought, as he looked around. Castoffs that no one else had wanted.

Like no one wanted him, he thought. He grabbed a small piecrust table and flung it across the room, where it shattered against the wall. He forged onward, tossing the flotsam of his life aside. He moved closer to the bed he had so carefully restored, intending the same mayhem, but as he neared, the last of his rage faded.

Blake fell to his knees and buried his head against the bed.

The comforter and sheets still bore her scent and he inhaled deeply, flogging himself with the memory of her.

With a sharp tug, he ripped the linens off the bed, wrapped them up into a ball and pitched them to the side.

His anger spent, he rose and swiped at the moisture on his face, refusing to admit to the tears. Right then and there he swore he'd prove them wrong, and then he'd pack up his things and leave. It was time for him to find somewhere new to live. Some place where he could start over, the way he had done so many times during his long existence.

For too long he had deluded himself that this place could hold something different for him. Could hold love for him.

I should have known better, he thought.

Lee gazed at the kiang-shi standing before him. The younger man visibly trembled, hands clasped before him and head downcast in a show of obedience. A living man might have been sweating, but as kiang-shi they had lost many of their human traits, unlike their European brethren. Since Euro vamps still had some vestige of life, they retained many distasteful human attributes. Breathing, sweating, eating, if they chose to do so.

Maybe that was the reason for the vampires' continued misbelief that they could still experience human things. Or why the call of mortal love remained so tempting.

The kiang-shi knew no such weaknesses. They cared nothing for love or honor because they had not concerned themselves with those things in their mortal lives.

But as in their mortal lives, they understood the punishment for failure.

Lee shot a glance at his two other minions as they waited by the entrance to the door of the office in the Blood Bank. Their faces were unsympathetic, stoic. Their stances were erect and unyielding, just as they had been when they had served as his trusted cadre on the battlefield.

They would not come to the assistance of their friend.

"Someone saw you at the restaurant?" he asked. As his lackey nodded, rage built within him.

"You realize how dangerous you have made it for us?"

The man's limbs shook so much that Lee could imagine the undead flesh on those bones falling away from the continued force.

Lee intended to put him out of his misery long before that, furious as he was with the man's failure. No one was supposed to know that it was he and his group supplying the drug to the vampires. He had planned on casting doubt on another of the vampire elders present in the city: Stacia, Hadrian or one of the others who mingled on the fringes of the wannabes.

Now this underling had jeopardized his plans.

In a burst of speed, he was before the man, gripping him by the throat. The soft, decaying flesh gave easily beneath his fingers until he encountered the harder shell of cartilage and bone.

"Please, master," the kiang-shi choked out.

Fury rose up stronger at the man's entreaty. At the weakness he could not stomach in one of his warriors. "You would beg for this miserable existence to continue?"

The kiang-shi nodded. Seeing Lee's anger, he quickly tried to explain in the hopes of swaying him. "Only the platinum-haired one saw me, but I was able to trick him, master."

Lee exerted a bit more pressure and lifted the man until the tips of his toes were barely brushing the ground. The weight created a shift of bones and a series of small little pops as the kiang-shi stretched to try and counteract the traction Lee was creating with his hold.

"Trick him? How?"

With a wheezing sound escaping his damaged

throat, the kiang-shi said, "I watched him afterward and saw where he kept his things. I snuck in and left a few vials there."

Brilliant, Lee thought. He had wanted to create discord amongst the wannabes and his flunky's actions would do just that. These misguided vampires placed so much value on honor that they would never stomach one of their own betraying them.

He released the man, who sagged with relief.

When he smiled as he considered what the wannabes would do to the white-haired vamp in retribution, the kiang-shi took it as a sign of approval. He dropped to his knees and grabbed hold of Lee's leg. He hugged it tight and rubbed his head along Lee's crotch, wanting reward.

Lee rubbed the back of the kiang-shi's head the way he might pet a favorite dog. He whimpered with pleasure and pushed even harder against Lee's growing erection, only Lee's satisfaction was not coming from sexual anticipation.

He took the man's head in both hands, shivered as the man shifted his mouth up and down his penis.

The kiang-shi moaned, anticipating his reward, and in that moment, Lee violently twisted the kiang-shi's head.

The decaying bone and flesh were easily rent and for the barest bit of time, the kiang-shi looked up at Lee, his mouth opened in a surprised *O* as his body fell in a heap to the ground.

Satisfaction finally filled Lee and he tossed the kiang-shi's head onto the floor beside the rest of his body. He looked up and stared at the two other kiang-shi bodyguards. They remained immobile by the door, faces still blank and uncaring of the fate of their friend.

Lee jabbed his finger in the direction of the door. "Go fetch the platinum-haired vampire. Foley should know where he keeps his lair."

Meghan dropped down on the terrace of Blake's apartment from the adjacent rooftop.

She hadn't expected his welcome, but she certainly hadn't expected this, she thought, as she twined a path through the spilled soil and trampled remains of Blake's garden. Fear slammed into her as she took note of the French doors that were almost hanging off their hinges.

If Blake had been telling the truth and someone had seen him leaving Otro Mundo and coming here...

She rushed forward, almost sickened by the thought that something might have happened to him because she had not had the strength to believe. She had been too afraid of what she was feeling for him. Too scared of where it might lead and had jumped on the opportunity to create distance between them.

She had never expected this kind of reaction from him, and she wanted to weep as she entered his home and noted the destruction. Pieces of broken furniture and of some of the mementoes he'd collected littered the floor. The rugs, which had once been pristine, bore the remnants of soil and greenery tracked in from outside. Dropping to one knee, she glanced at the footprints on the rugs and realized there was just one set.

Only Blake's, she thought. She did a slow pivot to

take in all the damage to his home. All the wrath he had unleashed on those things he had so lovingly collected.

She understood that now.

Fury had called him to obliterate all that he had once held dear. To destroy those things that he saw as the evidence of his failure.

She plopped down on the edge of the unmade bed, sadness sapping her strength. She couldn't leave everything like this. She had made a mistake. A big one.

She shouldn't have doubted him. She should have stuck up for him before the others, only she had been a coward. She had allowed herself to be ruled by her earlier feelings for him. By the anger and hatred that she had harbored toward him for turning her.

Emotions that he had thought to change.

Emotions that he *had* changed, she acknowledged. Over the last few weeks, she had come to feel differently for him. She cared for him. In fact, she loved him.

It was her fear of loving him that had made her look for an excuse to distance herself from him.

She swept her gaze over his place once again and felt the pull of the love he had put into it. She remembered the nights they had recently shared and the comfort of his arms.

She couldn't leave his home like this.

Slowly she began gathering up those things that could be salvaged and put them to the side. Those things that were still intact she put back in their place. Finally she bagged the debris.

The bed looked decidedly inhospitable without linens, and she searched through his drawer for more.

They were filled with his clothes—modest, like the simple, uncomplicated man that he was. T-shirts and jeans, although in one drawer there was a hideous blue polyester suit that bore the distinct aroma of camphor.

In a bottom drawer she finally found a fresh set of sheets. She pulled them out and remade the bed, running her hand lovingly to smooth the sheets before she covered them with the rich silk comforter he had crumpled in one corner of the room.

A noise outside drew her attention and her heart sped up at the thought that it might be Blake returning home.

She raced outdoors, and the cloying scent of cardamom overwhelmed her senses a second before someone grabbed her from behind.

Chapter 20

Moonlight lit the rooftops for Blake as he continued to vent his rage and frustration by extending his romp across Manhattan. From his terrace near Gramercy Park he headed uptown, leaping across the roofs of the low buildings in the Thirties until he neared the high-rises of Midtown. He detoured there toward the East Side, speeding up Second Avenue until he got to the Queensboro Bridge.

With a series of bounding leaps, he climbed to the pinnacle of the bridge and stared at the East River below him. The water glistened with the moonlight and the reflected the lights of Manhattan.

Turning around, he peered toward the Manhattan skyline, searching out the tip of Ryder's building in the

Sixties. He imagined Ryder and the prickly FBI agent acting out homey scenes in their chic little pied-à-terre.

Sickening, he thought, trying to drive away the pain that would consume him if he continued with such thoughts.

Returning to Manhattan, he fled up Second to the Seventies, where he turned westward and plunged into the thicket of Central Park, racing and swerving through the woods there on his way to the West Side. The branches lashed at him, but that was good. The pain of them flogging his flesh whipped up his ire until he was in a fine fury.

On Central Park West he detoured back to Diego's fancy digs, determined to give Meghan a piece of his mind, but as he reached the building, he noted the lack of any vampire power within.

Strange, he thought. Noting the lateness of the hour, he wondered where she might be.

Probably still plotting with Nancy Drew and the rest of the gang. Probably considering how to make sure he ceased to be a problem in their lives. Little did they know he intended to take care of that himself. By leaving. Once he cleared his name.

He imagined the scene when he'd make that revelation. The shocked look on Meghan's face and how she would beg for forgiveness. He smiled as he thought about turning his back on her and walking away.

Of course, he could only do that if he got the goods on whoever had framed him and was responsible for the shit going down at Otro Mundo.

Which meant that it was long past time that he head

downtown to the Blood Bank. Foley was there and might tell him more about what was going on.

Blake intended to drag it out of Foley, even if it meant a fight. He was up for a good fight. Maybe breaking a few bones and spilling a little blood would drive away the last of his upset.

With a swell of speed, he blasted down to Columbus Circle and then along the broad width of Fifty-seventh Street, taking delight in the astonished gasps of the few pedestrians on the street as he blew past them, invisible to their gaze at this speed.

Once on the East Side he headed beneath the FDR Drive, racing past the seamier side of the city that the tourists didn't see. In seconds he was in the tangle of cobblestoned streets where the Blood Bank was located.

He leapt upward, intending to scope out the place before entering. The last thing he wanted to do was to run into Meghan and the rest of them, certain that they would be on the lookout for him. He knew that the only reason they had let him go was because they thought he would lead them to whoever had given him the drug.

To his surprise, not one of them was there. Unless they had opted to go inside and wait for him.

He dropped to the ground below and straightened the black leather jacket on his shoulders. Sauntering to the door, he snarled at the bouncer, displaying his fangs and the vampire nodded and let him past the line of patrons waiting to get in.

Once inside, he opened up his senses, searching the crowd for other immortals, and was rewarded by the strong hum of vampire power. A number of undead were present tonight. But he was disappointed not to sense the erratic, uneven thrum of energy he had sensed from Lee and the other kiang-shi.

Preparing himself for a run-in with Meghan and the rest of the gang, he was actually frustrated not to find them within the club, since he had wanted to vent his hostility against them. Instead, he found Foley at the end of the bar, sipping a drink, his hands shaky and a jittery tension in his body.

Blake slowly approached, not wanting to surprise the other vampire, who was clearly on edge. Foley must have picked up on the pulse of Blake's power, because he turned and shot Blake a pained smile. He raised his glass in invitation and signaled for the bartender to bring another. Not that Blake was in the mood for sharing a cup.

Still, he slipped onto a stool beside Foley, thinking that he might be able to get the information he needed without a fight. Pity that, he thought.

"This is getting to be a habit, old man," he said.

"They say misery loves company." Foley drained his glass with a quick gulp and slammed it down onto the scarred surface of the black bar.

"Have you had company lately?" he asked, as the bartender laid two glasses of blood before them.

"Lots of company," Foley admitted. "Lee and his crew, minus the ladies and one smelly corpse. I'm getting a little tired of picking up after him."

"Drained them, did he?" Blake asked, intrigued for a run-down on Lee's activities and hoping that something Foley said would clue him about Lee's other endeavors.

"Women were nearly dead once he and his friends

finished with them. Luckily they survived or there would have been a real mess to deal with." Foley grasped his new glass and cupped it with his hands, almost fondling it, as he said, "Corpse was nasty to clean up. Too many pieces for my taste."

"Pieces," Blake repeated, and at Foley's nod added, "Must have been a right mess."

"Definitely. Told the same thing to your friends."

Blake sniffed roughly and gulped down a bit of the blood. "Don't have any friends, Foley. You should know that by now."

Foley shot him a half glance, his gray eyes stormy. Troubled. "Seems we're two of a kind after all."

"Possibly," Blake muttered. "So what did my 'friends' want?"

Foley took a slurpy sip from his glass. Blake knew him too well not to realize he wanted to annoy him. He'd seen him use much the same tactic on the FBI agent and Ryder. Blake wasn't going to fall for it and so he remained silent, waiting for Foley to answer.

After another noisy taste, Foley laid the glass down and said, "They were looking for you. Asking all kinds of questions about what you've been up to."

"Hmm. Not much, I'm sorry to say."

Foley reached over and plucked something from Blake's jacket, which he tossed onto the bar. A small pine twig that must have snared in his jacket during his wild race through the park. "I'm guessing that's there because you went uptown to pay the cheerleader a visit."

"She wasn't home," he admitted since there was no

sense lying to Foley. The other vampire was sure to see right through it.

"She wasn't with them, if you're wondering."

He tried to mask his surprise. *If Meghan hadn't been with them, where was she?*

"So where are my friends now? Waiting in the shadows for me? Ready to take in Big Bad Blake?" he scoffed, and held his hands out as if to be handcuffed.

"They left about an hour ago."

He failed to hide his shock this time and Foley chuckled wickedly. "Sorry, mate, but I guess they had bigger fish to fry."

Still smarting from Meghan and company's earlier distrust, he clenched his hand on the glass, mindful not to break it. No sense wasting good blood, he thought as he raised the tumbler and drained it with one long swallow.

The surge of energy raced along his body and he battled to keep the demon in check, but it was raring to go again, incited by the blood and his anger at his supposed friends and Meghan.

He rose and gestured to the empty glass. "Thanks for the drink. I owe you."

"You do," Foley said, and returned his attention to the glass in his hand, clearly uncaring of whatever was going on.

A little later Blake made his way through the crowd in the Blood Bank, keeping his demon senses on alert for any touch of undead power. As he passed a vampire here and there, he scoped them out, alert for the wild kind of look he had seen in the dead vampiress's face before she had ripped into her dining companion to feed.

All that greeted him were the challenging looks he would expect to see. The vampires were on the prowl for a meal and another vampire moving in on their intended prey didn't sit well. Unlike the human wannabes, most vampires made few friends and were fairly territorial by nature, especially at mealtime. For a long time he'd been the same way—a loner. It was only since meeting Meghan that he had changed, but he still understood what the other vampires expected, so he kept his distance as they hunted for dinner, and continued his investigation.

He worked the crowd for at least another hour, waiting for any sign of Meghan and the others, or of Lee and his entourage. Searching for anything that would point to the presence of the sanguinarium drug amongst his undead brethren.

But he discovered nothing that would help him clear his name.

Realizing the futility of the night, he decided to leave but then reconsidered. He had nowhere to go, having trashed his apartment. Not to mention that he was starting to feel a might peckish. As one tasty young thing swept passed him, tossing him an inviting look, he headed in her direction, intending to grab a quick bite.

But then his senses picked up on something off.

It was on the periphery of his powers, but strong enough to register. Uneven undead power along with something more familiar…Meghan's sympathetic energies calling to his own.

He slowly pivoted on one foot, hoping to see her or one of the kiang-shi, but they were nowhere in sight. As it occurred to him how weak the force of the power was, he realized she had to be some distance away.

But where? he wondered.

He didn't hesitate a second longer, racing off in search of the source of the power and the growing disturbance he had sensed.

Chapter 21

"**Y**ou can't do this," Foley said, gesticulating wildly as he paced before two of Lee's kiang-shi, who held a struggling Meghan. They were in the lair Lee kept for his infrequent visits, two stories below the Blood Bank. The lair was sumptuously appointed with a series of large beds covered with the richest of silks and plush pillows.

Lee demanded only the best for where he would take his rest, his meals and play his games, Foley thought. He shot an uneasy glance at Meghan as he considered Lee's plans for her. If he had seen them enter earlier, he might have tried to warn Blake or the others, but Lee had also selected the space because of a secluded staircase that allowed them undetected entrance into the building.

Foley had to get word to Blake, he thought, and repeated his prior plea. "Don't do this to her, Sun Tze."

Lee laughed out loud, stepped forward and snared his arm, stopping him in his tracks. "Becoming the white knight, are we?"

Foley sensed the menace beneath Lee's words and the tight grip on his arm. Of its own volition, his body began to quiver, knowing what would follow. He forced back his distress, knowing that he had to do this not just for himself and Meghan, but for all the vampires who would remain behind long after Lee had tired of his games and left.

"Just being logical," Foley replied, trying to appear calm. "If you feed her the drug and turn her loose on the humans, you'll expose all of us. You'll risk our lives to the mortals who will seek to destroy us as they did millennia ago."

Lee scoffed at his assertion. "We are superior, Foley. It is time we stopped hiding in our own little under-world. It is time we stopped wishing to be like them."

With each word Lee's voice escalated until he was nearly screaming. He punctuated each word that followed with an angry jab in Meghan's direction. "She is a prime example of what we should not become. She is an abomination. Her kind are a blight on the vampire name. Who better to use to make our statement?"

While Foley was no fan of Ryder and his human wannabes, he was also wise enough to realize that Lee's bloodthirsty ways could only bring destruction to their kind. "In time they will destroy themselves with their foolishness, Sun Tze. There is no need for this type of attack."

Lee's eyes slowly began to glow. When he spoke, an unearthly rattle sounded from deep in his chest and his hair bleached out to the glaring white of the kiang-shi.

"This is not an attack, Daniel," he said, using Foley's given name from a lifetime ago. "This is an example for all the undead." He pointed a finger in Foley's direction. Long, deadly, sharp nails *click-clack*ing together as he jabbed the air before him in emphasis.

"Master," Foley said, lowering his head in obedience as a way to deflect Lee's wrath. It only seemed to infuriate Lee more, and fear made Foley's stomach clench tightly.

"Do you have no guts, Daniel? Will you never rise up and defend yourself?" Lee taunted.

With those words, something finally snapped within Foley. He launched himself at Lee, aware that only he stood between this madman and the destruction of the life that he knew. The destruction of Meghan and her friends. His friends, he realized suddenly, but in that moment of epiphany came something else.

The realization that he had acted too late.

Foley's hands were on Lee's throat, the force of his grip bone-crushing, but the kiang-shi had driven those long, deadly nails deep into Foley's abdomen. With a vicious swipe, he ripped upward, slicing through muscle and viscera.

Foley's grip failed and his knees gave way as his abdomen split open, spilling blood and intestine at Lee's feet.

Foley crumpled to the ground and tried to pull himself together, literally, hoping he had enough strength to heal, but the rush of his blood came quickly on his hands and cold immediately filled his core.

"So you do have guts after all," Lee said, licking the blood and gore from his nails.

Foley's eyesight dimmed as he struggled to stay alive, focusing all of his energy on containing the rush of blood from his body. He prayed for the first time in centuries that he could hold on long enough to warn the others.

He had no doubt that if Lee's plan succeeded, it would lead to the destruction of the vampire underworld they had so carefully guarded for centuries.

"You…will…not succeed," he rasped, each word weaker and more painful than the last.

Lee stood directly above him, looking down at him with disgust. "My dear Daniel. The word failure is not in my vocabulary."

Meghan shook her head in disbelief as she met Foley's fading gaze. His lips moved weakly, as if he were trying to tell her something, but she couldn't hear him.

"Foley," she screamed. He was dying right before her eyes and she could do nothing about it. He had sacrificed himself on her account, dying as others might if she couldn't break free.

She renewed her struggles, but the grasps of the two kiang-shi were too strong for her in her mortal form. As much as she despised the vampire, she summoned the demon, hoping that the added strength might be enough to overpower the kiang-shi, yet knowing that even if she did get free of them, she would never be able to escape Lee.

Still, she had to try. She had to make an attempt to warn the others about what Lee intended to do to her and she needed to get Foley some help.

She drove her heel onto the foot of the one kiang-shi and as he grunted from the pain and bent, she drove upward with her elbow, flattening his nose.

The sickening crack of bone was followed by a splatter of fetid-smelling blood and the release of his grip.

The action distracted the other kiang-shi and with a dip of her hip, she tossed him up and over her, earning her freedom.

With a surge of vamp speed, she edged to one wall of the room and stared at the door across the way from her and Lee who stood in the way. Blood and gore dripped from his one hand as Foley lay at his feet, barely moving but alive. She could still sense the weak pulse of his power, although Lee's energy was beating against hers violently, making it hard for her to focus her vamp power on anything else.

Lee seemed amused by her actions and as his bodyguards surged to their feet, intending to imprison her once again, Lee raised one hand and gestured to them to leave her alone.

He then began to clap, the sound loud and hollow in the large room. He had an amused expression on his face as he approached slowly. "Quite a show, my dear, but you realize that it's not enough to stop me."

She couldn't argue with him. She didn't have the strength to stop him, nor did most of the vampires in her group. Possibly only Stacia was strong enough, but after the other night at her apartment, the vampire elder had gone missing.

Typical. She had gotten the sense from Stacia and the others that Stacia only did what benefited Stacia.

Meghan realized she was on her own until the cavalry came. If the cavalry ever came.

As Lee advanced toward her, his eerie crimson glow eating her up, she summoned all her demon power and sent out a call, hoping that someone would be close enough to pick it up.

The summons was more faint than before, confusing him.

Blake had thought that she was a short distance away, but this outcry was weak. Very weak. It could only mean one of two things—either Meghan was farther away than he had originally sensed, or she was injured and too powerless to put out a proper distress signal.

He assumed it was the former because he couldn't stomach the thought of the latter, no matter how angry he was with her.

Nearing the hall to the back rooms, he opened himself to determine the origin of the power, but couldn't sense it there.

He moved onward, slipping down another hall to Foley's office, but there was still no one there and the source of the faint call remained uncertain. He cursed beneath his breath and wondered where she was. Where Foley was, for that matter.

He had seen Foley making his rounds after their talk,

but the other vampire had been missing for some time now. That was unusual for him, since he always made a point of keeping his eye on the goings-on in the club.

Blake pressed onward through a storage area filled with bottles of liquor to a second storeroom that contained a number of refrigerators and freezers. He skipped past the freezers, certain they would hold the food that Foley kept for the bar's human patrons.

Opening the door on one of the fridges, he noted the blood bags hanging from a rod. He grabbed a few of the bags, thinking that if Meghan were injured, she would need to feed. Stuffing the bags into his jacket pockets, he slanted along the edge of the walls, hoping to feel the weak buzz of power once again.

He finally found a doorway deep in one corner of the room and something pulled at his senses. A smell, rich and exotic, wafting from somewhere nearby.

It was what he had smelled in the alley when he found the dead vamp, making him wonder if he might be on the right track. What had Meghan said about Foley? he thought, racking his brains and then the bits of conversation came back to him.

Decay and...cardamom. She had said that Foley smelled like decay and cardamom. He suspected the spice was the source of the unique aroma in the alley. Certain that the smell was the clue to follow, he approached the door.

It was locked, but with a quick twist of vampire strength, he made short work of the doorknob.

Beyond the door was a narrow staircase leading downward. What waited for him below? Lee and his kiang-shi? Blake knew that on his own he was no match for them.

But he was on his own. The others had abandoned him.

With no choice but to forge ahead alone, he took the first step down the narrow staircase, certain that his life would never be the same.

He inhaled deeply as he crept down the steps and the spicy smell grew stronger. Then he heard something from far below. The scuff of a footstep? A muted cry?

Knowing hesitation could mean death, he threw himself down the stairs, landing roughly at the bottom. He pushed forward along a short, narrow hallway until he reached another closed door at the end of the hall.

Blake grasped the doorknob, prepared to twist it open, but it turned easily beneath his hand. He reached out with his vampire senses but detected only the faintest hint of vampire power.

He flung open the door.

A few feet away, Foley lay on the ground in a large pool of blood, his hands feebly trying to keep together the tangle of guts that had oozed out of his abdomen.

"Sweet Jesus," Blake said. He raced to Foley's side, kneeling next to the badly wounded vampire.

"Easy, mate." He slid Foley onto his back and moved the other vamp's hands away, trying to see the extent of his injuries. They were severe, he realized, and he didn't know how Foley had managed to last as long as he had, judging from the size of the blood pool. He had to be nearly dry, Blake thought and grabbed a blood bag from his pocket.

Cradling Foley against his legs, he held the blood bag

up to Foley's mouth while with his other hand he patiently worked at tucking his intestine back into his abdomen. All the while he hoped it would be enough, although the damp and chill of Foley's skin warned him that it might already be too late.

Maybe his was the faint call Blake had heard and not Meghan's, he thought, as he watched Foley listlessly drain the bag dry. When Foley finished, Blake tossed the bag away and reached for another, but Foley stopped him, feebly grabbing his wrist.

"Meghan." Her name escaped Foley like a man's last dying gasp. His mouth flopped open and closed as he struggled with another breath and finally managed to say, "Lee has Meghan."

Shit, Blake thought. "Where is he?"

Foley inclined his head and with a bloodstained finger, pointed weakly to the far side of the room. There was a door on the opposite wall and Foley said, "Back staircase."

Damn. He had been going downward while Lee had probably been dragging Meghan upward to ground level to make his escape. *Bloody damn.*

Foley must have seen his frustration for he weakly patted the hand that Blake had placed over his abdomen and with a hesitant breath said, "Go."

Blake wanted to go. He wanted to save Meghan, but he also couldn't leave Foley to die alone. Not when Foley had clearly tried to help Meghan.

"I'll go in a second, mate. Try to feed some more," Blake said, and offered up the second blood bag, but Foley weakly pushed it away.

"Go," Foley said with forced strength that clearly taxed him.

"Listen here, Foley. I don't desert my friends when they need me. But you're right. An ice-cold bag of human blood isn't what you need." He dropped the bag to the ground and presented Foley with his wrist instead, but Foley turned his head away, refusing the offer.

"Bollocks, mate. Feed already. The longer it takes, the less chance I have of kicking Lee's ass."

A weak grin sprung on Foley's lips and he finally latched down onto Blake's wrist. Pain erupted there along with the lash of vampire passion that came with the bite. He hauled in a ragged breath, battling both as Foley sucked for long minutes, but with each suck, Foley seemed to rally even as Blake weakened from the offering.

Finally, reluctantly, Foley released him, aware that if he continued to feed, Blake's power would be too low to take on Lee. With a slight smile, he said, "Go kick his ass, my friend."

Blake nodded forcefully. He picked up the blood bag he had discarded earlier and handed it to Foley. "Feed and hang on. I'll be back for you."

He gently eased Foley back onto the ground and sped for the doorway. As he raced upward, he heard, "I know you will."

Chapter 22

Lee's grip on her neck was punishing as he thrust her up the last few steps ahead of him and out into the alley behind the Blood Bank.

A large, black SUV was parked at the curb by the mouth of the alley. Lee never released the tight hold he had on her neck, and since her toes were barely brushing the ground, there was little she could do to get any leverage. Once she was on terra firma, however…

He carted her by the scruff of her neck as his bodyguards followed him to the entrance to the alley. As they neared the SUV, the engine turned over and the lights snapped on. A second later, someone threw open the back door.

Lee pitched her into the backseat.

Hard hands grabbed her and she smelled the telltale aroma of cardamom.

Another kiang-shi, she thought, as the arms encircled her, holding her prisoner as Lee slipped in beside her while the two other vampires took seats at the front of the SUV.

She twisted back and forth in the kiang-shi's grasp, trying to loosen his hold. She kicked at him and then at Lee, but he snared her throat in his hand and squeezed until dark circles danced before her eyes.

She tried to claw at his hand but couldn't lift her arms, imprisoned as they were by the Asian vamp. Sucking in a rough breath, she found herself choking as Lee spilled something into her mouth. She had no choice but to swallow.

The liquid tasted bitter. It burned as it slid down her throat, and she coughed, trying to retch up the fluid.

Lee only laughed and grabbed her throat once again. He brought his hand up and this time she caught sight of the vial in his hand. A small glass encased in a fine golden web.

She whipped her head back and forth, fighting him, but was no match for his superior strength. He forced her mouth open and emptied the vial. She choked and sputtered on the liquid's biting flavor.

Lee shook her roughly, and the liquid slipped down her throat, burning its way to her stomach.

From within her she felt the sizzle of the double dose as it sent wildfire along her nerve endings, immediately igniting electric passion and want. Her breasts and nether lips swelled and throbbed. Sharp spasms of a burgeoning climax tore through her, and she moaned and shifted on the seat of the car, trying to assuage her need.

"Wonderful, isn't it?" he said, and flicked at the distended tip of her breast with his index finger. The rough touch rocketed through her body, triggering a release that shattered her will, but as soon as the climax ebbed, passion rose again, sharper and stronger than before.

With a loud moan, she arched her back and once again jerked back and forth in the kiang-shi's arms, the violence of the drug pulsing through her body, demanding satisfaction on so many levels that she was nearly dizzy from the sensations buffeting her.

Lee chuckled harshly and bent his head, teethed the tip of her breast, wanting to punish her yet again, but she fought back the climax, panting heavily as she struggled for dominion over the fury of the drug.

"You cannot battle it forever. In fact, you won't be able to battle the need for much longer," Lee said, as he met her gaze.

"I won't give in," she said from between her clenched teeth, almost hissing the words at him.

He just laughed once again, a rich deep sound that penetrated her senses and created a sympathetic vibration between her legs that lashed at her control. "We'll just see how long you can last, my treasure."

With a snap of his fingers, he called out to the driver, "Take us to the Lair."

Blake rushed from the staircase and out into the alley where the scent of the kiang-shi lingered, although the area immediately outside the Blood Bank was empty.

He heard a muffled scream—Meghan's scream—and tracked the sound to a big, black SUV parked at the end of the alley.

The SUV was rocking back and forth violently. A struggle was going on within and Blake raced in its direction, but it sped away from the curb, wheels screeching.

He summoned his demon and burst to the curb in time to see the SUV turn down the block. Racing forward, he hurtled onto the roof of the building on the corner, and the vantage point let him see the route of the SUV.

Although he had assumed that it would be headed farther downtown in the direction of Otro Mundo, the SUV was moving directly westward at a fast clip, ignoring red lights and swerving around the traffic in its way.

If it kept on going in that direction there was only one vampire hangout that he could think of in that part of town—the Lair.

Bounding from one rooftop to the next, he pursued the SUV as it traveled along the streets. The black car finally turned southward, going up on two wheels from the sharp movement before lurching back down on its way to the triangle of land beyond Canal Street.

No doubt remained that the SUV was headed to Tribeca and Ryder's club. Why it would go there he couldn't begin to guess.

He paused on one rooftop, tracking the red taillights of the car as it raced away from him. He considered whether to keep on chasing it or call in the cavalry.

If the cavalry would even believe him. If they didn't…

He made the jump to the next building, intent on handling the problem by himself. But then he thought of Foley, lying wounded in the subbasement of the Blood Bank.

Foley wouldn't survive if he went it alone.

He plummeted to the ground below and searched for a pay phone, continuing to move in the direction of the Lair as he did so. A few blocks away he finally found one and dialed Diana Reyes.

She answered on the first ring. "Reyes, here."

"It's Blake."

A fire truck raced by, creating enough noise to nearly obliterate Diana's response. He huddled tighter to the phone and heard her say, "Where are you?"

"Where I am isn't as important as where I'm going. Lee's got Meghan. I think he's headed to the Lair."

"Are you sure?" she asked and in the background came the muted sound of other voices. He covered one ear, trying to discern what was being said. He barely made out the muffled, "Can we trust him?"

Anger surged through him. He clenched the phone tightly and heard the crackle of plastic beneath his fingers. "Tell the blighters that I'm telling the truth."

"Why should we believe you?"

"Because I wouldn't risk Meghan's life and if you don't want a lot of dead humans on your hands—"

"We're on our way to the Lair," she said.

Before she hung up he added, "Lee hurt Foley. Real bad. He's in a subbasement at the Blood Bank."

"We'll get someone over there. And Blake…"

He waited out her hesitation, eager to hear what she would say next.

"Be careful," she urged, and relief flooded through him.

The cavalry might just arrive in time to help him after all, he thought.

The dangling phone swayed back and forth from the blast of vamp speed he put on as he forged ahead to the Lair.

Meghan's body quaked violently, every part of her excruciatingly alive and demanding that she satisfy too many different needs. She was sexually aroused, so tightly wound that the simplest of touches would set her off.

Lee took advantage of that during the wild ride to the Lair. He fondled her, bit the tips of her nipples and stroked the center of her to send her over the edge time and time again until she was drenched with sweat and the aftermath of her arousal. Each release only served to increase her need for not only more sexual satisfaction, but for blood.

Lee understood that. In fact, he delighted in it as he whipped up her lust, laughing as he did so.

"Why?" she asked breathlessly after one climax stole the last of her willpower. She struggled against the kiang-shi that held her, but not for freedom. She snapped and clawed at him so that she might feed and quench her runaway need.

"That's what I wanted to see. The demon you are. The demon who will stop at nothing to satisfy its hunger."

She wanted to deny his words, only the demand was so strongly upon her that she bit into the arm of the kiang-shi holding her.

The demon howled from her attack, but didn't release her.

As she sucked, a brackish weak liquid filled her mouth and she spit it out, earning yet more mirth from Lee.

"The kiang-shi are the walking dead, remember. You'll find no sustenance there, but at the Lair…"

He leaned close to her, nudging her nose with his while whispering against her lips. "Think of all the humans there. The richness of smooth flesh beneath your fangs. The earthiness of warm blood spicing your mouth."

She salivated in anticipation and growled with hunger at the images that came at her, courtesy of Lee's words and his elder power. She realized now that he was also playing head games with her, filling her mind with visions and sounds intended to stoke her hunger.

The beat of a human pulse, steady and true, throbbing beneath fresh clean skin. The slight trace of dampness where neck met shoulder and the blood would be closest to the surface.

She closed her eyes and battled back the thoughts he was drumming into her brain, even as her body shivered in anticipation of satisfaction.

"Soon, *baobei*. Soon you will be fulfilled and the world will remember how vampires are supposed to be," he nearly crooned.

The SUV came to an abrupt halt, jostling them. When the door flew open, Lee slipped out into the street seemingly without a care.

The kiang-shi holding her tossed her out, but two other kiang-shi were there to imprison her yet again.

As she looked around, she realized they were in the service alley behind the Lair. She renewed her struggles then, and this time the kiang-shi had a harder time of it as the drug was giving her added strength. They tightened their hold and dug in their heels to keep her steady as their master approached the back entrance to the Lair.

Lee opened the door to the club and the bouncer immediately stepped to the entrance.

Lee grabbed him by the throat and threw him across the width of the alley. The bouncer landed with a resounding thud against the brick wall and then slumped to the ground, unconscious.

Smiling, Lee held his hand out in the direction of the entrance with a flourish.

"Shall we?" he said.

The night air pushed against him as Blake raced the final distance to the Lair, but as chilly as the early spring air was, the knot of fear in his gut was colder. Blake imagined the reasons why Lee had grabbed Meghan and taken her to the Lair, and none of the reasons was good. None of the outcomes he imagined ended happily.

They all ended with death and destruction.

That was all Lee understood. That was all that mattered for vampires like Lee. But not for vampires like Blake or Ryder or Diego or even Foley, who possibly lay dying because he believed otherwise.

By the time Blake arrived at the Lair, the SUV was

parked in the alley. A few feet away on the cobble-stoned ground lay one of the bouncers, unconscious and bleeding, but alive.

Unbitten, he realized as he kneeled and examined the bouncer's neck That surprised him. He had thought Lee would have no care as to where or when he fed. That he had bypassed such an easy snack only worried him more.

Lee was on a mission, and Meghan was obviously a part of his plan.

He needed to get inside and find out what was going on.

He yanked on the door, but it was firmly secured. Not even his vampire strength was enough to break the lock, and he suspected that something had been jammed behind the door to ensure it wouldn't open from outside.

Forcing himself to remember the layout of the Lair, he recalled that the club had an entrance on the other side of the building in addition to the main doors along the street. Wanting to avoid the crowd that was always waiting to enter at the main doors, he raced around the back of the building and to the second entrance, but it had been barred from within as well.

Nothing that he did could dislodge whatever was sealing the door closed.

Bollocks, he thought, and raced to the front of the building.

Chapter 23

A chilled sweat covered Meghan's body, which shook uncontrollably from the desire ravaging it. She wrapped her arms around herself and huddled tighter against the wall, battling the effects of the drug as she searched for a way out of the club.

Once inside, Lee had set her loose and she had raced for her freedom, but the kiang-shi had circled around her. Determined to find a way out, she had dodged them and gone for the shadows created by the fake cavern walls Ryder had used to create the theme for the club.

As she moved along the shadows, praying to find an exit, she realized she would die if she didn't feed, recalling the out-of-control vampiress at Otro Mundo. But then Diego's words came back to her:

Human blood won't bond with the drug and neutralize it.

Whirling around, she realized she was adrift in a sea of humans, pulsing with life and blood that couldn't help her. But she imagined sinking her teeth into the soft flesh of a neck, feeding on the warm richness of humanity.

She had to get out of the club. She tightened her hold on herself and made a dash for the back exit. Only one of Lee's kiang-shi bodyguards stood there, barring her escape. She rushed at him, kicking and scratching, but he pushed her aside the way an ox might a gnat with a swipe of his tail.

The initial strength the drug had provided her was fading as the sanginarium ate away at her system. She would continue to weaken unless she fed—and once again, the call of the human life nearby, pulsing with blood, almost undid her.

Sucking in a shaky breath as she fought for control, she raced to a second exit but found it barred and guarded as well. Then she turned toward the front of the club, but found yet another kiang-shi at that entrance.

Lee's guards intended to keep her within the mass of humanity. In the midst of the walking blood bags that would do little to appease her need.

Her breath heaved in her chest as she retreated to the shadows of the club once again, hiding the demon she was barely mastering.

Lee's words kept on broadcasting in her brain, trying to shatter that fragile composure.

"Feed, my treasure. Imagine the satisfaction it will

bring." For good measure he followed it up with visions of rich blood pulsing beneath her fangs.

She closed her eyes and covered her ears, but the urge rose sharply. Intensely.

She knew she couldn't linger there, close to the temptation of so many people and Lee's constant urging to feed from them.

Wildly searching for any avenue of escape, she caught sight of the window of Ryder's office, high above the floor of the club. She remembered then about the door that led to that office and the back rooms of the Lair.

Swiftly skirting around the edges of the club, she was feet away from the door when she realized that it, too, was being guarded by one of Lee's cadre. She recognized him as the kiang-shi who had been at the main door just moments earlier.

She couldn't fail this time, she thought, and launched herself at the kiang-shi.

Blake risked entry through the main door, rushing past the bouncer in a blur of speed that he hoped would go unnoticed. As he came to a stop, he noticed the bouncer shooting an odd glance toward the entrance, as if to double-check whether someone was there, but then he returned to his duties, asking for the ID of the next patron in line.

A close call, he realized. The fit through the door had been tight, forcing him to pass closely to the humans lingering there. But now he was within the club, and the uneven energy of the kiang-shi beat at him along with the thrum of vampire power. Multiple vampires, he realized, and wondered whether the cavalry had arrived.

Searching the interior of the club, he saw no sign of Diana and her vampire pals.

Not good, he thought. There were too many kiang-shi, plus Lee, for him to handle alone, but he wasn't going to let that deter him.

He had to find Meghan and get her out of there.

Focusing his vampire power, he reached out for a touch of her sympathetic energy and felt a glimmer of it, only…

Something was wrong. He knew that immediately.

He moved along the fringes of the club, hiding in the shadows and nooks created by the fake rock outcroppings built into the side walls to mimic the appearance of a cavern. He'd always thought the theme hokey, but welcomed the cover it provided tonight.

As he neared the back door he hadn't been able to open, he detected the power of a kiang-shi and back-tracked. Along the other side of the space, back behind the cover of a partial wall intended to hide the workings of the club, he finally caught a glimpse of Meghan. She was fighting one of Lee's kiang-shi, seriously out-muscled but completely determined.

He rushed to her side, but as he did so, the out-of-sync thrum of energy warned him all was not right with her. As her gaze met his, he took note of the wild fierce look in her eyes.

He knew then what Lee had done. What he had planned and why she was here.

* * *

Meghan felt it. With their blood connection she knew the moment Blake realized what had happened. Though she shook with the force of his realization, there wasn't time to acknowledge it. Or to ask for his forgiveness.

She had to break past Lee's bodyguard and get to the safety of Ryder's office. Once she was there, the humans milling about the Lair would be safe.

She dug her nails deep into the kiang-shi's decayed flesh, her fingers slid in and she jerked at the flesh, stripping it away as she tried to break past him.

Blake joined the fray, but went straight for the kiang-shi's neck, his hand flattened, fingers extended. With a knife-like jab he pierced the side of the kiang-shi's throat. He pushed deeper until his hand almost disappeared in the demon's flesh. When he retracted his hand, bits of cartilage, flesh and bone came with it.

Meghan felt the kiang-shi weaken and took advantage, driving her fist upward into its throat. The loud snap and crackle of his throat flattening beneath her punch sickened her and she fell back, unable to finish.

Blake had no such problem.

With another vicious jab and yank, more of the kiang-shi's body landed at her feet. As the demon's knees buckled, Blake encircled its head in his arms and with a sharp jerk, finished the decapitation.

Shoving away the falling body of the Asian vampire, he rushed to her side and embraced her.

Comfort flooded her for the smallest fraction of time before other sensations buffeted her mind and body. The feel of his lean body stoked the inferno in her breasts and core while the pulse of his blood…

Beating. Strong. His vampire energy melded with hers and she shook as the longing to sink her teeth into him rose almost more sharply than she could control.

He knew it.

He urged her away, his arms holding hers, as he said, "Fight it, Meghan. We'll win this battle together."

She wanted to believe him, but the urge was almost unbearable now. The fury of the drug jolted her body over and over. She wrapped her arms tighter around her body, imagining that by doing so she could keep herself from shattering, but knew it was a futile battle.

"You can't save me, but you can save them," she said, and tilted her head in the direction of the dance floor.

Sadness darkened his eyes to the color of a stormy sea before he nodded with understanding. He grabbed her in his arms and raced for the door leading to Ryder's office.

He moved at a breakneck pace, aware her dominion over the drug's effects was near an end. When they reached Ryder's office, he tossed open the door and immediately moved to the large mahogany desk at one end of the office. Leaning her against the edge, she watched as he sped around the room, in search of what she didn't know until he returned with the thick cords for the curtains.

Shivering, her control nearly done, she hopped up onto the surface of the desk and lay down, releasing only one extremity at a time until she was tightly bound to the massive desk. Only then did she finally allow the lust and hunger of the drug to take over.

As another climax slammed into her body, she cried

out Blake's name and arched off the desktop. Her back bowed tightly in a spasm of ecstasy and need. The ropes bit deep into her wrists and ankles, so deep it drew blood and even the faintest whiff of that had her snapping and biting at the air as if that could bring satisfaction.

Blake stood by, immobile as a statue as he watched her writhe on the surface of the desk, battling the drug. Knowing that each second he stood by without doing something, she was slipping away as the sanguinarium took its toll on her body.

Unless she fed from another immortal.

With enough vampire blood flooding her system, he might be able to counteract the effects of the drug. But he suspected that just his blood alone wouldn't be enough. The lust would likely have her bleeding him dry before it made any difference.

He hurried to the window of Ryder's office and drew apart the curtains that had fallen closed. Down below, in the midst of all the humans, he detected nothing out of the ordinary, but as he used his vamp eyesight to scope out the darkness along the edges, he saw what was going on.

Ryder was grappling with one kiang-shi at the back door while Diego was hauling one from the front door toward the side of the club. By his count, that left only Lee to deal with.

His gut tightened as he realized only Diana remained to do battle down in the crowd. She was no match for the kiang-shi elder, but together they might be able to keep him distracted long enough for Diego and Ryder to come to their aid.

But first, he had to do something to keep Meghan alive.

He knew the fridge in Ryder's office likely held its share of blood bags filled with human blood, but they were useless.

Only his blood could make a difference now.

He approached Meghan as she thrashed on the surface of Ryder's desk, her body jerking and yanking on the cords, but he had done too good a job. She wouldn't get free of the bindings.

As he neared, she turned her pained gaze on him. The neon-blue green of her vampire eyes nearly blinded him with its intensity, and blood began to fill her eyes at the edges of her eyeballs. Drool escaped her lips and she snapped at the air with her fangs, hungry for something into which to sink her teeth.

He intended to give her just that, but first he had to calm her a little, fearing that she would savage him if he didn't. It wouldn't help any of them if he was too weak to fight.

Carefully he approached, and as he finally got close he reached out and took hold of her head in his hands. He applied gentle pressure to immobilize her and tenderly ran his fingers across her hair, soothing her the way he might a wild animal.

For good measure, he sought out the connection they shared and sent his thoughts to her. He poured out the emotions he had kept in check, knowing that this might be the last time to share them with her.

He wanted her to know all that she had been to him.

Chapter 24

The images invaded her mind, picture after picture of all that had ever been good between them. In between each image came emotion. Rich, unbridled sentiments that left no doubts in her mind about how he cared for her.

How he loved her.

Tears came to her eyes even as her body jerked as the drug racing through her system responded to the emotions. Her breasts swelled, tips pebble-hard until she imagined they might burst. Between her legs came the heavy throb of need.

"Please, Blake. Please," she begged, needing release, but he just tenderly cradled her head with his hands.

Softly stroking the sides of her face as he leaned close, he whispered, "Not like this, Meghan. Just hold on a bit longer."

Frustration swamped her and she snapped at him, the unfulfilled sexual need giving rise to the fury to feed and get satisfaction of another kind.

His touch came on her face once again, delicate and compassionate. His words soothing, trying to lull her rage as he said, "Nice and easy, Meghan. Just a little nip for now."

She popped her eyes open and realized he was bringing his wrist to her mouth. He was offering himself to sate her thirst and she couldn't hold back any longer.

Rearing up, she sank her fangs deep into his wrist.

Foley shook with the chill bathing his body, made even colder by the damp sweat covering him.

He knew the signs well. He had seen more than one vampire die during his hundreds of years of existence.

He had just never imagined that he would go like this—alone and in a pile of his own blood and filth.

An apt reward for the shitty way he had led his life up until now. At least at the end he had tried to make amends.

Maybe God would take that into account, he thought. He shivered from the cold and curled even tighter into a fetal position, trying to conserve what little life he had left.

He didn't know how long he had been lying there when he heard the soft footfall by the door.

Opening his eyes, he realized it was Diana Reyes. Or maybe he was imagining her. He'd always kind of had a thing for her, so it only seemed right that whatever angel had come to take him to meet his maker might look like her.

"Blake sent me," the angel said, kneeling beside him. As she reached down and picked him up in her arms, it occurred to him that this was no angel. She was all-flesh-and-blood woman holding him close.

"Damn you, Foley. Why did you have to go and get all White Hat on us?" she whispered, rocking him in her arms.

He smiled weakly and closed his eyes. It had been so long since he had been held like this. Tenderly and with caring. Too long.

"It's worth dying just for this moment," he said softly, as his body began to shake violently from the chill of death. As he began to lose all sensation in his extremities, he focused on the feel of her, soft and womanly beneath the side of his face.

As he did so, he sensed something he hadn't expected. But he was too weak to talk. Too far gone to ask.

"Oh, no, Foley. I am so not going to let it end like this." Diana raised him up, baring her neck and holding his head close to the pulse beating strong and steady beneath his lips.

He didn't wonder at what she was offering since even that second of hesitation would be the last thing he did.

Instead, he pierced the skin at her neck and fed, the first suck weak until the energy of her blood slammed into him, more potent than that of a human, nearly as rich and fulfilling as that of the undead.

Her soft cry of pain at one forceful suck tempered his feeding, but with each measured pull, the cold fled from his body replaced by the heat of her blood. The dull pain in his abdomen receded as his body slowly continued healing.

Beneath his lips her flesh was warm. The scent of her and the feel of her skin surrounded him. With greater consciousness as the threat of death left him, he imagined as he had on many a night how it might be to lie with her.

As she grew weaker from his feeding, he surrounded her in his arms and pulled away, aware that he could not keep on draining her.

He was still frail, as now she was, and they collapsed onto the floor together, unable to remain upright any longer.

As their gazes connected, he said in a soft whisper, "I don't know how to thank you."

She forced a smile to her lush lips, grasped his hand in her soft one, and said, "Don't go back to playing for the Dark Side."

Even if Diana hadn't asked it of him, he didn't think he could.

Things were different now. He was different and if he somehow survived, he knew that the eternal life that awaited him had to be different from the one he'd already lived.

Meghan bit down over and over again, rapaciously feeding from his wrist until he was light-headed from the loss of blood.

Pulling away his savaged wrist, he stumbled back, his knees weak.

Meghan howled in anger at his withdrawal and once

again began squirming and pulling at the ropes keeping her from satisfying her blood rage.

"Easy, love," he urged softly, taxed beyond what he had expected. Her feeding had been demanding and he plopped into Ryder's expensive office chair as his knees finally gave way. Blood continued to drip from his wrist onto the expensive Oriental rug on the floor.

He'd allowed her too much of his blood, he realized, as he failed to heal. He was too powerless to do much of anything else and wondered what was keeping Ryder and Diego. He had expected them long before now. With that thought came another.

He still had no clue what was up with Diana down in the crowd below.

Stumbling to his feet, he staggered across the short distance to the window and once again searched for her and the two other vampires. With an unfocused gaze, he thought he saw Ryder down below, still fighting with someone, but he wasn't sure.

He turned, intending to search for them, only to discover Lee standing by Meghan, a delighted smile on his face.

"Have you ever seen a dogfight, Blake?"

With a quick flourish of his hand, he whipped out a long, thin stiletto from beneath the sleeve of the elegant silk jacket he wore.

Blake knew he was done for. He wasn't strong enough to battle Lee in this condition. But if he kept him talking long enough...

"Can't say as I have, mate. Never much cared for sport like that." He wavered on his feet as the blood continued to leak from his ravaged wrist, forcing him to lean back against the window to keep upright.

Lee's full lips curved into an even broader smile. "It's quite a sight. Both animals biting and snapping. Sinking their jaws deep into each other's flesh." He bent and cut loose the first curtain cord at Meghan's ankle.

She responded to the freedom immediately, kicking out with her leg, but Lee easily dodged her blow.

He sauntered to her other leg, but before cutting it free, he leaned over Meghan's body and in soft tones whispered to her, "You will heed my summons, *baobei*. You will obey me when I command you to kill him."

At his words, Meghan instantly quieted and Blake realized Lee was using his elder powers to control her.

He glanced out the window out of the corner of his eye, but saw no sign of Diana, Ryder or Diego. Had they fallen to Lee's bodyguards?

Lee quickly picked up on that subtle glance and chuckled as he smoothly sliced through the cord, freeing Meghan's other leg. He strolled casually to the head of the desk, leaned down and whispered to her, "You will have him and then I will have you."

Bugger that, Blake thought, and catapulted himself at Lee with the last of his strength, tackling him to the ground. The knife went flying as they sprawled into a heap behind Ryder's desk.

Lee tried to toss him off, but Blake had the upper position and used it to his advantage. Much like he imagined Lee's dogs might have done, Blake sank his fangs through the silken fabric of his jacket and deep into the thick muscle in Lee's shoulder.

Wrenching and turning, Lee tried to force him off, but Blake somehow held on, one arm around Lee's neck while the other snaked beneath Lee's armpit, cementing his hold on the kiang-shi. He sucked intensely of Lee's blood, ignoring the odd taste of it. Instead he savored the power that surged into him, the power from the European vampires Lee had fed from. The blood empowered him enough to maintain his hold on the Asian vampire.

Realizing that Blake was not about to go so easily, Lee ceased his struggles and crawled a few feet away, moving out of the tight space behind the desk. Blake realized too late that the knife was now within Lee's reach.

The kiang-shi swiped the knife up in his right hand and crossed up and over his left shoulder, driving the blade toward Blake.

Pain seared through Blake as the silver of the blade skimmed along his shoulder blade, slicing him open before it plunged deep into his back. Somehow he held on to Lee, took another frantic suck of blood, but Lee pulled the blade out and reversed the direction of his strike.

He bent his elbow and pounded the blade from down below into Blake's side. He repeated the attack, plunging from above a second time and then a third from down below, each swipe stronger and deeper than the first.

Through the haze of pain, Blake registered the burn as the silver blade sank into his body each time. He felt the slight catch as the final blow snagged on a rib before it punctured his lung and slipped even further. The burn registered in his heart, stealing the strength from him.

He fell away, losing his grip on the kiang-shi.

Mustering his flagging energy, he tried to rise as Lee scrambled to his feet, but the knife blows had done their job too well. A gurgle came from deep in his chest as he struggled to draw a breath, forcing him to cough.

Bright red blood spewed from his mouth and onto the floor. The smell of his blood was thick in the air. As Meghan caught the scent of it, she went wild on the desktop, thrashing and howling, pulling the ropes and biting the air with her fangs.

Lee laughed, sensing victory. With a wild slash, he cut the cord from one of Meghan's wrists and then expertly reversed the bloody blade and quickly slashed through the other cord, releasing her.

She bounded off the desk and faced them, a feral look in her eyes. A wild tremor shook her body as she stood there, smelling the air.

Blake knew she was beyond reach, beyond caring for anything but blood, and Lee wasn't much better.

Gleeful laughter erupted from him as he sidestepped from where Blake lay, bleeding to death. As Lee moved, he crooned to Meghan, "He is yours, *baobei*. Savor him. Watch the light fade from his eyes as you devour him."

Meghan advanced on him, but something flickered in her gaze. Something that said to him that she might not be as far gone on the drug as he had thought.

Forcing himself into an upright position, he softly whispered, "Don't go chicken on me now, Meghan. A cheerleader can kick that Chinaman's sorry ass any day."

Another flicker danced across her eyes, but she still

moved toward him, almost as if stalking prey. Only he wasn't going anywhere. He would be an easy kill for her in his current condition. For that matter, he might be dead meat by the time she finally decided to attack.

On his back and along his side he felt the dampness of the blood draining rapidly from his body. Lee had gotten something vital with those knife thrusts, and the silver was interfering with his healing. When he drew a rough breath and felt a sharp pain at the center of his chest, it occurred to him that Lee had probably nicked his heart.

Black circles danced before his eyes, but he forced himself to focus and somehow rose to his feet. A mistake, maybe, as he noted what was left of his blood drain from his extremities and pool in his gut. His legs grew even more rubbery, and he couldn't stay upright against the wall.

Lee sensed it as well. He knew Blake's death was imminent, but that wasn't enough for him. Once again he urged Meghan onward. "Take him, *baobei*, before he robs you by dying."

Dying, Meghan thought.

That one word broke through the haze of the drug and she struggled to fix on that word. She somehow managed to converge all her senses into recognition of that one concept.

Dying.

Blake was dying. The smell of his blood was strong. She had the scent of it imprinted in her brain from the many times they had shared themselves. From the many times he had loved her.

"Feed from him, my treasure. Feed me." Lee intoned

his command but she pushed him out of her brain. Only one thought dominated her mind.

Blake was dying.

Then another thought assailed her. Her own death.

She knew the drug was sizzling in her veins, demanding blood to satisfy it and destroying her the longer she couldn't feed.

She imagined sinking her teeth into flesh and tasting the rich earthy warmth of blood. Imagined the rush of power through her veins.

She advanced on Blake again and in her head, she heard his soothing voice urging, "Feed from me to save yourself, Meghan. I understand."

Her mind rebelled at his request and somehow she managed to hold on to the connection with his energy. She used it to drive away the pull of Lee's power that commanded her to kill and enticed her with the promise of the satisfaction Blake's blood would bring.

Blake's blood, she thought again. The aroma of it was rich in her nose, so strong it was if she could taste it. With that awareness came another.

Blake's energy was fading quickly.

He was dying and only she could do something about that.

In a blur of movement she rushed across the room and attacked Lee, who slashed at her with the knife, catching her on the forearm. The momentary pain drove her away and let him rush to the door, but the pain only delayed her for a second.

With a long jump, she landed before him and snared the hand with the knife.

Lee made a play to grab her throat, but she caught his hand as it went for her. Locked together, they wrestled for control, pushing and pulling each other as they battled.

Lee was strong, and as an elder, he had the power of mental manipulation. He pummeled her brain with it, alternately threatening and cajoling in an effort to dominate her.

She forced his thoughts from her mind, concentrating instead on the physical as they struggled for the uppermost position. She didn't know how much longer she could fight. She could already feel her body weakening as the drug obliterated the cells that gave her vampire strength.

Lee sensed her waning energy and pressed onward, glee in his eyes as he realized she was losing the battle.

Meghan used that sudden physical push forward to her advantage. She relaxed her hold on him and he became unbalanced and fell toward her. She slipped beneath his guard, encircling his head in her arms and sinking her fangs into his neck.

Power quickly surged through her from the richness of his half vamp–half kiang-shi elder blood. The energy that immediate taste provided was enough for her to wrest control of the knife from him. Angrily she tossed the knife to the side and continued to feed.

Lee fell forward onto the ground, taking her with him. He rolled, trapping her below him before rolling again in the hopes of dislodging her, but his rich vampire elder blood was providing her with too much strength. Strength that helped her retain her hold on him. She pushed off with her legs and rolled him beneath her once again, pinning him to the ground.

Fighting for freedom, Lee tried to buck her off. He reared back with an elbow, catching her along the side of the head. Anger rose up in her at the pain of his blow. At the damage he had done to so many people in her life.

As the kiang-shi's blood flowing through her veins finally brought the sanguinarium drug under control, Meghan felt sanity slowly returned. One thought coalesced. *Blake.*

She fell away from Lee, breathing heavily but able to master herself, just as Ryder and Diego came racing through the door of the office.

She saw two angry-looking puncture wounds on Ryder's neck where his shirt was torn open.

Someone—or something—had slashed Diego's chest through his jacket, and the gash on his face still oozed blood.

Still, they were a welcome sight.

As her friends took in Lee on the ground and the blood all over her, she knew they realized what had happened.

Then as one, their gazes shifted to a spot behind her. As she tracked their gaze, she saw Blake, sitting drunkenly against the wall. His black T-shirt darkened from the blood he had lost. Dark cherry-colored blood pooled on the floor beside him. More blood dribbled down from the corner of his mouth. He sucked in a rough breath, and she heard the gurgle in his chest. He was drowning in his own lifeblood.

"God, no," she said, and rushed to his side, but she didn't know what to do for him.

He forced his lips into a semblance of his normally cocky smile. "You kicked his ass."

"Blake, please hold on." She slipped her arm behind his back to hold him close. As she did so, the wetness of the blood he had lost registered sadly against the palm of her hand. As she took hold of his hand and noticed the savage bite marks at his wrist, she recalled what he had done for her. How he had offered himself in order to save her life.

She could do no less.

Offering him her wrist, she said, "Lee's blood is rich in my veins. It may be enough—"

"It isn't," he said with a raspy breath. Then he coughed, bringing up yet more blood.

"Damn it, Blake," she cried, and held his head to her. "You can't leave me now."

"Don't…want…to," he somehow managed to say. But each word seemed weaker than the first to her, and his body sagged feebly against her.

"Then feed," she urged yet again.

Chapter 25

Everything he knew to be true was telling him that it was senseless to feed. He could no longer feel his body. All he could sense was a numbing cold in his center. That and the dampness along his back and side, and the metallic taste of his own blood in his mouth.

"Feed," she urged.

He realized that she was holding him in her arms, cradling him to her heat.

He gazed up at her and tried to focus on her face. Slowly her features became sharp and distinct. He wanted to remember them. Take them with him wherever it was that he would soon go.

The deep emerald of her eyes. The straight, pert nose and full lips. How those lips felt so wonderful when pressed against his. The soft skin of her cheek, smooth and silken.

He wanted to touch that skin and tried to pick up his hand, but it wouldn't answer his command, hanging uselessly beside him.

Tears shimmered in her eyes and she softly urged once again, "Please feed, Blake. I don't want to lose you."

Beneath his lips came the feel of the delicate skin of her inner wrist and the steady pulse that beat there. He imagined that it called to him, saying "Love me. Love me."

He did love her and as his gaze connected with hers, it occurred to him that she might just feel the same. After all this time, she finally loved him as he lay there dying. He realized how stupid it would be to not try to live and explore that glimmer of love in her eyes.

Gently he bit through that fragile skin and fed. Her blood was rich with the kiang-shi's, filled with energy and life, but the blood seemed to hardly make a difference. The barest trickle of heat began in his core, but it was like a candle in the wind. Erratic and uncertain. It blew out almost as soon as it had been kindled.

He released her wrist and this time, had enough strength to pick up his hand and run his fingers along her cheek.

"Sorry, luv. I wish we could have had more time."

"Shut up, Blake," said a voice beside him and he glanced in its direction.

Ryder was kneeling beside him. Diego was standing beyond him and had Lee all trussed up like a Christmas turkey.

To Blake's surprise, Ryder undid the cuff on his shirt

and thrust it up impatiently. He shoved his arm in front of Blake's face and said, "Don't argue. Just do it already."

Blake knew how much it was costing the other vampire, who wasn't one for sharing in vampire things. Because of that and because somewhere within him the spark had awakened once again, he didn't argue. He bit into Ryder's wrist and fed.

This time that spark didn't extinguish. It took hold firmly and slowly intensified.

The cold was beginning to leave his body and sensation slowly returned to his arms and legs. The first thing that became rooted in his brain was the soft press of Meghan's body against his as she held him. The tenderness in her arms as she cradled him.

He also noted the slight tension that had entered the muscles of Ryder's arm and knew it was time to let him go.

Ryder pulled away abruptly and quickly covered up the sign of his feeding by dragging down his sleeve over the bite marks.

Diego came next. He had discarded his suit and had already pulled back his sleeve. With a graceful brandish, he offered up his wrist, although Blake also understood the price of it. Just to make sure that his understanding was correct, Diego said, "If you survive, you'll owe us big-time for this."

If he survived, Blake thought. Even as he fed from Diego's blood, made richer by virtue of his age, he realized he was still incredibly weak. Maybe too weak.

But he fed nevertheless, longer and harder than he had with Ryder, since the treat of blood so old and lush was hard to refuse. He fed until the spark of life within him grew into a persistent glow and then released his bite on the lordly vampire.

Diego grunted something and then thrust Lee's neck close. Lee's head hung limply and as he gazed from Meghan to the other two vamps, he realized they had all taken their share of the Asian vampire. If he took his...

Diego was the first to understand his hesitation. He jerked Lee's body before him once again and said, "Take what you can. If he survives, the council will order his death."

He had no doubt about Diego's statement. Lee had risked revealing their existence with his actions; he had put them all in danger. When the vampires in the area assembled for the council, the punishment would surely be death.

As his gaze skittered to Meghan's, she nodded her acceptance.

He bit down on Lee's neck and fed greedily, sucking down the potent mix of vampire and kiang-shi blood. Experiencing the surge of energy that it brought through his being.

The glow within him burned ever brighter, and the fire spread through him, searing his back and side and even his heart, as his body slowly began to repair itself. Hope grew within him that maybe he might survive. That he might be able to explore the glimmer of caring he had seen in Meghan's eyes that night.

He fed until Diego finally commanded him to stop and jerked away Lee's body. "As much as I'd love to see you drain him dry, it might be best to let him expire at the hands of our fellow vampires."

Expiring was a euphemism for what their fellow vampires would do to him, but Lee deserved all that pain and more, he thought.

As he looked up at Meghan, he noticed her tears, but also the smile on her face as she said, "It's time to take you home to heal."

Home, he thought. The home he had trashed in his misery, but Meghan didn't give him a chance to warn her, nor was he in any condition to do anything about it.

He was still so weak that he couldn't stand, but Meghan had no such problem. She lifted him into her arms and with a hasty goodbye to the other two vamps, raced off into the night with him.

Blake had never fully appreciated the sensation of their speed and agility, he thought. It was impossible not to wonder at it now as she cradled him against her and dashed through the night. The spring air was chilly against his skin and his blood-soaked clothes. He shivered in her arms and she tightened her hold on him, warming him with the heat of her vampire body.

As they came to a stop, he could smell the spicy aroma of the trampled tomato plants and earthiness of the spilled soil.

They were home. Or rather, they were at his home, but Meghan must have picked up on his thoughts since she said, "*Our* home, Blake."

He cupped her cheek and brushed his thumb across the faint smile on her lips. "I should warn you, luv."

The smile broadened beneath his thumb. "You're a shitty housekeeper," she said. As she stepped through the French doors and into the space, he realized she had cleaned the mess and destruction he had left behind.

"You shouldn't have," he said, but emotion engulfed him at her actions. At her caring.

With that engaging smile on her face, she tenderly ministered to him, removing his clothes and wiping away the blood on his body. As she cleansed his back, the sting of her actions reminded him he had not completely healed. She used another of his T-shirts to fashion a bandage and bundled him into bed, since he was still too fragile to even sit up.

But he was alive, he thought. Still, he was unprepared for what she did next.

She stood by the opposite side of his bed and slowly undressed, baring all of herself to him. The full breasts with the rich caramel peaks. The toned muscles of her midsection with the perfect indent of her navel.

He groaned from pain of a different kind as his body responded weakly to the sweetness of her form.

She chuckled, and it was a sexy siren's acknowledgment of her power. "Not yet, luv," she teased, and picked up the edge of the clean sheets she had placed on his bed.

She eased beneath them and to his side, lying along the length of him with one arm propping her head up so that she could look down at him. The other hand she placed on the center of his chest, right above his heart.

"I was afraid to believe in you," she whispered. "To believe you when that was all you asked of me."

He covered her hand with his. "Why, Meghan? All I wanted—"

"Was my trust, but we both know it was about more than that." She turned her hand, twined her fingers with his. "We both know it was about admitting that this was about more."

"This? Even now you can't say it. Can't admit that—"

"I love you." She said it without hesitation or pretense, shocking him with the admission.

He knew what it had cost her, having known the price of rejection once too often in his own life. "Well, that's good because I didn't want to be the only one in this relationship who was in love."

She chuckled and leaned close, brushing her nose along his cheek as she said, "You love me."

He smiled, but it was weak as he felt his energy fading. "I do, Meghan. I love you, only I may have to wait a bit to show you."

She eased her arm beneath his head and snuggled down close to him. "Rest, Blake. You need some time to get stronger."

Time was something he had a lot of, he thought, as he allowed himself to slip off to slumber.

Meghan watched as he released his hold on wakefulness. Only then did she allow the fear to emerge. They had almost died tonight. He was still incredibly weak, and she was certain it would take some time before he was fully recovered. Even vampires had their physical limits, and she suspected Blake had been on the edge of his.

She allowed herself some rest, lying beside the hard muscular length of his body. Savoring the steadier beat of his heart. Sensing the subtle warmth of his skin, so far removed from the damp and chill that had earlier warned he had been near death.

But as an hour or two passed, she registered the weakening of that beat and the slight chill to his skin. She was about to wake him to feed when she sensed the strong hum of vampire energy nearby.

She eased from Blake's side and as she rose, noticed the shadows out on the patio. A rich velvet throw sat on the ornate wooden chest at the end of the bed and she snagged it, wrapped it around herself.

When she neared the doors, she realized it was Diego and Ryder out on the patio. Something else occurred to her at that moment. "Where's Diana? Foley? Is he—"

"Alive, but barely," Diego said.

"Diana is with him at the Blood Bank. We're going to them next." Ryder picked up the small cooler he held. "We thought you would need this."

He handed it to her just as Diego said, "Not much of a gardener, is he?"

He wrinkled his nose in distaste at the mess on the patio.

Meghan took the cooler and popped open the top. Nestled in ice were half a dozen or so blood bags.

Diego motioned to them and said, "*You* should feed often. It'll be your blood that makes the difference."

She understood the warning in his message.

With a curt nod, she acknowledged her understanding. But there was one thing she had to know before she returned to her lover.

"What about Lee?"

"Alive for now. We turned him and his two pals over for judgment," Ryder said.

Swift and sure justice, she was certain. Vampires left nothing unresolved and unavenged.

She bid her two friends goodbye and walked back into the apartment. Blake slept on, his skin pale, the rise of his chest nearly imperceptible.

Placing the cooler on a nearby table, she opened it and pulled out the first bag. She punctured the bag with her fangs and sucked down the blood and then drained another. By the third bag she wanted to retch since she hated feeding. In the nearly four years she had been a vampire, she had never gotten quite used to it.

She did it to survive and only when she had to keep the demon at bay.

This time she had to do it for Blake. Already she could feel her vampire body metabolizing the blood and making her stronger. Because of that, she sucked down the third bag of blood and sat there, feeling the energy surge through her veins and heat her body.

Heat that Blake would welcome, she knew. Heat that would keep him with her.

She let the throw fall to the floor and eased back into bed beside him. He roused as she pressed her body to his and warmed him.

Blake opened his eyes and thought he had gone to heaven. She was beside him, lush and warm. Her breasts brushing his chest and side as she threw her thigh over his leg, sharing the heat of her body and dispelling the chill that had worked its way into his once again.

The chill that told him this wasn't heaven, but hell.

Hell because he didn't want to leave her now. He didn't want to, but there was so little strength left in his body. The pain in his back and deep within his chest reminded him that he hadn't completely healed and the longer that the internal bleeding continued and he was injured…

He refused to entertain that thought. Not now. Not when she was finally beside him. Willingly. Lovingly.

"You feel good, Meghan," he murmured and wrapped an arm around her waist to urge her closer.

"I'll feel even better after you've had a bite," she teased, sensing the maudlin turn of his thoughts. She pulled aside the blond strands of her shoulder-length hair, baring the fine line of her neck.

"Are you sure?" He reached up and laid the pads of his fingers against the pulse there. He stroked the graceful line of her neck down to the crook of her shoulder.

"Never more sure," she answered, and lowered herself over his body, granting him easier access.

He didn't ask again.

She was offering him life and love, and he wasn't about to refuse such an offer.

Chapter 26

Meghan didn't know how long they had been repeating the cycle. She would feed from the blood bags that Diego and Ryder brought and grow stronger. In turn, she would sink back into their bed, nourish Blake and weaken from his feeding. But with each time he suckled from her, he grew stronger until with the last go, she finally felt comfortable that Blake would survive.

Diego had returned sometime during the course of those cycles, bringing not only more blood, but also the news that Foley was managing to hang on.

"And Diana?" she asked, wondering at what had happened with the determined FBI agent.

"Ryder's tending to her. What about Blake? Will I need to hire another hand for the kitchen?"

Meghan had given him a playful shove as they talked out on the patio. "Admit it. He came through for us."

Diego had chuckled and ruefully shaken his head. "If I did that, Blake might be insufferable."

With that he had leapt off the rooftop to the next building, and Meghan had returned inside to feed yet again.

When she slipped into bed this time, Blake was already awake and the gleam in his eyes said he was ready for more than a nip of her neck.

Her lips curved into a brazen smile as she sauntered toward him, eager to celebrate their victory over Lee and death.

Blake propped himself up on one arm as she moved toward him, the glide of her body sensuous and filled with promise. There was only a slight hitch high up on his shoulder blade as he did so, as if to caution him that he still needed to take care. But another part of him wasn't listening, rising up immediately and demandingly.

Her eyes narrowed and dropped to where the sheet shifted, straining against his arousal. One edge of her lips quirked up saucily as she laid a knee on the edge of the bed and said, "I see that you're feeling better."

He slid across the sheets and with his free hand, cupped her breast and gently squeezed. "You're feeling right fine yourself, Meghan."

She chuckled and eased in beside him, her front pressed to his. She insinuated her knee between his thighs and closed the distance at their hips, cradling his erection with the softness of her belly. He realized then she had no intention of rushing this moment, and he was totally on board with that.

As they lay side by side, he placed his hand on her waist and then slowly trailed it up to cup her breast once again. She did the same, running her hand up the muscle of his side, lingering by the pink skin where he had been wounded.

"Don't think about that now, Meghan," he urged. She nodded and raised her hand to his nipple, where she ran her finger around and around the edge of it.

Each circle of that sensitive nub sent a jolt between his legs, and siren that she was, she knew and pressed forward, applying gentle pressure with her thigh up into him. He moaned as she rubbed her thigh back and forth across him.

He tweaked her nipple with a little more force, yanking a soft gasp from her. Bending his head, he soothed the tip with a soft lick. When she cradled his head to her, he accepted the invitation, loving her with his mouth while he eased his hand down between their bodies and found her center.

He stroked the swollen nub between her legs and sucked a little more roughly on the hard tip of her breast.

Meghan dragged in a shaky breath and cradled the back of his head, loving the feel of him. Of the way he treasured her with his mouth and fingers. Heat built within her, and as he eased one finger and then another into her, she clenched her muscles around him and tilted her hips, wanting more.

He picked up his head from her breast, brought his mouth to hers and whispered against her lips, "Love me, Meghan."

Shifting onto his back, he cradled her waist and urged her onto his body.

Her belly pressed into him a second before her thighs straddled his. She rubbed her body up and down the length of him, her softness enticing him, not that he seemed to need it.

He grasped her waist firmly and urged her upward, settling her over his hardness. Dampening him before he urged her to lift her hips, she positioned him at her entrance.

The tip of him breached her, but she stopped there, the moment suspended in time. The moment she had been waiting for in two lifetimes now.

"There's no going back after this," she said, wanting him to understand.

He reached up and cupped her jaw, shot her a boyish grin that stopped her heart for a moment. "There's only one woman I've loved in both my lifetimes."

As she slowly sank onto him, burying him inside, she said, "It had damn well better be me."

He surged up off the bed and sank his fingers into her hair, keeping her immobile as he chuckled and whispered against her lips, "Damn well is, Meghan."

She smiled and shifted her hips, giving herself over to the wonder of loving him. To the tenderness in the way he treasured her body. To the laughter and joy that seemed never far from their hearts. They loved each other until neither of them could move.

Later, cuddled beside him, their legs entwined and his softening erection tucked safely within her, she slipped her arm around his body and brushed a kiss across his lips. Beneath her mouth she felt his grin and pulled him tight until they were touching from belly to breast.

His hand at the small of her back brushed up and down lazily, soothing her. She sighed with pleasure and said, "Will it always be like this?"

Blake bit back the too-quick rejoinder on his lips about being immortal. For them, nothing would change. There would be no sagging chins or bulging bellies. No children to interrupt them in the middle of the night because he hadn't known that was a gift it might have been possible to give.

How he wished he had known. How he wished to see her round with child, to see his babe suckling at her breast.

But that was all impossible because of his one selfish act.

She must have sensed the tension that crept into his body with his thoughts. She raised her index finger and smoothed the frown line across his forehead. In a soft whisper, she said, "Don't think about that."

"I've taken so much from you. How can you ever—"

She laid her fingers across his lips. With a shake of her head, she said, "I hated you for stealing my life. But when I think about all that I almost just lost and all the love you've given me…"

She stroked her fingers across his lips and with another shake of her head, said, "I have no regrets, Blake. I love you."

He smiled and with a cocky jerk of his shoulder said, "I guess things turned out well after all."

"Damn you, Blake," she said and rolled over him,

imprisoning him beneath her, which quickly had him hardening within her. "Can't you be serious just this once?"

Chuckling, he reversed their positions and pinned her arms above her. He shifted his hips, drawing a mewl of pleasure from her as he said, "Is this serious enough? I'll love you forever, Meghan. Forever."

And as he moved in her again, they both knew it was a promise he intended to keep.

Epilogue

Otro Mundo
A few days later

Blake hadn't really been sure that he could muster a shift of work. Although the wounds Lee had inflicted on him had completely healed, he knew his strength was not what it should be, but Meghan had insisted that he return to the restaurant that night.

Like most things involving Meghan, he hadn't been able to say no.

As he walked through the service entrance, he realized that only the vampire employees were waiting within. At his quizzical look, they began to clap and cheer, dragging a blush of color to his face. He wasn't used to that kind of praise and it created the kind of warmth in him that his mother's gentle touch had once roused. Or Meghan's caring caress.

Meghan, he thought with a happy sigh as she stepped up beside him and grabbed his hand. At his puzzled look, she said, "They all appreciate what you did to help keep this place safe."

He gave a nonchalant shrug and accepted the well wishes as he walked farther into the kitchen area. He felt guilty about the reception, since he hadn't really done it to save the restaurant for them. He had done it for Meghan, although all had benefited from his actions.

Ryder and Diego stood by the hall leading to the pantry and the office, their faces stern as he approached, but Ryder quickly broke into a grin as Diego whipped out something from behind him—a suit bag.

Diego held it out to him and he hesitantly accepted it, unzipped the bag for a peek. Inside was a navy blue suit, but nothing like the polyester one he had sported for his interview a few weeks ago.

As he brushed his thumb across the fabric, he realized the suit was made of the finest wool. Beneath the suit on the hanger was a pale blue cotton shirt that would make his eyes quite striking.

"What's this?" he asked, shooting anxious glances from Diego to Ryder and then to Meghan, who was standing off to the side.

"Figured you wouldn't be up to any lifting and we could use some help up front. Can't have one of our hosts looking like that," Diego said, a mock curl of disdain as he motioned to Blake's black ensemble of jeans, T-shirt and a new leather jacket to replace the one Lee had ruined with his knife attack.

"I won't let you down," he said, with a little bounce of the bag.

"We know you won't," Ryder said. "You can get changed in our office."

He nodded and was about to walk away when something else occurred to him. "How's Foley?"

Ryder immediately answered. "He's in one of my guest rooms, healing slowly. Melissa is helping him get better with her doctoring."

"And the missus? Is she okay?" he asked. Meghan stepped to his side, slipped her hand into his.

"Go get changed," she urged, but Ryder held up his hand, his face serious once again.

"Diana is… Since she's on leave and everything is fine here, she decided she needed a little rest and relaxation. She's headed to Miami for a visit with her mother."

Contrary to Ryder's assertion, Blake suspected that not all was fine with the FBI agent and his friend Ryder.

His friend, Blake thought with some surprise. He stepped forward, laid a hand on Ryder's shoulder and gripped it tightly. "I'm here when you need me."

Ryder nodded and said, "Let's hope that we've all had our share of excitement for the immediate future."

But as Blake considered just how much had happened to their little circle of friends in the last few years, he suspected they were in for quite a few more adventures together.

And he planned to be in the thick of them.

As Meghan tightened her grip on his hand, he met her gaze and realized he wouldn't be alone this time.

She would be with him, and the strength of their love would sustain them no matter what the future brought.

* * * * *

*Mills & Boon® Intrigue brings you
a sneak preview of…*

Delores Fossen's Expecting Trouble

*Special agent Cal Rico lives by the rules. He would
never get involved with someone he has sworn to
protect, which is why it comes as a shock that Texas
heiress Jenna Laniere would name him as the father of
her baby. With an assassin hot on Jenna's trail, though,
and Cal falling hard for both mother and daughter, he
faces his most important
assignment yet.*

Don't miss the thrilling third story in the new
TEXAS PATERNITY: BOOTS AND BOOTIES
*mini-series, available next month from
Mills & Boon® Intrigue.*

Expecting Trouble
by
Delores Fossen

A deafening blast shook the rickety hotel and stopped Jenna cold.

With her heart in her throat, Jenna raced to the window and looked down at the street below. Or rather what was left of the street, a gaping hole. Someone had set shops on fire. Black coils of smoke rose, smearing the late afternoon sky.

"Ohmygod," Jenna mumbled.

There was no chance a taxi could get to her now to take her to the airport. And worse were rebel soldiers, at least a dozen of them dressed in dark green uniforms. She'd heard about them on the news and knew they had caused havoc in Monte de Leon. That's why by now she'd hoped to be out of the hotel, and the small South American country. She hadn't succeeded because she'd been waiting on a taxi for eight hours.

One of the soldiers looked up at her and took aim with his scoped rifle. Choking back a scream, Jenna dropped to the floor just as the bullet slammed through the window.

She scurried across the threadbare rug and into the bathroom. It smelled of mold, rust and other odors she didn't want to identify, and Jenna wasn't surprised to see roaches race across the cracked tile. It was a far cry from the nearby Tolivar estate where she'd spent the past two days. Of course, there'd been insects of a different kind there.

Paul Tolivar.

Staying close to the wall, Jenna pulled off one of her red heels so she could use it as a weapon and climbed into the bathtub to wait for whatever was about to happen.

She didn't have to wait long.

There was a scraping noise just outside the window. She pulled in her breath and waited. Praying. She hadn't even made it to the please-get-me-out-of-this part when she heard a crash of glass and the thud of someone landing on the floor.

"I'm Special Agent Cal Rico," a man called out. "U.S. International Security Agency. I'm here to rescue you."

A rescue? Or maybe this was a trick by one of the rebels to draw her out. Jenna heard him take a step closer, and that single step caused her pulse to pound in her ears.

"I know you're here," he continued, his voice calm. "I pinpointed you with thermal equipment."

The first thing she saw was her visitor's handgun. It was lethal-looking. As was his face. Lean, strong. He had an equally strong jaw. Olive skin that hinted at either Hispanic or Italian DNA. Mahogany-brown hair and sizzling steel-blue eyes that were narrowed and focused.

He was over six feet tall and wore all black, with various weapons and equipment strapped onto his chest,

waist and thighs. He looked like the answer to her unfinished prayer.

Or a P.S. to her nightmare.

"We need to move now," he insisted.

Jenna didn't question that, but she still wasn't sure
what she intended to do. Yes, she was afraid, but she
wasn't stupid. "Can I trust you?"

Amusement leapt through his eyes. His reaction
was brief, lasting barely a second before he nodded.
And that was apparently all the reassurance he
intended to give her. He latched on to her arm and
hauled her from the tub. He allowed her just enough
time to put back on her shoe before he maneuvered
her out of the bathroom and toward the door to her
hotel room.

"Extraction in progress, Hollywood," he whispered
into a black thumb-size communicator on the collar of
his shirt. "ETA for rendezvous is six minutes."

Six minutes. Not long at all. Jenna latched on to that
info like a lifeline. If this lethal-looking James Bond
could deliver what he promised, she'd be safe soon.
Of course, with all those rebel soldiers outside, that
was a big *if*.

Cal Rico paused at the door, listening, and eased
it open. After a split-second glance down the hall, he
got them out of the room and down a flight of stairs
that took them to the back entrance on the bottom
floor. Again, he looked out, but he must not have liked
what he saw. He put his finger to his lips, telling her
to stay quiet.

Outside, Jenna could still hear the battery of gunfire

and the footsteps of the rebels. They seemed to be moving right past the hotel. She was in the middle of a battle zone.

How much her life had changed in two days. This should have been a weekend trip to Paul's Monte de Leon estate. A prelude to taking their relationship from friendship to something more. Instead, it'd become a terrifying ordeal she might not survive.

Jenna tried not to let fear take hold of her, but adrenaline was screaming for her to run. To do something. *Anything.* It was a powerful, overwhelming sensation. Fight or flight. Even if either of those options could get her killed.

Cal Rico touched his fingers to her lips. "Your teeth are chattering," he mouthed.

No surprise there. She didn't have a lot of coping mechanisms for dealing with this level of stress. Who did? Well, other than the guy next to her.

"Try doing some math," he whispered. "Or recite the Gettysburg Address. It'll help keep you calm."

Jenna didn't quite buy that. Still, she tried.

He moved back slightly. But not before she caught his scent. Sweat mixed with deodorant soap and the faint smell of the leather from his combat boots. It was far more pleasant than it should have been.

Stunned and annoyed with her reaction, Jenna cursed herself. Here she was, close to dying, only hours out of a really bad relationship, and her body was already reminding her that Agent Cal Rico smelled pleasant. Heaven help her. She was obviously a candidate for therapy.

"I'll do everything within my power to get you out of here," he whispered. "That's a promise."

Jenna stared at him, trying to figure out if he was lying. No sign of that. Just pure undiluted confidence. And much to her surprise, she believed him. It was probably a reaction to the testosterone fantasy he was weaving around her. But she latched on to his promise.

"All clear," he said before they started to move again.

They hurried out the door and into the alley that divided the hotel from another building. Cal never even paused. He broke into a run and made sure she kept up with him. He made a beeline for a deserted cantina. They ducked inside, and he pulled her to the floor.

"We're at the rendezvous point," he said into his communicator. "How soon before you can pick up Ms. Laniere?" A few seconds passed before he relayed to her, "A half hour."

That was an eternity with the battle raging only yards away. "We'll be safe here?" Jenna tried not to make it sound like a question.

"Safe enough, considering."

"How did you even know I was in that hotel?"

Cal shifted his position so he could keep watch out the window. "Intel report."

"There was an intelligence report about me?" But she didn't wait for him to answer. "Who are you? Not your name. I got that. But why are you here?"

He shrugged as if the answer were obvious. "I'm a special agent with International Security Agency—the ISA. I've been monitoring you since you arrived in Monte de Leon."

Still not understanding, she shook her head. "Why?"

"Because of your boyfriend, Paul Tolivar. He is bad news. A criminal under investigation."

Judas Priest. This was about Paul. Who else?

"My ex-boyfriend," she corrected. "And I wish I'd known he was bad news before I flew down here."

Maybe it was because she was staring craters into him, but Agent Rico finally looked at her. Their gazes met. And held.

"I don't suppose someone could have told me he was under investigation?" she demanded.

He was about to shrug again, but she held tight to his shoulder. "We couldn't risk telling you because you might have told Paul."

Special Agent Rico might have added more, if there hadn't been an earsplitting explosion just up the street. It sent an angry spray of dirt and glass right at them. He reacted fast. He shoved her to the floor, and covered her body with his. Protecting her.

They waited. He was on top of her, with his rock-solid abs right against her stomach and one of his legs wedged between hers. Other parts of them were aligned as well.

His chest against her breasts. Squishing them.

The man was solid everywhere. Probably not an ounce of body fat. She'd never really considered that an asset, but she did now. Maybe all that strength would get them out of this alive.

© Delores Fossen 2009

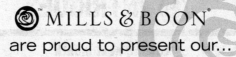

INTRIGUE

Coming next month

2-IN-1 ANTHOLOGY

EXPECTING TROUBLE by Delores Fossen

Special agent Cal lives by the rules. He would never get involved with someone he has sworn to protect. That is, until heiress Jenna names him as the father of her baby!

PRINCE CHARMING FOR 1 NIGHT by Nina Bruhns

Lawyer Conner needs down-on-her-luck dancer Vera as bait to catch a thief. But could a crash course in social graces turn Vera into the woman of his dreams?

2-IN-1 ANTHOLOGY

NATURAL-BORN PROTECTOR by Carla Cassidy

Melody has returned to her home town following her sister's murder. Tough single dad Hank is determined to keep Melody safe – as her bodyguard *and so much more...*

SAVED BY THE MONARCH by Dana Marton

Judi once refused an arranged marriage to sexy prince Miklos. Yet when the pair are kidnapped, he is determined to save her life and win her heart in the bargain!

SINGLE TITLE

VANISHED by Maureen Child
Nocturne™

After his destined mate abandoned him Rogan had no use for desire. When mortal Allison inspires his passion he's bewildered. Could she be his *real* true love?

On sale 19th February 2010

millsandboon.co.uk Community

Join Us!

The Community is the perfect place to meet and chat to kindred spirits who love books and reading as much as you do, but it's also the place to:

- Get the inside scoop from authors about their latest books
- Learn how to write a romance book with advice from our editors
- Help us to continue publishing the best in women's fiction
- Share your thoughts on the books we publish
- Befriend other users

Forums: Interact with each other as well as authors, editors and a whole host of other users worldwide.

Blogs: Every registered community member has their own blog to tell the world what they're up to and what's on their mind.

Book Challenge: We're aiming to read 5,000 books and have joined forces with The Reading Agency in our inaugural Book Challenge.

Profile Page: Showcase yourself and keep a record of your recent community activity.

Social Networking: We've added buttons at the end of every post to share via digg, Facebook, Google, Yahoo, technorati and de.licio.us.

www.millsandboon.co.uk

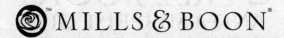

2 FREE BOOKS
AND A SURPRISE GIFT

We would like to take this opportunity to thank you for reading this Mills & Boon® book by offering you the chance to take TWO more specially selected books from the Intrigue series absolutely FREE! We're also making this offer to introduce you to the benefits of the Mills & Boon® Book Club™—

- **FREE home delivery**
- **FREE gifts and competitions**
- **FREE monthly Newsletter**
- **Exclusive Mills & Boon Book Club offers**
- **Books available before they're in the shops**

Accepting these FREE books and gift places you under no obligation to buy, you may cancel at any time, even after receiving your free books. Simply complete your details below and return the entire page to the address below. You don't even need a stamp!

YES Please send me 2 free Intrigue books and a surprise gift. I understand that unless you hear from me, I will receive 5 superb new stories every month, including two 2-in-1 books priced at £4.99 each and a single book priced at £3.19, postage and packing free. I am under no obligation to purchase any books and may cancel my subscription at any time. The free books and gift will be mine to keep in any case.

Ms/Mrs/Miss/Mr _____ Initials _____

Surname _____

Address _____

_____

_____ Postcode _____

Send this whole page to: Mills & Boon Book Club, Free Book Offer, FREEPOST NAT 10298, Richmond, TW9 1BR